PENGUIN BOOKS

Up Close and Personal

Leonie Fox is a former magazine journalist. She has written two novels, *Private Members* and *Members Only*, both of which are published by Penguin. She lives in Kent.

Up Close and Personal

LEONIE FOX

PENGUIN BOOKS

Published by the Penguin Group
Penguin Books Ltd, 80 Strand, London WC2R 0RL, England
Penguin Group (USA) Inc., 375 Hudson Street, New York, New York 10014, USA
Penguin Group (Canada), 90 Eglinton Avenue East, Suite 700, Toronto, Ontario, Canada M4P 2Y3
(a division of Pearson Penguin Canada Inc.)
Penguin Ireland, 25 St Stephen's Green, Dublin 2, Ireland
(a division of Penguin Books Ltd)
Penguin Group (Australia), 250 Camberwell Road, Camberwell, Victoria 3124, Australia
(a division of Pearson Australia Group Pty Ltd)
Penguin Books India Pvt Ltd, 11 Community Centre, Panchsheel Park, New Delhi – 110 017, India
Penguin Group (NZ), 67 Apollo Drive, Rosedale, North Shore 0632, New Zealand
(a division of Pearson New Zealand Ltd)
Penguin Books (South Africa) (Pty) Ltd, 24 Sturdee Avenue, Rosebank, Johannesburg 2196, South Africa

Penguin Books Ltd, Registered Offices: 80 Strand, London WC2R 0RL, England

www.penguin.com

First published 2010
1

Set in Garamond MT Std on 12.5/14.75 by Palimpsest Book Production Limited,
Grangemouth, Stirlingshire
Printed in England by Clays Ltd, St Ives plc

ISBN: 978-0-141-03705-9

www.greenpenguin.co.uk

Penguin Books is committed to a sustainable future
for our business, our readers and our planet.
The book in your hands is made from paper
certified by the Forest Stewardship Council.

Acknowledgements

A big thank you to all at Penguin, especially Mari Evans, Lydia Newhouse, Naomi Fidler, Katy Szita, Tom Chicken, Julia Connolly and John Hamilton.

I

In the first week of April, the weather turned suddenly, unseasonably, insistently lovely. At this time of year, the historic market town of Loxwood was at its prettiest. Hyacinths and anemones filled the hanging baskets outside the town hall and the well-kept churchyard was dotted with clusters of wild daffodils, their golden heads turned to catch the watery sunshine. As her mini-cab turned off the high street and headed towards open countryside, Juliet Fisher caught her first glimpse of Ashwicke Park. She'd spent the winter in Aspen, staying with her cousin Harry, who owned a ski school and a string of luxury condominiums. Initially, she'd turned down his invitation, generous as it was, unwilling to abandon Ashwicke for an entire season. Managing the hotel was a demanding job – especially for someone who, like Juliet, had no experience in the hospitality industry. But Harry wouldn't take no for an answer and eventually Juliet had relented. With hindsight, it was the best decision she could have made.

Feeling as if she might burst with happiness, Juliet turned to Dante, her husband of ten days. 'I'm so excited to be back in England,' she said. 'I hope you are too.'

'You bet,' said Dante, gazing at her worshipfully. 'Although, to be honest, I'm feeling kinda nervous too.'

Juliet's eyes widened in sympathy. 'I'm not surprised; your whole life's been turned upside down . . . new wife, new home, new country. It's bound to take you a little while to adjust.' She gave his hand a comforting squeeze. 'I can't wait to show you the house – and introduce you to all my friends.'

Dante smiled shyly. 'I sure hope they like me.'

'Of course they will.' Juliet looked at her new husband, taking in his long eyelashes, strong jaw and the pectorals bulging beneath his thin cotton sweater. 'I should think most of them will be green with envy. One look at you and they'll all be wanting toyboys of their own.'

Dante frowned. 'I wish you wouldn't use that word.'

'I'm only teasing,' Juliet said, resting her head on his shoulder. 'You know the age difference means nothing to me; I married you because I love you.'

'And I love you too,' Dante replied. 'I loved you the minute I saw you.'

He broke into a grin as he recalled the occasion in question. It was the third night of Juliet's stay in Aspen and she'd arranged to meet her cousin in one of the resort's more exclusive après-ski watering holes for pre-dinner cocktails. She'd already been sitting at the bar for half an hour when Harry called to say he'd be late. One of the condos had been inadvertently double booked and, it being high season, he was struggling to find alternative accommodation for his well-heeled and very irritable guests. Flipping her mobile shut with an exasperated sigh, Juliet leaned across the bar and ordered a second margarita from the cute bartender with the blue eyes. 'Have one yourself,' she added as an afterthought.

Dante, who tried to avoid drinking on the job, smiled at her. 'Thanks. I'll just take a Coke.'

It was a full two hours later when Harry finally arrived, flustered and full of apologies – by which time Juliet and Dante had struck up quite a rapport. The bartender was used to women coming on to him and, most of the time, he was immune to their charms. As far as his work was concerned, Dante was a perfectionist and he resented anything that took his mind off the job. But that night he welcomed the distraction, for there was something deeply fascinating about this cool blonde with the cute English accent and the slightly aloof air. In those two hours, as he expertly mixed one cocktail after another for the slick team of waiters to ferry to the thirsty punters, Dante found himself opening up to Juliet. He told her about dropping out of college and how he'd left his family and friends in Montana to come to Aspen, fuelled by a love of skiing and the dream of setting up his own bar. Although she was rather less forthcoming about her own background, Juliet had apparently enjoyed herself every bit as much as he had, because before she left she handed him a napkin with her mobile number scrawled across it.

'In case you feel like some company on the slopes on your next day off,' she said as a faint wash of colour spread from her jaw to her earlobes.

This casual offer turned out to be the start of a passionate, and entirely unexpected, love affair. At first, Dante found the enigmatic Englishwoman rather reserved. She preferred to listen, rather than to talk, and didn't give up her secrets readily. But, after some gentle probing, her story slowly emerged – the blissfully happy childhood, the private-school education, her marriage to a high-flying businessman, followed, some years later, by her husband's tragic death.

At twenty-eight, Dante was seven years Juliet's junior but, from the very beginning, the age gap didn't seem to matter. What started as a holiday fling quickly turned into something much deeper and when, nine weeks after their first meeting, Dante got down on one knee in the powdery snow at the foot of a blue run and proposed to Juliet she didn't hesitate to say yes. Dante had envisioned a long engagement and he was stunned when Juliet suggested they get married, right then and there in Aspen. Unable to think of any good reason to refuse her, they had tied the knot without fuss in a log cabin nestling at the foot of the mountain, with a bemused Harry and his wife as witnesses.

There hadn't been much discussion about where they should live – it seemed only natural that Dante, who had fewer ties than Juliet, should move to England. A six-month tourist visa was hastily arranged and a single airfare booked. Dante didn't stop to think whether or not he was making the right decision. All he knew was he was in love with Juliet and, given that he would have gone to the ends of the earth for her, England didn't seem so very far away. It was only now, as the cab turned right, heading for a pair of tall iron gates open wide to the long drive beyond, that he was beginning to realize just what a huge jump into the unknown he had taken.

'We're here,' Juliet said excitedly as the cab sailed through the gates. 'Welcome to your new home.'

Dante had been expecting something on a fairly grand scale. He knew Juliet's late husband, Gus, came from a well-off family. But nothing could have prepared him for the full splendour of Ashwicke Park. With its ivy-covered colonnades and graceful arched windows, it looked like a

Roman temple and seemed quite surreal, nestling there amid the sprawling gardens – which were, Dante couldn't help noticing, rather overgrown.

'Well,' said Juliet after a few moments. 'What do you think?'

'It's huge.' Dante licked his lips, which were suddenly dry. 'And very beautiful.'

'It's Grade-I listed,' Juliet told him. 'Built in the eighteenth century for the second Lord Brownlow.'

Dante dragged his eyes away from the house and frowned at his wife. 'Second Lord *who*?'

'He was a member of parliament and a bit of a rogue by all accounts. He's said to have impregnated half a dozen housemaids during his time at Ashwicke.'

Dante couldn't help smirking. 'Sounds like a busy guy.' His eyes returned to the house. 'I didn't know people actually *lived* in places like this. It looks like the kind of thing you'd see in a guidebook.'

'Yes, but Ashwicke's no museum piece,' Juliet said. 'It's a much-loved family home. Gus's great-grandfather bought it for a song after the war, and when he died it was passed on through the male line. And then Gus died . . .' Her voice wavered. 'He'd be horrified if he knew I'd turned the place into a hotel – but needs must.'

Dante looked at Juliet. It was barely a year since her first husband's death. She'd found him herself in the garden, early one morning. He was hanging from the lowest bough of a horse chestnut, his last breath long extinguished. She hadn't talked a great deal about the circumstances surrounding his suicide, but Dante could see his death had affected her deeply. How could it *not* have? Seeing the concern in his eyes, Juliet gave him a faint smile and mouthed, *I'm fine.*

A few moments later, the cab drew to a halt outside the house. Dante could see it wasn't quite as well maintained as it appeared from a distance. There were tiles missing from the roof and the stucco façade was streaked with cracks. As his gaze travelled upwards, he noticed a row of faces ranged at one of the first-floor windows. They were very young – some no more than teenagers – and they were staring down at the car, wide-eyed and curious. 'It looks like we've got a welcome committee.'

Juliet looked up and smiled. 'That's the hotel staff.' Craning her neck, she waved at them. 'They're a nice bunch, if a little high-spirited.'

Right on cue, one of the figures at the window turned and dropped his trousers, before pressing his bare buttocks up against the glass.

Dante burst out laughing. 'I guess that's one word for it.'

'I suppose I ought to be a bit stricter with them,' Juliet continued. 'But I don't want to drive them away. It's so hard to get staff these days. Nathan did a great job finding them for me.'

'Who's Nathan?' Dante asked.

'The general manager. He used to work at one of the big hotels in town and nearly doubled their turnover during the four years he was there. I was hoping he'd be able to do the same at Ashwicke. Heaven knows, we need all the help we can get.'

'Oh? I'd have thought folks would be queuing up to stay at a place like this.'

Juliet grimaced. 'Before I left for Aspen, we were barely

covering our costs – but, then again, it is only our first year of trading. I'm sure things will improve.'

'How many guest rooms do you have?'

'Eight – and it's bed and breakfast only. I've deliberately kept things on a small scale. I want the guests to feel as if they're at an exclusive country-house party . . . you know, somewhere comfortable and intimate, where they can really unwind.'

'Right,' said Dante, who'd never been to a country-house party in his life.

Suddenly, a man in a well-cut suit appeared at the side of the car. He was forty-five or thereabouts – tall, and handsome in a swarthy sort of way. As Dante's fingers closed round the door handle, the man yanked the door open from the outside, jerking Dante's arm almost out of its socket.

'Welcome to Ashwicke Park,' the man said, as Dante lurched sideways. 'Did you have a pleasant flight from the States?'

'Yes thanks,' Dante replied as he stepped out of the cab.

'I'm Nathan Woods,' the man said, taking Dante's hand in a firm grip. 'The general manager.'

'Oh yeah, Juliet was just telling me about you.'

'Nothing bad I hope.'

'Don't be silly,' Juliet said, emerging from the other side of the car. You've been an absolute godsend, Nathan.'

The general manager nodded. 'Thank you, Mrs Ingram.'

'It's Mrs *Fisher* now,' Juliet said lightly as she passed a handful of notes through the driver's window before walking round to join her husband.

'Ah yes, of course, my apologies.' Nathan turned towards

the front door and snapped his fingers. 'Come on, Charlie, jump to it,' he said officiously, whereupon a pale-faced youth in a burgundy uniform emerged from the shadows. In his arms he carried a garish bouquet of flowers, wrapped in cellophane.

'On behalf of myself and all the staff at Ashwicke,' the manager said as the boy handed the flowers to Juliet. 'To congratulate you on your marriage.'

Juliet's face lit up. 'Ahh, how thoughtful of you, Nathan.'

'Thanks,' Dante added. 'We really appreciate the gesture.'

Nathan dipped his head in acknowledgement. 'You're most welcome. I hope you're going to be very happy at Ashwicke Park, Mr Fisher – and if there's anything I can do to make your stay more comfortable, please don't hesitate to ask.'

Juliet gave a dry laugh. 'Dante hasn't come for a holiday, Nathan; this is his home now.'

The ghost of a smile played about Nathan's lips. He looked at Dante. 'I do beg your pardon, Mr Fisher . . . a slip of the tongue.'

'No worries,' Dante said casually.

'Will you bring our luggage in, Nathan?' Juliet asked as the cab driver popped the boot.

'Certainly.' The manager jerked his head economically to his subordinate. 'Mr and Mrs Fisher's bags, please.'

As Charlie began wrestling with an oversized suitcase, Juliet linked her arm through Dante's. 'Come on, darling, let's go inside.'

A few moments later, they were walking through the front door and into a vestibule filled with a haphazard collection of walking sticks and waxed jackets, and on to a large, honey-coloured hall, dominated by a tarnished chandelier. Beyond it, a wide, carpeted staircase swept upwards, the walls on either side lined with gilt-framed oil paintings, each depicting some energetic, and occasionally violent, countryside pursuit.

'Wow, this place is awesome.' As Dante's words echoed around the hall, a dog came bounding towards them, leaving a trail of muddy paw prints in its wake. It ran straight to Dante and sat at his feet, beating its tail on the smart black and white tiles. 'Hello, boy,' Dante said, bending down to stroke the animal's soft, liver-coloured head. 'What's your name?'

'Actually, Jess is a girl,' Juliet said.

Dante smiled as the dog thrust its wet snout into the palm of his hand. 'She's gorgeous. What breed is she?'

'An English pointer. Bred for hunting. She and Gus used to go shooting together. They were pretty much inseparable.'

Dante felt a stab of envy, the way he did every time Juliet mentioned his predecessor. He knew it was silly to be jealous of a dead man, but he couldn't help himself. He loved Juliet with a ferocity he wouldn't have believed possible and the thought of her lying in another man's arms made him feel quite sick. A sudden thought struck him. 'Shit,' he said. 'I didn't get to carry you across the threshold.'

Juliet smiled. 'Never mind.' She bent down and patted Jess's flank. 'How have you been, old girl? Did you miss me?'

The dog gave a little shudder.

'No? I didn't think so.' Juliet looked at Dante. 'Jess has always preferred men to women. She's been following

Charlie around the house like a lovesick schoolgirl since Gus died.'

There it was again: *Gus, Gus, Gus*. The sound of his name was like fingernails down a blackboard. Dante looked around, surprised that the house seemed so still and quiet. 'Where are all the guests?'

'I expect they've gone out for the day. The countryside around here is so beautiful people generally like to take full advantage of it.'

Nathan reappeared on the threshold. 'All your bags are here in the vestibule now. Charlie's going to take them upstairs for you.'

'Great,' Juliet replied. She went over to a modern blonde-wood reception desk, which looked strangely out of place among all the antiques. 'How have things been?' she asked Nathan.

'The immersion heater broke down last week, so we didn't have any hot water for a couple of days.'

Juliet groaned. 'Not again.'

'Oh, and I had to give Ellie her marching orders.'

'What! But she was one of our best chambermaids.'

'I know she was, but I caught her late one night in the lounge. She was sitting on one of the guests' laps.'

'Silly girl, I've warned her enough times about inappropriate flirting,' Juliet sighed. 'But, all the same, there was no need to sack her. Surely, a written warning would've sufficed.'

Nathan cleared his throat. 'She was naked from the waist down.'

Behind him, Dante stifled a laugh.

'Ah,' Juliet said. 'In that case you did the right thing.' She began flicking through the pages of a ledger. 'What's our occupancy?' she asked.

'Only two guests at the moment, I'm afraid.'

Juliet looked at the general manager in horror. 'You're kidding.'

Nathan raised an eyebrow. 'Last week we didn't have any.'

Juliet sighed and slammed the ledger shut.

'Don't worry, Mrs Fisher, the winter season's always tough,' Nathan added. 'I'm sure things will pick up now the weather's warmer.'

'I hope so,' Juliet said wearily. She stepped out from behind the desk. 'We've had a very long journey. Would you be able to rustle up some tea and biscuits for us?'

'Of course,' Nathan said. 'Why don't you go through to the drawing room and take the weight off your feet?'

'Good idea. Thank you, Nathan.'

As the manager disappeared through a vaulted stone archway, Juliet walked over to Dante. 'I'm sorry about all this. It wasn't the sort of homecoming I'd imagined for you.'

Dante smiled. 'No problem. I'm just glad to be here.'

Juliet pointed towards one of the corridors that led off the hall. 'The drawing room's the last door on the left. Why don't you make yourself comfortable while I pop upstairs to freshen up? I won't be long.'

As she turned to go, Dante caught her arm and drew her towards him. It was the first moment they'd had any privacy since boarding the plane in Aspen. 'Haven't you forgotten something, Mrs Fisher?' he asked.

'What's that?'

'A hug for your husband.'

Grinning, Juliet stood on tiptoes and threw her arms round his neck. She was a petite woman – only five feet three, and very slender. Dante always felt as if he might crush her if he held her too tightly.

'I can't wait to show you the bedroom,' Juliet murmured into his neck.

Dante grinned. 'There's no time like the present,' he whispered back.

'Let's have some tea first, shall we? It's been three months since I've had a decent cup.'

'Hey, there's nothing wrong with American tea,' Dante replied.

Juliet wrinkled her nose. 'You've got to be joking.'

'Are we having our first row, Mrs Fisher?'

'Absolutely not,' said Juliet with mock indignation. 'It's a difference of opinion, that's all.' She patted Dante's bottom playfully. 'Now get that gorgeous arse of yours into the drawing room; I won't be long.' She twisted away from him and walked towards the stairs, turning to add over her shoulder: 'And take that mutt with you.'

Dante looked down at Jess, who was lying on the floor, head between her front paws. 'Come on, girl,' he said, patting his thigh. The pointer rose to her feet obligingly and together they set off down the corridor.

When Dante pushed open the door of the drawing room, he found himself in a well-proportioned room, lavishly decorated in shades of green and purple. The furniture looked expensive and the walls were lined with more paintings – these ones in a softer Renaissance style. With Jess at his heels, he wandered around, pausing every now and then to admire some *objet d'art* – an antique globe, a tiny hand-painted Limoges, a lead crystal paperweight. On the mantelpiece was a porcelain heron with a struggling fish clamped in its beak. Dante picked it up and turned it over in his hand, marvelling at the detail.

'I'd be careful with that if I were you.'

Dante looked towards the door. Nathan was standing on the threshold with a tea tray in his hands.

'It's Minton,' the manager continued. 'It's been in Mr Ingram's family for the best part of a hundred and fifty years.'

Feeling like a schoolboy caught shoplifting, Dante returned the ornament to the mantelpiece. 'Sorry,' he said. 'I was just looking.'

'There's no need to apologize.' Nathan entered the room and set the tray down on an occasional table. Jess came trotting over to investigate, resting her chin on the edge of the tray. 'No!' Nathan said firmly, pushing the dog's head roughly away with his knee. He offloaded two china cups and saucers, a fat brown teapot and a plate of shortbread fingers.

'Are all these things family heirlooms?' Dante asked, gesturing around the room.

'Some of them are, but I believe most were bought at auction by Mr Ingram. He had an excellent eye for collectibles, as you can see.' Nathan's voice, which hitherto had been flat and expressionless, suddenly took on a new life. 'Mr Ingram had expensive tastes, but then again he could afford to be extravagant; by all accounts, his shipping company was terribly successful. He was a generous man too. Every Christmas he'd host a carol concert at Ashwicke with all the money going to a local charity for children with terminal illnesses.' Nathan sighed. 'No wonder everyone in the town held him in such high regard.'

'Well,' said Dante, who felt compelled to offer some sort of comment, 'he sounds like a great guy.'

'Sadly, I never had the pleasure of meeting him, but I know lots of people around here miss him a lot.'

Dante shifted from foot to foot, suddenly feeling awkward. 'Do you live nearby?' he asked.

Nathan smiled tightly. 'Actually, I'm in the lodge. It's just by the entrance gates. You might have seen it when you drove past.'

Dante nodded, though he didn't remember seeing the building in question – there had been so much else to take in.

'It's rather bijou, but perfectly adequate for one.'

'Do all the staff live in?'

'No, just me. Mrs Ingram likes me to be close by, even when I'm off duty.' The manager moistened each corner of his mouth with his tongue. 'Just in case.'

'Oh . . . okay,' Dante said. He suddenly had an overwhelming urge to be alone, away from Nathan's penetrating stare. 'Well, it's been nice talking to you.'

The manager bowed his head obsequiously. 'Likewise – and if you need any more information – regarding Ashwicke itself, or the local amenities – then don't hesitate to ask.'

'Thanks. I might just take you up on that; I'm not used to all this opulence.'

The manager blinked. His eyes were cold and hard, like chips of ice. 'No, I shouldn't think you are.'

When Nathan had gone, Dante sank into one of the

wingback armchairs beside the fireplace. Jess immediately got up from her hidey-hole under the console table and settled at his feet with a great yawn.

'At least somebody around here likes me,' Dante muttered, as he petted the dog.

A few moments later he heard the sound of Juliet's heels clicking down the corridor. When she appeared at the door, he saw that she'd tied her hair back in a high ponytail and swapped her T-shirt for a light cashmere sweater.

'I hope you haven't been too bored,' she said, flopping onto the armchair's twin with a great sigh.

'Nope, I've been chatting with Nathan.'

'That's nice.' Leaning forward, Juliet picked up the teapot and began filling their cups.

'He was telling me about Gus's charity work,' Dante went on.

'Oh?'

'I didn't realize your late husband was such a pillar of the community.'

Juliet made a little moue. 'Everybody in Loxwood knew Gus; he was one of those larger than life characters.'

Dante carried his tea to the window and looked out across the lawn. Dusk was falling and the sky had darkened to the colour of an old bruise. In the gloom he could just make out a wooden swing hanging from a large oak. Suddenly, the wind caught it, sending it rocking backwards and forwards as if propelled by an invisible hand. 'I don't think Nathan likes me,' he said glumly.

Juliet came to stand beside him, resting her head against his arm. 'Don't be silly, darling. He's just a bit prim and proper, that's all. He'll soon loosen up once he gets to know you.' She wrapped her arm round his waist. 'I'll take you on a guided tour later, if you like. There's tons to show you.'

'I bet there is; I can't wait to see it,' Dante said, trying to sound as if he meant it. He knew he should be excited about the prospect of exploring his new home, but instead all he felt was a sense of being hopelessly out of his depth.

2

It was lunchtime in Loxwood High Street and Chez Gaston was bustling with life. Sitting at one of the restaurant's coveted window tables was journalist Yasmin O'Brien. The exotic product of an Irish father and a Malaysian mother, she was tall and olive-skinned, with glossy chestnut hair and startling green eyes. Since making her entrance, five minutes earlier, Yasmin had drawn plenty of admiring glances, but she was too engrossed in her mobile phone to notice them. She'd just received a text from her current lover, David, a fellow journalist, who lived in London. They'd met at a press conference in the city and, after some flirtatious small talk as they waited for the conference to begin, David had invited her to join him for dinner that evening. Dinner became a nightcap at Yasmin's hotel and so on to bed. They'd been seeing each other for nearly two months now – though, given the distance between them, their dates were usually confined to weekends.

In the beginning, things had been great. Just lately, however, David had grown clingy and now here was a text demanding to know why Yasmin wasn't coming down that weekend. Rolling her eyes in exasperation, she punched out a brief reply, promising to call him that evening. She'd break the bad news to him then. Even for someone as single-minded as Yasmin, dumping a lover by text was a no-no.

The text safely despatched, she leaned back in her chair

and smoothed a hand over her Miu Miu pencil skirt. The designer suit had cost her the best part of a month's wages, but it had been worth every penny. Whenever she wore it, she felt powerful, invincible even. Not that she wasn't pretty self-assured already, but just occasionally she needed an extra boost of confidence, especially when it came to dealing with some of the *Sunday Post*'s curmudgeonly hacks, who resented her rapid rise through the ranks.

Yasmin had wanted to be a journalist for as long as she could remember. After graduating with a first in media studies, she'd joined a local free sheet as an unpaid intern. Six months of making tea and photocopying followed before she landed a proper job as the editor's PA. By her own admission she was a useless secretary, too busy looking over the reporters' shoulders and bombarding the features editor with ideas to take dictation. Within a year, she was working as a junior reporter on the showbiz desk of a well-regarded evening paper. Equipped with a socialite's charm and a racehorse's stamina, Yasmin rose steadily through the ranks until, at the age of thirty-one, she defected to the *Sunday Post*, becoming the first female showbiz editor in the paper's long and proud history – not to mention the youngest.

Yasmin checked her watch; her friends were running late. Feeling bored, she pulled her compact out of her handbag and flipped it open, checking her teeth for lipstick marks. The face that stared back at her looked tense – which, given her current workload, was hardly surprising. Sighing, she snapped the compact shut. When she was stressed, there was only one remedy and, with the soon-to-be-dumped David miles away in London, she was going to have to seek a cure closer to home.

Looking up, she saw Gaston himself standing at her table. 'Good afternoon, Mademoiselle O'Brien. What a pleasure it is to see you – as always,' he lisped. 'And may I say how lovely you're looking today?'

'Thank you, Gaston,' Yasmin replied, though she knew his compliment was meaningless, given that he took the same toadying tack with all his rich and/or well-connected female customers.

'Can I get you something to drink while you're waiting for your friends? A glass of Chablis, perhaps?'

'Just some sparkling water, thanks; I need to keep a clear head for work.'

'Of course.' Gaston threw a hand camply in the air. 'And how *is* the world of show business?'

'Oh, you know, the same as usual: fickle, fatuous, ferocious.' She smiled. 'And utterly fabulous, of course.'

'I enjoyed your gossip column last weekend,' Gaston said, raising his voice slightly so the nearby diners would realize he was talking to a local luminary. 'How do you dig up all that dirt?'

Yasmin tapped the side of her nose. 'A good journalist never reveals her sources.'

'I understand,' the restaurateur said with a smile. 'I'll be right back with that drink.'

'Wait,' Yasmin said, touching his arm as he turned to go. 'Your nephew from Grenoble . . . is he working today?'

'Pascal? Yes, as a matter of fact he is.'

'How's he shaping up?'

'So-so.' Gaston lowered his voice. 'I know he's my sister's boy, but, between you and me, he has a bit of an attitude problem. He wants to be a top chef, but, as I keep telling him, he's got to start at the bottom. That's why I've got him waiting tables.' He shook his head despairingly. 'He thinks it's a waste of his talent, but he'll thank me for it one day. He needs to work on improving his English too. Some of our customers find his accent a little thick.'

'I wouldn't mind giving him private lessons,' Yasmin murmured.

'I didn't know you spoke French, mademoiselle.'

'I don't. I had something else in mind.' Yasmin cocked her head to one side. 'Perhaps you could send Pascal out with my water. That way I'll be able to discuss my proposition with him directly.'

Gaston gave a small nod and disappeared.

A few minutes later a stocky man wearing the restaurant's regulation black suit approached Yasmin's table. He was very young with flashy dark looks and black hair that curled over the collar of his jacket. While most of Chez Gaston's waiters were deferential and understated, this one wore a distinct air of arrogance. He strutted rather than walked, shoulders pulled back as if to emphasize the broadness of his chest. After depositing an ice-filled glass onto the table, clumsily knocking Yasmin's butter knife out of alignment in the process, he began to fill it with sparkling water. Then he straightened up and stood with his legs aggressively akimbo.

'Gaston – 'ee said you wanted to see me,' he said in heavily accented English.

Yasmin's eyes flickered from Pascal's crotch to his face and back to his crotch again. 'You're new here, aren't you?' she said. 'I spotted you last week; you served me a delicious duck pâté.'

Pascal gave a little pout and a shake of his head. 'Zee chef 'ere, 'ee is very good, but 'is pâté is not as good as my grandmère's. She gave me zee recipe when I came to England. I make it all the time to remind me of 'ome. It is . . .' Pascal kissed the tips of his fingers. 'Out of zis world.'

'I'll take your word for it.' Yasmin leaned forward, resting her elbows on the table, and looked the waiter in the eye. 'I expect you're wondering why I asked to see you.'

Pascal nodded.

'I was keen to find out how you were settling in,' Yasmin continued. 'I know Gaston has very high standards. Family or not, working for him must be pretty tough.'

Pascal stuck out his bottom lip. ''Ee's okay, but 'ee gets angry wiz me because my Engleesh is not so good.'

This was the opening Yasmin had been waiting for. 'You know,' she said, 'I'm not a qualified language teacher or anything, but I'd be happy to spend some time with you, talking English – just, you know, to bring you up to the required standard.'

Pascal looked at her, confused. 'You would do *zat*, for me – a stranger?'

'Why yes,' Yasmin replied. 'I'm a journalist, so I work with words all day. I'd be delighted to help you.'

The waiter rubbed his jaw, which was covered in decidedly non-regulation stubble. 'Zat would be very kind, mademoiselle. But I would 'ave to do somezing for you in return.'

'Oh, I'm sure we can come to some arrangement.' Yasmin's eyes flitted over Pascal's crotch again. 'I know.' She paused and bit her bottom lip provocatively. 'Perhaps you could cook me dinner.'

A lazy smile spread across the waiter's face as the penny dropped. 'Okay,' he said. 'I zink I would like zat.'

As Pascal made his way back to the waiter's station, one of Yasmin's business cards now nestling in his jacket pocket, he passed a curvaceous brunette wearing a baby sling. The woman paused for a moment, scanning the room, before making her way towards one of the window tables.

Seeing her approach, Yasmin sprang to her feet.

'Hi, Nicole,' she said, kissing her friend on the cheek. She turned to the sleeping infant pinned to the other woman's chest. 'Hello, Tilly, darling,' she whispered, bending her head so she could inhale the baby's sweet scent.

'She wasn't such a darling last night when she was screaming her lungs out,' Nicole said as she eased herself into a chair. 'She's got colic; I've been up half the night with her.'

Yasmin winced. 'Poor little thing. Can't Connor prescribe something for that?'

Connor Swift, Nicole's husband of three years, was a GP and a well-known figure in Loxwood.

'No, apparently there's no treatment for it, so I guess I'll just have to get used to the sleepless nights.' She patted the area under her eyes. 'Look, even my bags have got bags.'

Yasmin smiled sympathetically. 'You should have stayed at home and grabbed a couple of hours' rest while the baby was asleep.'

'What – and miss seeing Juliet for the first time in months? You've got to be kidding.'

Yasmin tapped her watch. 'I hope she gets here soon. I'm doing an interview at two thirty.'

'Who is it?' Nicole said eagerly. 'Anyone exciting?'

'Just some second-division soap star who's written her

autobiography. I daresay I'll be clawing the walls by the end of it.'

'Don't knock it . . . showbiz editor of the highest circulation newspaper in the south-west of England? I wouldn't mind swapping with you. All those launches and after-parties . . . sounds like heaven to me.'

Yasmin raised an eyebrow. 'It's not all glitz and glamour, you know. Some of it's bloody hard work.'

'Don't give me that, Yaz. You love it . . . you know you do.'

Yasmin broke into a grin. 'Yeah, you're right, I can't deny it: I *have* got the best job in the world.' As she spoke, she caught sight of a familiar figure crossing the Square. 'Look!' she cried excitedly. 'Here's Juliet.'

Nicole turned towards the window. '*Ohhh*,' she groaned in disappointment. 'She's on her own. I thought she was going to bring Dante.'

'That's a shame. I'm dying to meet him.' A frown nicked Yasmin's brow. 'I hope she knows what she's doing, getting married again so quickly. It's barely a year since Gus died and you know how close those two were. I'm worried she hasn't given herself enough time to grieve properly.'

'She did take his death very hard,' Nicole agreed. 'Poor Gus. I still can't believe what he did . . . and for Juliet to be the one to find him.' She gave a little shudder. 'It makes me go cold just thinking about it.'

'Do you remember when we went to see her at Ashwicke, just a few days after it happened?' Yasmin asked.

'How could I forget? She could barely string a sentence together; the poor woman was in pieces. Do you remember how she kept saying how it was all her fault? That was the worst thing.'

Yasmin nodded. 'For a while I was really worried about her. She seemed so . . . I don't know . . . broken. And rattling around that big old house on her own couldn't have been good for her.'

'That's why setting up the hotel was such a brilliant idea. Apart from having people around the place, it must really have helped take her mind off things.' Nicole gave a long sigh. 'I really admire Juliet. I don't know how I'd find the strength to go on if anything happened to Connor. After everything she's been through, she really deserves a bit of happiness.'

'Well, judging by her emails, it looks as if she found it in Aspen,' Yasmin said. 'Let's just hope this Dante's as crazy about her as she obviously is about him.' She broke into a smile as Juliet entered the restaurant and waved to attract the other woman's attention. A moment later, they were hugging warmly. 'It's wonderful to see you,' Yasmin said as she released her friend. 'I can't tell you how much we've missed you.'

'And I've missed you too,' Juliet replied as she bent down to hug Nicole. 'More than you know.' She planted a kiss on top of Tilly's head. 'I can't believe how much this little one's grown.'

'She's crawling now,' Nicole said proudly.

'Clever girl! I'm looking forward to giving her a great big cuddle when she wakes up.' Juliet took a seat at the table. 'Sorry I'm late. There was a bit of a crisis at the hotel this morning – Jack, our kitchen porter, has gone down with the flu.' She rolled her eyes. 'Although, knowing Jack, it's more likely to be a hangover. Normally, we could've managed without him, but I've agreed to lay on a special birthday dinner for one of the guests and there's no way Chef could've done all the prep on his own. I've spent the morning on the phone, trying to find a temp, without any luck – and then Dante very kindly agreed to step into the breach.'

'Wow,' said Nicole. 'I'm impressed.'

Juliet pressed a palm to her breast. 'Honestly, girls, I can't believe how lucky I am. Dante's so strong and dependable . . . the sort of person that would never let you down.'

'How can you tell when you've only known him a couple of months?' Yasmin's hand went to her mouth. 'God, that must've sounded really rude. I'm pleased for you, Juliet, really I am. It's just –'

Juliet finished the sentence for her: 'You're worried I might have rushed into things?'

Yasmin blushed. 'Well . . . yes.'

'I know how it looks – a woman of my age falling for a barman on holiday. You probably had a heart attack when you read my emails.'

'I was a bit concerned for you.' Yasmin flashed a look at Nicole. 'We both were. You've been through a tough time this past year; no one could blame you for wanting a bit of fun.'

Juliet shook her head. 'Dante is more than a bit of fun,' she said firmly. 'I realize we haven't known each other very long, but we're soul mates; I feel it in my heart.'

Nicole smiled at her friend. 'Then that's all that matters.'

'We were gutted to miss the wedding,' Yasmin interjected. 'Couldn't you at least have waited till you got back to England?'

Now it was Juliet's turn to blush. 'Sorry, but it just felt

so right at the time. Aspen's such a magical place. I felt like a different person while I was there . . . so relaxed and carefree. Dante and I did things I'd never dream of doing back home, like knocking back tequila in some backstreet dive, or having a massive snowball fight, or staying up all night to watch the dawn break over the mountains.' Her eyes misted over, as she relived each memory. 'And as well as being funny and kind Dante's incredibly sexy too. Sometimes, when we're lying in bed at night and I look at him, lying asleep next me, I almost have to pinch myself.' She smiled impishly. 'Not that either of us is getting much sleep at the moment.'

Nicole sighed wistfully. 'Lucky you. I can't remember the last time I had sex.'

'You're kidding!' Yasmin cried. 'I thought you and Connor couldn't keep your hands off each other.'

Nicole looked down at the sleeping infant in her arms. 'Things have changed since Tilly was born. I don't think Connor finds me sexually attractive any more.'

'In that case he needs his head examining,' Juliet said. 'Because any idiot can see you're absolutely gorgeous.'

'Thanks, it's sweet of you to say that, but I'm still struggling to get rid of this baby weight.' Nicole's hand went instinctively to the overhang of flesh at the waistband of her skirt. 'I wish I could be like one of those celebrity mums whose stomachs miraculously snap back into shape two days after giving birth.'

'No you don't,' Yasmin said firmly. 'The women that do that put themselves through hell – and for what? Just so they can look good in front of the camera. Who gives a shit if you're carrying a few extra pounds anyway?' She threw Nicole a sharp look. 'Has Connor said something to you?'

'Not in so many words. He did buy me a gym membership for our wedding anniversary last week, though.'

Yasmin snorted. 'And they say romance is dead.'

'He didn't even take me out for dinner like he usually does; he had to work late at the surgery.' Nicole's mouth tightened. 'He's always working late these days. I sometimes think he does it on purpose, just to avoid being at home.'

'Why would he do that?' Juliet asked. 'Surely he'd want to spend every spare minute with his family.'

Nicole shrugged. 'I get the impression he's finding fatherhood quite difficult. I don't think he realized just how much our lives were going to change when Tilly came along.'

'Honestly, men can be so pathetic sometimes,' Yasmin snapped. 'When a woman has a baby, she's thrown in at the deep end and just expected to get on with it. Why can't guys be the same?' Her gaze wandered to Juliet. 'You know, I'm surprised you and Gus never had kids. I think he would've made a brilliant dad.'

'Do you?' Juliet said, fiddling with the stem of her wine glass.

'Yeah . . . maybe it's because he seemed like a big kid himself. He was so full of life, always laughing and joking, and he had that wonderful mischievous grin, as if he'd just put a whoopee cushion on the teacher's chair.' She smiled. 'Do you remember that time he hosted the auction at the cricket-club dinner?'

'God, yes,' said Nicole, giggling at the memory. 'He had us all in stitches, didn't he?' She turned to Juliet, but the other woman was staring out of the window with a faraway look in her eyes.

'Anyway, let's not dwell on the past,' Yasmin said briskly, sensing Juliet's discomfort. 'Why don't we order some food and then Juliet can tell us all about Dante?'

'And you mustn't leave out a single detail,' Nicole said, squeezing Juliet's arm. 'We've missed out on far too much already.'

Over the course of the next hour, Juliet regaled her friends with the story of her whirlwind romance. Although the three women had been in regular email contact during her stay in Aspen, this was the first chance they'd had to talk face to face. As Juliet relived her low-key wedding, her eyes shone with happiness. 'It was amazing – just me, Dante and the mountains,' she said. 'And afterwards we went for dinner at this wonderful Italian restaurant Dante knows. He'd persuaded the owner to let us have the private dining room all to ourselves and when we walked in the whole place was filled with candles and dozens of long-stemmed roses.'

'Dante sounds ever so romantic,' Nicole said enviously. 'I can't wait to meet him.'

'Why don't you both come to dinner next weekend? I've invited my family over.' Juliet winced. 'And Piers and Eleanor, Gus's parents. They're going to want to meet Dante sooner or later and I thought I might as well get it out of the way.'

'So they know you've got married again?'

Juliet nodded. 'I called Eleanor from Aspen a couple of days after the wedding to break the news. It seemed the right thing to do.'

'How did she react?'

'She wasn't exactly thrilled, put it that way,' Juliet said with a sigh. 'No doubt she thinks I'm desecrating Gus's memory by getting married again so soon, but it's my life, not hers.' She reached out and rested a hand on each woman's arm. 'It would be great to have you two there on Saturday for moral support – and Connor too, of course. The Ingrams are terrible snobs . . . I have a feeling they're not going to approve of Dante.'

'We wouldn't miss it for the world,' said Yasmin, leaning to one side as the waiter deposited a trio of cappuccinos on the table.

'And if the in-laws give Dante a hard time, we'll spring to his defence,' said Nicole, reaching for the sugar bowl. 'How's he settling in to life at Ashwicke? It must be very different to Aspen.'

'I think he finds it all a bit overwhelming, to be honest,' Juliet replied. 'And I don't blame him; I felt the same way when Gus brought me back to Ashwicke for the first time.'

'I'm sure he'll soon settle in,' said Nicole. 'And it sounds as if he's going to be a great help running the hotel. How are things going on that front? Did the staff cope okay while you were away?'

Juliet shrugged. 'So-so. Nathan seems to have kept everybody on a tight rein, but our occupancy rates are still low. We've only got a couple of guests staying at the moment – *two* piddling guests, can you believe it?' She raised her coffee cup to her lips. 'I'm going to make that business succeed if it's the last thing I do. I've decided to try targeting the American market. Loxwood's full of tourists in summer and Dante reckons they'd really appreciate

Ashwicke's olde worlde charm. I've already written to a couple of the big American guides in a bid to get us listed.'

'That sounds like a great idea,' Yasmin said. 'I can speak to the *Post*'s travel editor if you like. He's planning a "historic hideaways" special in a couple of months' time. I'm sure I can persuade him to include Ashwicke.'

Juliet smiled gratefully. 'That sounds wonderful. Right now we need all the publicity we can get, because if things get much worse I might have to start thinking about selling some of the furniture.'

Nicole gasped. 'I didn't think things were that bad.'

'The place is haemorrhaging money,' Juliet said glumly. 'The heating bill alone would pay off a Third World debt.' She shifted awkwardly in her seat. 'If only Gus hadn't been quite so reckless with his investments, I wouldn't be in this position now.'

'He left you a bit of money, though, didn't he?' Yasmin asked.

'Yes, but it's all gone now. Most of his wealth was tied up in the house and even that's turned out to be a bit of a white elephant.' She noticed Yasmin looking at her watch. 'You don't have to get off already, do you?'

''Fraid so,' Yasmin said. 'Jumped-up soap stars generally don't like to be kept waiting.'

'In that case I'll get the bill.' Juliet turned and gestured to Pascal, who was skulking behind the coffee machine. The Frenchman winked in acknowledgement.

Juliet turned back to her friends. 'I think I've pulled,' she whispered. 'That waiter just winked at me.'

'He better not have,' Yasmin said, reaching for her

handbag. 'He's coming round to my house on Thursday to improve his linguistic skills.' She ran her tongue slowly round her lips. 'I've heard that Frenchmen are *very* good with their tongues.'

Juliet burst out laughing. 'I see nothing much has changed since I've been away. I take it you're still single, then.'

'You're seeing that journalist down in London, aren't you?' Nicole interposed.

'Not for much longer,' Yasmin replied. 'He's getting too serious.'

Nicole groaned. 'What's wrong with that? It's called *having a relationship*, in case you didn't know.'

'But I don't want a relationship,' Yasmin protested. 'I haven't got the time *or* the energy.'

Juliet raised a doubtful eyebrow. 'Are you sure you're not just scared of commitment?'

'No.' Yasmin hesitated. 'At least I don't think so. It's just that right now I need to concentrate on my career.'

'But there's more to life than work,' said Nicole. 'Isn't it time you started thinking about settling down?'

'Just because you've got the husband and the baby and the Audi estate doesn't mean I have to follow suit,' Yasmin said.

'No, of course not. I just want you to be happy, that's all.'

Yasmin grinned. 'And do you know what makes me happy?'

'No, but I'm sure you're about to tell us.'

'A well-chilled bottle of Dom Pérignon and hot, no-strings sex.'

Nicole threw back her head and laughed. 'I won't argue with that.'

3

It was three days after Juliet's return and Reg Cundy was performing a random inspection of Ashwicke Park's guest bedrooms. Since Nathan had hired him as head of housekeeping four months earlier, Reg had carved out a nice little niche for himself. His job was relatively straightforward and involved overseeing the hotel's small team of chambermaids, as well as maintaining a daily inventory of laundry and cleaning materials. But still Reg managed to perform his duties with the maximum amount of grumbling and the minimum amount of effort, his working days punctuated by twice-hourly tea breaks, sly reads of the paper and even the occasional snooze.

A more experienced hotelier would have been able to see they were being taken advantage of – but Juliet was a complete novice. Besides which, she was far too busy in her role as hostess-cum-receptionist to keep tabs on everything that went on behind the scenes. All the staff knew this, and the vast majority milked the situation for all it was worth. It was a shame, Reg thought as he pushed open the door to the magnificently proportioned, if slightly shabby, Wordsworth Suite. Having worked in a number of country-house hotels during his long career in the hospitality industry, he knew that Ashwicke Park could be a highly profitable business in the right hands. In fact, he could've given Juliet a few useful pointers – but Reg, who was only two years away from retirement, wanted an easy life. What's more, he wasn't being paid enough to act as unofficial consultant. His employer, he told himself as he began a tour of the room, would just have to learn the hard way.

Pausing, Reg ran his finger along the top of a picture frame, sighing as it came away thick with dust. Still, he told himself as he wiped his hand on the side of his uniform trousers, what the eye can't see the heart can't grieve over. The bedroom having passed muster, he went through to the en suite and immediately spotted several pubic hairs decorating the soap dish. As he wiped them away with a wodge of toilet paper, he made a mental note to reprimand the chambermaid responsible. He knew he was fighting a losing battle. Most of Juliet's staff were inexperienced youngsters; it was hardly surprising that they cut corners.

Re-emerging into the bedroom, Reg spotted a scrap of fabric poking out from under the bed. He bent down to pick it up and saw, to his amusement, that it was a pair of knickers. The correct protocol would be to obtain the name and address of last night's guest, before posting the freshly laundered underwear back to her, but that would require far too much time and effort. Chuckling to himself, Reg stuffed the knickers into his trouser pocket. Then, worried that he may have over-exerted himself, he sank down on the bed. A few feet away, the mini-bar stood tantalizingly. Reg found himself licking his lips as he looked at it. He knew that drinking on the job was a sackable offence, but he *was* awfully thirsty.

After less than a minute he gave in to temptation. Reaching into the refrigerated cabinet, he removed a miniature of Glenfiddich. 'Bottoms up,' he said, raising the bottle to an imaginary companion before draining it in a single gulp.

All he had to do now was conceal the evidence – and Reg was a past master. Heading over to the complimentary beverages tray, he placed a teabag in one of the china cups. Then he carried the cup to the bathroom and filled it with water from the tap, prodding the teabag with his finger until it turned the water a convincing shade of amber. All that remained was to fill the empty whisky bottle with tea and return it to the mini-bar. As and when a guest discovered the switch, it would naturally be blamed on the room's previous occupant.

Having completed his cursory inspection, Reg departed the Wordsworth Suite and set off down the corridor towards his next port of call. As he passed the cleaning supplies cupboard, he noticed the door was slightly ajar. Through the aperture he could see porter-and-sometime-laundry-assistant Charlie standing in the semi-darkness, staring fixedly at the tiny flickering screen of one of the newfangled handheld gadgets all the youngsters seemed to have these days.

'What are you doing in there?' Reg bellowed as he yanked the door open.

Charlie started and stumbled backwards, sending a mop clattering to the floor. 'Nothing,' he said, gulping hard.

'Well, it doesn't look like nothing to me.' Reg held out his hand. 'Give it here. You know very well that electronic devices are banned at work.'

Charlie hugged the handheld to his chest like a child reluctant to be parted from his favourite toy. 'It won't happen again,' he said. 'I was just texting my mum to see if she could pop round and feed the cat tonight.'

'Like hell you were,' Reg said. 'Come on, Charlie, hand it over. You'll get it back at the end of your shift.'

Heaving a sigh, Charlie did as he was told.

Reg stared at the unfamiliar device, looking for the *off* key. He couldn't help but notice the moving image on the screen above the keypad. It was a woman and she was wandering around her bedroom – naked. He looked at Charlie. 'So *that's* what you were doing . . . surfing the internet for porn.' He frowned disapprovingly. 'You filthy little bugger.' Reg's eyes returned to the screen. The woman was closer to the camera now. He found himself admiring her hourglass shape and the delicate shell-like pink of her nipples. Suddenly, she reached towards the bed and picked up a bra that was lying on top of a strangely familiar floral counterpane.

Reg held the device closer to his face, noting the toile de Jouy wallpaper and the handsome Windsor armchair with its faded upholstery. 'That looks like the Coleridge Suite.' He glanced at Charlie, whose cheeks had ripened to the colour of plums.

'It is,' Charlie admitted.

Reg looked at the screen again. The woman had put the bra on and was now stepping into a tiny G-string. 'How the devil . . .' he muttered.

'It's a hidden camera,' Charlie explained sheepishly. 'I bought it off the internet.'

Reg let out a long low whistle. 'You've got some nerve,' he said. 'If that young lady discovers she's being spied on, you'll be in big trouble.'

'She won't,' Charlie said. 'The camera's practically invisible. It's hidden inside the smoke detector.'

Reg studied the woman's face. He recognized her now. She was part of a six-strong hen party that had arrived at the hotel the night before. 'Is this *live*?' he asked.

'Uh-huh,' Charlie replied. 'The picture quality's pretty good, isn't it?'

'Yeah, not bad,' said Reg, watching, transfixed, as the woman began performing an elaborate stretching routine in front of the full-length mirror. 'Have you got cameras in all the rooms?'

'On *my* wages? You must be joking.'

Reg was intrigued. 'So how come you can see the footage on this gizmo?'

'The camera's got a motion sensor and it streams real-time video direct to my handheld.'

Tearing his eyes away from the screen, Reg thrust the device into his jacket pocket. 'You do realize this is a very serious matter, don't you?' he said in a stern voice. 'Not to mention highly illegal.'

Charlie nodded. 'Please don't tell Mrs Fisher or I'll lose my job. I know I shouldn't have done it, but I just thought it would be a bit of a laugh. As soon as she's gone down to breakfast, I'll go in there and get rid of the camera, I promise.'

Reg sucked in his breath. 'Now let's not do anything hasty, lad. I think we'd be better off waiting until the young lady's checked out on Monday. After all, we wouldn't want her walking in while you're up there fiddling with the smoke detector or she might get suspicious.' He patted his jacket pocket. 'And, in the meantime, I'd better keep a hold of your equipment. We wouldn't want it falling into the wrong hands now, would we?'

‘Erm, no, I guess not,’ said the bemused porter.

Reg tapped the side of his nose. ‘And not a word about this to anyone. Let’s keep it between ourselves.’ He stepped out of the broom cupboard. ‘I’d better get on with my rounds. And you’d better get down to the laundry room. The fella in the Betjeman had a little accident last night. Something he ate disagreed with him apparently and his bed needs stripping. You’ll need to give everything a good boil wash, mind.’

Charlie’s shoulders drooped at the thought of the unappetizing task that lay ahead. ‘Right you are.’ He watched as the older man lumbered down the corridor. Reg Cundy was a dirty old dog and no mistake.

4

Dante was taking Jess for her usual early morning walk in Ashwicke's sprawling grounds when, quite without warning, the heavens opened. When he left the house half an hour earlier, the sky had been bright and filled with cottony clouds. Unfamiliar with the vagaries of the British weather, he'd ventured outdoors without an umbrella. Big mistake: in another few minutes he'd be soaked to the skin. Sighing, Dante patted his hip and called to Jess, who was having great fun chasing wood pigeons. The second she heard his voice, the pointer wheeled round and came bounding across the lawn towards him. Dante smiled; it was only his third week at Ashwicke, but already he and Jess had formed a strong bond.

Shoving his hands in his pockets, Dante started back to the house with Jess at his side. As he walked, head bowed against the driving rain, his thoughts turned to his old life back in Aspen. There, his days typically started with a breakfast of pancakes and strong black coffee, followed by a two-hour session on the ski slopes. Afterwards, he did chores or met a friend for lunch, before heading to the bar mid-afternoon to start his shift. He was never bored or at a loose end; in a bustling resort like Aspen, there was always something to do or someone to see. Indeed, it had often seemed to Dante that there weren't enough hours in the day. Here in Loxwood, however, it was a different story. To fill the long hours he'd been doing odd jobs at the hotel – putting up shelves, fixing leaky taps and doing bits of painting and decorating. He was happy to help out, but it was mind-numbing stuff. It wouldn't have been so bad if he and Juliet had been working side by side, but during the day they hardly saw each other. Juliet was either manning reception, chasing after staff, or holed up in her tiny office under the stairs, hunched over a spreadsheet. Evenings were better – but even then Juliet was on permanent call in case one of her guests needed a spare blanket or there was a problem with the hot water.

By the time Dante arrived back at the house, he looked like something the cat had dragged in. His clothes were sodden and droplets of rainwater were running off the ends of his hair and down the back of his neck. Stepping into the vestibule, he kicked off his trainers, then reached for one of the old towels Juliet kept for the dog. After giving his own hair a brisk rub, he bent down and started wiping the mud from Jess's paws, but she managed to wriggle free before he'd finished.

'Bad girl,' Dante scolded as the pointer hurtled into the hall. He followed her, towel in hand, frowning when he saw the muddy trail she'd left in her wake. With the dog now nowhere in sight, he squatted down and began rubbing at the nearest set of paw prints.

'You should've taken an umbrella.' The voice made Dante jump. Looking up, he saw Nathan standing behind the reception desk. With his deep-set eyes, prominent cheekbones and thick lips, the general manager had a rather simian look.

'Yeah,' Dante said, sitting back on his haunches. 'I guess I'll have to buy one.'

'There's no need for that.' Nathan gestured to the elephant's foot umbrella stand in the corner. 'We keep these for guests. Just help yourself.'

Dante glanced at the stand. He found it quite grotesque, even though Juliet had explained that it was an antique and, as such, fell outside the remit of modern-day conservation laws. 'Great,' he said, turning his attention back to the paw prints.

Nathan walked over to him. 'I'll have one of the chambermaids bring out a mop and bucket,' he said in a voice unsettlingly lacking in peaks or troughs.

'It's okay, I'm nearly done.' Dante wiped away the final set of paw prints and stood up.

Nathan whisked the towel out of his hands and tucked it under his arm. 'I'll take this to the laundry.'

'It's okay, I can do it myself.'

'Honestly, it's no trouble,' Nathan replied.

'Fine,' Dante said, fighting the urge to yank the towel back out of the general manager's grasp.

'Have you had breakfast yet?'

'No, I was just going to grab some cereal.'

'Are you sure you wouldn't like something more substantial? I can have Chef prepare a full English for you.'

Dante patted his stomach. Two weeks of full Englishes were already beginning to take their toll. 'No, honestly, cereal's fine.'

'Muesli, cornflakes or Weetabix?'

'Er, muesli, thanks.'

'And would you like that with hot milk or cold?'

'Cold, please.'

'Can I bring you some toast as well?'

'Uh, okay.'

'White, wholemeal or granary?'

'Wholemeal.'

'Jam, honey or lemon curd?'

'Just butter, thanks.'

'Salted or unsalted?'

Dante tried not to show his irritation. The exchange had left him feeling drained. He'd always thought that the point of having staff was to make one's life easier, but here at Ashwicke they only served to make even the simplest decisions a hundred times more complicated. 'I really don't care.'

'And to drink?'

'Coffee: black, caffeinated, no sugar.'

'And where will you take it?'

Dante sighed. 'Where would you suggest?' he said in a faintly sarcastic tone.

'Why don't you go in the snug? It's awfully cosy.'

Dante frowned. The day after their arrival from the States, Juliet had taken him on a whistle-stop tour of Ashwicke's many rooms, but he still hadn't had time to explore them all properly – never mind learn their names. 'I don't think I know where the snug is,' he said, embarrassed that he had to ask for directions in his own home.

Nathan nodded towards one of the corridors that led off the hall. 'It's down there, third door on the right. I'll bring your breakfast shortly.' And before Dante had a chance to protest the manager had turned on his heel and walked away.

Suddenly, Dante felt something warm and soft nudge his hand. Looking down, he saw Jess staring up at him with her big eyes. 'Well,' he told the dog, 'I guess we're having our breakfast in the snug this morning.'

The snug, as its name suggested, was a small, low-ceilinged room, comfortably furnished with a well-worn Chesterfield and several mismatching armchairs. The curtains were made of plum-coloured damask and the walls were covered with a richly patterned paper depicting various types of game bird. Nothing about the room was remotely familiar; Dante was certain he'd never set foot in it before. Jess, by contrast, seemed instantly at home, flopping down on the faded rug in front of the fireplace.

Dante went over to one of the windows and flung open the sash. The snug was certainly cosy, as Nathan had indicated, but the air in the room smelled stale and faintly musty, as if it hadn't been used in a long time. Just below the window was an antique desk, clearly positioned to make the most of the view across the garden. A blotter lay across the top, covered in old ink stains. There were doodles too, very masculine in nature: a sports car, an intricate pirate ship, a rocket launching into space. Lying across one corner of the blotter was a pipe – well used, judging by the teeth marks on the stem. Dante assumed that, like the doodles, it belonged to Gus. He picked the pipe up and raised the bowl to his nose. It still bore the sickly-sweet scent of tobacco. He felt a twinge of jealousy, knowing that the lips that had gripped this pipe had kissed Juliet a million times. Above the blotter was a paperback: a Robert Ludlum spy thriller. A dog-eared page revealed the reader had stopped fourteen pages from the end.

With a vague sense of unease, Dante slid open the top drawer of the desk. The first thing he saw was a pewter paperknife with the initials *GI* engraved on the handle. Next to it was an old diary. The pigskin cover felt soft and expensive under his fingertips. He opened a page at random and saw that it contained several mundane entries, written in a strange, sloping hand. Feeling like a carrion crow, picking over the remains of a dead body, he shut the drawer and took a step back, deep in thought. It was then that he noticed a pair of men's leather slippers beneath the desk. He bent down and picked one up. It was huge: a size twelve, at least.

'I think those will be a bit big for you. I can give you a pair of guest slippers if you like.'

Dante looked up. Nathan was standing in the doorway with a breakfast tray in his hands.

Feeling slightly foolish, Dante set the slipper down beside its twin. 'I wasn't figuring on wearing them,' he said. 'I was just looking.'

'Curious, eh?' Nathan said, smiling sardonically. 'I don't blame you.' The manager came into the room and set the tray down on a long low coffee table in front of the Chesterfield. 'Would you like me to pour your coffee?'

'Yes, please.' He watched as Nathan pushed the plunger down on the cafetière. 'Are those Gus's things on the desk – the book and so on?'

'I believe so. Everything's been left just as it was the day he died. Those were Mrs Ingram's instructions.' The manager gestured to the breakfast things. 'Why don't you eat your toast, before it gets cold?'

Dante sat down on the Chesterfield. He didn't fancy

eating his breakfast in the snug any more; the room seemed suddenly oppressive. But, not wanting Nathan to see he was spooked, he picked up a slice of toast and began buttering it vigorously. When he looked up again, the manager had gone.

After polishing off two rounds of toast – with a little help from Jess who, he was rapidly discovering, would eat anything put in front of her – Dante was about to start on his muesli when all at once he heard Juliet's voice out in the hall. 'Dante?' she was saying. 'Dante, darling, where are you?'

He turned his head over his shoulder. 'In the snug,' he called back.

A moment later Juliet appeared at the door. The last time Dante had seen her she was still in her nightdress, but now she'd changed into jeans and a white linen blouse. She seemed shocked to see him there. 'What on earth are you doing?' she demanded, hands on hips.

The spoon stopped halfway to Dante's mouth. 'Having my breakfast.'

'Yes, I can see that,' Juliet said impatiently. 'But why are you eating it in *here*?'

'It was Nathan's idea.'

Juliet's nostrils flared. 'Was it now?' She swept over to the open window and slammed it shut. 'Look at this,' she said, picking up a corner of the curtain. 'The rain's come in – this is sopping wet.' Her voice was tremulous. She seemed upset.

'Don't worry, babe, it'll soon dry out.'

Juliet dropped the curtain and gave a little shiver. 'What were you thinking of anyway, opening the window? It's blowing a gale out there.'

'I wanted to get some fresh air; this room smells as if it's been shut up for ages.' Dante stood up and walked over to his wife. 'What's wrong? Is this place off-limits?'

Juliet shook her head. 'No, no, it's fine,' she said in a calmer tone. 'It's just that this was Gus's special room. I've hardly used it since he died; it holds too many memories.'

What do you expect, when you haven't even cleared his things out? The place is like some kind of grisly shrine. Dante pushed the thoughts aside. 'Nathan's such a jerk, telling me to come in here,' he said gruffly. 'He must've known it would upset you.'

'I'm sure he meant well.' Juliet hooked her arm through Dante's and led him back to the Chesterfield. 'Sorry if I overreacted. I didn't expect to find you in here, that's all. Why don't you finish your breakfast?'

'Do you miss him?' Dante said. It was a question he'd been dying to ask Juliet since the first night he'd met her.

'Who?' Juliet said as she sat down beside him.

'Gus.'

A slight hesitation. 'Sometimes.' She rested her head on his shoulder. 'But I've got you now, haven't I?'

Dante stroked the side of her face with his fingertips. 'And, believe me, I feel like the luckiest guy alive.'

She reached up and wrapped her fingers round his. 'Are you starting to feel at home here? I know it must be hard for you . . .'

Dante didn't get a chance to answer, because at that moment the door burst open and one of the chambermaids ran into the room, skidding to a halt in front of the Chesterfield. 'Oh, Mrs Fisher!' she cried. 'Thank fuck I've found you.'

'I do wish you'd knock first, Leah,' Juliet said wearily. 'And we can do without the swearing, thank you.'

The chambermaid took a few hiccuping breaths. 'Sorry, Mrs Fisher, but it's an emergency.'

Juliet arched her eyebrows. Leah was prone to exaggeration. Only last week, she'd claimed to have seen a rat the size of a terrier in one of the outhouses. 'What sort of emergency?'

'It's Mr Weinberger, the American bloke who arrived yesterday.'

'What about him?'

'There's water pouring through the ceiling in his room.'

Juliet turned pale. 'Please tell me you're joking.'

'I'm not. Apparently it's coming from a dodgy pipe in the room above. Reg is up there now trying to fix it.'

'And where's Mr Weinberger?' Juliet asked, the panic evident in her voice.

Leah shrugged. 'Dunno. Last time I saw him he was rampaging down the first-floor corridor like a rhinoceros with a red-hot poker up its arse.'

'Why on earth didn't you apologize and escort him to another room?'

Leah scowled. ''Snot my job.'

Suddenly a portly figure in a paisley silk dressing gown appeared in the entrance hall behind Leah. His brushy eyebrows were knitted together in fury and his complexion was a worrying shade of aubergine.

'Ah, Mr Weinberger,' Juliet said, nudging Leah aside as she moved towards her irate guest. 'I hear there's a small problem with your room.'

'Small!' the man growled. 'If you think waking up to find

your bed drenched in water constitutes a small problem, I'd sure as hell like to know what your idea of a big one is.'

'You're quite right,' Juliet said quickly. 'I'm so sorry for this dreadful inconvenience, Mr Weinberger. We'll move you to another room right away.'

The man seemed unmoved by her apology. 'What kind of half-assed establishment are you running here?' he said in a loud voice. 'The plumbing sucks, the towels are too small, the staff are incompetent.' He stamped on the floor with his slippered foot. '*And* my mattress is lumpy.' As his voice reverberated around the entrance hall, another guest appeared at the top of the stairs and looked over the balustrade, curious to see what the kerfuffle was about.

Juliet took Mr Weinberger's arm and tried to lead him in the direction of the dining room. 'Why don't you come and have some breakfast while we get this mess sorted out?'

The man yanked his arm free. 'I won't be needing a new room. As soon as I've packed my suitcase, I'm leaving. But, before I go, allow me to introduce myself,' he said, reaching into the pocket of his dressing gown and thrusting a business card into Juliet's hand.

Juliet was confused. 'But I already know your name, Mr Weinberger.'

'Yeah, but you don't know what line of work I'm in,' the man said triumphantly as he turned round and began marching up the stairs.

Juliet looked down at the card in her hand: *Carson Weinberger, Senior Inspector, Schwartz's Hotel Guide.*

'I don't fucking believe it,' she said, clapping a hand to her head.

Leah tutted loudly. '*Language*, Mrs Fisher!'

5

It had taken Nicole the best part of the afternoon to get ready for Juliet's dinner party. Since giving birth, she hadn't had the time, or the energy, to lavish much attention on herself – but tonight was a special occasion and it deserved a special effort. After dropping Tilly off at her mother's, she headed for Loxwood's most upmarket salon, emerging two hours later with her frizzy mop blowdried into a sleek bob, her eyebrows freshly waxed and her fingernails shining with a subtle peony polish. Later, as she walked along the high street, she happened to glance in the window of a chic vintage boutique, where she spotted an adorable black satin cocktail bag. She baulked when she saw the price tag but, knowing how well the bag would go with the full-skirted shirtdress she was planning to wear, she couldn't resist splashing out.

Back at home, Nicole's plans received a setback when she discovered the shirtdress still bore an unpleasant residue of baby sick on the collar, despite two washes in biological detergent. Vigorous rubbing with a damp cloth only succeeded in fading the dye around the stain, so that now it looked twice as bad. Eventually, after trying on at least a dozen deeply unflattering outfits, she settled on a geometric print skirt and a pretty tunic top that did a good job of disguising her swollen breasts and soft stomach.

Connor was sprawled across the bed, observing his wife's

preparations with some degree of amusement. The doctor's face was wide, the features on it almost too expressive, like those of an actor who'd made a career of crowd pleasing and grown expert in cheap effects. 'You're pushing the boat out a bit, aren't you?' he said. 'It's only a dinner party.'

'It's more than that,' Nicole replied, frowning as she tried to brush the clumps of mascara out of her eyelashes. 'We're meeting Juliet's new husband for the first time.'

Connor yawned. 'Big deal.'

'You might show a bit more enthusiasm,' Nicole said, giving up with the mascara and reaching for a neutral lipstick. 'And I want you to be nice to Dante. He doesn't know anyone in England; he's bound to be feeling a bit at sea.'

'But he's just a kid – I doubt we'll have anything in common.'

'Well, *find* something.' Nicole glared at her husband in the mirror. 'Please . . . do it for me.'

Connor rolled off the bed. 'All right, all right,' he muttered. 'Anything to stop you nagging.'

He didn't see the wounded look in his wife's eyes.

Half an hour later, the Swifts' Audi was making its way along Ashwicke's long drive. Magnificent trees lined the way, their highest boughs arching to meet, so the drive became a dark, whispering tunnel. At the end of the tunnel stood the house itself, rearing up from the shadowy mass of grass and trees, its façade fabulous with amber light cast from a series of outdoor lamps.

At the door, Nathan was waiting to greet them. 'Good evening, Doctor and Mrs Swift,' he said in a solemn voice. 'Won't you come in?'

Nicole, who'd met the general manager on several previous occasions, smiled. 'You're working late, aren't you, Nathan?'

He nodded. 'I know it's a big night for Mrs Fisher so I offered to lend a hand at her little soirée. That way she can concentrate on her guests.' The manager ushered the couple into the hall, before returning to the vestibule to hang up their coats. 'The others are having drinks in the drawing room. If you'd like to follow me . . .'

As he turned to lead the way, an elderly lady came shuffling along the corridor towards them. She presented a neat figure in a tartan skirt and angora cardigan. A cameo brooch pinned to the neck of her blouse kept in place, not just the lace collar, but also the strands of wrinkled skin that stretched from her throat to her chin and swayed gently as she spoke.

'Hello, dear,' she said as Nathan approached.

'Hello, Mrs Hibbert,' he replied. 'What are you doing here? The west wing is out of bounds to hotel guests.'

The woman's rheumy eyes blinked. 'Oh, I'm sorry. I didn't mean to go off piste. I was looking for my knitting. I thought it was in my room, but I can't find it anywhere.'

'I expect you left it in the residents' lounge,' the manager replied. 'Why don't I take you there?'

'Oh, yes, please,' the woman said, linking her arm through Nathan's. 'It's a while since I had an escort, especially one as handsome as you.'

Nathan grimaced at the Swifts over the top of her head. 'Sorry, folks, would you excuse me for a moment?'

'It's okay,' Nicole said, smiling. 'We can see ourselves to the drawing room. I know the way.'

Nathan and Mrs Hibbert were barely out of earshot when Connor turned to Nicole. 'This place is a joke,' he said. 'Mark my words, Juliet will be out of business by the end of the year.'

Nicole looked at her husband in surprise. 'I beg your pardon?'

'I mean, whatever was Juliet thinking, setting up a hotel in the first place? She doesn't know the first thing about it.' He gestured towards a zig-zagging crack in the wall that ran from floor to ceiling. 'And if the guest accommodation is anything like the rest of the house it's no wonder she's struggling to attract guests. When Gus died, she should've sold up, taken the money and run.'

'Actually, I rather admire Juliet for taking a risk,' Nicole said tightly. 'It takes a lot of guts to do what she did.'

Connor gave a sneering laugh. 'Guts? Stupidity, more like.'

Nicole felt a retort rising in her throat but, not wanting to sour the mood, she swallowed it back down. 'I hope you're going to make an effort tonight,' she said as they approached the double doors leading to the drawing room. 'Like Nathan said, it's a big night for Juliet.'

'Don't worry,' Connor muttered as he straightened his tie and summoned up one of the fake smiles he usually reserved for patients. 'I won't let the side down.'

It was a modest gathering, six people in all, and yet the room gave the impression of being full. The air was thick with excited voices and a rather strident aftershave. Vivaldi was playing softly in the background and a large champagne bucket had pride of place on top of the baby grand.

In the midst of the group stood Juliet. She was talking to a weaselly character in a Harris tweed jacket that Nicole recognized as Gus's father, Piers, a prominent local businessman. Standing next to them both was a good-looking young man with tawny hair, flecked with gold, and a deep tan. He was smiling and nodding, but his posture was awkward and his eyes bore the bewildered expression of a cartoon character who had just been flattened by a steamroller.

For a couple of seconds nobody seemed to have noticed the Swifts' arrival; then suddenly Juliet was walking over to them, smiling with what looked to Nicole very much like relief. 'Perfect timing,' Juliet hissed in her friend's ear as they exchanged kisses. 'I've been stuck with Piers for ages. I don't think he likes Dante.'

'How can you tell?' Nicole whispered back.

'It's glaringly obvious,' Juliet said. Without elaborating further, she ushered the couple towards the others. 'Everyone, I'd like you to meet my good friends, Nicole and Connor Swift.'

Brief introductions followed with the Ingrams and Juliet's parents, before finally it was Dante's turn. Connor took the American's hand in a firm grip and pumped it in a good-humoured, matey fashion.

'Connor's a GP,' Juliet told Dante. 'His surgery only opened a few months ago, but it's already got a waiting list as long as your arm. It's not like your average NHS surgery either; the décor's really sleek and minimalist . . . you must've spent a fortune on the refurb, Connor.'

The doctor shrugged good-naturedly. 'Only the best for my patients. What line of business are you in, Dante?'

'I worked in a bar back in Aspen. But, uh, I'm not doing anything right now.'

Behind his back Nicole saw Gus's mother flinch.

'It's great to meet you at last,' Dante told Nicole. 'Juliet talks about you a lot. I guess you guys are pretty close.'

Nicole smiled at Juliet. 'Yes, I like to think so.'

'Have you known each other long?'

'Five years or so; we met at a yoga class.'

'We were the useless ones at the back who couldn't even master the breathing techniques,' said Juliet. As she spoke, the double doors opened again and Yasmin appeared, looking effortlessly stunning in a floaty bandeau dress and lots of ethnic jewellery. 'Unlike that exotic creature over there who could wrap both legs round her neck on day one.' She linked her arm through Dante's. 'Come on, let's go and say hello.'

When Yasmin had done the round of introductions and the guests' champagne flutes had been refilled, Juliet clapped her hands together to get everyone's attention. 'Now that we're all here, I'd like to propose a toast,' she said. She looked at Dante adoringly and raised her glass to him. 'To my new husband.'

'Dante,' the guests chorused, some more enthusiastically than others.

Nicole smiled as Dante unselfconsciously took Juliet in his arms and buried his face in her hair. 'Don't they make a lovely couple?' she remarked to Juliet's mother, Catherine, standing next to her.

'Lovely,' Catherine echoed. She fingered the rope of pearls at her neck and added in a low voice, 'He's very different to Gus, though. I do hope Juliet knows what she's doing.'

Before Nicole could reply, Nathan arrived to announce that dinner was about to be served.

The dining room looked beautiful. The walls were painted a soft sage green and decorated at regular intervals with brass sconces in the shape of shells. On the sixteen-foot walnut dining table, silver cruets and bulbous carafes of iced water jostled for position with Waterford candelabra and stiff white napkins folded in the shape of swans. In the midst of it all, flanked by sparkling clusters of glassware, was a towering centrepiece of frosted fruit, skilfully arranged on a glittering salver.

'I thought it might be fun to mix all the couples up,' said Juliet, resting her hands on the back of a Regency carver. 'I've laid out place cards, so if you'd all like to find your seats . . .' She turned to Nathan, who was standing by the door, fingers neatly laced together. 'We're ready for the starter now, thank you.'

Nathan nodded and slipped out of the room discreetly.

As Nicole took her seat, she glanced at Dante, who was sitting opposite her. He still looked rather anxious. Nicole felt a rush of sympathy for him. She tried to catch his eye so she could give him a reassuring smile, but he was too busy gazing in confusion at the battalion of cutlery laid out in front of him.

A few moments later, Charlie appeared, struggling under the weight of a heavily laden tray.

'Charlie's our porter,' Juliet explained as the youth moved round the table distributing bowls of onion consommé under Nathan's hawk-like gaze. 'He very kindly agreed to act as waiter tonight.'

At this, Gus's mother, Eleanor, an elegant woman, whose good looks were spoiled somewhat by the vulpine curve of her mouth, gave her hostess a spiky look. 'Don't you have any proper waiters?'

'There are so few guests it's not worth hiring any,' Juliet replied. 'I usually serve the breakfasts myself.'

Eleanor frowned. 'Isn't that a bit beneath you, dear?'

'Not at all,' Juliet replied, picking up her soup spoon. 'Actually, I rather enjoy it.'

'Business is still slow, then,' said Piers.

'Yes, unfortunately. We've only got five guests at the moment. I'm hoping things will pick up in the summer.'

''Fraid we're down to three now,' Charlie said as he set down a basket of bread rolls. 'Mr and Mrs Johnson checked out of the T. S. Eliot this afternoon. They found mouse droppings in their wardrobe.'

'How embarrassing,' Juliet murmured. 'Ask Reg to put down some traps when he comes in tomorrow, would you?'

Eleanor gave a little shudder. 'Do they have free run of the place?'

Juliet nodded. 'I'm afraid mice are inevitable in an old place like Ashwicke, although we do try to keep them under control.'

Eleanor sighed. 'I was talking about the guests.'

'Oh,' said Juliet, giggling at her mistake. 'No, the guest accommodation is confined to the east wing. Dante and I have the west wing to ourselves – although guests do occasionally get lost and wander in by mistake.'

'I wouldn't care to share *my* home with strangers,' Eleanor remarked.

'Oh, it's not so bad. Most of the guests keep themselves to themselves.'

Piers wiped his bushy moustache with his napkin. 'Can't think why you wanted to turn the place into a hotel in the first place.'

'I'm with Piers on this one,' Connor said. 'I really think you're being overambitious, Juliet. The hotel business is a tough old game, especially for someone like you with no experience.'

Across the table, Nicole glared at him.

'I had to do something,' Juliet said. 'It's the only way I can afford to keep the place going.'

Eleanor had the look of a hawk about to strike. 'Gus must be turning in his grave.'

At this, Dante looked up from his soup. 'The house is Juliet's now,' he said quietly, but firmly. 'It's up to her what she does with it.'

A heavy silence descended on the table. Yasmin looked at Eleanor and saw she was wearing an annoyed, tooth-achey expression. Fearing that an atmosphere might be brewing, she turned to her hostess. 'This is delicious soup. You'll have to give me the recipe.'

'I'm afraid I can't claim credit for it,' said Juliet, flashing her friend a grateful look. 'Chef made it before he left this morning.'

Another silence, and then Piers cleared his throat noisily. 'So, Dante,' he began in a hearty tone. 'How are you finding life at Ashwicke?'

'The house is awesome,' Dante replied. 'I had no idea Juliet lived in such a cool place.'

Eleanor bared her teeth in a parody of a smile. 'It must be quite a culture shock for a barman, eh?' she said.

'Senior cocktail waiter,' Dante corrected her.

The smile faded. 'Pardon?'

'That was my job title: Senior Cocktail Waiter.'

'Oh, you were a *waiter*,' Eleanor said. 'In that case, shouldn't you be the one dishing up the soup?' She started tittering. 'Only teasing,' she added insincerely. 'Did you live above the bar?'

Nicole could see a vein in Dante's temple throbbing.

'No,' he replied. 'I shared an apartment a couple of miles away.'

'You *shared*,' Eleanor said, as if it were quite the most appalling concept she'd ever heard of. 'In that case living here must be quite a step up for you. I bet you couldn't believe your luck when you saw the house for the first time.'

'Of course he couldn't,' Nicole said, painfully aware of the blush unfurling across Dante's face. 'Any one of us would be grateful to live in a beautiful place like Ashwicke.'

'Absolutely,' said Yasmin. 'And I'm sure Dante's going to be a huge help with the business.'

'Invaluable,' Juliet agreed. 'He's worked in the service industry ever since he left school. I daresay he'll be able to teach me a thing or two.' She smiled in her husband's direction. 'Actually, I was thinking about making him Customer Liaison Manager. Nathan's so busy these days; it would be nice to offload some of his responsibilities onto Dante – and I'm sure he's more than capable of doing it. Aren't you, darling?'

Dante, who seemed to be growing more uncomfortable by the minute, nodded mutely.

Juliet's father, Richard, a tall, gingery man who'd barely said a thing all evening, smiled at Dante. 'Have you had a chance to explore the local area?'

Dante seemed grateful for the change of subject. 'Not really,' he said. 'I'd like to, though. Juliet tells me there's beautiful countryside around here.'

'I've been so busy with the hotel I haven't had much time to show Dante the sights,' Juliet explained.

'I'm happy to take Dante on a recce,' Piers piped up.

Juliet looked vaguely alarmed at the prospect. 'That's very sweet of you to offer, but really there's no need.'

'Nonsense,' said Piers, tossing down his napkin. 'How else are we going to get to know each other?' He turned to Dante. 'Tell you what, I'm going deer hunting with a few other chaps next week. Why don't you tag along?'

Dante's soup spoon stopped halfway to his mouth. 'Thanks for the offer, but I think I'll give it a miss. Hunting's not really my thing.'

Catherine clucked disapprovingly. 'Oh go on, Dante. It'll be heaps of fun.'

'The thing is . . .' Dante squirmed in his seat. 'I don't agree with killing animals for sport.'

'Oh for goodness' sakes, man, don't be such a namby-pamby,' Piers said with a startling degree of vitriol. 'Hunting's part of everyday life in the country.'

'I'll take your word for it,' Dante replied. 'But that doesn't mean I have to participate in it.'

'But those deer are a bloody pest. They cause millions of pounds' worth of damage to forestry and agriculture. Killing them is the only way to keep the blighters under control.'

Dante shrugged. 'If you say so.'

His nonchalant demeanour seemed to rile the older man. 'Now look here, old chap,' Piers said, his face flushed with emotion, 'if you're going to live in the country, you can't afford to be so bloody sensitive, or else –'

'No offence, Piers, but yours is actually quite an outdated view,' Yasmin suddenly broke in.

He glowered at her. 'What the devil are you talking about?'

'I work for one of the highest circulation regional newspapers in the country,' she said smoothly. 'We ran a poll a couple of months ago. More than seventy per cent of our readers were against hunting of any kind.'

Piers made a harrumphing noise. 'Were they now?' He looked at Dante. 'I didn't mean to get on my high horse,' he said gruffly. 'It's just that hunting is something I'm very passionate about.'

'It's okay,' Dante replied as he helped himself to a wholemeal roll. 'I know you guys do lots of things differently over here.' He pulled the butter dish towards him and picked up a knife.

Eleanor, who was sitting next to him, rapped his wrist. 'Not that knife, Dante,' she said in a loud voice. 'That's for the fish.' She tapped her own butter knife. 'In *this* country, we start from the outside and work our way in.'

'Don't you have knives and forks in America?' Piers quipped.

Dante's jaw tightened. 'All us Yanks eat with our fingers, didn't you know?' he said. 'After all, who needs cutlery when our diet consists almost entirely of hamburgers and fried chicken?'

At this Piers threw back his head and laughed uproariously. 'I like a chap with a sense of humour.'

He failed to notice that Dante wasn't laughing.

During the main course of herb-crusted monkfish with roasted vegetables, talk turned, as it often does at dinner parties, to the price of property.

'I see that timbered cottage opposite the church is up for sale again,' remarked Catherine. 'I can't believe it's on for 1.3 million. Who in their right mind is going to pay that sort of money for a house with no off-street parking?'

'You'd be surprised,' said Piers, tweaking the cuffs of his tweed jacket ostentatiously. 'Property in Loxwood's always in demand. When houses come onto the market, they're snapped up almost before the details have been printed.'

His wife pursed her lips. 'But if that new development gets the go ahead, house prices in the area will plummet,' she declared. 'Isn't that right, Piers?'

'Damn right they will,' he said. 'Buyers like Loxwood because the properties are so individual. A modern estate is certainly going to lower the tone.'

Yasmin turned to Dante. 'A developer has put in a planning application for twenty executive homes on the site of the old fruit farm. It's about half a mile from here.'

'It'll be a bloody eyesore,' Eleanor said. 'Let's just hope those planning officers at the council see sense.' She gave a long, heavy sigh that made her shoulders droop. 'Gus would've been up in arms about it – and he'd have got the whole town behind him.' She banged the table with the palm of her hand, making the cutlery jump. 'Wouldn't he, Juliet?'

'I expect so,' Juliet murmured as she drove her fork through a roasted tomato. 'Gus was certainly never backwards about coming forward.'

Piers released a sudden chuckle. 'Do you remember when he heard the council was threatening to revoke the licence at the cricket-club bar after those allegations of underage drinking?'

'How could we forget?' Catherine cried, clapping her hands together. 'I thought I was going to die laughing when I saw him.'

Yasmin nodded. 'He even made it into the paper. It was quite a talking point on our letters page.'

'What happened?' asked Dante.

Yasmin smiled. 'Gus was so incensed at the prospect of an alcohol-free cricket club that he chained himself to the railings outside the pavilion in protest.'

Connor grinned. 'She's left out the best bit . . . Gus was completely starkers.'

'On a Saturday lunchtime,' Richard added.

'People couldn't believe their eyes,' said Eleanor. 'Drivers were stopping their cars to gawp at him – it caused a tailback through the town a mile long.'

'He spent most of the afternoon chained to those railings,' said Piers. 'He would've stayed even longer, but some old dear called the police. They were going to charge him with indecent exposure but, Gus being Gus, he managed to charm his way out of it.' He looked at his daughter-in-law. 'He certainly had the gift of the gab, eh, Juliet?'

'He certainly did,' Juliet agreed. As she spoke, Nicole thought she heard a catch in her voice.

'Poor Gus,' said Eleanor, hanging her head. 'He had so much to live for.'

For a few moments, the only sound in the room was the scrape of cutlery on fine china as each of the guests was lost in their own private thoughts. Yasmin's gaze fell on Dante, who had stopped eating and was staring fixedly at his plate. She supposed it must be rather awkward for him . . . sitting there, listening to the others talking about his predecessor's exploits with a mix of affection and awe, especially when the whole point of the dinner party had been to celebrate his own arrival in Loxwood. Suddenly, Dante pushed his chair away from the table.

'Excuse me,' he said, tossing down his napkin. 'I need to use the john.'

As he got up from the table, Yasmin caught Eleanor's barely concealed look of disgust. Whether it had been provoked by Dante's use of slang, or his breach of etiquette by leaving the table mid-course, was anyone's guess.

It was with a certain degree of relief that Nicole and Connor set off on the short drive home, just after midnight.

'I'm glad that's over,' Connor said as their car passed through the entrance gates. 'You could have cut the atmosphere in that dining room with a knife.'

'Gus's parents are vile,' Nicole said. 'I know it must be hard for them, seeing Juliet with another man – especially in the house where Gus grew up – but they didn't have to give Dante such a hard time.' She turned to her husband. 'Will you give him a call in the next few days and offer to take him out? We don't want him thinking everyone in Loxwood's obsessed with blood sports and the finer points of table etiquette.'

Connor groaned. 'Look, Nic, I've got an awful lot on my plate at the surgery just now.'

'You're *always* busy,' Nicole snapped. 'I'm beginning to wonder just what goes on at that surgery of yours.'

'I didn't say I wouldn't do it,' Connor said quickly. 'I just need to check my diary first.'

Nicole stared out of the window as the hedgerows flashed by. Although the lane was unlit, the moon was full and it cast an ethereal glow over everything that, for some inexplicable reason, Nicole found arousing.

'You know what,' she said, turning to Connor. 'We should take advantage of the fact Tilly's staying the night with Mum.' She laid a hand on his upper thigh. 'How about it? You could even bend me over the kitchen table, just like old times.'

Connor's eyes remained fixed on the road. 'Do you mind if we give it a miss? I'm absolutely knackered and I've got to get up early to play golf.'

Nicole made a resigned face. 'Of course not,' she said tersely.

Back at Ashwicke, Juliet and Dante had retired for the night.

'Did you have a nice evening, darling?' Juliet said as she sat at her dressing table, brushing her long hair.

'Yeah, it was interesting,' Dante replied, quickly pulling his shirt over his head so his wife wouldn't see his face and know that he was lying.

'I didn't know you were opposed to hunting,' Juliet said lightly.

'I guess there's a lot we don't know about each other.' Dante sat down on the hand-carved Jacobean four-poster that had accommodated three generations of Ingrams and started taking off his socks. 'Like I didn't know you were planning to make me Customer Liaison Manager.'

Juliet turned to face him and smiled. 'Isn't it a great idea?'

Dante shrugged. 'I don't even know what a Customer Liaison Manager is.'

'It's quite straightforward really. You'll be responsible for looking after the guests and dealing with any problems or enquiries they might have. I'll get Nathan to show you the ropes. I'm sure you'll pick it up in no time.'

Dante held up his hand. 'Hold your horses, missy. Did it even cross your mind to discuss your grand plan with me first before you went shooting your mouth off to everyone?'

Juliet's face darkened. 'Actually, the idea only popped into my head this afternoon when I was chatting through some ideas with Nathan. I didn't have a chance to mention it to you before dinner.'

'Oh, so Nathan was the first to know, was he?' Dante said angrily. 'How nice to know you two have been talking about me behind my back.'

'Darling!' Juliet cried, rising to her feet. 'I don't know why you're being so sensitive about this. Nathan and I weren't talking about you; he was just saying he could do with some help. I thought you'd jump at the chance to work at the hotel.'

'Why, because being at Ashwicke is such an enormous

privilege?' Dante said. 'Well pardon me if I don't just fall to the ground and kiss your feet in gratitude, but actually I'd rather get my own job, thanks very much. I don't want to be dependent on you – I want to earn my own money.'

Juliet frowned. 'Doing what?'

'Bartending. There must be lots of pubs in Loxwood. I'm sure I could find something.'

Juliet wrinkled her nose. 'Isn't there something else you could do?'

'Why, what's wrong with being a bartender?'

'It's a bit . . .' Juliet hesitated. 'You know . . . menial.'

'It didn't seem to bother you when we were in Aspen.'

'Yes, but nobody knew me in Aspen.'

A hurt look crossed Dante's face. 'What's that supposed to mean?'

Juliet sighed. 'Sorry, I shouldn't have said anything. Look, I'm not going to stop you looking for a job if that's what you really want to.'

'How incredibly generous of you,' Dante scoffed. Then, not trusting himself to keep his temper in check any longer, he marched to the en suite, slamming the door shut behind him. Once he was alone, he sat on the edge of the bath, taking deep breaths as a huge wave of anger threatened to engulf him – except it wasn't Juliet he was angry at. It was the Ingrams.

Back in the bedroom, Juliet went to the window seat and sat by the open window, staring vacantly ahead as the night breeze brought goose bumps to her bare arms. She didn't see Nathan in the garden below. The general manager was enjoying a cigarette on the terrace after his night's labours before heading back to the lodge. He'd overheard most of the Fishers' conversation and now, as he ground out his cigarette on the wall, he gave a curdled smile, confident that the beautiful prize he lusted after would soon be his.

6

'Shit!' Yasmin muttered as a dollop of cream-cheese frosting slid off the spatula and landed on the sleeve of her favourite Whistles cardie. Sighing, she threw down the implement and reached for a cloth. In less than half an hour, Nicole and Juliet would be arriving for afternoon tea. Usually, they met at Nicole's spacious Edwardian semi, but the doctor's wife was having new kitchen units fitted, necessitating a change of venue.

Nicole was a veritable domestic goddess, who always laid on homemade cake and a selection of exotic teas. Yasmin, by contrast, didn't know the first thing about baking, and usually drank PG Tips, or black coffee, the stronger the better. Against her better judgement, she'd decided to make a cake, when it would've been far easier – and probably far cheaper too – to buy one from the local baker's. After scouring the internet for a suitable recipe, Yasmin had followed the instructions to the letter but, to her disgust, both sponges had turned out lopsided and the frosting was suspiciously runny. Having wiped the worst of it off her cardie, she turned her attention back to the misshapen cake, scattering walnuts on top in a vain attempt to improve its attractiveness. 'Oh well,' she said as she carried it over to the dining table where cups and side plates were already laid out. 'That'll have to do.'

*

On the other side of Loxwood, Nicole was preparing to leave the house. 'Now, don't forget Tilly's five o'clock feed,' she told her husband, raising her voice so she could be heard above the sound of drilling.

Connor looked at his wife in horror. 'Five o'clock? Surely you'll be back by then.'

'I doubt it,' Nicole replied. 'The girls and I have got lots to catch up on.'

'But you only saw them at the weekend.'

When Nicole failed to reply, Connor kicked the leg of the sofa like a sulky teenager. 'I don't know why you have to spend so much time with those women anyway,' he grumbled.

'Because they're my *friends*,' she said shortly. 'In any case, it will be good for you and Tilly to spend some quality time together.'

Connor winced as a loud bang issued from the kitchen, followed by a string of expletives. 'What am I supposed to do with her?' he asked. 'We can't stay in the house with that bloody racket going on.'

'I don't know,' Nicole said impatiently, wishing Connor were the sort of father who was bursting with ideas for fun-filled afternoons with his infant daughter. 'Go for a walk . . . Take her to feed the ducks in the park. Or, if you're really desperate, you could always go round to my mother's.'

Connor's face lit up. 'Brilliant! That's what I'll do.'

Nicole's heart sank. She should've known Connor would take the easy option. 'You'd better go and wake Tilly up,' she told him. 'If you let her sleep too long now, she won't go down tonight.'

'Okay,' Connor said in a bored tone. He turned as if to go, then glanced back over his shoulder. 'Is that what you're wearing to Yasmin's?'

Nicole looked down at her cotton wrapover dress. Admittedly, it was a size 14 when she was more like a 16 these days, but it *was* one of her favourites. 'Why, what's wrong with it?'

Connor rubbed a hand over his jaw. 'I think it makes you look a bit . . . you know . . . paunchy.'

'Really?' Nicole said, frowning. 'I thought I looked quite nice.'

Connor shrugged. 'It's fine, honestly. I shouldn't have said anything.'

'Then why *did* you?' Nicole snapped as she snatched up her handbag and headed for the front door.

Juliet was the first to arrive. It was a while since she'd visited the apartment and, as her hostess fetched cold drinks from the vast, American-style refrigerator, she found herself gazing around the open-plan space in envy. Housed in a former jam factory, Yasmin's apartment was achingly chic, with exposed brickwork, mood lighting and a breathtaking Brazilian walnut floor. She'd softened the industrial architecture with clever use of texture and colour, and the bare walls had been brought to life with huge, fabric-covered canvases.

'You are lucky,' Juliet said as the younger woman joined her on the smart modular sofa. 'I'd love to live in a place like this.'

Yasmin wrinkled her nose disbelievingly. 'Oh come on, why on earth would you want to live in a one-bedroom apartment when you've got Ashwicke?'

Juliet took a sip of apple juice. 'Yes, but the house is incredibly high maintenance and so . . . well . . . big. Even with the guests I sometimes feel quite lost in there.'

'So why don't you sell it?'

Juliet looked at her aghast. 'I couldn't do that. Gus's mother would never speak to me again.'

'What's it got to do with Eleanor?' Yasmin replied. 'It's like Dante said the other night – the house is yours. You can do whatever you like with it.'

Juliet sighed. 'Well, yes, in theory – but I can't help feeling a certain obligation to the Ingrams. Ashwicke used to be their family home after all, and it would be awful if it fell into the wrong hands. Imagine if the developers got hold of it . . . Eleanor and Piers would never forgive me.'

'Well, I hope they appreciate all your efforts to keep Ashwicke going,' Yasmin said. 'They certainly didn't seem very grateful the other night. I couldn't believe it when Eleanor said Gus would be turning in his grave.'

Juliet winced. 'Yes, it was a bit embarrassing, wasn't it?'

'She was very rude to Dante too. I don't know how he managed to keep his cool.'

'With some difficulty, I suspect.'

'Still,' Yasmin continued, 'I'm sure once the Ingrams see Dante's getting involved in the upkeep of Ashwicke they'll be a bit nicer to him.'

Juliet licked her lips. 'Actually, I don't think Dante's going to be getting involved.'

'But I thought you said he was going to be Customer Liaison Manager.'

'Apparently not. We had a huge row about it afterwards.

Dante was pissed off because I hadn't discussed it with him first.'

Yasmin shrugged. 'Oh well, I suppose that's understandable. I'm sure he'll come round to the idea.'

'No, he won't. He's going to get a bartending job. He says he doesn't want to be dependent on me.'

'That's not a bad thing, is it?'

'I suppose not.' Juliet looked down at her hands, absent-mindedly rubbing her wedding ring. 'I think I'm just disappointed because I assumed he'd want to be involved in the business.'

'Didn't you discuss that sort of thing before you got married?'

'No, it sounds crazy now but I was so caught up in the moment I didn't really think about the practicalities of our life together. Actually, there were lots of things we didn't discuss. Before we came to England, I didn't even know what Dante's favourite movie is or how he takes his coffee. She frowned. 'Come to think of it, I still don't know what his favourite movie is.'

Just then the intercom buzzed into life, making them both jump. 'That'll be Nicole,' Yasmin said, rising to her feet. After pressing the entry button, she opened the front door and stood on the threshold until the lift doors parted.

'Hi, Nic,' Yasmin said as her friend emerged from the lift, looking harassed. 'Is everything all right?'

The furrow between Nicole's brows deepened.

'You look as if you're chewing a wasp,' Yasmin added.

Nicole's hand went to her forehead. 'Do I?' She followed

Yasmin into the apartment and sat down heavily on the sofa. 'It's Connor,' she said, after she and Juliet had exchanged a brief greeting. 'He's just so bloody selfish.'

'What's he done now?' Juliet asked.

'He resents me having a social life,' Nicole said, folding her arms crossly in front of her chest. 'He seems to think it's perfectly okay for him to spend hours at the gym, or stay out all night drinking with his golfing buddies, but the minute I want to set foot outside the house he kicks up a fuss.'

'Is it because you've left him looking after Tilly?' Yasmin enquired.

'That's part of it,' Nicole conceded. 'I know babies can be hard work, but given that he's barely laid eyes on his daughter all week I thought he'd really enjoy spending some time with her. But, no, all he can do is moan about the fact I'm going out and ask me how he's supposed to entertain her.'

Yasmin groaned in sympathy. 'This is the reason I'm never getting married.'

'Naturally, the lazy sod jumped at the chance when I suggested taking Tilly to my mum's,' Nicole continued. 'No doubt he'll sit there reading the paper like he always does, while Mum keeps her granddaughter amused.' Her mouth tightened. '*And* he said I looked fat in this dress.'

'He didn't!' Juliet gasped.

'As good as.' Nicole pulled thoughtfully on her lower lip. 'Honestly, I don't know what's got into him these days. He's not the man I married, that's for sure.'

'I'm sure it's just a temporary blip,' Juliet said. 'All marriages go through rough patches. Have you told him how you're feeling?'

'Yes, several times,' Nicole said wearily, 'but it doesn't seem to have much effect. Connor just sits there with a strangulated look on his face, like he'd rather be examining some old dear's haemorrhoids than listen to me going on. And when I've finished he'll apologize for being ratty and say it's only because he's feeling under pressure at work. Afterwards, he'll be on his best behaviour for a couple of days and then he'll slip back into his old ways.' Her eyes blazed with frustration. 'Our love life's still non-existent too. I tried to initiate sex the other night while we were lying in bed together and do you know what he did?'

Both women shook their heads.

'Started snoring. I knew damn well he wasn't asleep, though.'

'So what do you think the root of the problem is?' Juliet asked.

'Connor's always had a low boredom threshold. The truth is I just don't think our marriage is exciting enough for him.' Nicole sighed. 'I don't know if it ever has been.'

'I'm sure that's not true,' Juliet said. 'You two just need to inject some romance back into your relationship.'

'And how am I supposed to do that when we hardly ever see each other?'

'Lure him back from the surgery one evening with a spurious excuse, something he can't just ignore.'

Nicole looked at her doubtfully. 'Like what?'

'Oh come on, Nic, use your imagination. Say a water pipe's burst or the garden shed's on fire. Then, when he walks through the door, surprise him with a candlelit dinner.'

'Yeah, and make sure you're wearing your sexiest underwear,' Yasmin said. 'I know it's a cliché, but all the blokes I know go wild for lingerie.'

Nicole raised an eyebrow. 'That's because you've got a gorgeous toned body. I, on the other hand, am a big fat blob that no man – least of all my fitness fanatic husband – could possibly find attractive.'

'No you're not,' Juliet said staunchly. 'You're a gorgeous, voluptuous woman and it's high time Connor started appreciating you more.'

'Something's got to change,' Nicole muttered. 'Otherwise our marriage is heading for the divorce courts. I know what it's like to come from a broken home and I don't want Tilly going through the same thing I did.' She mustered a smile. 'Anyway, that's quite enough about my marital problems. Let's talk about something else, shall we?' She turned to Yasmin. 'I didn't get a chance to ask you at Juliet's dinner party about your date with the waiter. How did it go?'

Yasmin grimaced. 'It was a massive letdown. I wish I hadn't bothered.'

'Oh, that's a shame,' Juliet said. 'What happened?'

Yasmin kicked off her sandals and folded her legs underneath her. 'Well, for starters Pascal was supposed to be cooking me dinner, but when he arrived – forty-five minutes late and reeking of aftershave – all he'd brought were two frozen pizzas.'

Juliet tutted. 'Not a good start.'

'He was looking pretty hot, though, so I was prepared to overlook it. In any case, I wasn't that hungry.'

'So what did you do?' Nicole asked.

'We had a couple of glasses of wine – *my* wine, I might

add; he hadn't bothered to bring any – and chatted for a bit. He talked mainly about himself, which was pretty boring, so after half an hour or so I decided to cut to the chase.'

'Meaning?' Juliet asked, wide-eyed.

'Meaning, I excused myself to go to the bathroom and when I came back I was wearing my short silk dressing gown.'

Nicole giggled. 'You are brave. I'd never have the nerve to do something like that.'

'We both knew what we were there for,' Yasmin said nonchalantly. 'And Pascal didn't need a second invitation. He came over and started kissing me. Then he picked me up in his arms and carried me into the bedroom.'

Nicole squealed. 'How exciting! I thought that sort of thing only happened in Mills and Boon novels.'

Yasmin snorted. 'Believe me, Pascal's no hero – at least not in the sack. After taking off his clothes he spent at least ten minutes parading around my bedroom naked, showing off his bod, which, I must admit, was pretty spectacular.'

'And then . . .' Nicole prompted.

Juliet shuddered. 'I'm not sure I want to hear this.'

'I do,' said Nicole. 'I'm not having sex with my husband, so how else am I supposed to get my thrills?' She turned to Yasmin. 'Go on.'

'And then we got down to business,' Yasmin said matter-of-factly. 'I'll spare you the gory details. Suffice to say that, like a lot of good-looking men, Pascal's incredibly selfish in bed. When he climaxed, he even called out his own name.'

'You're joking . . .' Juliet said.

'Well yeah, actually I am,' Yasmin conceded. 'But if he

had done I wouldn't have been the least bit surprised.' She rolled her eyes. 'And afterwards he even had the cheek to ask me to give him a lift home.'

'What did you say?'

'I gave him his coat and told him where the nearest bus stop was.'

Nicole clapped her hands together. 'Good for you.'

'I don't know why you bother having these one-night stands,' Juliet said, frowning. 'It sounds like an awful lot of effort for not very much reward, if you ask me.'

'Not as much effort as a relationship,' Yasmin replied.

'Isn't there anyone nice at work?' Juliet enquired hopefully.

'Nope. They're all married, ugly, emotionally retarded or all of the above.' Yasmin frowned. 'Actually, there is *one* bloke . . . Rob. He's the sports editor.'

'What does he look like?' Juliet said eagerly.

'He's tall and dark, with amazing brown eyes,' Yasmin began. Suddenly she batted her hand in front of her face. 'No, forget it . . . We're always arguing in the office; it would never work.' She stood up. 'Shall we have tea, ladies?'

Nicole nodded. 'Yes, please, I'm starving.'

'Don't get too excited,' said Yasmin, walking over to the kitchen to put the kettle on. 'I made the cake myself and it's a pretty amateurish affair.'

'Well, I think it looks lovely,' Nicole said as she took a seat at the dining table.

'And I bet it tastes delicious,' Juliet added.

'Thanks, ladies,' Yasmin said, beaming over the breakfast bar. 'I knew I could rely on you two to lie through your teeth.'

7

Nicole could feel her eyelids drooping as she pushed the buggy along the deserted lane. She'd been up several times in the night with Tilly who, having got over her colic, was now teething. Amazingly, Connor had barely stirred while his daughter was bawling her lungs out – an achievement which had succeeded in making Nicole not only sleep-deprived, but resentful too. In the morning, she glared at him as he emerged from the shower looking handsome and well rested. 'Good sleep, darling?' she enquired.

'Great, thanks,' he replied, oblivious to her sarcasm.

Unable to help herself, Nicole picked up a slipper and hurled it across the room, catching Connor on the shoulder.

'What the hell was that for?' he snapped.

'You try surviving on four hours' sleep a night!' she screamed at him.

He shrugged nonchalantly as he pulled a shirt from the wardrobe. 'I said ages ago we should get an au pair.'

'But I don't want somebody else looking after my child,' she retorted.

'I can't bloody win, can I?' Connor muttered, before stalking out of the room.

Ten minutes later he left for the surgery with only the most cursory of goodbyes, shouted from the foot of the stairs.

With her husband gone, an exhausted Nicole would

have liked nothing better than a lazy morning at home, but she'd promised to call in at Ashwicke with some cookbooks. In a bid to increase her profit margins, Juliet was introducing afternoon teas at the hotel, and needed some quick and easy cake recipes she could fling together at short notice.

It was such a glorious day that Nicole had decided to walk the mile or so to Ashwicke. She was hoping the exercise would have the dual effect of waking her up and lulling Tilly to sleep, but sadly it didn't seem to be working on either front. As she prepared to turn into Ashwicke's long drive, she paused to adjust the hood of the buggy, so the sun wasn't shining in Tilly's eyes. She was so distracted she didn't see Charlie's ancient Ford Escort speeding round the bend until it was too late. With a loud scream, Nicole hurled herself across the buggy, sending it tipping backwards into the grass verge at the side of the road – and her with it. Seconds later the car roared past, its driver seemingly oblivious to the chaos he'd left in his wake.

'Bloody lunatic!' Nicole shrieked after him. 'You could have killed us!'

'Are you all right?'

Nicole rolled onto her back. A man was standing over her, blocking out the sunlight. He was tall – well over six feet – with broad shoulders and a shock of sandy hair.

'Erm, I think so,' she replied, peering anxiously at Tilly, who offered a gummy grin.

The man bent down and righted the buggy. 'This little lady doesn't seem to be any the worse for wear,' he said, stroking Tilly's cheek with the back of one of his huge hands.

'Hmm . . . well, it's no thanks to that stupid idiot.'

'He was going a bit fast, wasn't he?' The man took Nicole's hand and helped her to her feet. 'I'm Bear, by the way.'

Nicole looked up at him. He was so tall she had to shade her eyes from the sun. 'I've never met a Bear before,' she remarked.

'It's not my real name; I was christened James. Bear's a throwback to my rugby days.'

'Well, it's nice to meet you, Bear, and thanks for coming to our rescue,' she said. 'I'm Nicole and this is my daughter, Tilly.'

Bear smiled, a slow, deliberate smile that made the corners of his eyes crinkle sexily. 'Are you staying at the hotel?' he asked.

'No, I live just down the road. The hotel owner's a friend of mine. I was popping in to see her.'

'Juliet?'

'That's right. I take it *you're* a guest.'

'Sort of. I'm camping in the grounds.' He pointed to a row of conifers, which shielded a handful of ramshackle outbuildings from view. 'My caravan's parked just behind those trees. I only arrived last night. I was just heading into town for some provisions.'

Nicole looked surprised. 'I didn't realize Juliet was taking campers.'

'She's doing me a favour,' Bear said. 'I turned up at the campsite down the road, only to find my pitch had been double-booked. When I drove past this place and saw the hotel sign and the size of the grounds, I decided to chance my arm and see if the owner could accommodate me for a few weeks – at the going rate, of course. Luckily for me, Juliet agreed.'

'Well, you've certainly picked a beautiful spot for a family holiday.'

'Actually, it's just me.' Bear held her gaze for a long moment. She noticed that his eyes were an unusual shade of blue, so dark they were almost navy. 'And I'm not on holiday – I'm working. My caravan's a lot cheaper than staying in a hotel; it's cosier too.'

'What line of work are you in?'

'I'm a freelance journalist.'

'Really?' Nicole hooked her hair back behind her ears and tried to remember if she'd bothered with mascara before leaving the house. 'One of my best friends is a showbiz reporter. What's your speciality?'

'I write about the environment, which means I spend a lot of time travelling around the country, doing research.' Bear gave a self-deprecating grimace. 'It's not particularly glamorous, but it's something I'm very passionate about.'

'What story are you covering in Loxwood, if you don't mind me asking?' said Nicole, her interest piqued.

'One of the broadsheets has commissioned me to write a piece about the old fruit farm. A big-name developer's hoping to build some executive homes on the site, but it seems there's a lot of local opposition.'

'Oh yes, some friends and I were talking about it at dinner only the other night,' Nicole said. 'It's quite a hot topic of conversation in Loxwood – although I can't imagine why a national newspaper would be interested.'

'You'd be surprised,' Bear said. 'For one thing, that land's Greenbelt. For another, it's home to one of the largest badger setts in the country.' Seeing the blank look on Nicole's face, he added, 'Badgers are a protected species; it's illegal to kill or injure them, or to interfere with a sett.'

'So the developers can't just go tearing up the ground with their JCBs willy-nilly?'

'That's right – although I've heard the local council's under enormous pressure to grant planning permission. The development's going to include a section of affordable housing, you see – and there's precious little of that around these parts. It's looking as if this could turn out to be something of a test case as far as the badgers are concerned.'

'Poor things,' Nicole murmured. 'It doesn't seem fair they should be evicted.'

'My feelings exactly,' agreed Bear. 'They're fascinating creatures. I was planning on going on a badger watch later in the next couple of weeks to get some pictures for my piece.'

Nicole looked at her daughter. 'Hey, did you hear that, Tilly? Our new friend here is going to visit some badgers.' She turned back to Bear. 'She loves animals; so do I, actually – although I must admit I've never seen a badger in the flesh before.'

Bear smiled. 'You're welcome to come with me. You really are missing out if you haven't seen one at close quarters. The best time to see them is at dusk when they're foraging for food.'

Nicole felt a blush rising to her cheeks. She'd only just met Bear, and now here he was inviting her to spend the night with him, so to speak. 'Er, I'm not sure I'll be able to get away,' she said. 'Evenings are a bit difficult, what with the baby and everything.'

Bear shrugged. 'I understand; it was just an idea. In any

case, I'm sure you're far too sensible to head into the woods with a man you've only just met – although I promise you I *am* completely trustworthy.'

Nicole's blush deepened. 'I'm sure you are.'

She suddenly became aware that Bear was staring at the top of her head.

'Do you mind if I, um . . . ?' he said, reaching out a hand. Without waiting for a reply he plucked a sprig of cowslip from her hair. 'A little souvenir from your near-death experience,' he said, tossing it away. He beamed at her, the whiteness of his teeth contrasting pleasingly with his lightly tanned skin. 'I hope you don't mind me saying this, but you have beautiful hair.'

Nicole's hand went to her unruly mane. It was a long time since any man had paid her a compliment. 'You're joking, aren't you?' she said. 'This hair's the bane of my life; one drop of rain and it turns to frizz. Connor – that's my husband – keeps telling me I should have it cut short.'

'Oh no, you mustn't do that,' Bear said.

Suddenly Tilly gave a kittenish mew. Nicole looked down at her, startled, as if she'd forgotten she had a child in tow. 'I think this little madam's getting impatient,' she said, picking up the stuffed rabbit that was lying abandoned in a corner of the buggy and thrusting it into her daughter's arms.

'In that case I won't detain you any longer.' Bear laid a hand on Nicole's bare forearm. His touch was light, but it made her nerve endings tingle. 'But before you go I don't suppose I could ask you a favour, could I?'

Nicole found herself nodding, even though she didn't have the faintest idea what he was going to suggest.

'Could I interview you for my piece?'

'Me?' Nicole said. 'But I don't know the first thing about environmental issues.'

'Maybe not, but you live locally and you'd be able to give me a useful insight into the way local people are feeling. The dinner-party gossip you mentioned . . . that's exactly the sort of stuff I'm after.'

Seeing her hesitation, Bear reached into his jeans pocket and pulled out a battered leather wallet. 'Look, I don't want to put you on the spot. Why don't I give you my number and, if you're up for it, you can give me a call?'

'Oh . . . okay,' Nicole said as she accepted his business card.

Bear stepped aside so she could wheel the buggy off the verge. 'It was nice talking to you, Nicole.'

'You too,' she said. 'Enjoy your walk.'

Halfway along the drive, she looked over her shoulder, but disappointingly Bear had disappeared from view.

Half a mile away, the Willows Surgery, a modern, low-rise building just off Loxwood's historic market square, was preparing to close for lunch. As receptionist Carol McCarthy began bolting the entrance doors, an attractive brunette in her late twenties appeared. She was wearing a smart double-breasted trench coat and carrying an expensive-looking tote bag in the crook of her arm.

Carol smiled pleasantly. 'I'm sorry, dear, the surgery's closed.'

'I just wanted to ask Dr Swift a question about my prescription,' the woman said in a breathy voice.

'The surgery's closed now,' Carol replied. 'Perhaps you could pop back this afternoon.'

The woman's eyes grew larger. 'Oh, but please . . . it'll only take a minute.'

Carol shook her head. 'I'm sorry,' she said again. 'I really can't.'

The woman wrinkled her nose in annoyance and half turned as if she were about to go. Then, all at once, Carol heard the distinctive rich voice that always made her nether regions tingle.

'It's okay, Carol. I'll see Mrs Tripp.'

The receptionist looked over her shoulder. Dr Swift was standing by the reception desk. His hair was rumpled and there was a red patch on his cheek as if he'd been leaning his face on his hand. It was all Carol could do to stop from pressing him to her sagging, fifty-four-year-old bosom. 'Are you sure, Doctor?' she said.

'Yes, you get off home,' Connor replied. 'I'll lock up behind you.' He patted her on the shoulder. 'And thanks for all your hard work this morning.'

The receptionist gave him an adoring smile. 'You're more than welcome, Doctor.' She gave him a little wave. 'See you at two.'

As she set off down the pathway in her sensible shoes, the brunette stepped into the surgery.

'Hello, Zoe,' Connor said. 'This is an unexpected pleasure.'

His patient shot him a haughty look. 'Follow me,' she commanded as she swept past him. 'And do hurry up. I haven't got all day.'

Connor's pulse was racing as he quickly locked the entrance doors and followed her to his office. The minute he was inside, Zoe tossed her bag on the desk and began unbuttoning her trench coat. When it fell to the floor, Connor saw to his astonishment that she was wearing a vintage army uniform: a figure-hugging pencil skirt in lovat green wool and a matching jacket, cinched at the waist. On her shoulder were three gold stars signifying a rank – unless he was very much mistaken – of captain. Beneath the jacket was a starched khaki shirt and tie. Completing the look were old-fashioned seamed stockings and three-inch patent-leather stilettos. It was all Connor could do to stop himself groaning out loud.

As the doctor gazed at his patient admiringly, she reached into her bag and removed a green wool cap, decorated with a red band and an impressive silver badge. She placed it on her head and gave the peak a businesslike tug. Suddenly, her top lip curled in a contemptuous sneer. 'Do you know why I'm here, Private Swift?' she snapped.

Connor shook his head.

'I performed a surprise inspection of your barracks today.'

'Did you?' said Connor, feeling a familiar frisson of excitement.

'Yes, and I was quite horrified by what I found.'

Connor licked his lips. 'What *did* you find?'

'Dirty boots and an unmade bed.'

'Oh dear,' said Connor.

'And that's not all.' Zoe folded her arms across her chest. 'Your weapon hadn't been polished.' She began walking back and forth in front of the doctor. 'You know what this means, don't you?'

Connor bit his lip. 'Some sort of punishment?' he ventured.

'Got it in one, Private Swift.' A cruel smile formed on Zoe's pink-glossed lips. 'Now drop down and give me twenty.'

Connor hesitated. 'Twenty what?'

'Press-ups!' Zoe shrieked impatiently.

Instantly, Connor dropped to the floor. He was in good shape for a man of his age and he managed the first ten press-ups easily but, as he attempted the eleventh, he felt Zoe's spiked heel in the small of his back. As he moved upwards, she dug the heel in hard, sending a flood of endorphins surging through his body. Gritting his teeth, Connor struggled through the remaining ten press-ups, before collapsing onto his stomach.

'I hope you've learned your lesson,' Zoe said, as she removed her foot from his back.

Connor grinned. 'You bet.' He raised himself onto his forearms and looked up at her. 'Is there anything else I can do for you, Captain?'

'Yes, actually, there is.' Zoe went over to her tote bag and removed a cardboard cake box. 'I'm feeling rather peckish,' she said as she sat down on Connor's Eames chair, purchased at vast expense, despite his wife's protestations that the money could be better spent elsewhere. She gave him a meaningful look. 'All I need now is an occasional table.'

Connor knew exactly what was required. During previous encounters with Zoe, he'd assumed the role of footstool, chaise longue and even, on one memorable occasion, a coat stand. Picking himself up off the floor, he went over to Zoe and positioned himself on all fours in front of her.

Smiling approvingly, she placed the cake box on his back.

'You don't know how much I'm going to enjoy this,' she said, lifting the lid.

For the next ten minutes, Connor remained perfectly motionless while Zoe ate. She selected a chocolate éclair first, pulling it apart and licking off the cream, before gobbling the buttery pastry. Next, she attacked a scone filled with jam and clotted cream, smacking her lips at regular intervals to convey just how delicious it was, and finally a rich custard slice. When she'd finished eating, she extended a foot and pointed out some crumbs on the dark wool carpet. 'Look at this terrible mess,' she said, as if Connor were somehow to blame. 'I need a vacuum cleaner.'

Smiling, Connor bowed his head to the ground and began licking up the crumbs, chasing them with his tongue. When the carpet was perfectly clean, he looked up at Zoe, eagerly waiting for her next whim to be communicated.

'Excellent work, Private Swift,' she said. 'You can get up now.'

Connor rose to his feet and began wiggling his toes to try and relieve the pins and needles in his feet.

Meanwhile, Zoe was strutting over to his examination couch. 'What shall we do now?' she said, sitting down and crossing her legs, so that her skirt rode up, exposing a tantalizing glimpse of stocking top.

Connor swallowed. 'How about I give you a good hard seeing to?'

Zoe gave a throaty laugh. 'I think I'd like that, Private.'

Connor Swift was faithful to his wife, make no mistake about it. It was simply that his definition of monogamy differed from most other people's. In Connor's book, becoming emotionally attached to another woman constituted infidelity. Sex for sex's sake, on the other hand, was perfectly acceptable . . . just so long as his wife didn't find out about it. During the five and a half years he'd been with Nicole, Connor had slept with three other women. The first was a one-night stand with a fellow GP he'd met at a resuscitation refresher course in the Midlands. Sturdy and bespectacled with short, mannish hair, she wasn't really his type. But she was frighteningly clever and when, after a few drinks on the last night, she'd asked him to pleasure her anally, he thought it rude to refuse. His second conquest was a blonde, waifish thing, who served him cappuccino every morning at the coffee shop next door to the surgery. For several weeks they'd flirted outrageously, and then one day Connor had impulsively scrawled his mobile number on a paper napkin and passed it across the counter to her. 'Call me,' he said, 'if you ever fancy hooking up.' Half an hour later they were fucking like mink in the coffee-shop staff toilet. It was a scenario that was destined to be repeated many times and in various locations over the next few months, until the waitress found herself a proper boyfriend.

Connor's third and final lover was Zoe Tripp. They'd met five months ago, not long after Tilly's birth. Zoe had just moved to Loxwood with her husband, a high-flying city lawyer who worked long hours. One day, she'd come to the Willows complaining of watery eyes and an itchy rash. Connor had diagnosed an animal-hair allergy and sent her away with a prescription for anti-histamines. The following week she was back again, apparently concerned about a small mole beneath her left breast. As Connor examined the blemish – which turned out to be perfectly normal – Zoe had propositioned him. Ordinarily, patients were strictly off-limits for Connor. Such a liaison would be awkward, not to mention highly unethical. But Zoe was very insistent – and stunningly beautiful to boot. In the end, Connor had been powerless to resist, and he hadn't regretted it for a minute. Zoe was quite the most exciting lover he'd ever had, regularly eschewing vanilla sex in favour of intricate role play and light bondage. Sexually speaking, she liked to be in charge and, much to his surprise, Connor discovered he liked being dominated. So much of his daily life involved being strong and assertive that it was nice being told what to do for a change. His new lover was very imaginative and he never knew who she was going to be from one session to the next – sometimes she played the part of a sexy schoolteacher in angora sweater and horn rims, administering discipline to her recalcitrant pupil; other times she was a smart-suited executive and he her hopeless subordinate.

It wasn't long before Connor became hopelessly addicted. The more sex he had with Zoe, the more he wanted. In stark contrast, his marital relations had dwindled to practically nothing – though this was only partly due to the affair. A large part of Connor's lack of sexual interest in his wife stemmed from her new status as mother. Since Tilly's birth, Nicole had swapped the figure-hugging jeans and G-strings she knew he loved for rather less attractive drawstring trousers and granny knickers. To make his home life even more unappealing, Connor found his new domestic responsibilities unspeakably tedious. Not that he didn't love his daughter; far from it. It was just that he found the practical aspects of parenthood – the bathing, the night-time feeds, the endless nappy changing – boring in the extreme. His wife, by contrast, seemed to revel in the most mundane of tasks. Only that morning, she phoned him on his mobile, triumphant because she'd found a new hypo-allergenic brand of baby wipe that didn't irritate Tilly's sensitive skin. Fatherhood made Connor feel boring, predictable. He craved excitement in a way he had never done before – and excitement was precisely what he got from Zoe.

Now, as he lay on his examination couch with her, their limbs damply intertwined after a particularly frenzied bout of lovemaking, his thoughts turned once again to his responsibilities. 'I'd better nip out and grab a sandwich,' he said, glancing at the funky retro wall clock he'd had imported from Italy. 'Afternoon surgery starts in half an hour.' He reached for his trousers. 'We must do this again soon, but it's probably best if you don't drop into the surgery unannounced again, or Carol will start to get suspicious.'

Zoe rose up onto her elbows and arched her back, thrusting her impressive breasts ceilingwards. 'Actually, I did have another location in mind,' she said provocatively. 'And a rather unusual activity.'

'Oh yes?' Connor said eagerly.

'It might be a bit kinky for you.'

Connor grinned. 'You know me – I'm always open to new experiences.'

'Okay, then, how are you fixed for next Thursday evening?'

Connor scratched his head. He and Nicole had tickets for the theatre that night. 'I'm pretty sure I can get away,' he said.

'Great, I'll let the others know we're coming.'

Connor flinched. 'You mean there are other people involved?'

'Yeah – why, is that a problem?'

'Of course it is,' Connor said impatiently. 'A man in my position . . . It could be very embarrassing.'

Zoe laughed softly. 'Trust me, Dr Swift, no one's going to recognize you.'

Connor mugged at her. 'Huh?'

'Don't worry, all will be revealed on Thursday. I'll make the arrangements and let you know where to meet me.'

'Well, okay,' Connor replied warily. 'But I reserve the right to back out if it gets too weird.'

Zoe swung her legs over the side of the couch. 'It's a deal.'

They finished getting dressed in silence. Both had got what they'd come for; there was no need for small talk.

Connor was smiling as he tidied his room in readiness for afternoon surgery. He wasn't the only one in a good mood. Several miles away, in the offices of the *Sunday Post*, Yasmin had just emerged from an editorial meeting. A couple of days earlier she'd interviewed a hot young singer-songwriter who owned a luxurious country retreat in one of Loxwood's satellite villages. She'd been in negotiations with his agent for weeks, and was thrilled when she'd eventually been granted an hour-long audience with the notoriously reclusive star. The interview had gone brilliantly and, thanks to a combination of flattery and flirtation, she'd got the singer-songwriter to go on record about his recent marriage split for the first time. The story was so good it might even be picked up by the nationals. With this in mind, the *Post*'s editor had decided the interview should have pride of place on the front cover of the paper's colour supplement. Yasmin's victory was another journalist's loss, however, and, as she collected a celebratory cup of coffee from the vending machine and carried it back to her desk, sports editor Rob Pritchard barged past her with a face like thunder.

'Oi,' Yasmin said, as coffee slopped over the edge of the plastic cup and onto the carpet. 'Look where you're going, can't you?'

'My apologies,' Rob said, not sounding sorry at all. 'I didn't see you – which, given the size of your head, is a minor miracle.'

Yasmin stopped in her tracks. 'What the hell's that supposed to mean?' she fired at her colleague's departing back.

Rob didn't break stride. 'Just that you're in danger of getting too big for your boots,' he replied.

'Aw, diddums, is ickle Robbie upset because he didn't get the cover of the supp?' Yasmin put her hands on her hips. 'Face facts, Rob: I got the cover because my interview's better than your piece on match-fixing. Simple as that.'

'You haven't even written the bloody thing yet,' Rob retorted. 'For all I know, you're going to turn out a complete pile of crap – and even if the guy did open up about his marriage split, it's hardly Pulitzer Prize-winning stuff, is it?'

Yasmin snorted, aware that half the office was listening to their heated exchange. 'And your piece *is*?'

Rob sat down at his desk, where a framed photograph of his two young sons jostled for position with piles of press releases and reference books. 'My piece is a meticulously researched, thoughtfully written, hard-hitting exposé,' he said, without a trace of irony. 'Yours, on the other hand, is pointless showbiz fluff.'

Yasmin sighed. 'Why do you always feel so hard done by? Can't you just accept defeat graciously for once?'

Rob picked up his phone and punched out a number. The conversation, apparently, was at an end.

Yasmin walked back to her own desk. She and Rob had never got along. From day one he'd been unfriendly and obstreperous and in recent weeks they'd had several public spats. And yet, despite this, Yasmin had a grudging admiration for Rob. He was sharp and witty and brilliant at his job – and, although she'd never admit it, she actually found him quite attractive. He was older than her – nearer forty than thirty, with a cute dimple in his chin and a tendency to wear clothes that a cynic might suggest were slightly too young for him. According to the *Post*'s editorial assistant, who seemed to know all the office gossip, Rob was single after going through an acrimonious divorce a couple of years earlier. His wife and her new partner had recently moved to Dublin and now he only got to see his kids every couple of months, which must, Yasmin supposed, be pretty tough.

Usually, Yasmin enjoyed sparring with Rob, but today's contretemps had just left her feeling annoyed. 'That man is such an ignorant pig,' she muttered to Pete, the junior showbiz reporter, as she sat down. 'He can't stand it if anyone gets one up on him, especially if it happens to be a woman.'

Pete leaned back in his chair, a stupid smirk on his face. 'Why don't you just admit it, Yasmin . . . You fancy him, don't you?'

'Oh, puh-lease!' she said, as she checked her email.

'I bet Rob wouldn't say no to a quick one, either.'

Yasmin looked up. 'Why, has he said something to you?'

'No, but anyone with half a brain can see you two have got the hots for each other.'

Yasmin gave him a scornful look. 'You're having a laugh, aren't you?' she said witheringly. 'I wouldn't shag Rob Pritchard if he was the last man on earth.'

It was four months since Yasmin had started work at the *Post* and here she was, still eating lunch at her desk. The realization depressed her. She would've loved to spend her lunch hour wandering around the shops with a colleague or gossiping over skinny cappuccinos in Starbucks – and, as she sat alone, poking at the limp salad she'd brought from home, she couldn't help thinking she only had herself to blame.

Yasmin had arrived at the *Post* full of enthusiasm and determined to make her mark. In meetings she was outspoken and, if she felt she was in danger of being overlooked, downright belligerent. When it came to chasing stories, she was like a dog with a bone: persistent, tenacious, occasionally aggressive. She often arrived in the office half an hour before everybody else and was rarely home before eight – not because she had nothing else to fill her time with, but because she loved her job with a passion: the thrill of meeting talented people, the adrenalin rush of breaking an exclusive, the fact she got to go places and see things that ordinary mortals didn't. Somewhere along the line, however, her colleagues seemed to have mistaken ambition for aggression, confidence for arrogance, dedication for ruthlessness. Why else did she feel like an outsider? Sighing, Yasmin clamped the lid on her Tupperware and picked up her handbag. She needed to get out of the office. A brisk walk in the park would soon set her to rights.

When Yasmin returned half an hour later, she was carrying a giant box of Krispy Kremes. She paused in the lobby to offer one to Val, the *Post*'s long-serving receptionist.

'Ooh, thank you, lovie,' Val said, falling hungrily on a glazed chocolate ring. 'What's the occasion?'

'Nothing in particular,' Yasmin said with a smile. 'I just felt like treating everyone.'

Inside the open-plan office, she continued distributing her booty. The doughnuts were such a small thing, but the gesture elicited a surprising degree of warmth from her colleagues and Yasmin found herself wondering why she hadn't thought of it sooner. She was halfway round the room when she spotted Rob. He was talking to Sue, one of the picture researchers, a doll-like thing with a sheet of silky blonde hair that shone like a halo. Yasmin felt an unexpected prick of envy as she watched them together, heads bowed over a portfolio, bodies so close they were almost touching. As she approached, they both looked up. Rob was scowling, clearly annoyed at the interruption.

'Sorry, I don't mean to barge in,' Yasmin said.

'Don't be silly; we were just going through some photographers' books,' Sue said pleasantly. She eyed the box of doughnuts. 'Ooh, can I have one of those?'

'Go for it,' Yasmin said. When Sue had made her selection, she held the box out to Rob. 'Can I tempt you?'

'No, thanks, you've probably poisoned them.' He smiled sardonically. 'Anything to get ahead, eh?'

Suddenly Yasmin's cheeks were burning hot. She tried to think of something smart to say back, but her usual wit deserted her.

'What's the matter?' Rob jeered. 'Hit a nerve, have I?'

Yasmin turned away. 'Fuck you, Rob.'

8

Dante adjusted his grip on the golf club and focused on the fifteen-foot stretch of turf that lay between his ball and the ninth hole. Tensing his forearms, he swung his upper body, then watched in satisfaction as the ball rolled smoothly towards its target before disappearing from view.

'Nice shot,' Connor called out. 'You were obviously telling porkies when you said you were out of practice.'

Dante smiled. 'I haven't played in ages; I just got lucky.'

'Puh! Luck doesn't come into it. You're a bloody good player and that's all there is to it.'

It was a week since Juliet's dinner party and the two men were enjoying a round of golf. The doctor's invitation had come out of the blue, and Dante – who was finding Ashwicke's gloomy corridors increasingly oppressive – had accepted immediately. Connor, meanwhile, had his own reasons for wanting to escape the house. After a busy week at the surgery, he'd been looking forward to a relaxing weekend. Unbeknown to him, however, Nicole had planned a relentless schedule of infant-friendly activities, all of which he was expected not only to participate in, but also to *enjoy*. The first of these was a visit to a farm park more than an hour's drive away where, Nicole had gleefully informed him, newborn lambs could be seen.

'I don't know why we can't just have a nice quiet day at

home,' Connor remarked as he watched Nicole stuff a garish jungle-print bag with nappies and wet wipes.

His wife shot him a censorious look. 'We've got a baby now; we can't just think of ourselves.'

'I'm sure Tilly wouldn't say no to a nice long nap, while Mummy and Daddy read the papers,' Connor said, glancing at his daughter who was sitting on the floor in her car seat. 'Would you, sweetheart?'

'But she needs stimulation,' Nicole replied. 'I'd have thought you of all people would know that. You are a doctor, after all.'

'Yeah, and as a doctor I've had a bloody hard week at work and I really don't fancy tramping around some shitty farm in the middle of nowhere just to see a flaming sheep.'

'But just think of Tilly's face when she sees those adorable lambs.'

'Mmm . . .' Connor muttered. But he wasn't thinking of Tilly; he was thinking of Zoe Tripp and her magnificent breasts.

And so, unable to talk Nicole out of the excursion, Connor had made the long drive to the next county and then spent two mind-numbing hours pretending to admire a series of domestic beasts he was already perfectly well acquainted with. He pushed the buggy dolefully from enclosure to enclosure, while his wife cooed and burbled with Tilly as if baby talk were her mother tongue.

After a very mediocre meal at the farm park's ludicrously overpriced café, they'd set off for home, their journey time nearly doubled because of an accident on the bypass. When they finally arrived, Nicole had taken Tilly straight upstairs for her bath, leaving Connor to shake the mud from the car mats and unpack the changing bag. Afterwards, he'd slumped on the sofa, utterly exhausted and slightly nauseous at the thought of tomorrow's activity: a parent and baby swimming session.

'I can't wait to see Tilly in that dear little costume I bought her,' Nicole had gushed earlier that morning when Connor was lying in bed, still half asleep. 'She's going to have such fun in the water. Not that it's just about having fun, of course; she'll be improving her coordination and motor skills at the same time and that's so important when they're this age.' She'd nudged him in the ribs. 'You're going to love it too.'

No, I won't, Connor thought to himself as he sat on the sofa listening to the sounds of splashing and laughter overhead. *I'll hate every sodding minute.* And so, while Nicole had her hands full with Tilly, he'd looked up the Fishers' number in the address book by the phone. Connor knew his get-out-of-jail-free card had to be Dante, for if he arranged to meet any of his *real* mates for a jolly, Nicole would've thrown a strop and forced him to cancel. But, seeing as she was the one who'd suggested he take the young American under his wing in the first place, he thought he might just get away with it. He was right.

'Oh, but it's Waterbabies tomorrow,' she said when he told her he'd made plans to see Dante the following day. 'I thought I told you.'

'Shit,' Connor said, clapping the heel of his hand to his head. 'I completely forgot about it. Sorry, Nic.' He reached for the phone. 'No problem, I can easily cancel Dante.'

'No, don't do that,' she said. 'He'll be really looking forward to it.'

'Well, if you're sure . . .' Connor began.

His wife nodded. 'Tilly and I can easily go to Waterbabies on our own. What are you and Dante going to do anyway?'

'I thought I'd take him to the golf club for nine holes. Then maybe I'll introduce him to some of the other guys.'

'That's a great idea,' Nicole said, leaning over the back of the sofa and wrapping her arms round his neck. 'Thanks for taking the initiative, darling. I really appreciate it and I know Juliet will too.'

Connor couldn't help grinning as he congratulated himself for pulling off such a nifty manoeuvre.

'You don't have to rush home, do you?' Connor asked as the American retrieved his ball from the hole.

'Nope,' said Dante. 'Why, what did you have in mind?'

'A couple of drinks in the clubhouse?'

Dante shoved the ball in his pocket. 'Sounds good to me.'

After stopping off in the locker room to deposit their cart bags and change their muddy footwear, the two men headed for the clubhouse bar. It was late afternoon and the place was bustling. As they found a spot at the horseshoe-shaped bar, Dante looked around with interest. Apart from the dinner party and a few visits to the local pub, it was his first foray into Loxwood society and he was keen to soak up the atmosphere. The bar was pretty plush and had an exclusive feel. Most of the clientele were fellow golfers, dressed in expensive-looking separates, but there were also several youngish, prettyish girls wafting around, as well as a gaggle of horsey types at a large corner table, gossiping over a bottle of Prosecco.

‘What are you having?’ asked Connor, pulling his wallet out of his pocket.

‘No way,’ Dante said. ‘This one’s on me.’

Connor smiled. ‘Okay, if you insist. I’ll have a Scotch and soda, thanks.’ He patted Dante on the shoulder. ‘Excuse me for a minute, will you? I need to use the Gents.’

As he waited to be served, Dante perused the leather-bound cocktail menu. The choice was modest and, in the American’s opinion, rather unimaginative. On impulse, he ordered a Cosmopolitan, keen to see how it compared to his own effort. He watched closely as the bartender mixed the drink and poured it into a martini glass, frowning when he made an amateurish mistake, flaming the orange-peel garnish too close to the surface of the liquid so it left a nasty black film. After paying for the drinks, Dante looked around for a place to sit. In one of the cosy corner booths, two men had stood up and were putting on their jackets. Assuming they were about to leave, Dante went over and stood a few feet away while they gathered their belongings. As he hovered, snatches of their conversation drifted over to him above the general hubbub.

‘Have you tried the new Nike SasQuatch Sumo?’ the older man said to his companion as he adjusted the belt on his garish checked golf trousers. ‘It’s an ugly bastard, but I reckon it’s just about the most forgiving driver on the market.’

The other man nodded. ‘Yeah, and let’s face it, Mike, with a swing like yours, you need all the help you can get.’

The first man was about to say something smart back when he noticed Dante watching them. ‘Sorry, are you waiting for the table?' he said pleasantly. 'We're just going.' He turned to pick up a rucksack, which was lying on the leather banquette. Suddenly, he looked back at Dante. Instantly, his face hardened. 'Hey,' he said, elbowing his friend. 'Look what the cat's dragged in.'

For a few moments, the two stared at the young American with undisguised hostility. Dante was nonplussed. The man called Mike was distinctive – tall and lean, with lots of gold jewellery and a circle of dark hair that perched like a wreath round his shiny pate. He was certain he'd have remembered if they'd met before. 'I think you must be confusing me with someone else,' he said curtly.

'You're that Fisher fellow, aren't you?' The man's upper lip was curled in a sneer.

'Yeah,' Dante said warily. 'I'm sorry, do I know you?'

The second man stepped forward. 'Your sort aren't welcome here,' he said in a threatening tone.

Dante held his gaze. 'And what sort might that be?'

'Gold-diggers.' He spat rather than said the word.

The hairs on the back of Dante's neck prickled. 'What are you talking about?' he said, setting the drinks down on the nearest table.

'Don't play the innocent,' the man called Mike retorted. 'Everyone knows you only married Juliet Ingram for her money and if she wasn't still in pieces about Gus – who, I might add, happened to be a good friend of mine – then I'm sure she'd be able to see that for herself.'

Dante counted silently to five. It was a technique he'd often used back in Aspen when faced with a difficult or aggressive customer. 'Look, I don't know who you guys are, or what your problem is, but all I want to do is have a quiet drink, okay? So I suggest you get out of my face before I really lose my temper.'

The man turned to his friend. 'Did you hear that, Andy? The Yankee boy's going to do his Hulk impression. I'm pissing my pants.' He gestured towards Dante's pink cocktail. 'That looks like a girl's drink to me,' he remarked. 'Wouldn't that just be the icing on the cake? Not just a gold-digger, but a *gay* gold-digger.' He gave a cruel laugh. 'Poor Juliet.'

Sighing in disgust, Dante turned to go, but before he'd taken a single step, Mike had grabbed his arm. 'Hey, don't walk away when I'm talking to you.'

It was too much for Dante. He'd been bottling up his feelings ever since he'd arrived in England and now weeks' worth of pent-up emotion came bubbling to the surface like molten lava. Whirling round, he shrugged Mike's hand off his arm. 'Take your freaking hands off me or I swear I'm gonna kick your butt across this room,' he hissed, thrusting his face close up to the other man's.

Mike seemed shocked by Dante's reaction. He began backing away, hands held up defensively. 'Steady on, mate. There's no need to get your jockstrap in a twist.' His speech was slightly slurred and it occurred to Dante for the first time that his adversary might be the worse for wear.

'What's going on here?'

Looking over his shoulder, Dante saw Connor standing behind him. Before he could open his mouth to explain, Mike had brushed past him. 'Dr Swift, great to see you!' he exclaimed, grabbing Connor's hand in both of his and pumping it up and down.

'Hi, Mike,' Connor replied in a clipped tone. 'I see you've already met my friend Dante.'

The man's smile vanished. 'You two are *friends*?'

'We certainly are.' Connor withdrew his hand and folded his muscular arms across his chest. 'So if you've got a problem with Dante I'm afraid you've got a problem with me too.'

'Problem? Who said anything about a problem?' Mike said quickly. 'We were just having a laugh with Dante here.' He looked at his friend. 'Isn't that right, Andy?'

The other man nodded. 'But he took our little joke the wrong way.' He curled his hand round his mouth and whispered stagily to Connor, 'I don't think these Americans appreciate our English sense of humour.'

Mike flashed a fake smile at Dante. 'Sorry, mate. I always get a bit lippy when I've had a few drinks.' He looked at his companion. 'Come on, Andy, let's get going. Our wives will be wondering what's become of us.'

As the two men sidled off, Connor and Dante took their seats in the booth. 'Don't take any notice of them,' Connor said as he sipped his Scotch. 'Mike Henderson's an idiot. He's always shooting his mouth off, especially when he's pissed. You're not the first person he's got into a ruck with, and you certainly won't be the last.'

For a few moments, Dante stared at his drink, silently working over Mike's words. Then he looked at Connor. 'He called me a gold-digger . . . Is that what everyone around here thinks?'

'Not at all,' Connor said firmly. 'What you've got to understand is that this is a very close-knit community and people love to gossip – especially about newcomers. You just need to put yourself about a bit, and pretty soon people will realize that they've got you all wrong.'

'I guess . . . It's going to take time, though.' Dante sighed and rested his chin on his hand. 'Can I ask you something, Connor?'

'Sure. Fire away.'

'What was Gus like?'

The GP took a drink of whisky. 'He was one of those larger-than-life types – the sort of bloke who was always in the thick of things. He was chair of the Rotary Club, vice-president of the cricket club, a leading light in the Loxwood amateur dramatics society . . . I don't know where he found the time, to be honest. He was a bit of a showman too; he liked to play to a crowd. Every year the cricket club holds a formal dinner, followed by a charity auction. Gus used to act as compère and he was really good at whipping the audience into a frenzy, playing one bidder off against another. His tactics were a bit theatrical for my tastes – but, fair play to him, he helped raise an awful lot of money.'

'Did you know him well?'

'Not really. We met socially, of course . . . played golf a few times. That's about it.'

'What did he look like?'

Connor looked at him in surprise. 'Haven't you seen a picture?'

Dante shook his head. 'Nope. There are photos and portraits all over Ashwicke, but not a single one of Gus . . . It's kinda weird, don't you think?'

'Not necessarily. Perhaps Juliet put them all away because she knew they'd make you feel uncomfortable.'

'I guess . . . or maybe she just finds it too painful looking at him – that's my theory,' Dante said. 'Gus's death must've been a huge shock, and sometimes I think she's still grieving for him. Whenever his name comes up, she gets this kind of misty look in her eyes, like she's thinking about all the good times they had together. It was there the other night at the dinner party.'

'Oh well, it's only been a year since he died. It takes a long time to come to terms with the death of a loved one, especially when you lose them in such appalling circumstances.' Connor frowned. 'Anyway, what were we saying? Ah yes, Gus's physical appearance. He was a good-looking bloke and he kept himself fit; I used to see him at the gym all the time. I remember Nicole always used to say how well groomed he was. He always wore designer gear – even on the golf course – and he never had a hair out of place.'

Dante felt suddenly self-conscious in his khaki trousers and plain white T-shirt. He was the most casually dressed person in the bar – by a mile. 'He sounds the complete opposite of me.'

Connor gave a strange, knowing smile. 'Yeah, you could say that.' He swirled the ice cubes round his glass. 'I appreciate it can't be easy for you, coming to a new country, stepping into a dead man's shoes . . .'

Dante winced at the GP's turn of phrase. 'Yeah, it's weird not having people I can talk to. I really miss my friends back home.'

'They must've been pretty surprised when you got married and took off to England with a woman you hardly know.'

Dante scratched his chin. 'Mmm, a couple of them even tried to talk me out of it. But I knew I was making the right decision.'

Connor drained the rest of his whisky in one gulp. 'And do you still think that?'

'Of course I do,' Dante replied.

'Good for you.' Connor waggled his empty glass. 'Let's get another drink, shall we? Nicole's not expecting me home any time soon.'

Dante was in a good mood when the cab dropped him off at Ashwicke, shortly after seven p.m. Despite the unpleasant confrontation in the bar, he'd enjoyed his afternoon with Connor. He just had enough time for a quick shower before Juliet returned from her Pilates class.

He'd almost reached the top of the stairs when he heard the distant strains of music. Frowning, he stopped beside the portrait of one of Gus's illustrious ancestors, who gazed down sourly at him through layers of blackened varnish. The music was coming from the far end of the west wing. Wondering if one of the chambermaids was working late, he decided to investigate.

He set off down the corridor, his footsteps muffled by the thick carpet. The music seemed to be coming from a room midway down the corridor. Its door stood slightly ajar and, as Dante approached, he felt a flicker of apprehension for this, he already knew, had been Gus's dressing room.

He'd caught a brief glimpse of it the day after his arrival at Ashwicke, during Juliet's whistle-stop tour of the house. There was just time to take in the custom-made floor-to-ceiling wardrobes and the large cheval mirror before Juliet was closing the door. 'I've been meaning to give that room a good clear-out for months,' she'd remarked. 'It's just finding the time.'

A few days later, Dante had made a second, unaccompanied visit to the room, while Juliet was busy in the kitchen discussing some new additions to the breakfast menu with Chef. Even though it was his home, Dante felt like a trespasser as he pushed open the door to the dressing room, which was at least twice the size of the bedroom in his apartment back in Aspen. It was very much a man's room, purposeful and unfussy, the furniture large and linear, the walls covered in a bold striped wallpaper. He opened one of the wardrobes and found it full of designer suits, some still in their dry-cleaning wrappers. The next wardrobe contained a rainbow of shirts, grouped in corresponding colours, and, on a shelf unit, a selection of aftershaves. Picking up the nearest bottle, Dante puffed a spray of scent into the air. It was fruity, with citrus undertones, and rather pleasant. He returned it to the shelf and went to the tall chest of drawers. The top drawer contained several dozen silk ties, all neatly rolled; the second, a stack of handkerchiefs with Gus's initial embroidered on them in navy thread. Dante had no appetite for the third drawer; he'd seen enough. After checking that he'd left the room exactly as he'd found it, he slipped back out into the corridor and pulled the door to.

Now that he was mere feet away, Dante could hear the music quite clearly. It was a classical piece – a haunting violin concerto. He stopped and cocked his head, ears straining for sounds of human activity: the hum of a vacuum cleaner, the hiss of an aerosol, the squeak of a cloth against glass. He heard nothing. Frowning, he stepped closer and peered through the two-inch crack in the door.

The next instant his heart was in his mouth. A tall figure with dark hair was standing in the middle of the room, with his back to the door. He was wearing one of the suits Dante had seen in the wardrobe; the dry-cleaning wrapper was lying on the floor. Over his shoulder, Dante could see a radio on the windowsill that hadn't been there on his previous visit to the room. Just then, he became aware of a distinctive smell: aftershave – or, to be more specific, *Gus's* aftershave. Dante swallowed, his mouth suddenly dry. He watched as the man's hand went to his throat, as if he were adjusting a tie. A few moments later, the hand went to his left sleeve and plucked off a stray hair. It suddenly dawned on Dante that the man must be studying his reflection in the cheval, which lay frustratingly out of view. After telling himself firmly that there were no such things as ghosts, he reached out and pushed the door open. The man turned round and Dante realized with a jolt of surprise – and a hefty measure of relief – that it was Nathan.

Dante's eyes flickered over the general manager. Now that they were standing face to face, he saw he was wearing a silk tie with a distinctive purple stripe and beneath it, a pink shirt. For a few seconds, Dante stood staring at Nathan in shocked silence. The strangest thing of all was not that he was wearing Gus's clothes, but that he didn't seem in the least bit embarrassed. The manager was the first to speak.

'Good evening, Mr Fisher,' he said calmly. 'I didn't expect you back till later.'

Dante frowned. 'What are you doing in here?'

'I was just checking Mr Ingram's wardrobe,' the manager replied in a tone that suggested the answer was perfectly obvious to anyone with half a brain. 'We had a terrible infestation of moths a few months ago. I had to throw out several of Mr Ingram's good lambswool sweaters, so now I come in here once a month to shake everything out.' He smiled tightly. 'It seems to do the trick.'

Dante folded his arms across his chest. 'Yeah, but why are you *wearing* that stuff?'

'It's easier to check things this way.' Nathan brushed some invisible lint off his lapel. 'A little macabre, I know, but if a job's worth doing . . .'

Dante frowned. 'Wouldn't it be easier to give it all to charity?'

'I couldn't possibly do that; Mrs Fisher would be devastated.'

Dante's nostrils flared. 'Would she now?'

'Absolutely. She likes to have Mr Ingram's things around her.'

His words were like a knife twisting in Dante's chest. Swallowing hard, he glanced at his wristwatch. 'It's getting late. How much longer are you going to be?'

'Only another ten minutes or so.' Nathan's hollow eyes bored into Dante. 'Is that all right with you?'

Dante shrugged. 'I guess it'll have to be.'

Nathan went to the open wardrobe and began rifling through the line of suits, rattling the wooden hangers noisily as if to demonstrate how industrious he was being.

As Dante started back down the corridor, he felt a creeping sense of unease. When he reached the top of the stairs, he glanced back over his shoulder. Nathan was standing in the doorway of the dressing room like a sphinx guarding the entrance to the pharoah's tomb.

9

'Cheers, ladies,' Yasmin said, taking several gulps of wine in quick succession.

Juliet smiled. 'Tough day at the office, was it?'

'Mondays are always the worst, and today was an absolute pig,' Yasmin replied, turning her face upwards to catch the watery rays of early evening sunshine that flooded Nicole's west-facing garden. 'I was supposed to be meeting a TV contact for lunch – he's a press officer for *South West Tonight*.'

'Oh, I love that show,' Nicole said. 'Especially the new presenter . . . the one with the sideburns and the puppy-dog eyes. What's his name?'

Yasmin took another drink of wine. 'Jason Noble.'

'He's gorgeous,' Nicole said.

Yasmin snorted. 'He also happens to be a pervert.'

'No!' Nicole cried.

''Fraid so. Apparently, young Jason gets his kicks peeking under ladies' toilet cubicles at his local health club. I'm itching to put it in my gossip column, but the editor's worried Noble will sue.'

Nicole and Juliet looked at her in horror.

'I know, it's totally sick,' Yasmin continued. 'But when you're a famous TV personality with a million-pound farmhouse, a model girlfriend and a Porsche 911, I guess there's nothing much that can still thrill you – except perhaps grabbing a flash of knickers as you kneel on all fours, desperately craning your neck to peer under a khazi door.'

'How do you know about this?' Juliet asked.

'My contact at the TV company told me.' Yasmin drained her wine glass and sighed in pleasure. 'Ahh, that's taken the edge off.'

Nicole picked up the bottle of Pinot Grigio. 'Another one?'

'Yes, please.' Yasmin slid her wine glass across the table. 'I was hoping he'd spill lots more juicy gossip today at lunch, but the bastard stood me up. I sat there for nearly an hour getting hungrier and hungrier, and then, when I called him to see where he'd got to, he told me he'd just been sacked. Apparently, his boss found out about our little meetings and wasn't very happy.'

'Poor guy,' Juliet murmured.

'Yeah, and poor me too,' Yasmin rejoindered. 'He was one of my best sources.' She picked up her second glass of wine and held it close to her chest, as if she were afraid it might be snatched away. 'And that was just the beginning. When I got back to the office, I discovered the subs had cut my piece on "fab to flab" celebs in half to make way for a late-breaking story on a football transfer deal. Naturally, Rob was delighted to have got one up on me.'

'Ah, your nemesis, the sports editor.' Nicole glanced down at Tilly, who was lying in her buggy sucking on a set of plastic keys. 'There's no ceasefire in sight, then?'

Yasmin sighed. 'I've tried to get along with him, believe me, but for some reason we just keep rubbing each other up the wrong way.'

'That's a shame,' Juliet said. 'It must make things difficult for you at work.'

'Oh, I dunno . . . In a weird way I enjoy it.'

'Masochist,' Nicole muttered, rising to her feet. She waggled the near-empty wine bottle. 'I'll get another one of these, shall I?'

'Ooh, yes,' Yasmin said. 'And some crisps too, if you've got them. I'm starving.'

When Nicole returned a few minutes later, she was carrying dishes of tortilla chips and olives, as well as another bottle of chilled Pinot Grigio. 'These should keep us going till dinner,' she said as she offered the dishes round.

'What's Dante up to tonight?' Yasmin asked, helping herself to a handful of snacks.

'Watching TV, I should think,' Juliet replied.

Nicole tutted. 'Why didn't you bring him along? There's plenty of food.'

'I couldn't,' Juliet replied. 'It's Nathan's night off and someone has to keep an eye on the guests.' She smiled wryly. 'I don't know why I'm using the plural. We've only got old Mrs Hibbert with us at the moment and she's usually in bed by nine.'

'Why do you bother paying a full-time general manager?' Yasmin asked. 'If the hotel's that quiet, surely you and Dante could manage by yourselves.'

'Actually, I spoke to Nathan about reducing his hours the other day. I couldn't believe it when he offered to take a pay cut instead. He said he wouldn't know what to do with himself if he wasn't working.'

Nicole uncorked the second bottle of wine and set it in the middle of the table. 'That was nice of him.'

'It was, wasn't it? I'm very lucky to have him.'

'And what about Dante? Has he managed to find a job?' asked Yasmin.

'Not yet. He's contacted loads of pubs and wine bars, but nobody seems to be hiring at the moment.'

'He'd probably be better off waiting till summer when all the tourists are in town.'

'That's what I told him.' Juliet turned to Nicole. 'It was nice of Connor to invite Dante to the golf club yesterday, by the way. He really enjoyed himself.'

'So did Connor,' Nicole said. 'Actually, I'd like to get to know Dante better myself. Perhaps Yasmin and I could take him out for lunch one day.'

'He'd like that,' Juliet said. 'He's keeping himself busy by decorating one of the guest rooms, but I'm sure he's tearing his hair out with boredom.'

'He's not having second thoughts about that customer liaison job, then?' asked Yasmin.

Juliet shook her head. 'And, who knows, maybe it's better that we don't work together. We'd probably drive each other mad if we were together twenty-four seven.'

'What makes you say that?'

'Oh, I don't know . . . We just seem to be getting on each other's nerves lately,' Juliet said, dropping a fat green olive into her mouth. 'It's nothing major – just silly bickering.' A shadow briefly crossed her face. 'It's strange. When we were in Aspen, we couldn't get enough of each other, but here . . .' She paused and stared at her wine glass. 'It's different, that's all.'

Yasmin touched her friend's shoulder. 'You know, there's no shame in admitting you made a mistake, Juliet. I'm not saying you *have* or anything – but if you, you know . . . further down the road . . . decide Dante's not the one for you after all, no one will think any less of you.'

'I hope to God it doesn't come to that.' Juliet's eyes flickered from side to side, as if her brain were trying to disassociate from the notion.

'Of course it won't,' said Nicole. 'In fact I don't think we should even be discussing it; it's bad karma.' She picked up the wine and topped up Juliet's glass. 'How are the afternoon teas going?'

'Slowly,' Juliet replied. 'I've only had a couple of takers so far, which is hardly surprising when the hotel's practically empty.'

'Why don't you offer them to non-hotel guests too?' Yasmin suggested. 'I'm sure plenty of locals would like the chance to see inside the house.'

Juliet smiled. 'That's a good idea.'

'And if it takes off I could help you bake the cakes,' Nicole said. 'God knows, I'd be glad of the distraction.' Smiling guiltily, she reached down and took one of Tilly's chubby hands. 'Not that I don't love being a mum. It's just that sometimes it does get a bit repetitive.' She glanced up at Juliet. 'Have you seen Bear lately?'

Juliet nodded. 'He came in for breakfast this morning as usual. Mrs Hibbert has taken quite a shine to him. She even invited him to share her table.'

'Who the hell's Bear?' Yasmin said through a mouthful of tortilla chips.

'His caravan's parked up at Ashwicke,' Juliet explained. 'The campsite down the road was fully booked so I took pity on him. Nicole met him the other day when she came round to drop off some recipe books.'

'He's a journalist,' Nicole added. 'He writes about the environment.'

'Oh yeah? Who does he work for?'

'Lots of different people; he's freelance. He's working on a piece for *The Times* about the redevelopment of the old fruit farm.'

Yasmin's eyes widened. 'Blimey, I knew it was a contentious issue but I'm surprised the nationals have picked up on it.'

'It's all because of the badgers,' Nicole told her.

'*Badgers?*' Yasmin repeated.

'There's a huge sett on the site, and the law says no building work can take place within a twenty-metre radius – but rumour has it the developer's trying to find a way to get round it.'

Yasmin frowned. 'Since when were you such an expert?'

Nicole lifted a grizzly Tilly out of the buggy. 'I'm not really. Bear was telling me all about it when he interviewed me yesterday.'

'He *interviewed* you?' Juliet said.

Nicole nodded. 'It was more of a chat really. Bear just wanted to get some idea of the strength of local feeling.'

'And where did this chat take place?' Yasmin asked.

'In my kitchen.'

Yasmin pursed her lips in mock outrage. 'I expect Connor had something to say about that, eh . . . a strange man visiting his wife in the middle of the day?'

'Actually, I didn't tell him.' Nicole licked her lips. 'Not that I've got anything to hide. I just thought it would be easier . . . You know how jealous Connor gets.'

'So what's he like, this Bear?' Yasmin asked. 'Is he good looking?'

'Oh yes,' Juliet said. 'He used to play semi-professional rugby when he was younger; he's built like a tank. He's really interesting too. I could sit and listen to him all day.'

'I know what you mean,' Nicole murmured.

Yasmin's eyes widened. 'Is he single?'

'I'm not sure; he's never mentioned a girlfriend.'

'Nicole?' Yasmin prompted.

'Um, I don't honestly know. I haven't asked him.'

'Well next time you see him, be sure to find out.' She gave Nicole a sly, sideways look. 'I take it you will be seeing him again?'

Nicole, who was suddenly feeling rather self-conscious, began fiddling with the Peter Pan collar of Tilly's gingham dress. 'I'm not sure. He's invited me to go on a badger watch on Thursday, but Connor and I have got tickets for the theatre.'

Yasmin started giggling. 'A *badger watch*? That's an unusual seduction technique.'

'He's not *trying* to seduce me,' Nicole replied, feeling her face grown warm. 'He just wanted to get some pictures for his article and he fancied some company. I'm the only person he knows in Loxwood.'

'Are you sure that's all it is?' Yasmin persisted.

'Quite sure,' Nicole said firmly. She thrust Tilly into Yasmin's arms. 'I'd better check on my fish pie. Keep an eye on her, will you – and if she starts getting grumpy again, just push her up and down in the buggy.'

'Will Connor be joining us for dinner?' Juliet asked.

Nicole shrugged carelessly. 'Your guess is as good as mine. He did say he'd be home in time to put Tilly to bed, but I'm not holding my breath.'

*

Unbeknown to Nicole, Connor had already forgotten his promise to her. He wasn't working late at the surgery. Instead, he was approaching the reception desk of an upmarket – and therefore exceedingly discreet – hotel on the outskirts of Loxwood.

Zoe's summons had come out of the blue. He hadn't been expecting to see her until Thursday, but earlier that day she'd called to say her husband was out of town unexpectedly. As usual, she'd masterminded the arrangements – a room was booked in his name; he should wait for her there.

He'd been holed up for nearly fifteen minutes when there was a knock at the door. 'Room service,' a familiar voice called out. In an instant, Connor was on his feet, almost tripping over an antique armoire in his haste to get the door. His breath caught in his throat when he saw what she was wearing: a figure-hugging black dress, cropped to mid-thigh, with white lace cuffs and collar, and, over it, a white frilled apron. Her hair was piled into a bun, trimmed with a lace headpiece. Seamed stockings and black patent-leather stilettos completed the outfit.

With a small superior smile, Zoe sashayed into the room and began flicking her feather duster over the desk, hip thrust out provocatively. 'I'm terribly sorry about this, sir,' she said, 'only we didn't have time to clean the room before you arrived.' She turned her attentions to the bedside table, bending low so he could see her stocking tops and the black silk of her underwear. It was predictable, end-of-the-pier stuff, but Connor found the performance unspeakably arousing.

Zoe glanced over her shoulder. 'Would you like me to turn the bed down, sir?' she murmured silkily.

Connor's erection made its own feelings known by twitching in his pants. 'Yes, please,' the doctor said.

She threw her duster on the floor and bent over the king-size bed, drawing back the coverlet slowly, sensuously, seductively. Then she turned to face him. 'Is there anything else I can do for you, sir?'

'Oh, I'm sure I can think of something,' the GP said hoarsely as his hand went to his zipper.

10

The day was fading when they reached their destination. Although it was mild for the time of year, a freshening breeze snatched at Nicole's skirt and the pale blue scarf at her throat. Her companion looked around furtively, before removing a pair of wire cutters from the folds of his army surplus coat. 'Keep a lookout, will you?' he said, as he squatted down at the base of the flimsy metal fence that was designed to keep out intruders. Nicole knew what they were doing was probably illegal but, as she scanned the dusty lane for any sign of life, she couldn't help feeling a frisson of excitement.

This wasn't how Nicole was supposed to be spending her Thursday night. She and Connor had tickets to see a lavish touring production of *42nd Street* that had received rave reviews. Nicole had been looking forward to it for ages, but two days earlier Connor had announced that the date clashed with a life-saving demonstration he was giving at the local scout group.

Nicole was furious. 'But we bought those tickets months ago,' she snapped. 'How could you have gone and double-booked yourself?'

'It's Carol's fault,' Connor replied, placing the blame squarely on his receptionist's shoulders. 'She got the dates muddled up. She definitely told me the demo was on the seventeenth. It was only when I called the scoutmaster to check the arrangements that I discovered it was actually the fifteenth.' He gave her a quick appeasing smile. 'I'm really sorry, Nic. I'd get out of it if I could, but thirty young lads are expecting to learn CPR on Thursday night. I can hardly let them down now, can I?'

'I suppose not,' she conceded reluctantly.

'Why don't you take one of your friends instead?'

'Mmm . . .' she said. 'I suppose I'll have to.'

Finding someone to accompany her to the theatre at such short notice proved more difficult than Nicole anticipated, and in the end she'd given the tickets to her cleaning lady. 'Have a night out on me,' she'd said as she pressed an envelope into her delighted employee's hand. 'You'll have a great time; they're the best seats in the house.' Afterwards, Nicole was just about to call her mother to inform her that her babysitting services would no longer be required, when all at once a daring idea popped into her head. A moment later, she was rummaging through the jumble of items in her handbag until she finally unearthed Bear's business card.

'About that badger watch,' she said when he answered. 'I'm free on Thursday night after all.' And now here she was, standing at the entrance to the old fruit farm, keeping watch while Bear attempted to break and enter. She hadn't told Connor where she was going. He would only worry about her; he might even be jealous – although, as Nicole kept telling herself, her relationship with Bear was entirely platonic.

A few more snips with the wire cutters and Bear had created a gap big enough for an adult to squeeze through. 'Okay, we're in,' he said, folding back the section of fence. 'You first.'

After a quick look left and right to check they were still unobserved, Nicole dropped to her knees. As she lowered her head and started crawling under the fence, her movements somewhat restricted by the pencil skirt and high-heeled boots she was wearing, she couldn't help thinking that jeans and trainers would've been a more sensible option. Unfortunately, vanity had got the better of her. It wasn't that she was hoping to impress Bear, she reassured herself as she stood in front of the bathroom mirror, applying smoky grey shadow to her eyelids, it was simply that she wanted to show him she had another look beside 'mumsy'.

Suddenly, Nicole's progress under the fence was halted by a sharp tugging sensation in her scalp. 'Aaargh!' she cried, putting her hand to the back of her head. In an instant, Bear was on his knees beside her. 'Your hair's got caught on the fence,' he said. 'Stay still a minute.' Leaning forward, so that he was almost on top of her, he set about unsnagging the curl of hair. He was so close Nicole could feel his warm breath on the back of her neck.

'Sorry if I'm hurting you,' he said. 'I'll be as quick as I can.'

'Don't worry,' replied Nicole, who was enjoying the fleeting moment of intimacy. It was a long time since anyone had touched her so tenderly. She got lots of affection from Tilly, of course, but her hands were rough and greedy. As for Connor, he was too absorbed in his precious work to pay her much attention – physically *or* emotionally. All too soon the curl was free and Bear was following her under the fence. 'We'd better get a move on,' he said, looking up at the sky. 'It'll be dark soon.' He pointed to a patch of woodland in the distance. 'The Badger Protection League sent me a copy of the last survey that was carried out on the site and by my reckoning the sett should be situated just over there, on the outskirts of that copse.'

Nicole rubbed her hands together in anticipation. 'Lead the way.'

As they walked, they fell into easy conversation. Bear was an engaging companion and there was a refreshing simplicity about him – a simplicity that was reflected not only in his lifestyle, which seemed to Nicole to be blissfully free of responsibilities, but also in the open way he talked about himself and the things he was passionate about.

'I'm glad you changed your mind about coming,' he said as they made their way across an abandoned strawberry field. 'Badger-watching's twice as much fun when you've got company.'

'I'm really looking forward to it,' Nicole said. 'The most excitement I get these days is taking Tilly to baby yoga.' She sighed in irritation as she felt her heels sinking in the soft earth. 'I just wish I'd dressed a bit more appropriately.'

Bear gave her a shy sideways glance. 'I think you look lovely. I hope your husband knows how lucky he is.'

Nicole blushed. 'I shouldn't think Connor would notice if I were wearing sackcloth, quite honestly. He's been very distracted recently.' Then, not wanting to sound disloyal, she added quickly. 'But then again he does have an awful lot on his plate at work.' She cleared her throat. 'Are *you* attached, Bear?'

'Not any more. I split up with my girlfriend at Christmas.'

'Was she a journalist too?'

'No, a human-rights lawyer.'

'Oh,' Nicole said, feeling rather deflated. She knew she was being ridiculous, but she couldn't help wishing Bear's girlfriend had been something less high-flying. A secretary, for example – or a shop assistant. 'Had you been together long?'

'Two and a half years. In the end, she got fed up of me being away from home so much. She wanted us to get married and start a family.'

'But you didn't want to settle down?'

'I would – if I met the right person – but *she* wasn't the one. I think I always knew that in my heart.' He stopped and studied the copse, shielding his eyes against the setting sun. 'Okay, we're nearly there now, so we should move quietly from here on in. Keep your voice low and try to avoid stepping on any twigs. If there are badgers around already, we don't want to frighten them off.' He smiled at her. 'They're beautiful animals. I really hope we get lucky tonight.'

When they arrived at the copse, Bear slipped off the backpack he was wearing and dropped it at Nicole's feet. 'I'm going to do a quick recce. You'd better wait here; the fewer scent trails we leave, the better.'

'What are you looking for?' Nicole whispered.

'Tracks, spoil heaps, claw marks on trees. Anything to indicate badgers have been here.'

Bear began pacing the area, squatting down every now and then to examine a rock or a patch of earth more closely. It wasn't long before his eye was drawn to a large bramble bush. Nicole watched him bend over and pull something from one of the bush's thorny stems, before walking back over to her. 'Look,' he said, opening his palm to reveal a clump of whitish hairs. 'This is definitely from a badger. There's a scratching post over there too and some fresh droppings. There's an active sett in this area, no doubt about it.'

'So what do we do now?' Nicole asked eagerly.

'From here on in, it's a waiting game.' Bear reached down and picked up a handful of dead leaves. He held them aloft, then let them go, watching carefully as the wind carried them away from the copse. 'Badgers have a very keen sense of smell,' he explained. 'We don't want the wind blowing directly from us to them.' He looked around, his gaze finally settling on a grassy bank about ten feet away. 'I think we should set up camp over there. That way, if and when the badgers appear, we'll have a grandstand view.'

Hooking the backpack over his shoulder, he took Nicole by the hand – an intimate gesture that, strangely, felt perfectly natural to her. Together, they walked to the top of the bank, where Bear instantly took charge. Reaching into the backpack, he produced a picnic blanket with a waterproof backing, as well as a large torch, a pair of binoculars, a digital camera, a Thermos flask and two plastic cups.

'It looks like you've come well prepared,' Nicole remarked as she settled on the blanket.

'We might be in for a long wait. I just hope you're not easily bored.'

Nicole looked up at the sky, which was glowing mauve and orange as the last shimmer of the sun's corona slipped behind the treetops. 'How could I be bored on a beautiful night like this?'

*

Less than half a mile away, Nicole's husband was embarking on an illicit mission of his own. A scout-group demonstration wasn't planned for that evening and never had been. In reality, Connor was meeting his lover. Zoe had been frustratingly coy about the arrangements, telling him simply to meet her in a secluded lay-by on the outskirts of the town.

Her Mercedes was already there when he arrived. As Connor parked up, Zoe emerged from the car and walked over to him, looking hot in a pair of well-cut jeans and a tight pink T-shirt.

'Hi, gorgeous,' he said, grabbing her curvaceous rump through the open window of his Audi. 'I've missed you.'

'Mmm, me too,' she said, bending down to kiss him. 'We're going to have a lot of fun tonight. I can't wait.'

Connor looked around the deserted lay-by. 'So where's the action?'

'Five minutes' drive away.'

The doctor frowned. 'So what are we doing here?'

'We need to change into our costumes first.'

'*Costumes?* What are you talking about?'

Zoe put her hands on her hips. 'I gave you my word that no one would recognize you, remember?'

'Yeah, but fancy dress . . . What sort of event *is* this?'

'You'll see soon enough,' Zoe said mysteriously. 'But for the time being you're just going to have to trust me. Come on.'

Connor got out of his car and followed her to the Mercedes. She opened the boot to reveal two large zip-up garment carriers.

'Here you go,' she said, handing one to him. 'I hope you

approve. I chose the one I thought fitted your character the best.'

Connor draped the garment carrier over his arm. Its contents were soft and unexpectedly heavy. 'Are you sure this is really necessary?'

'Absolutely,' Zoe said firmly. 'We won't get in otherwise. Oh, and you'll need this too.' She opened the car door and removed a bulging black bin bag from the passenger seat.

'What the fuck's this?'

Zoe just smiled. 'Patience, Dr Swift.'

'So where am I supposed to get changed?'

'Over there.' She nodded to a dour concrete structure, which housed some public toilets. A light shining through the grimy window revealed that, despite the lateness of the hour, they were still in service. She picked up her own costume, which, like Connor's, was accompanied by a knotted bin bag. 'Meet you back here in five minutes.'

When Connor emerged from the Gents, he felt like a prize idiot. The costume was not what he was expecting and consisted of an orange plush jumpsuit with a contrasting white chest, accessorized with orange fur gloves and a large bushy tail. The bin bag turned out to contain the head of his costume. It was eye-catching to say the least, with a long snout, trimmed with leatherette nostrils, and a pair of pointed ears.

Outside, a giant rabbit was waiting beside the car. Connor recognized it as Zoe only by the two large humps straining against its white fur chest. When she saw him, she lifted a paw and waved. 'Looking good, Mr Fox.'

Connor was not amused. Pulling off his animal head, he marched over to her. 'Is this your idea of a joke?'

'Not at all; I think you look great.' Zoe pressed the full length of her fur-covered body against him and ran her hand over his right buttock. 'Who says hairy arses are a turn-off?'

'I look like a complete knob,' Connor wailed. 'I thought we were supposed to be having some adult fun, not going to a flaming football mascots' convention. Either you tell me what's going on, or I'm going straight home.'

At that moment, a passing car caught them in its headlights. Connor just had time to catch the shocked face of the driver before it sped away. 'You do realize that if anyone sees me dressed like this I'll never be able to hold my head up in public again,' he bleated.

Zoe shook her bunny head incredulously. 'And here was I thinking you were the adventurous sort.' She opened the car door. 'Get in and I'll put you out of your misery.'

'Now I know this is going to sound a bit freaky, but I want you to reserve judgement until I've finished explaining,' Zoe began.

Connor put his hand on her arm. 'Do you mind taking your head off? Only it's really disconcerting trying to have a conversation with a giant rabbit.'

'Sure.' Zoe pulled off her furry head and shook out her shoulder-length hair. 'Happy now?'

Connor nodded. 'Go on.'

'We're going furring,' Zoe said, tossing her rabbit head onto the back seat.

The word meant nothing to Connor. 'We're going *what*?'

'You've heard of dogging, right?'

'Um, yeah. That's when a bunch of strangers meet up in a car park and shag each other.'

'Well, it's like that,' Zoe continued. 'Except with animal costumes. And instead of car parks, all the action takes place in woodland.' She smiled. 'It's more natural that way.'

Connor's mouth gaped open. '*Natural?* Are you having a laugh? What sort of pervert gets turned on by shagging a giant rabbit?'

'Actually, we call ourselves *fur*-verts,' Zoe said disdainfully. She ran her paws over her fur-covered breasts. 'Don't you think I look sexy in this outfit?'

Connor looked her up and down. 'Well, yeah, in a weird kind of way, I suppose you do,' he conceded.

'In any case, it's not just about the costumes. It's about being completely anonymous and having the freedom to satisfy a sexual urge in the most basic way imaginable.' Zoe gave a little shudder. 'There's something deliciously thrilling about being on all fours in the woods and getting a good hard seeing to from a complete stranger.'

Connor raised an eyebrow. 'I'll take your word for it.'

'So you'll give it a go, then?'

Connor rubbed his jaw thoughtfully. 'So let me get this straight: a whole pile of people in animal suits turn up at some prearranged location and, even though they haven't got the faintest idea what anybody else looks like, they have sex with each other.'

'Exactly, except furverts call it *yiffing*.'

Connor smirked. 'Do they now?'

'Of course you don't have to have full sex. Some people are happy just *skritching*.'

'Which is?'

'Scratching and rubbing each other – the sort of stuff you might do with a pet dog or cat.'

Connor tried to imagine what it would be like having his tummy tickled, and decided it might be rather pleasant. 'Anything else I need to know?'

'Some furverts like to make the noises their chosen animal would make when they're having sex. It can be a little off-putting the first time round, but you soon get used to it.'

'And they're all strictly hetero, right? I don't want some bloody geezer in a gorilla suit trying to mount me.'

'Absolutely. And tonight's event is couples only. That way, the organizers can guarantee equal numbers of men and women. Oh, and you won't see any gorillas; it's woodland creatures only. The guys will be dressed as foxes, wolves or stags, and the girls are rabbits, mice or squirrels. That way you'll be able to tell what sex they are.'

'So where does this animal orgy take place?'

'On private land. After all, we don't want to risk giving any late-night dog walkers a coronary.'

'And you won't be jealous if I make a move on someone else?'

'Of course not.' Zoe licked her lips salaciously. 'I might want to watch, though.'

Connor laughed wolfishly. 'That's fine by me.'

'So, are you up for it – yes or no?'

Connor stared down at the fox head that was lying in his lap. Despite his initial reservations, he was beginning to find the idea of furring rather arousing. 'Go on, then,' he said. 'But I'm warning you, if we get there and I feel at all uncomfortable, I'm leaving. Understood?'

'Understood,' she said solemnly.

'Oh, and one more thing – how am I supposed to, you know, perform? These costumes are pretty snug.'

Zoe smiled. 'I've come prepared.' Reaching into the glovebox, she removed a small tool the size of a pencil. She pulled off the plastic cap at one end to reveal a curved metal blade.

Connor squinted at the device. 'What's that?'

'A seam ripper. Every furvert's best friend.' Without warning, Zoe grabbed the crotch of Connor's fox costume and hooked the instrument into the stitching.

'Hey, be careful with that! I might want to have more kids one day.'

'Relax, I'm an old hand.' Zoe tugged gently at the seam and soon she'd created a two-inch tear.

'Hmm, is that going to be long enough?' she said, inspecting her handiwork. 'You're quite a big boy, so I'd better give you a bit more room to manoeuvre.'

'Won't the fancy-dress shop be a bit pissed off when they get these back?' Connor asked as Zoe extended the tear by another inch.

'Don't worry, I'll sew the seam back up before I return them.' Zoe spread her legs and performed a similar operation on the crotch of her own all-in-one. 'Although, if the costumes get really dirty, they'll probably charge us extra for dry-cleaning.'

'*Dirty?*'

Zoe giggled. 'Use your imagination.'

A few minutes later, the pair were driving down one of the twisting country lanes that criss-crossed Loxwood. Connor had decided to leave his car in the lay-by. Costume or not, he didn't want to risk being recognized. After a couple of miles, Zoe turned off onto a dirt track. After half a mile or so, it came to an abrupt end, the way ahead blocked by a high wire fence. A dozen or so vehicles were parked at the side of the track. Worried that someone might recognize him, Connor pulled his fox head on.

A few feet away was a Toyota pick-up. Beside it, a six-foot stag was deep in conversation with a giant mouse.

'I think that's Harvey and his wife Anne,' Zoe said. 'They're the organizers.' She wound down the window. 'Harvey, is that you?'

The stag strolled over. 'Yeah, hi, Zoe, glad you could make it.'

'This is my friend Connor.'

Harvey bent down to peer through the window, wincing as his foam antlers smashed against the car's soft-top. 'Damn these bloody things,' he muttered as he took a step back and bent down again.

'Nice to meet you,' Connor said. His gaze drifted to the mouse, who now had her back to them and was rummaging for something in the back of the pick-up. Her costume was very tight and showed off her slender waist and full buttocks to mouth-watering effect. Connor swallowed hard. There was no getting away from it: the rodent was hot. He turned his attention back to Harvey. 'Where's everyone else?'

'They've gone ahead to the woods. I said I'd wait here to collect any stragglers.'

Zoe glanced at the clock on the dash. 'Shit, I didn't realize we were so late. Sorry, Harvey. Connor's a first-timer. He was having a few last-minute nerves, but I managed to talk him round.'

'I'm very pleased to hear it. You don't need to be nervous, Connor; we're a friendly bunch.'

Suddenly, the mouse appeared at Harvey's side. 'We're not expecting anyone else now,' she said in a husky voice. 'Shall we join the others?'

'Yeah,' Harvey replied. 'Come on, guys, let's get this party started.'

It was only a short walk to the woods and Connor was amazed by what he saw there. In a clearing, illuminated by the soft glow from dozens of outdoor candles, around thirty furverts were congregated. Most were chatting in small groups, but two of their number – a squirrel and a wolf – were openly fondling on a plastic groundsheet that had been scattered with hay. Two stags were watching from the sidelines. One, Connor couldn't help noticing, was sporting an erection.

'Couldn't you two hang on till everyone was here?' Harvey said in a jocular tone as he turned off his torch and set it down on a nearby tree stump. The wolf looked up. 'Sorry, mate, we couldn't help ourselves.'

Harvey clapped his hands together and called for silence. 'Now listen up, everyone, we've got a first-timer here tonight.' He turned and patted Connor on the shoulder. 'So I'd like you all to be very gentle with him.'

Connor raised a paw. The evening was growing more surreal by the minute. 'Hi, everyone.'

All at once, a bunny rabbit stepped forward out of the shadows. Her costume was more cartoon-like than Zoe's and instead of a full head she was wearing a pair of pink ears on a headband and her face was skilfully made up with paint. 'I'll take care of you, Mr Fox,' she said, going up to Connor and linking her arm through his. 'Would you like to see my burrow?'

'You bet I would,' said Connor. The night was still young, but he had a feeling he was going to enjoy this furring lark.

It was nearly two hours since Bear and Nicole had begun their vigil, but disappointingly they had yet to sight a single badger. To pass the time, they talked about all sorts of things: their childhoods, their families, their favourite films. Nicole was intrigued to discover that Bear had been privately educated before starting work as a gopher at his local paper.

'How did you end up specializing in the environment?' she asked as she sipped tea from a plastic cup.

'Pure chance,' he replied. 'Although I prefer to think of it as fate.' He picked up the Thermos and gave them both a top-up. 'Do you believe in fate, Nicole?'

'Yes,' she replied. 'At least I think I do.'

'So do I,' Bear said. He looked into her eyes as if searching for something, the way a teacher might look into the eyes of a child to see if they were telling the truth. Feeling self-conscious, Nicole turned away and fiddled with the buckle on her boot. 'Anyway, you still haven't answered my question.'

Bear shook his head. 'Sorry, where was I? Oh yes, fate's hand in my career. Okay, well, after my stint as a gopher, I got a job as a junior reporter at a local paper up in Yorkshire. One day, I was sent to interview a group of protesters who were claiming squatters' rights on an area of woodland that was scheduled for clearance to make way for a new bypass. They were living in tree houses and surviving on food donations from sympathetic members of the public. Some of them had been there for months. It was such a great story that my news editor suggested

I join the camp for a week and write a daily column for the paper.'

'Ooh, that must have been an exciting assignment for a rookie reporter,' said Nicole.

'I'm afraid I didn't see it that way, at least not at first. There was no running water or electricity at the site, and the toilet was a hole in the ground. I'd never even been camping before, so it was all a bit of a culture shock. But, within a few days, my view had completely changed. The passion and commitment of those protesters was unlike anything I'd ever seen before. That piece of woodland was so important to them they were prepared to do anything to save it, even if it meant putting the rest of their lives on hold.' Bear's eyes took on a distant look, as if he were imagining himself back at the camp. 'And then, when they explained to me just what a huge environmental impact the loss of the woodland would have, I started to feel that passion myself – so much so that by the end of the week I'd forgotten I was a journalist; I was a protester just like the others, and I made up my mind that I'd do everything in my power to help them. Luckily, my column proved a big hit with the paper's readers, so when the week was up I persuaded my editor to let me stay on. After that, the column seemed to take on a life of its own. My daily reports helped attract huge publicity for the campaign, and people from all over the county started turning up at the site to lend their support.'

Nicole's eyes grew round. 'Wow, that's amazing. How long were you there for in the end?'

'Seven weeks – and I would've stayed longer, even if it meant losing my job.'

'So what happened?'

'When the bailiffs realized we were in it for the long haul, they dropped their softly, softly approach and moved in with their wretched cherry pickers. It was six in the morning; most of us were still asleep. Against strong-arm tactics like that, we were powerless.'

'So the bypass went ahead?'

'Yep, and another precious piece of countryside was lost forever.'

Nicole winced. 'Oh dear, I thought there was going to be a happy ending.'

'Not that time unfortunately, but the campaign had a profound impact on me. My column ended up winning quite a prestigious journalism award and as a result I started getting commissions from the nationals. Eventually, I packed in my job at the newspaper and became a freelance.'

'What a great story,' said Nicole, smiling. 'Your work sounds fascinating. It makes my life seem terribly dull by comparison.'

'Oh come on, Nicole; you're bringing up a child. How can your life be dull?'

'Don't get me wrong – I love Tilly to bits – it's just that sometimes I think being a wife and a mother isn't enough.' Nicole sighed. 'I suppose I shouldn't really complain. I have a very comfortable life; Connor's a fantastic provider. Tilly and I don't want for anything.'

'And what about your emotional needs?'

Nicole was taken aback. She wasn't used to being questioned in such a direct way, especially not by someone she'd only just met. She knew that the sensible thing to do would be to lie – to smile politely and say that, yes, her marriage was perfectly fulfilling and Connor was a dutiful and attentive husband, thank you very much. But she didn't.

'Connor's your typical alpha male, so sensitivity's not his strong point,' she said in a quiet voice. 'His work takes up a lot of his time and emotional energy. I don't think he has much left to give by the time he comes home at the end of the day – or at least that's the way it seems.'

Bear's face crumpled in concern. 'Oh dear, that doesn't sound very good.'

Just then, Nicole caught a movement out of the corner of her eye. 'Oh my God, I think I just saw a badger,' she said in an excited whisper.

Tossing his plastic cup of tea aside, Bear sprang to his feet and shone his torch into the woods. 'Where? I can't see anything.'

'Over there,' said Nicole, pointing to the left. As Bear swung the torch, its beam picked out the glinting amber eyes of a tawny owl that was perched on a low branch. It stared at them for a few seconds before taking flight on soft, silent wings.

'Hmm,' said Nicole as she stared after the bird. 'I guess I was wrong.'

Bear frowned. 'The badgers should be out well before sunset. I wonder if something's scared them away.' He glanced at his watch. 'We may as well call it a day. Your husband will probably be wondering where you are.'

'I doubt it,' Nicole said under her breath.

They didn't say much to one another as they trekked back across the strawberry field. Now that it was dark, the field had become treacherous with its hidden furrows and trails of rotting vegetation. Nicole's progress in her high-heeled boots was painfully slow. She trod carefully, not wanting to risk turning her ankle – for how would she explain *that* to Connor? Despite her caution she nearly lost her footing a couple of times and was disappointed when, instead of offering her his hand, Bear simply asked if she was okay and waited for her to catch up. They were halfway to the boundary fence when he suddenly stopped in his tracks and lifted his nose in the air like a beagle scenting a fox.

'Did you hear that?' he said.

Nicole listened. At first there was only silence, but then she heard the unmistakeable sound of laughter. She looked back towards the copse. Through the trees, she could just make out some flickering yellow lights. More noises drifted through the thin night air, though these ones seemed less human: a series of sharp yelps, followed by a high-pitched keening. 'I wonder what's going on over there,' she said. 'Whatever it is, they seem to be enjoying themselves.'

Bear's jaw tightened. 'Badger-baiting,' he said grimly. 'I'd put money on it.'

'Goodness, does that sort of thing still go on?'

'Yes, unfortunately. Thousands of animals die every year in the name of the so-called "sport" – not just the badgers themselves, but the terriers they send down into the sett to catch them. It's one of the most brutal activities imaginable, but I'll spare you the grisly details.' Bear rubbed his chin thoughtfully. 'No wonder we didn't see any badgers. They'll have sensed the danger and gone to ground.'

'Should we call the police?'

Bear gave a hard laugh. 'By the time the cops get here, those guys will be long gone – and in any case, we're trespassing, remember? We'd probably end up getting arrested ourselves.' He stared at the flickering lights in the distance. They seemed to be coming from the very heart of the copse, where he knew there were likely to be other entrances to the sett. 'I'm going to take a look,' he said.

Nicole felt a twinge of anxiety. 'You're not going to do anything silly, are you?'

'Don't worry, I'll keep my distance. They won't even know I'm there. I just want to get a fix on their location and see how many of them there are. At least then I'll be able to report them to the Badger Protection League.' He pushed the torch into her hands. 'Why don't you go on through the fence and wait for me on the other side? I won't be long.'

Nicole shook her head. 'No, I'm coming with you.'

'I don't think that's a good idea. The people involved in this sort of thing are vicious thugs. If they see us, they'll probably set their dogs on us.'

'But they aren't *going* to see us, are they?' Nicole said as she began walking purposefully back towards the copse. 'Come on.'

Bear sighed. Then, after a few seconds' hesitation, he set off after her.

When they arrived at the edge of the copse, Bear stopped to rummage in his rucksack. 'We need to take some precautionary measures,' he said, pulling out a dark wool balaclava. 'Here, put this on. It'll give you some camouflage.'

Nicole did as she was told, pushing her shoulder-length hair up into the hat. 'What about you?' she asked.

'This'll do me.' Bending down, Bear scooped up a handful of mud and began daubing it over his cheeks, nose and forehead. 'Okay, now turn off the torch,' he said. 'We don't want them to see us coming.'

Nicole flicked the switch. Now the only light came from the moon and the millions of twinkling stars.

Bear touched her arm lightly. 'Are you ready?'

Nicole nodded.

'Good, then follow me.'

Nicole was feeling more than a little apprehensive as they set off, but she knew instinctively that, whatever happened, Bear would protect her. As they continued deeper into the woods, the noises grew louder. There was giggling – female as well as male – accompanied by strange grunts and snorts.

'It sounds as if there are quite a few of them,' Bear whispered. 'We need to be very careful; stay close to me.'

They advanced further, their footfalls muffled by the mulchy ground. Up ahead, Nicole could see a clearing staked out by flaming torches. There were figures too, moving in the shadows, though from this distance their forms were indistinct.

Bear pointed out a fallen tree that lay over to the left, twenty feet or so from the clearing. 'That'll give us some good cover,' he whispered. 'Let's make a run for it, but remember to stay low or they might see us.'

Together, they scuttled forward, heads bowed, so all they could see was the ground in front of their feet. When they arrived at the tree trunk, they collapsed behind it and sat with their backs to the tree, praying they hadn't been seen. They needn't have worried – their targets had other more pressing matters to attend to. While Bear and Nicole waited for their hearts to stop thumping, new and strange vocalizations rent the air.

'*Baaad* Mr Fox!' a female voice squealed loudly. 'Aaah . . . yes . . . harder . . . yes . . . faster . . . yes . . . ooooh!'

Nicole looked at her fellow eco warrior. 'What the . . . ?' she mouthed. Bear, who seemed as nonplussed as she, simply shrugged. Unable to contain her curiosity a moment longer, Nicole rolled onto her knees and raised her balaclava'd head a few inches above the tree trunk.

What she saw made her skin prickle and her eyes bulge. In the clearing were a large group of animals – or, rather, human beings *dressed* as animals. Even more startling, the vast majority were engaged in sexual acts of one sort or another. Nicole's gaze was drawn to an exceedingly vocal grey mouse, who was kneeling on all fours on a groundsheet, while 'Baaad Mr Fox' serviced her from behind. As well as her cries of encouragement, little squeaks issued from the rodent at regular intervals. The fox, by contrast, remained resolutely silent, his bushy tail quivering with each thrust. Nicole's gaze wandered to the other side of the clearing where a rabbit with gigantic pink ears was performing enthusiastic fellatio on a stag. A wolf sat on a nearby tree stump watching them as he masturbated with a fur-gloved hand.

Bear had now joined Nicole above the tree trunk and he too was stunned by what he saw. 'Jesus,' she heard him murmur. 'I think we've interrupted a private party. We'd better make ourselves scarce.'

'Hang on,' Nicole whispered back as her eyes were pulled by some invisible force back to the fox. Although the man's face was completely obscured, she could see how hard he was concentrating on the task in hand by the rigidity of his shoulders and the way his paws gripped his partner's hips, pulling them towards him in rhythmic movements. As she watched, mesmerized by the surreal scene, the fox threw back his head and began panting loudly as he approached orgasm. And then, quite without warning, his head fell to the side and he was looking directly at Nicole. The next moment, he was pulling out of the mouse and stuffing his penis – still with its condom on – back into his costume.

The mouse looked over her shoulder. 'What are you doing?' she said crossly.

The fox jabbed a finger towards the tree trunk and muttered something before running off into the undergrowth.

Bear grabbed Nicole's arm and pulled her back behind the tree – but it was too late.

'Watch out, everyone!' the mouse cried. 'We've got company. There are people spying on us . . . over there, behind that fallen tree.'

'Shit,' Bear said. 'Come on, let's run for it.'

As they took to their heels, a series of angry cries rang out. 'Piss off! . . . Bloody peeping Toms! . . . Don't you know this is private land?'

The fugitives didn't look back – not until they were halfway across the strawberry fields when Nicole had to stop and bend over double to catch her breath.

'Are you okay?' Bear said, looking anxiously around to make sure they weren't being pursued by irate animals.

Nicole peeled off the balaclava. 'I'm fine, just a bit unfit. I haven't run that fast since I was at school.' She looked back towards the copse. 'Can you believe that? Isn't it funny how some people get their kicks?'

'Yeah, for a minute back there I thought I was seeing

things.' He smiled. 'Anyway, I think that's enough excitement for one night. Come on, I'd better get you home.'

As they walked across the field, hand in hand, Nicole looked up at the beautiful night sky and smiled. It had been a strange and eventful night, but she wouldn't have missed it for the world.

11

The gardens of Ashwicke Park were almost unrecognizable. Clusters of trestle tables dotted the front lawn, each one groaning under the weight of a different homemade delicacy – from jams and chutneys to lavishly decorated cakes, towering pyramids of scones and exotic varieties of fudge wrapped in greaseproof paper. Positioned a safe distance away, against a line of oak trees, was a coconut shy and next to it a hoopla, a shooting range and a strongman striker. To the east, on the elevated terrace, a row of hay bales marked out a small arena – this was where the Loxwood Players would enact excerpts from Gilbert and Sullivan, before a troupe of dancers from Miss Golightly's School of Ballet, Tap and Mime performed an energetic encore. To the west, overlooking the rose garden, stood a timber-framed gazebo. Its windows had been draped with colourful voiles and a hand-painted sign on the door read: *Madame Zsa Zsa, Fortune Teller.* Inside sat Harriet Heaver, the local postmistress. For one day only, she had swapped her usual uniform of pussy-bow blouse and pleated skirt for a turban of cerise silk and a diaphanous gown that did little to flatter her ample curves. Truth be told, Harriet's only knowledge of the future had been gleaned from the horoscopes page of the *Daily Mail* – but none of the people who crossed Madame Zsa Zsa's palm with a crisp five-pound note objected to her lack of experience. At the end of the day, it was all for charity.

There had been great excitement in Loxwood when, just before she left for Aspen, Juliet announced her intention to host the town's annual summer fête. The Ingram family had generously staged the fête at Ashwicke for as long as anyone could remember, but the previous year it had been cancelled at the last minute, following Gus's sudden and shocking death. There had been some talk of moving the event to an alternative location, but everyone agreed it wouldn't be the same. And so, as a mark of respect to Gus who, for many years had presided over the fête like a proud ringmaster, a memorial service was held instead at the local church. Juliet, understandably, hadn't felt well enough to attend. Rumour had it she spent the day in hospital, heavily sedated. But now it seemed the chatelaine of Ashwicke had put those nightmarish times behind her and was keen for things to get back to normal. Nobody doubted her when she promised that this year's fête would be bigger and better than any that had gone before.

The day in question dawned clear and bright. At two p.m. precisely, Juliet made her way to the entrance gates, where a large crowd of locals was already gathered in the sunshine. A ripple of applause broke out as she took her place in front of the red ribbon that was stretched across the drive. 'My husband and I would like to declare the Loxwood summer fête open,' she said, smiling at Dante, who was standing at her shoulder. 'And I do hope everyone has a wonderful afternoon. I certainly shall.' With that, Juliet raised her scissors and snipped the ribbon, then stood aside as the fête-goers swept into the estate, eager as a bunch of bargain-hunters on the first day of the Harrods sale.

Yasmin and Nicole joined the procession heading

towards the front lawn, Nicole tutting irritably as a woman in a garish floral dress charged past them, almost upending the buggy in her eagerness to get to the cake stalls.

'Honestly, some people are so rude,' Nicole said, as she checked to make sure Tilly was securely strapped in.

Yasmin pushed her sunglasses up into her hair and scanned the lawn. 'When's Connor getting here?'

Nicole glanced at her watch. 'Any minute now. He promised me he wouldn't be late.'

'I can't believe he's working on a Saturday. The surgery's not even open, is it?'

'No, but he's expecting a bunch of test results in the post and he wanted to call the relevant patients before Monday.' Nicole gave a long sigh. 'I suppose I should be proud I'm married to such a dedicated doctor, but I can't help feeling resentful. Connor works such awfully long hours; he's missing out on great swathes of Tilly's babyhood. I thought when he set up his own practice he'd have more free time, but it's turned out to be quite the opposite.' She wheeled the buggy round. 'Come on, let's get to those cake stalls before all the best goodies get snaffled.'

As the two women wandered from stall to stall, it wasn't long before Yasmin spotted a familiar face. 'Look,' she said, nudging Nicole. 'Isn't that Charlie, Juliet's porter, standing behind that table over there?'

Nicole squinted into the distance. 'I think you're right. Let's go and say hello, shall we?'

When the women arrived at the stall, Charlie was busy serving a customer. Behind him, chambermaid Leah lay sprawled on the grass in a pair of denim shorts and a skimpy bandeau top.

'Hi, Charlie,' Yasmin said, as the customer wandered away. 'I didn't expect to see you here. I wouldn't have thought summer fêtes were your thing.'

The porter grinned. 'They're not usually, but I'm hoping this one will turn out to be a nice little earner.'

Yasmin looked down at the table, which was draped in dark green velvet, presumably in an attempt to make Charlie's misshapen chocolate brownies, clumsily wrapped in clingfilm, look more appetizing. 'Did you make these yourself?'

'I certainly did – with a little help from Leah here.'

The chambermaid raised a languid arm and let it fall again. 'Hey,' she said in a sleepy voice.

Nicole prodded the nearest package of cakes with a forefinger, testing it for moistness, then gasped as she noticed the price label. 'Ten pounds for four brownies? That's a bit steep, isn't it?'

'Ahh, but you see these aren't just any old brownies,' said Charlie, pointing out the words *Extra Special* on the handwritten label. He reached for an identical-looking package on the other side of the table. 'If it's the ordinary variety you're after, these ones are a quarter of the price.'

'So what's the difference – are the extra-special ones organic?' Nicole asked.

Leah giggled. 'You could say that.'

Charlie's eyes flickered from side to side like a cobra's as he checked to see who was in earshot. Then he leaned across the table. 'They're hash brownies,' he whispered. 'Available to discerning customers only. Obviously, if some old dear tries to buy some, I'll fob her off with the other ones.'

Nicole's eyebrows shot up. 'Does Juliet know about this?'

'You've got to be kidding.' He eyed her suspiciously. 'You're not going to grass me up, are you?'

Yasmin tutted. 'Don't be silly, of course she isn't – *are* you, Nicole?'

'Well, I'm not sure . . . drug-dealing is illegal, after all,' Nicole said primly.

'Oh, don't be so boring,' Yasmin said, reaching for her purse. 'I'll take a package of the extra-special variety, please.'

'Yasmin!' Nicole exclaimed. 'I didn't know you indulged.'

'Just occasionally,' her friend replied airily. 'And today I happen to feel like spoiling myself.'

Ignoring the other woman's clucks of disapproval, Yasmin pressed a ten-pound note into Charlie's hand. 'And don't worry,' she told him. 'Your secret's safe with us.'

'Cheers,' he said. 'And there's plenty more where they came from.' He produced a small white card from the cashbox and handed it to Yasmin. 'Here's my mobile number . . . just in case you feel like spoiling yourself another time.'

Yasmin's eyes lit up. 'Great, I'll bear that in mind.'

Next to her, Nicole gave a theatrical shudder.

'You should try one,' Yasmin told her friend as she picked up the cakes. 'You never know, you might like it.'

'I wouldn't bet on it,' Nicole said as she turned and began walking towards a stall selling hand-knitted toys.

Twenty minutes later, their shopping bags bulging with purchases, the two women found themselves wandering towards the amusements. As they drew nearer, they noticed that a large crowd had gathered in front of the strong-man striker.

'I wonder what's happening over there,' Nicole mused out loud.

'I'll go and have a look,' said Yasmin, striding ahead. She stopped at the edge of the crowd, peering between the shoulders of the people in front of her. A second later, she turned and beckoned to Nicole. 'Hurry up, Nic. You don't want to miss this.'

Nicole wheeled the pushchair towards her. 'What is it? What's going on?'

'See for yourself,' Yasmin replied, stepping aside to make room for her friend.

When Nicole saw who was standing beside the strong-man striker, looking disreputably handsome in a pink shirt and faded Levi's, she gasped out loud. 'Connor!' she exclaimed. But her husband was too busy playing to the crowd to notice her.

'Stand well back, ladies,' the GP declared as he picked up the hammer. 'I don't want anyone to get hurt.'

'It looks as if your husband's quite a hit – in more ways than one,' Yasmin remarked as she looked around at the sea of adoring female faces turned towards Connor.

'He's a bloody show-off, I know that much,' Nicole muttered.

The next moment, Connor brought the hammer down, sending the puck flying all the way up to the bell.

'Yessss!' he shouted, dropping the hammer and punching the air with his fist triumphantly. He turned to face the applauding crowd and took a bow. 'Thank you, ladies and gents, you're too kind.' Just then he saw Nicole. The smile seemed to freeze on his face. 'Darling!' he cried, breaking through the crowd and gripping his wife in a bear hug. 'There you are. I've been looking everywhere for you.'

'Really?' Nicole said, raising a disbelieving brow. 'In that case you can't have looked very hard.' She nodded towards the rapidly dispersing crowd. 'That was quite a show you put on.'

Connor looked annoyed. 'It wasn't intentional,' he said. 'The guy running the stall is one of my patients. I happened to be walking past and he begged me to have a go. The next thing I knew there were loads of people watching me.' Seeing Yasmin hovering in the background, he raised a hand in greeting. 'Hi, Yasmin, how are you?'

'Not bad, thanks. Did you get all your work done?'

Connor frowned. 'I'm sorry?'

'Your work . . . at the surgery. Isn't that where you've been all morning?'

'Oh, that . . . yes, of course,' Connor said quickly. 'I managed to get through most of it.'

Yasmin pointed at his torso. 'Get dressed in a hurry this morning, did you?'

Glancing at his shirt, Connor saw that several of the buttons were done up the wrong way. 'It certainly looks that way,' he said, smiling genially.

Nicole tapped her watch. 'Yasmin and I have arranged to meet Juliet in the tea tent in five minutes. Will you look after Tilly?'

Connor made a face. 'Can't you take her with you?'

'No, I can't,' Nicole said, her irritation evident. 'I've had her all morning. I think it's about time you did your share.'

'Fine,' Connor said, wresting the handle of the buggy from her grasp.

'I'll meet you on the terrace at three thirty for the Best Dressed Pet competition.'

Connor gave a mock salute as he began walking away. 'Yes, *sir*!'

Nicole's eyes narrowed, but she didn't say anything.

Inside the tea tent – a gleaming, open-fronted pavilion overlooking Ashwicke's splendid Italianate fountain – Juliet was waiting. As the others approached, she stood up and smiled apologetically. 'Sorry, girls, this was the last table and as you can see there are only two chairs. We'll have to find another one from somewhere.'

Nicole scanned the packed tent and saw that every seat was taken. 'I guess we'll just have to wait for someone to leave.'

'Oh no we won't,' said Yasmin. She marched over to a table a few feet away, where two elderly ladies were guzzling scones with strawberry jam and clotted cream. Both were somewhat overdressed for the occasion – one resplendent in a mother-of-the-bride peach crêpe de Chine two-piece, the other sporting a tweedy suit and green felt hat, complete with quivering pheasant quill. Beside them, on a third chair, sat a Yorkshire terrier with a blue bow on its head.

Yasmin drummed her fingers on the back of the terrier's chair. 'Is *he* having afternoon tea?' she demanded.

The woman in the hat bristled at the interruption. 'I beg your pardon?'

'I said,' Yasmin repeated, speaking so loudly that several inquisitive heads turned in her direction, 'is *he* having afternoon tea?'

'Don't be ridiculous,' the woman snapped. 'He's a dog.

Of course he isn't.' As if to indicate that Yasmin was now dismissed, she picked up a half-eaten scone and crammed it into her mouth.

'Good. In that case, he won't be needing this.' Without warning, Yasmin grabbed the back of the chair and tipped it forward, so the terrier went tumbling to the ground, his claws skittering across the chair's painted wooden seat as he tried in vain to get a purchase on it.

The dog owner's eyes glittered. 'How dare you!' she cried through a mouthful of scone.

Yasmin eyed the Yorkshire terrier, who was now trembling in shock. 'Didn't anyone ever tell you it's not hygienic to have an animal at the table?' Without another word, she picked up the chair and started carrying it away. She'd only gone a few paces when she turned back over her shoulder. 'Oh, and in case you didn't know, it's rude to talk with your mouth full.'

When she arrived at her own table, Juliet and Nicole were gawping at her with a mixture of shock and admiration.

'Blimey, Yasmin, you're scary when you're angry,' Nicole said, moving her own chair closer to Juliet's to make room for her friend.

'That bloody mongrel shouldn't even be in here.' Yasmin waved at a passing waitress. 'Afternoon tea for three, please.' As she turned back to the others, she caught sight of a familiar face on the other side of the pavilion.

'I don't believe it,' she said. 'What's *he* doing at the fête?'

Juliet followed Yasmin's gaze. 'Who are you talking about?'

'Rob Pritchard. He doesn't even live around here.'

Nicole shrugged. 'Maybe his girlfriend does.'

Yasmin's stomach lurched. 'What girlfriend?'

'That woman sitting with him,' Nicole said. 'They look pretty close.'

When Yasmin craned her neck, she saw that Rob was indeed accompanied by a pretty – no, *stunning* – girl, red hair tumbling down her back pre-Raphaelite style, her heart-shaped face pale and ethereal. She was talking animatedly, using her hands for emphasis, and Rob was listening to her, rapt. He looked happy and relaxed, quite different from the brooding face he usually presented at work. 'I'm surprised anyone would have him,' she muttered, turning back to the others. 'So,' she said, resting her elbows on the table, 'what's new?'

'Bear took me badger-watching on Thursday night,' Nicole offered.

Yasmin frowned. 'I thought you said you were going to the theatre.'

'Connor couldn't make it because of a work thing; I gave the tickets to my cleaner.'

'That's a shame,' Juliet said. 'Did the badgers make up for it?'

'Actually, we didn't see any, but . . .' Nicole broke into a grin. 'We did inadvertently stumble across a bunch of people in animal costumes shagging each other in the woods.'

Juliet's hand flew to her mouth. 'Ewww! Why would anyone want to do that?'

'It's called furring,' Yasmin said, shaking out her napkin as she saw their waitress approaching with a heavily laden tray. 'We did a story in the *Post* a while back. Apparently it's the hottest trend in outdoor sex since dogging. I can't say the idea of being rogered by a man dressed as a giant wombat makes me go weak at the knees, but each to their own, eh?' She nodded in the waitress's direction. 'Look out, girls, we've got company.'

The tea tent was run by members of the Loxwood branch of the Women's Institute – an organization which, besides its sterling work for charity, was the town's chief conduit for rumour, gossip and hearsay. Nicole and co. were fully aware that any tasty morsel their waitress happened to overhear in the course of her duties would be gobbled up, partially digested and then regurgitated at the earliest available opportunity. And so, by unspoken agreement, they fell silent.

'Good afternoon, ladies,' the waitress trilled as she rested her tray on the edge of the table. 'Are you enjoying yourselves this afternoon?'

'Yes, thank you,' the women chorused.

The waitress began unloading her tray. A fat teapot was followed by three china cups and saucers, matching side plates, milk jug, sugar bowl and tongs and finally, the pièce de résistance, a three-tier stand of assorted cakes and fancies.

'Do let me know if you need more cakes,' the waitress said with a syrupy smile. 'I'd be happy to top you up. Our members have really done themselves proud this year. We've got éclairs, flapjacks, double chocolate brownies, date and walnut slices, Viennese whirls . . .'

'Super!' Juliet interrupted. 'We'll let you know.'

Still the waitress lingered. 'Would you like me to pour the tea?'

'I think we can manage,' said Yasmin in the sort of brisk

tone that was meant to discourage further chitchat. The waitress took the hint, pursing her lips before beetling off, tray in hand.

'Now, where were we?' said Yasmin, as she selected a fat vanilla slice, oozing with custard. 'Ah yes, the furring. Do tell us more.'

Juliet fluttered her eyelashes like a maiden aunt forced to watch *Deep Throat*. 'Please, spare us the sordid details. I think we get the picture.'

'There isn't much more to tell,' said Nicole. 'Bear and I had only been there for a couple of minutes when a man in a fox suit spotted us and we had to do a runner.' She frowned and rubbed her chin. 'It's funny, but there was something familiar about that fox. I can't for the life of me think why.' She picked up the teapot. 'I'll be mother, shall I?'

'Lovely,' said Juliet, pushing her cup forward. 'And Connor didn't mind you spending the evening with Bear?'

Nicole shifted guiltily in her seat. 'Erm, I haven't mentioned it to him.'

Yasmin's eyes narrowed. 'Is there something you're not telling us, Nic?'

'I don't know what you mean,' Nicole said, rubbing an imaginary stain on the Cath Kidston oilcloth.

Juliet leaned forward conspiratorially. 'I think what she means is, do you want to shag the arse off Bear?'

'Oh, for goodness' sakes!' Nicole cried shrilly. 'We're friends, that's all.'

'You're not fooling anyone,' Yasmin said, grinning. 'You'd just better hope Connor doesn't find out.'

Nicole's lower lip quivered. 'I shouldn't think he'd care less.'

The next moment she was pushing her chair away from the table. 'Will you excuse me? I need to use the Ladies.'

As she scooped up her handbag and headed towards the Portaloos at the rear of the pavilion, Yasmin turned to Juliet. 'Do you think she's all right?'

'She looked as if she was about to burst into tears just then.' Juliet tossed down her napkin. 'I'd better go after her.'

'Great,' Yasmin muttered as Juliet walked away. 'Leave me all on my own, why don't you?' She picked up the teapot and refilled her cup. 'And here was I thinking the fête was going to be such a laugh.' Suddenly, a mischievous look flashed across her face. 'I know what'll cheer everyone up,' she said as she reached for her shopping bag.

Gleefully, she unwrapped the package of brownies and began arranging them on the cake stand's heavily depleted bottom tier. Afterwards, she stuffed the incriminating cling-film in her bag and sat back in her chair, pleased with her handiwork.

'Look at this,' she said when Juliet and Nicole returned a few minutes later. 'The waitress has just replenished our stock of cakes.' She pointed to the stand. 'These brownies were fresh baked this morning.'

Juliet leaned forward. 'They look a bit amateurish to me.'

'I think you mean *rustic*.'

Nicole patted her stomach. 'I really shouldn't eat any more. I'm supposed to be watching my weight.'

'Come on, Nicole, today's a special day,' Yasmin urged. 'You can start the diet tomorrow.'

As Nicole vacillated, Juliet helped herself to one of the cakes. 'Well, I'm going to have one.' She broke off a corner of brownie and popped it into her mouth. 'Mmm . . . they taste better than they look,' she said, chewing meditatively.

Unable to resist temptation any longer, Nicole reached for a brownie. 'I'm going to regret this in the morning,' she said as she took a bite. 'Ooh, yes, you're right, Juliet, they *are* nice.' She chewed some more. 'They've got some interesting chewy bits in too.'

Yasmin bit her lip as a smirk threatened to erupt across her face. 'I think I'll have one too,' she said, picking up a brownie. 'Cheers, ladies.'

Half an hour later, the women emerged from the pavilion into the bright afternoon sunshine. Outside, Ashwicke's front lawn stretched before them like a brilliant green carpet, an affront to the implacable summer sun.

'What time is it?' Nicole asked.

Yasmin pointed to her friend's wrist. 'Why don't you look at your watch?'

Nicole started giggling. 'Silly me, I forgot I was wearing one.' She stroked the back of her hand across her brow. 'My head feels all muzzy; it must be the heat.' Looking down at her watch she saw that it was twenty past three. 'I'd better find Connor and Tilly,' she said. 'The Best Dressed Pet competition starts in ten minutes. Are you two coming?'

'You bet,' Yasmin said. 'A little bird told me Lydia Ormerod hired a top London costumier to make her outfit this year. Apparently it cost the best part of a thousand pounds.'

Juliet shuddered. 'That woman's so vulgar. It's only supposed to be a bit of fun.' Suddenly, she pointed over Nicole's shoulder. 'Look, there's Bear.'

Nicole turned round. Bear was standing on the other

side of the garden, perusing the secondhand-book stall as he munched on an ice cream cornet. In his T-shirt and black jeans, he made all the other men at the fête, dressed in their baggy shorts and leather sandals, look somehow effete and immature. She raised her hand above her head and started waving wildly. 'Bear! Bear! Over here!'

He looked up, smiling when he saw Nicole.

'God, he's gorgeous,' Nicole whispered as he started walking towards her.

'Sorry, what was that?' Juliet asked.

'Nothing.' Nicole licked her dry lips. Her tongue felt like cotton wool in her mouth and her heart was beating so hard she felt sure the others could see it jumping beneath her thin cotton blouse. 'Hi, Bear,' she called out when he was a few feet away.

'Hi, there,' he replied. 'I wondered if I might bump into you today.'

'Me too,' Nicole said breathily. Now that he was within touching distance, she found her gaze drawn to the neck of his T-shirt. Above it a cloud of tawny curls sprouted tantalizingly. For some reason she couldn't quite fathom, Nicole couldn't tear her eyes away from it.

Bear looked down at his chest. 'What is it?' he said, frowning. 'Have I dropped some ice cream on myself?'

'No,' Nicole replied, forcing herself to look away. 'I was just, um, admiring your T-shirt.'

Bear looked slightly bemused. 'I see.' He smiled at Juliet. 'This is a fantastic fête; you've done Loxwood proud.'

'Oh, I can't take all the credit,' Juliet replied. 'I had a lot of help.'

'She's just being modest,' Yasmin piped up. 'I've seen

how hard she's worked to pull all this together.' She held her hand out to Bear. 'I'm Yasmin, by the way.'

'Ah, the showbiz queen,' Bear said, shaking her hand. 'Nicole's told me a lot about you.'

Yasmin arched a well-shaped brow. 'Has she now?'

Nicole nodded energetically. As she did, she felt slightly dizzy. It seemed as if her head were no longer securely attached and might be about to roll off her shoulders and land at Bear's feet. All at once she started giggling uncontrollably. 'I'm sorry,' she said as her giggles turned to snorts. 'I don't know what's wrong with me; I'm not myself today.'

'I think the poor love's got a touch of sunstroke,' Juliet said, taking Nicole's arm.

Bear's eyes filled with concern. 'In that case, you'd better get her into the shade. Sunstroke can be a nasty thing.'

'We will,' Yasmin said, taking Nicole's other arm. 'Come on, Nic, let's go and find a nice big tree.'

The two women started leading Nicole away before she could embarrass herself further.

'Bye, Bear!' Nicole yelled over her shoulder. 'See you soon!'

'Bye, Nicole,' Bear said, shaking his head in amusement.

12

Inside Ashwicke's elegant drawing room Dante was kneeling in front of a baroque bureau, where earlier that day he'd placed a secret stash of clothing. Until two days ago, Dante had never even heard of the Best Dressed Pet competition. It was Nathan who'd mentioned it as he delivered coffee to the Betjeman suite, where Dante was painting the skirting boards.

'I thought you could do with some refreshment,' the general manager had said, placing the mug on the floor beside Dante.

'Thanks,' Dante replied, leaning back on his haunches.

Nathan, who seemed in no hurry to leave, went to the window. 'I expect you're looking forward to the fête on Saturday,' he remarked as he gazed out across the lawn.

Dante cleared his throat. Ever since their bizarre confrontation in Gus's dressing room a few days earlier, he'd felt awkward around Nathan. 'You bet,' he said.

'The weather forecast looks promising.'

'Yeah?' Dante said. 'That's good.'

Nathan turned away from the window and leaned against the sill. 'Were you thinking of taking part in any of the events?'

Dante shrugged. 'To be honest, I hadn't given it much thought.'

'That's a shame,' Nathan murmured, shaking his head.

'From what I've heard, Mr Ingram always liked to join in. One year he did a performance with the local Morris dancers. Apparently, he was so good he got a standing ovation.'

Dante felt a twinge of irritation. 'It's not that I don't want to join in,' he said, picking up the paintbrush, 'but I don't have any talents: I can't act; my singing's lousy and as for my Morris dancing . . . well, I don't even know what that is.'

'That doesn't matter. You could always offer to man one of the attractions – the tombola, perhaps, or how about the welly-wanging?'

Dante shook his head. 'I'd rather not commit myself to helping out for a whole afternoon. I want to spend some time with Juliet.'

'Yes, of course you do. It was silly of me even to suggest it.' Nathan straightened up as if he were about to go. 'There's always the Best Dressed Pet competition,' he said nonchalantly. 'That wouldn't take up much of your time. All you'd have to do is parade Jess round the ring a couple of times and you'd be done.'

Dante looked over at Jess, who was lying on the floor beside the bed, eyes half closed. Over the weeks, he'd grown fond of the gentle pointer – and, given that she now followed him everywhere like a shadow, the feeling was apparently mutual.

'It's up to you,' Nathan continued. 'But it might be a nice idea. If nothing else, it would show people you're keen to be part of the community.'

Dante thought for a moment. The general manager had a point: if his frosty reception at the golf club was anything to go by, he needed to ingratiate himself with the locals somehow. In any case, the competition sounded like fun – and Jess would certainly enjoy showing off. 'So what would I have to do, exactly?' he asked.

'It wouldn't require much effort,' Nathan reassured him. 'The rules are very simple: owner and pet have to wear coordinating costumes; each competitor parades round the ring a couple of times and then a team of judges decide the winner. That's all there is to it.'

'It's a neat idea, but how am I going to pull a costume together at such short notice?'

'Why don't you head up to the attic? There's bound to be some dressing-up things in the store room.'

Dante frowned. 'The store room? I don't even know where that is.'

'Third floor, the little room under the eaves. It was servants' quarters once upon a time, but now it's used for storage. I haven't been up there in a while, but I'm sure you'll find all sorts of interesting bits and pieces.' Nathan gave an odd, lopsided smile. 'Anyway, I mustn't keep you from your work. Don't forget to drink your coffee before it gets cold.'

With nothing better to do after lunch, Dante found himself climbing to the top of the house with Jess to see what, if any, treasures were waiting to be unearthed in the attic. The first door he tried led to a tiny room, sparsely furnished with an iron bedstead and a desperately unfashionable avocado sink unit. The door on the other side of the landing gave onto a larger room with a sloping ceiling and a handsome cast-iron fireplace. The air inside was muggy and smelled of mothballs, and the rosebud wallpaper was yellowed with age. There was no furniture in the room, save for a chipped mahogany wardrobe squatting under the eaves, and every available inch of floor space was crammed with packing crates and boxes.

While Jess began exploring the boxes, pushing her long nose into the crevices between them, Dante's eye was drawn to a stack of framed film posters that were propped up against the wall. He began flicking through them. They were all classics: *True Grit*, *Butch Cassidy and the Sundance Kid*, *For A Few Dollars More*. They looked like originals and, Dante supposed, would probably be worth something to a collector.

He pushed the frames back against the wall and walked over to the wardrobe, which seemed an obvious place to start hunting for potential costumes. There was a brown felt Stetson hanging on one of its polished wooden door-knobs. Almost without thinking, Dante picked it up and put it on his head. To his disappointment, there wasn't much inside the wardrobe – some long evening dresses, covered in transparent plastic sheaths, a mink coat, a tailored tweed riding jacket, some well-worn jodhpurs and, hanging at the end of the rail, a pair of soft leather chaps. Lifting the chaps off the rail, he held them against his legs, checking them for size. He looked over at Jess, who was wrestling with something behind one of the packing cases.

'What have you got there, girl?' he called out.

At the sound of his voice, Jess emerged from behind the crate and came over to him, dropping her find at his feet. Dante bent down and picked it up. It was a large stuffed teddy bear. Jess had all but chewed one of its legs off and both its button eyes were hanging by a thread. 'I sure hope this isn't a family heirloom,' Dante said, as he inspected the damage. The bear was dressed, somewhat incongruously, as a Red Indian in a fringed suede waistcoat and a red-and-white feather headdress which, miraculously, had escaped Jess's attack relatively unscathed. As he set the bear on the windowsill, out of harm's way, he caught sight of a Zorro-style eye mask, hanging from the catch of the sash window. He picked it up and looped the elastic over his finger.

'You know what, Jess,' he said, breaking into a smile. 'I think I've got an idea.'

The rest of the costume was easy. Dante already had jeans, cowboy boots and a denim shirt, and he managed to find a red scarf in one of Juliet's drawers that, when folded double, made a good neckerchief. Together with the chaps and the Stetson and the mask, he looked every inch the Lone Ranger. Jess, meanwhile, was a canine version of his trusty sidekick Tonto. Amazingly, the teddy bear's fringed waistcoat fitted her lean body perfectly, while the feathered headdress only required a length of string, tied to her collar, to stop it slipping off her sleek head.

As he left the drawing room with Jess, both newly outfitted and bound for the terrace, Dante couldn't help chuckling to himself as he imagined his wife's reaction when she saw them. He hadn't told her he was entering the competition, wanting to surprise her instead.

Outside, lots of people were congregated around the hay bales that marked out the arena. The Best Dressed Pet competition was always one of the day's highlights and generally gave rise to a good deal of merriment. At the appointed hour, the event's compère – retired Royal Navy captain Robert Lundy – emerged from the tent where all the competitors were waiting, clipboard in hand.

'Good afternoon, everyone,' Captain Lundy began in his booming voice. 'I know you're all looking forward to the Best Dressed Pet competition, and you certainly won't be disappointed because there are some spectacular entries this year. However, before we begin could I ask you all to bow your heads for just a moment as we remember our dear friend Gus Ingram, who died last year in terribly tragic circumstances. With his wonderful sense of fun and mischief, Gus always added an extra splash of colour to the fête and I'm sure there are many of you here today who feel his absence keenly.' Captain Lundy paused and bowed his head respectfully, as did those in the audience. As she dropped her own head, Juliet raised a white cotton handkerchief to her face and slowly dabbed each eye.

'And now, without further ado,' Captain Lundy continued, 'I would like to welcome our first contestant into the arena – Mrs Lydia Ormerod with Precious.'

As the Captain stepped aside, a stout woman in her early fifties strode purposefully into the arena. She was wearing a purple bra top, trimmed with gold brocade, and matching silk harem pants, over the top of which a sizeable muffin-top bulged. Her long, dark hair was piled into an elaborate beehive, decorated with shimmering, multicoloured jewels, and the lower part of her face was covered by a lilac veil, from which ersatz coins dangled. Accompanying her was a four-year-old springer spaniel clad in a miniature version of the same outfit, minus the beehive. As the eye-catching pair set off round the arena, enthusiastic applause broke out. Behind her veil, Lydia smiled, certain as she could be that victory was hers. Everything seemed to be going according to plan but then, as Lydia rounded the second corner, she realized that Precious was no longer beside her. Turning over her shoulder, she saw to her horror that the spaniel was sitting down and scratching furiously at her veil with her hind leg.

'Bad girl!' Lydia cried shrilly. 'Come here this instant.' The dog ignored her and continued scratching. The next moment her sharp claws ripped through the gauzy veil, sending gold coins skittering across the ground. 'Naughty girl, now look what you've done!' Lydia cried as she marched over to the dog. There were titters and good-natured catcalls from the audience as she wrenched what was left of the veil from Precious's head and flung it at the nearest hay bale.

'That poor mutt,' Nicole said. 'Imagine living with someone as bad-tempered as Lydia.'

'It's her husband I feel sorry for,' Yasmin replied. 'He's so henpecked that the last decision she let him make was whether to wash or dry. Look, that's him, over there.' She nodded towards the contestants' tent. Outside was a tall man with sloping shoulders, dressed nondescriptly in beige cords and a white shirt. At his feet was a large portable stereo.

'That's Lydia's husband?' Nicole said disbelievingly. 'I expected him to be more flamboyant; he's an art dealer, isn't he?'

Juliet nodded. 'And a millionaire several times over.'

Nicole's mouth dropped open. 'No wonder his wife can afford to blow a grand on fancy dress.'

'Mind you, it looks as if it was a spectacular waste of

money,' said Yasmin as she watched Precious break free from her owner before sinking her teeth into the silk pantaloons that covered her back legs.

'Stop that!' Lydia cried, smacking the spaniel on the nose. 'Now heel!' She started walking again, with a cross-looking Precious trailing several paces behind.

Each competitor performed two circuits of the arena. During the first, they were only permitted to walk with their animals, but the second could incorporate tricks or dance routines. As she completed her first circuit, Lydia waved at her husband, who was staring disconsolately into the middle distance. 'Arthur!' she screeched. 'Cue the music.'

At the sound of his wife's voice, Arthur's body jerked as if he'd just received ten thousand volts. Collecting himself hurriedly, he bent down and pressed a button on the stereo. As jangling, middle-eastern music blasted through the speakers, Lydia extended her arms outwards and began undulating her soft stomach in an amateurish belly dance. Precious, meanwhile, skulked behind her, head bowed in embarrassment. After shimmying in front of her stunned audience for a full minute, Lydia dragged a reluctant Captain Lundy into the arena and began performing a series of excruciating hip bumps against his crotch and buttocks. At this juncture, Connor covered his face with his hand.

'This is hideous,' he said to Nicole. 'Has that woman got no shame at all? If I had a body like that, I'd keep it well covered up.'

'I think she's very brave,' said Nicole, her hand straying to her own spare tyre.

Connor looked at his wife and frowned. 'Are you all right, Nicole? Only your eyes look a bit glazed.'

Nicole's hand went to her head. 'Actually, I am feeling rather peculiar.'

'What – like you might be sick?'

'No, just peculiar.'

Connor made a face. 'Can you be more specific?'

Nicole giggled. 'You know what, I don't think I can.' She smacked her lips. 'I don't suppose you've got anything to eat, have you?'

Connor looked at her in surprise. 'How can you be hungry when you've just had afternoon tea?'

'I just am, *okay*? Have you got anything or not?'

'No,' snapped Connor, turning back to the arena, where Lydia had now released a relieved Captain Lundy and was performing a rather ambitious back bend.

Nicole unzipped her changing bag that was stashed beneath the pushchair and pulled out a packet of baby rusks. She popped one in her mouth and began chewing it noisily. When it was gone, she reached for a second rusk, moaning in pleasure as she ate. A third followed in quick succession. 'These are yummy,' she said, reaching for a fourth. 'I can't believe I've never tried them before.' She held out the packet to her husband. 'Do you want one?'

'No thanks,' Connor said, quivering in disgust.

A few feet away, Juliet was also beginning to feel the effects of the hash brownies. 'Do you feel okay?' she whispered to Yasmin, as Lydia and Precious took a bow before leaving the arena.

Yasmin smiled. 'Never better. Why, don't you?'

'I feel a bit spaced out. And everything around me seems so much . . .' Juliet blinked hard. 'I don't know . . . brighter somehow.'

'Perhaps it was something you ate,' Yasmin said, suppressing a smile.

'Maybe . . . My mouth's really dry too.'

'Well, it is awfully hot.' Yasmin handed her a bottle of water. 'Here, have some of this.'

'I do hope I'm not coming down with something,' Juliet said, unscrewing the lid of the bottle.

'You'll be fine,' said Yasmin, smiling lazily as she felt the effects of her own hash brownie kick in. 'Just relax and go with the flow.'

Juliet eyed her friend suspiciously. 'Go with the flow? What are you talking about, Yasmin?'

'Ooh look, the next pet's coming on,' said Yasmin in an attempt to distract her friend.

Juliet looked towards the arena, where a goat in a fitted peplum jacket, diamanté collar and sunglasses was being led round the ring by the teenage daughter of a local farmer. Immediately, she exploded into laughter, spraying the woman next to her with a mouthful of water. 'That's the funniest thing I've ever seen,' she cried.

'Oh, things are going to get a lot better,' Yasmin said softly. 'Just you wait.'

After four more competitors had taken to the arena, it was finally Dante's turn.

'And now, ladies and gentlemen,' Captain Lundy said, beaming as he saw the name on his clipboard. 'I'd like you all to give a very big Loxwood welcome to our next competitor. All the way from the US of A . . . Mr Dante Fisher!'

When she heard his name, Juliet gasped. 'Oh my God,' she said, standing on tiptoes for a better view. 'Dante didn't tell me he was entering the competition.'

Beside her, Nicole gave a long, contented sigh. 'I feel all warm and fuzzy,' she said to no one in particular.

There were butterflies in Dante's stomach as he heard his name being announced. This was a golden opportunity to make a good impression on the locals. He couldn't afford to squander it. Stepping out of the contestants' tent, he made his way towards the arena with Jess walking beside him, her noble head held aloft. The pointer looked so cute in her waistcoat and feather headdress, he knew she'd give the other animals a run for their money, but for Dante the competition wasn't about winning. He'd already made up his mind that if he bagged first prize – £100 and a meal for two at Gaston's – he'd hand it to the runner-up. It seemed just the sort of magnanimous gesture Gus might have made.

Like all the contestants before them, pet and owner received an enthusiastic reception as they made their way towards the arena. Dante was grateful for the support and he was feeling surprisingly confident as he began his first turn round the ring. He was so busy concentrating on walking with a swaggering gait, just like a real cowboy, he didn't notice the applause was faltering. By the time he reached the first bend, it had died away altogether. However, it wasn't until people stopped talking that Dante realized something was seriously wrong. He stopped and looked about him in confusion. All he saw was row after row of stony faces. Nobody spoke, nobody moved. They all stared at him, their expressions a disquieting mix of shock and loathing. Dante spun round, his eyes scanning the crowd for a friendly face. There was none. Suddenly, he caught sight of his wife, standing with Yasmin and Nicole. Juliet's face was ashen and her eyes were blazing.

Suddenly, the silence was shattered by the sound of manic giggling. Yasmin turned towards the culprit. 'Jesus, Nicole, shut up, can't you?' she hissed.

'I'm sorry, I can't h-h-help it,' Nicole hiccupped, sucking in her cheeks in a desperate attempt to stop the next uncontrollable wave of laughter.

Yasmin was laughing now too. Other people were looking at them, glaring accusingly, as if they were gatecrashers at a funeral. Yasmin stuffed her fist in her mouth and looked across at Juliet. Juliet wasn't laughing. She was white as a sheet.

Nicole, meanwhile, had lost all her inhibitions. With tears rolling down her face, she pointed at Dante. 'It's the Lone Ranger,' she cried. 'And Tonto!'

'For God's sake, pull yourself together, woman,' Connor muttered.

Dante turned towards them. 'What is it?' he pleaded. 'What have I done?'

'Your outfits,' Connor barked. 'They're the same ones Gus and Jess wore at the last Best Dressed Pet competition.'

When he heard this, Dante's face crumpled in horror. Tearing the mask off his face, he turned and ran blindly across the lawn. By the time he arrived back at the house, his chest was heaving and the back of his neck was damp with sweat. After the emotion of the arena, the coolness and tranquillity of the entrance hall came as a welcome relief. He stood in the centre of the room, hands on his head, breathing in the smell of flowers and wax polish. All at once, he had a sense that he was being watched. He looked up and saw Nathan standing halfway up the staircase. The look on his face was leering, triumphant.

'Is everything all right?' the manager enquired calmly.

'No, it damn well isn't,' Dante said. Then he ran up the stairs, pushing past Nathan roughly, desperate to be alone.

13

The fête was long over by the time Dante woke up. At first he didn't know where he was. Then he realized he was lying on the lumpy mattress in the attic bedroom he'd stumbled across two days earlier. He sat up with a start, wondering what time it was. He hadn't meant to fall asleep; he just wanted to get away from the omnipresent Nathan and the sea of staring faces at the Best Dressed Pet competition. The last thing he remembered was lying down on the bed and gazing at the opposite wall where a small painting hung. It showed a primitive hunting scene – an impaled deer, eyes wide with fright as blood spilled from its pierced flank. A group of huntsmen stood nearby, their faces triumphant as they watched the wounded animal's life ebb away. He must have drifted off as he studied that brutal scene, and now here he was, still alone, goodness knows how many hours later.

The small room felt like a sauna. Rubbing his eyes, Dante went to the window and flung it open. It was still light outside and down below he could see dozens of workmen scurrying about the lawn as they dismantled the various stalls and attractions, before piling the component parts onto a series of flatbed trucks. He watched them for a few moments, marvelling at their efficiency, before staggering to the avocado sink in the corner of the room. Gripping the sides of the basin, he stared at his reflection in the tarnished mirror that hung above it. A shank of hair was glued to his forehead and his right cheek bore the imprint of the pillowcase's scalloped edge. He splashed his face with cold water and used his wet hands to push back his hair. Then, he decided, it was time to confront Juliet.

He found her in the conservatory. She was standing by the French windows, watching the tea tent coming down, arms wrapped across her chest as if she were cold. Although she must have heard his footsteps on the tiled floor, she didn't turn round. Thrown by her lack of response, Dante stopped and rested his hand on a button-backed easy chair. 'Juliet?' he said tentatively.

She didn't answer straight away, and when she did speak her voice sounded tired and flat. 'I was wondering where you'd got to.'

'I fell asleep in one of the attic rooms,' he said. 'Why didn't you come and find me?'

'I was going to,' she replied. 'Just as soon as I'd got rid of these workmen.'

Dante took a step towards her. 'I'm so sorry about the competition. All I wanted to do was surprise you.'

Juliet glanced over her shoulder. 'You certainly did that.' She turned back to the garden. 'I just wish you hadn't run away.'

'So what happened after I left?'

'Everyone was pretty stunned. They all seemed to be waiting for me to provide some sort of explanation, but of course I didn't have one. I just stood there, rooted to the spot like a rabbit caught in headlights, until Captain Lundy, God bless him, came dashing back into the ring and introduced the next contestant as if nothing had happened.'

'Who won?'

'The goat. It was a unanimous decision by the judges.'

Dante hung his head. 'I had no idea Gus had ever entered the competition, let alone what outfit he wore.'

'Of course you didn't know – how could you? It was just a horrible coincidence.' Juliet put her hand up to the window frame. 'Although I expect some mean-spirited souls will think you did it deliberately.'

Dante groaned. 'How could anyone think I'd pull a sick stunt like that on purpose?'

'I don't know . . . to assert your position perhaps. What better way to show you're every bit as good as Gus than by stepping into his shoes, quite literally?' Juliet turned to face him. 'Of course, that's not *my* opinion, but I've lived in Loxwood my whole life; I know how people talk.'

'But that's crazy,' Dante said, feeling the anger welling up inside him. 'I don't want to be Gus. Why would I? I didn't even know the guy.' He began pacing up and down the room. 'In any case, how could I ever match up to a guy as goddamn perfect as him?'

Juliet turned round. Her face was pale and stoical. 'You mustn't feel insecure, darling,' she said.

'It's hard not to when everyone keeps telling me how awesome Gus was,' Dante retorted. 'It seems like he never put a foot wrong.'

'Gus was no saint, I can assure you of that,' Juliet said emphatically. 'But he was a charismatic man – people were drawn to him. He made them feel good about themselves. Everyone was devastated when he passed away. It's only natural that they remember the good things, rather than the not-so-good. Don't try to compete with him. He's dead, Dante, dead and buried.'

Dante shook his head. 'It doesn't matter what I do, folks round here are never going to accept me. Everybody was staring at me like I'd murdered someone.'

'Don't be silly. They were just in shock, that's all.' She tilted her head to one side. 'Where did you find those costumes anyway?'

'In the attic. Nathan sent me up there.'

Juliet looked at him in surprise. 'Really?'

'Yeah, in fact he was the one who suggested I enter the competition in the first place.' Dante frowned. 'You know, the more I think about it, the more I'm beginning to think he set me up.'

'What are you talking about?'

Dante stopped pacing and put his hands on his hips. 'C'mon, Juliet, it's a bit of a coincidence, don't you think? First, he encourages me to enter the competition, then he sends me up to the attic, having strategically placed the Lone Ranger and Tonto costumes where I couldn't help but find them. Hell, he even got out some old film posters – Westerns, every last one of 'em – just to ram the message home.'

Juliet pressed her fingertips into her eye sockets as if she were trying to think. 'What possible motive could Nathan have for doing something like that?'

'To make me look like a jerk,' Dante said. 'I get the feeling Nathan doesn't much like having me around.'

'Now you're being ridiculous. I know you're upset, but –'

'Too right I'm upset,' Dante snapped. 'Have you got any

idea how difficult it's been for me these past few weeks? Coming to a strange country, having to say goodbye to my family and friends – and then, just when I think I'm starting to adjust, I'm ritually humiliated in front of the whole town.'

Juliet sighed. 'I know it's hard for you, darling, but I'm doing my best to help you settle in.'

'Are you?' Dante said. 'Only from where I'm standing it looks as if all you care about is this damn house.' He gave a sour laugh. 'But then again that's hardly surprising when everywhere you turn there's a reminder of the late, great Gus.'

Suddenly, there was a discreet cough from the garden. Juliet wheeled round. Eleanor Ingram was hovering by the French windows, looking curiously overdressed in a Chanel two-piece and a pillbox hat trimmed with marabou.

Juliet forced herself to smile. 'Eleanor, what a lovely surprise.'

'I hope I haven't called at an inconvenient moment,' Eleanor said as she stepped into the conservatory. 'I was just passing on my way back from the wedding.'

'Ah yes,' Juliet said, belatedly remembering that Eleanor had been attending the nuptials of her best friend's daughter. 'How was it?'

'Perfectly delightful.' Eleanor fingered the rope of pearls at her neck absent-mindedly. 'The reception was at Goodhurst House. I'm afraid I got rather emotional – and it wasn't because of the speeches.'

Juliet's smile faltered. Goodhurst House was where she and Gus had had their own wedding reception.

'How was the fête?' Eleanor asked.

'It was wonderful,' Juliet replied quickly. 'Gus would've been very proud.'

Eleanor's raptor-like gaze settled on Dante. 'The summer fête was very dear to my son's heart,' she informed him. 'It pained me greatly to miss it.'

Unsure of the correct response, Dante gave a small, sympathetic smile. In return, Eleanor issued a weary look, like a judge scoring a lacklustre performance: one out of five for effort.

'Isn't Piers with you?' Juliet asked.

'No, he had one of his migraines this morning, so he stayed at home.' Eleanor gave a theatrical swallow. 'I'm dreadfully thirsty, dear. A cup of tea wouldn't go amiss. Earl Grey, if you've got it.'

'Of course,' Juliet said. She flashed a quick look at Dante. 'I won't be long.'

'And don't forget the lemon,' Eleanor called out after her.

Now that he was alone with Eleanor, a spider of anxiety crawled up the back of Dante's neck. 'Please . . . take a seat,' he said, jangling the coins in his trouser pocket.

'How kind of you,' she replied. 'But, really, I don't need an invitation to sit down in my own son's home.'

Dante bristled. 'I guess not.'

She walked over to him, filling the air with her asphyxiating perfume. 'Did *you* enjoy the fête?' she said.

'Uh, yeah, it was nice, thanks.'

She stared at him, her eyes the cold blue of Venetian glass. 'Really?' she said. 'Only my good friend Lydia Ormerod called me not half an hour ago. According to her, you were involved in a rather ugly scene at the Best Dressed Pet competition.'

Dante knew in that moment that Eleanor's request for a cup of tea had simply been a ruse to get Juliet out of the way. 'The outfits were an accident,' he said, meeting her gaze head-on.

'How dare you,' she hissed as if she hadn't heard him. 'How dare you desecrate my son's memory?'

'I told you, it was an accident,' Dante repeated. 'Juliet knows that.'

Eleanor's lip curled. 'You might have pulled the wool over Juliet's eyes, young man, but unfortunately for you I'm not quite so gullible. I don't know what game you're playing, but you listen to me and you listen hard. I loved my son and I feel his loss every minute of every day – and I have no doubt Juliet feels the same.' She spoke in a strange, staccato manner, enunciating every syllable, as though she were talking to a slightly dense child. 'You can try as hard as you like, but you'll never take Gus's place, never. He was a bigger man than you will ever be.'

Dante felt his blood come to a rising boil. 'Now hang on –' he began.

Eleanor raised a hand to silence him. 'I have no idea why Juliet married you – I can only assume she suffered some momentary, catastrophic lapse of judgement – but I don't suppose it really matters. Judging by what I just heard, you won't be around for much longer.' The next moment, Eleanor's face was wreathed in smiles. 'Cakes too . . . you're spoiling me!' she cried, clapping her hands together.

Dante turned round. Juliet was walking towards them bearing tea and some slightly squishy chocolate éclairs, left over from the tea tent. He began backing away towards the door. If he didn't get out of there, he was liable to do something he might regret. 'If you don't mind, I'll leave you two ladies to it,' he said.

Juliet looked disappointed. 'Aren't you going to at least stay for a cup of tea?'

'Oh, let him go,' Eleanor said, picking up a teacup. 'I'm sure he's got better things to do than listen to our chitter-chatter.'

As Dante escaped down the corridor, head bowed and cheeks blazing, he almost cannoned into a young couple walking in the opposite direction. They'd checked in a couple of days earlier and were celebrating their first wedding anniversary. The man smiled at him. 'We're heading out to dinner,' he said. 'Do you happen to know if Gaston's is open yet?'

'No idea, sorry,' Dante said. As he continued towards the entrance hall, he thought of Juliet and how horrified she would've been by his unhelpful response. Sighing, he stopped and turned over his shoulder. 'Hey, why don't I call the restaurant and find out?' he said. 'And if they're not open, I'll find you some place that is.'

The woman smiled shyly. 'If you're sure it's no trouble . . .'

'No trouble at all,' Dante said. 'If you'd like to follow me to reception . . .'

A few minutes later, a reservation at Gaston's secured, the couple was walking through the front door and Dante was finally alone. In the absence of anything better to do, he sank into the high-backed chair behind the reception desk and covered his eyes with his hands. A few moments later, Jess came padding down the corridor. It was the first time Dante had seen her since fleeing the Best Dressed Pet competition.

'Hello, girl,' he said, reaching down to rub her back. He smiled as she sprawled at his feet, pressing her snout against his ankles. 'At least I've got one buddy in England.' As he spoke, Dante's thoughts turned to home. He'd left behind so much: his job, his friends, his freedom. It hadn't seemed like such a big sacrifice at the time – but now he wasn't so sure. He looked at the grandfather clock at the foot of the stairs: seven thirty British time, twelve thirty in Montana. He hadn't spoken to his family in weeks. On impulse, he picked up the phone and punched out a number. A few seconds later, tears sprang to his eyes as his mother's voice came on the line.

'Hi, Mom, it's me,' he said, his voice nearly cracking as he spoke the words.

'Dante!' she cried in delight. 'How are you, hon?'

'I'm fine, Mom,' he replied. 'Just fine.'

'You don't sound fine,' she said. 'Has something happened?'

Dante hadn't meant to dump all his shit on her, but he found that once he started he couldn't stop. He told her everything that had happened since his arrival in England: his shock at Ashwicke's size and grandeur, his continuing loneliness, his fear that Juliet regarded him as a poor substitute for Gus and, finally, the humiliating turn of events at the fête. Every now and then his mother would offer a sympathetic comment, but mostly she just listened.

'Oh, honey,' she said when he was through. 'I wish I was there now so I could give you a big hug.'

Dante produced a buckled smile. 'Me too.'

'It's only natural you're finding things tough,' she said. 'But you hang on in there, okay? The Fishers aren't quitters; I know you and Juliet can make this work.'

'I hope so, Mom,' he said. 'I really hope so.'

By the time Dante put the phone down he felt a lot better. His mom was right: he wasn't a quitter. More importantly, he loved Juliet with a passion he wouldn't have believed possible. She'd have to do something really awful to make him leave her. He glanced down at Jess. Although she was asleep, her tail was twitching and her paws were making scrabbling motions as if she were chasing rabbits. Dante would have left her to her dream, but then the thought struck him that, rather than chasing something, perhaps she herself was being chased, and that the whimpers she was making were the sounds of fear rather than delight, so he sank down beside her and stroked her head until she was soothed.

14

Juliet held on to the pelmet with one hand and reached the other towards Dante. 'Pass me a couple more curtain hooks, would you, darling?'

'I wish you'd come down from there and let me do that,' Dante said as he fumbled in a cellophane bag.

Juliet looked down at him from her precarious position on the windowsill and found herself thinking how absurdly handsome he was – a curious mixture of delicacy and strength, with his long eyelashes and sinewy skier's physique. 'You're so protective,' she said.

Dante smiled. 'That's my job.'

It was a week since Dante's humiliating experience at the Best Dressed Pet competition. Although he'd been subdued for a few days afterwards, Juliet was surprised to see how quickly he'd bounced back. She'd found their row in the conservatory quite upsetting and since then she'd been making a concerted effort to make him feel more at home – discreetly donating some of Gus's belongings to charity, taking time out from the hotel to make sure she and Dante always ate lunch together, even passing on the contact details of a friend of a friend who managed a bar in town and might have some work going. Hopefully now they could shake off the ghosts of the past and get on with their lives together.

'How much did those curtains cost?' Dante asked, as he handed her the hooks.

'Only a few pounds. I got them from a charity shop on the high street.' Juliet smoothed a hand over the thick, chintzy fabric. 'I know they're a bit unfashionable, but new ones would've cost a fortune.'

'They look just fine,' Dante said. 'And with any luck they'll do what they're supposed to.'

The previous day, the room's occupant, a ruddy-faced specimen with dandruffy shoulders, had complained about the sunlight coming through the – admittedly rather threadbare – curtains first thing in the morning. Eager to please, Juliet had wasted no time replacing them.

'And now that they're up,' Dante continued, 'will you please get down from that windowsill before you break your neck?'

'Just a sec.' Juliet was staring out of the window. Something – or rather, *someone* – in the distance had caught her eye. 'You know, I'm sure that's Nicole,' she said.

Dante peered through the glass. 'Where?'

'Over there, at the end of the drive.'

'Were you expecting her?'

Juliet shook her head. She tracked Nicole's progress down the drive, smiling as her friend suddenly dived behind a row of conifers. 'Ah, so it isn't me she's come to see. It's Bear.'

'That journo guy in the caravan?' Dante said. 'Are they friends?'

'Sort of. Nic's been helping Bear with an article he's writing. She won't admit it, but she's developed a bit of a soft spot for him.'

'I don't reckon Connor's going to be too happy about that.'

Turning away from the window, Juliet lowered herself into Dante's arms. 'Frankly, he's only got himself to blame.'

Nicole was impressed when she saw Bear's caravan. She'd been expecting a bog-standard model – the sort of dull white box she and her parents had toured Scotland with, the summer before their divorce. Instead, she found herself gazing at a vintage aluminium Airstream, glittering like a bullet in the afternoon sunshine. She should've known better, she chided herself: Bear was an extraordinary man and it was only natural that he should have an extraordinary home.

Nicole hadn't seen him since the fête and now, as she walked up to the Airstream, she tried to ignore the butterflies beating against her ribcage. She told herself she was simply being neighbourly, dropping by with homemade cake – and, if Bear wasn't home, no big deal. She would simply leave the cake on his doorstep with a note. She smoothed her hair with a hand and rapped on the door of the caravan. A few moments later, the top half of the door swung open and Bear appeared. He was wearing a pair of jeans and nothing else. Nicole found herself admiring his torso, which was deeply tanned with well-defined pectorals.

'Nicole!' Bear exclaimed. 'This is a nice surprise.' He clapped a hand to his naked chest. 'Sorry about my state of undress; I wasn't expecting company.'

'I haven't called at a bad time, have I?' Nicole asked. 'I can always come back later.'

'Don't be silly,' Bear said, unbolting the door's bottom

section. 'I was just doing some writing, but it can wait. Come on in.'

If the outside of Bear's home had taken Nicole by surprise, then the inside was even more of a revelation. There was a compact kitchen area, with a retro fridge in pastel blue and a row of mismatching enamelware hanging from butcher's hooks. Beyond it lay a comfortable living space, boasting a built-in shelf unit crammed with books, two red leather banquettes and a tubular steel table that wouldn't have looked out of place in a fifties' diner.

Nicole looked around her in amazement. Everywhere she turned, another stylish detail caught her eye: a Mark Rothko print, a squat piece of Troika, an old Bakelite radio.

'This place is stunning,' she said. 'When you said you lived in a caravan, I didn't imagine anything like this.'

'She's not bad for a fifty-year-old, is she?' Bear said. 'I refurbished her myself – plumbing, electrics, the works.' He opened a door to reveal a fully tiled wet room. 'I built this too.'

'I had no idea you were so talented,' said Nicole, noting the bottle of cologne on the shelf under the mirror, and the stack of neatly folded towels.

'Oh, it wasn't so difficult; it just took a bit of time and patience.' Bear closed the bathroom door and pointed to one of the banquettes. 'Why don't you take a seat and I'll make us some tea?' He went to a chest of drawers and pulled out a faded blue T-shirt. 'But first let me put some clothes on.'

The words *Must you?* threatened to erupt from Nicole's lips. 'I won't stay long,' she said, as she produced a Tupperware box from the carrier bag she was holding and placed it on the table. 'I didn't come round for anything in particular. I just wanted to drop this off.'

'What is it?' asked Bear, as he pulled the T-shirt over his head.

'Banana cake – I made it myself.'

Bear looked disproportionately pleased. 'How very kind,' he said, scooping up the Tupperware in one of his giant hands. 'We can have some with our tea.'

'Think of it as an apology,' Nicole added.

'Whatever for?'

'My behaviour at the fête.'

A hint of a smile played about Bear's lips as he lit the gas under the kettle. 'What was wrong with your behaviour?'

Nicole sighed. 'It's okay, you don't have to be polite. I know I made a complete tit of myself.'

'I wouldn't go that far,' Bear said magnanimously. 'In any case, you had sunstroke, didn't you?'

'Erm, no, actually. I was stoned.'

Bear gave a throaty chuckle. 'I didn't know you indulged.'

'I don't. Somebody served me a hash brownie in the tea tent.'

Bear's eyebrows shot up. 'Blimey, has the Women's Institute got a secret sideline?'

'It wasn't the WI; it was Yasmin,' Nicole replied. 'I think she wanted to liven things up a bit.'

'And did it have the desired effect?'

'Let's just say we were all in pretty high spirits by the time we left the fête.' Nicole gave a rueful smile. 'My husband wasn't very impressed, though.'

'Ah yes . . . Connor, isn't it?'

'That's right. As a doctor, he takes a dim view of recreational drug taking.' Nicole pursed her lips. 'In fact, he seems to take a dim view of quite a lot of things these days.'

Bear opened the Tupperware box and lifted out the banana cake. 'This looks amazing,' he said, as he cut two thick slices. 'Is Connor looking after Tilly, then?'

'Yeah, he's taken her into town to buy some new clothes. I did offer to go with them, but Connor said he wanted to go on his own.' Nicole smiled. 'Actually, I was quite pleased. I sometimes worry he's not bonding with Tilly as well as he should be.'

Bear opened a cream enamel caddy and dropped teabags into two striped mugs. 'Why do you think that is?'

Nicole shrugged. 'Who knows? I think he finds it all rather wearing . . . You know, the shit and the vomit, the teething, the colic, the night-time feeds.' She made a face. 'Not that Connor ever bothers getting up in the night. He leaves that to muggins here. I'm averaging five hours' sleep a night at the moment.'

'You must be exhausted.'

Nicole sighed. 'It's amazing how you adapt.'

Bear placed the tea and cake on the table and sat down beside Nicole. 'I expect Connor's got quite a lot on his plate, hasn't he, what with work and everything?'

'Yes,' Nicole said, picking up her tea. 'Although he does seem to be an awful lot busier lately. We're like ships that pass in the night these days.'

'That must be tough.'

'It is – especially since Connor doesn't seem to be particularly interested in family life.' Nicole stared into her mug. 'He's changed a lot since we got married. I wish things could be like they used to be between us.' Then, realizing she was in imminent danger of over-sharing, she changed the subject abruptly. 'So how's the article going? I can't wait to read it.'

'Really well, thanks,' Bear replied. 'The developer's still refusing to go on record, but I interviewed the council's Planning Services Director the other day. She reckons the badger sett isn't active any more.'

'But that's ridiculous,' Nicole said indignantly. 'We saw the evidence with our own eyes.'

'I know we did. But, unfortunately, I couldn't tell her that because then I'd be admitting to trespassing. However, I did say I'd been in discussions with the Badger Protection League about the planning application and that they were very keen to inspect the site themselves. That seemed to put the wind up her.'

'Good,' Nicole said. 'I'm assuming you didn't tell her about the other wildlife we saw . . . you know, the *furverts*.'

Bear laughed. 'Is that what they're called?'

Nicole nodded. 'According to Yasmin, half of Loxwood is shagging in the woods.'

'Ah well, whatever turns them on.' Bear broke off a piece of cake and popped it in his mouth. 'Mmm . . . this is delicious. How did you know banana cake was my favourite?'

Nicole felt a warm glow of pleasure. 'It was a lucky guess.'

The rest of the afternoon passed by in a flash and, before Nicole knew it, it was six o'clock. Bear looked genuinely disappointed when she said she had to go.

'You're welcome to stay for dinner,' he said. 'I've got a casserole in the pressure cooker. There's plenty for two.'

'Oh no, I can't, I'm sorry,' Nicole said. 'Connor's expecting me back.'

'God, yes, of course,' Bear said. 'I was just being selfish. It can get a bit lonely on my own in the caravan sometimes.'

For a moment he looked so forlorn that Nicole wanted to reach out and hug him. 'Well, any time you want to meet for a coffee . . .' she said. 'I'm pretty much free on weekdays – that's if you don't mind Tilly tagging along.'

'Of course not. I love kids,' Bear said, getting up to see her out.

At the door, Nicole stopped on impulse and kissed him lightly on the cheek. He smelled pleasingly of cologne and freshly mown grass. 'Enjoy the rest of your evening,' she said, scarcely able to believe her own daring.

'You too,' he replied. 'I'll be in touch soon.'

Nicole was smiling to herself the whole way home. She knew she was attracted to Bear, but it was only a harmless crush, she told herself; it didn't mean anything. Married people had crushes all the time – and this wasn't the first one she'd had either. There'd been that gorgeous bloke who sold organic goats' cheese at the farmers' market, the one with the floppy blond fringe and the dazzling smile. She'd bought cheese from him for weeks, practically lived on the stuff, and one night she'd even dreamed about him. About his strong hands. Had woken up in a hot sweat imagining them slowly undressing her, cupping her bare breasts . . . *Stop it, Nicole*, she told herself firmly. *Stop it right now!*

While Nicole was getting to know Bear, Connor was making a home visit. The home in question was a stunning oak-beamed barn conversion, complete with trout lake, guest annexe and two acres of secluded grounds. But instead of sitting beside a bed, tending the barn conversion's poorly occupant, the GP found himself at the top of a ladder. Connor had never been very good with heights and now, as he looked down at the unforgiving flagstones below, he felt a distinct wave of nausea. Turning back to the house, he peered through the half-open first-floor window. Frustratingly, there was no sign of life on the other side. Connor was confused. He'd followed Zoe's written instructions, hand-delivered to the surgery the day before, to the letter. Connor's eyes flitted to the Audi, where he'd left Tilly asleep in her car seat, the passenger window slightly open, so he'd hear her if she woke up. He'd driven for miles before she finally nodded off and with any luck she'd stay that way for the rest of the afternoon. He would rather not have brought her at all but, with the surgery closed on a Saturday, the spurious shopping trip was the only way he could get out of the house without arousing Nicole's suspicions.

Turning back to the window, Connor began rubbing his chamois half-heartedly against the glass – and then, quite suddenly, the genie of the lamp appeared. And what a foxy genie she was.

Zoe gave no sign that she'd seen Connor, didn't even glance in his direction. She was wrapped in a peach towel and her damp hair was piled seductively on top of her head. She stood in the doorway for a few moments, posing languidly against the doorframe, showing off her beautiful body. A few seconds later she padded across the creamy carpet and sat down on the bed, drawing one foot up onto the mattress so that the towel rode up, exposing her toned thighs and the inviting cleft between them. Connor watched with mounting excitement as she picked up a bottle that was lying on the bed and unscrewed the lid. She poured a generous amount of body lotion onto her palms and began massaging her left calf, throwing back her head as if she were being propelled towards orgasm by some invisible hand. After several minutes of this, she got up and walked across the room. When she reached the reproduction Louis Quatorze chiffonier, she reached up, as if she intended to pull open the top drawer. As she did, she took a deep breath, causing her chest to expand and the towel to loosen. As it fell to the ground, Zoe turned to face the window, hands on her cheeks, mouth pantomiming a wide O. This was the sign Connor had been waiting for. Without hesitation, he grabbed the edge of the window and pulled it towards him, creating an aperture wide enough for him to climb through. 'You dirty bitch,' he said, as he hooked one leg over the windowsill. 'You're going to get it now.'

15

Nicole was surprised when she arrived home to find the house empty. She tried to remember if Connor had taken a bottle with him. Tilly would be cranky if she missed her afternoon feed. Feeling a little anxious, she picked up the phone and called his mobile. When Connor answered, he sounded irritated and slightly breathless. 'Don't panic; we're on our way home now,' he told her. 'What's for dinner by the way? I'm starving.'

'I didn't have time to go to the supermarket,' Nicole replied. 'I thought we could get a takeaway.'

Connor sighed. 'What have you been doing all day?'

'Visiting a friend,' Nicole said vaguely. 'What do you fancy – Chinese or Indian? I'll order it now.'

Connor thought for a moment. 'Uh, Chinese. I'll have a sweet and sour pork with special fried rice.'

'Okay.'

'Oh, and, Nicole, I'd give the prawn crackers a miss this time if I were you. Think of the old waistline, eh?' The next moment the phone went dead.

With the jibe still ringing in her ears, Nicole opened the drawer where the takeaway menus were kept. She wished Connor would stop going on about her weight. She was tempted to abandon her romantic plans for the evening, but that would be defeatist. In any case, one of them had to make an effort or the thin threads that held their marriage together would stretch to breaking point. And so, having placed her order at the Chinese, she went upstairs to shower and change into her new purchases.

Half an hour later, as she was in the kitchen, pouring gin into two glasses, she heard the sound of the front door slamming. 'I'm in the kitchen,' she called out.

As Connor entered, Nicole mustered her best welcoming smile. 'Hi, darling,' she said as he placed Tilly, still strapped in her car seat, on the kitchen table. 'How did it go?'

'Not so well. Tilly was really playing up.' He nodded at the gin bottle. 'Make mine a large one, will you?'

Nicole looked at Tilly, who was fast asleep. 'She seems okay now.'

'You should've seen her an hour ago. She wouldn't stop crying. I thought my eardrums were going to burst.'

'Did you try giving her a bottle?'

'Yeah, but she didn't want it.'

Nicole touched Tilly's cheek to see if she was feverish. 'Do you think she's sick?'

'Of course not. She was just being her usual cranky self.'

'She's teething,' Nicole said defensively. 'What do you expect?'

'Hmm,' Connor muttered, as if he wasn't convinced. He went to the fridge for tonic and poured some into his own glass, but not Nicole's. 'Have we got any lemon?'

'No, sorry. I'll go to the supermarket tomorrow.'

Clucking in irritation, Connor picked up his glass and started walking towards the door.

'Aren't you going to show me?' Nicole asked.

Connor stopped. 'What?'

'Tilly's new clothes.'

Connor replied over his shoulder. 'She hasn't got any new clothes. You don't think I was going to carry a screaming brat round the shops, do you?'

At that moment, Nicole could have quite happily picked up the gigantic, hand-thrown fruit bowl and thrown it at Connor's head. Instead, she took in a big lungful of air and held it there for several seconds while she tried to summon up a shred of sympathy for her husband. 'So where have you been?' she asked. 'Please tell me you didn't dump her on my mother.'

'No,' he said, his voice heavy with a weary exasperation. 'We've been driving.'

'What – for two hours?'

'Yes, it was the only way I could get her off. When she finally went to sleep, I parked up at the golf club.'

Nicole frowned. 'You didn't leave her alone in the car, did you?'

'Of course not,' Connor snapped. 'What do you take me for?'

'Sorry,' Nicole mumbled.

'My head was throbbing so I closed my eyes. The next thing I knew, I was waking up an hour and a half later. That's why we're back so late.'

'I see,' Nicole said tautly.

Connor took a slug of gin and tonic. 'Is the food here yet?'

'Yes, it's keeping warm in the oven. I'll just put Tilly in her cot and then I'll serve up.'

Connor grunted something in reply and disappeared in the direction of the sitting room.

As soon as he was gone, Nicole lifted up a tea towel on the worktop to reveal a half-eaten bag of prawn crackers.

She tore the bag open and started cramming them into her mouth, one after another, until they were all gone.

They ate their takeaway in front of the TV. Nicole did her best to engage Connor in conversation, but he seemed engrossed in the quiz show they were watching, shouting out answers to the questions and whooping noisily whenever he got them right. When they'd finished eating, Nicole gathered up the plates and carried them through to the kitchen. As she stacked the dishwasher, she felt drained of energy, but she couldn't go to bed, not yet. So instead she dried her hands on a tea towel, knocked back a second, much stronger, gin and tonic, and returned to the sitting room.

Connor was now sprawled the full length of the sofa. The quiz show had ended and he was watching an American drama series he'd been following for weeks. Without a word, Nicole picked up the remote control and turned down the volume.

'Hey, what are you doing? I was watching that,' Connor said crossly.

'I thought we could make our own entertainment,' Nicole replied. She stood over Connor and pulled the tie on her wraparound dress. It fell apart to reveal a black lace G-string and matching balconette bra, which only just contained her swollen, post-pregnancy breasts. 'I treated myself to some new underwear,' she said, striking what she hoped was a seductive pose. 'What do you think?'

'Very nice,' Connor said, twisting his head for a better view of the TV screen. 'Now can I watch my programme?'

'No, you bloody can't.' Shrugging off her dress, Nicole

straddled him in one swift move. 'It's been ages since we made love,' she said, running her hands over his pectorals.

'That's what happens when you have a baby,' Connor said. 'Sex goes out the window.'

'But it doesn't have to be that way,' Nicole said, as she unbuttoned his shirt and bent over him, nuzzling her face against his chest hair.

'What if Tilly wakes up?' Connor said.

'She won't.' Nicole turned her attention to his nipples. 'And don't try and tell me you're feeling tired when you had a nice long nap this afternoon.'

She smiled as Connor's hand reached for her left breast. They started kissing, and then his hand crept downwards.

'Mmm, that's nice,' she said as he pulled her G-string to one side and began stroking her with a forefinger. Foreplay was something of a novelty for Nicole. Connor didn't usually put much effort into the task. She got the impression that, for him, her body was like a village that over time had grown until it became a bustling town, criss-crossed with new roads and multi-storey developments, some of them rather unsightly. It had changed beyond all recognition, but it was where he lived so he'd had to make the best of it.

After only a couple of minutes, her breaths started coming quicker. 'I want you inside me,' she said, reaching for his crotch. To her surprise, Connor wasn't erect. Didn't even have a semi. Frowning, she rolled off him and took up a kneeling position on the floor beside the sofa.

'What are you doing?' Connor asked.

She smiled and unzipped his flies. The next moment, his flaccid penis was in her mouth.

Connor flinched as she began teasing the tip of his glans with her tongue. He'd been having frenetic sex with Zoe all afternoon. He didn't think his cock could take much more punishment. 'Sorry, Nic,' he said, twisting his hips so he fell out of her mouth. 'I'm just not in the mood.'

Nicole sat back on her haunches and glared at him. 'That's a shame.' She picked up her dress and put it on. She wished she hadn't bothered buying the underwear now; it had cost a fortune. 'I'd better go and check on Tilly,' she said.

'Good idea,' Connor said, reaching for the remote. 'Get me another G and T before you go up, will you?'

Nicole rose to her feet. 'Get it yourself.'

On the other side of Loxwood, the offices of the *Sunday Post* lay in darkness. It was the Chief Sub's retirement do and all the staff had decamped to their local to give him one of the paper's traditional alcoholic send-offs. All, that is, except Yasmin. The showbiz editor was still at her desk putting the finishing touches to her interview with a former game-show host and recovering coke addict who was promoting his autobiography. Her subject had been edgy and uncooperative and – when he'd visited the bathroom for the second time in the space of an hour – she found herself wondering if he really had kicked the drugs. Back in the office, she'd struggled to salvage enough decent quotes from her transcript to make up the fifteen hundred words the editor was expecting in the morning – but finally, after a lot of writing and rewriting, she'd managed to pull something decent together.

By eleven p.m., Yasmin was exhausted. The introductory

paragraph still needed a few tweaks, but she was as good as there. All she needed was one last hit of caffeine to help her on her way. Executing a giant yawn, she stood up and wandered over to the vending machine in the hallway. After selecting a watery cup of cappuccino, she carried it to the window, which overlooked the empty car park. Sighing, Yasmin shut her eyes and massaged her lids with a fingertip, trying to relieve the scratchy veil of fatigue. When she opened them again, the car park was no longer deserted. A lone figure dressed in low-slung jeans and a leather jacket was walking towards the building. As he passed under a street lamp, she realized it was Rob.

By the time the sports editor walked into the office, Yasmin was back at her desk.

'You're working late,' he said gruffly as he walked past her.

'I'm just finishing off this piece for the supplement,' Yasmin replied. She watched as her colleague switched on his desk lamp and began foraging in his pen tidy.

'Forgotten something, have you?' she asked.

The sports editor held up a set of house keys. 'Just these,' he said. 'I'm not going to get very far without them.'

Yasmin noticed his voice was slightly slurred; he'd obviously had a few. 'Good evening was it?'

'Yeah, you missed out big-time.' Rob shoved the keys in his jeans pocket and clicked off the desk lamp. 'You know, you really should make more of an effort to be sociable,' he remarked. 'Tony's been with the paper for the best part of twenty years. Didn't you want to say goodbye to him?'

Yasmin's eyes didn't leave her computer screen. 'I've already told you – I've got a deadline.'

Rob snorted. 'Hoping to earn more brownie points with the editor, were you?' When she didn't reply, he went over to her desk and began reading her copy over her shoulder.

'Your opening paragraph's a bit clunky,' he said. 'If I were you, I'd start by describing what the guy looked like. That's the sort of thing female readers are interested in.'

Yasmin glared at him. 'Piss off, Rob. If I need your help, I'll ask for it.'

'Suit yourself,' he said, shuffling off towards the door. She thought he'd gone, but a few moments later he was back with a black coffee in his hand. He perched on the corner of the desk next to hers and began to slurp it noisily. Trying her best to ignore him, Yasmin highlighted a chunk of text and moved it to the next paragraph.

'Doesn't it bother you?' Rob said conversationally.

'Doesn't *what* bother me?' she replied through gritted teeth.

'The fact you're so unpopular.'

Yasmin spun round in her chair. 'I know you think I'm a hard-faced bitch, but I do have feelings, you know.'

He held her gaze. 'Do you? You're so cold I was beginning to think you were half woman, half android.'

Yasmin's eyes narrowed. 'Why don't you like me, Rob?'

'Because you try too hard.'

'And what's wrong with being ambitious?'

'Nothing,' he replied evenly. 'But there's a fine line between ambition and ruthlessness.'

'Meaning?'

'Meaning, I think you'll do whatever it takes to get what you want – even if it means shitting on other people along the way.'

Yasmin's nostrils flared. A moment ago she'd been mildly irritated; now her overriding emotion was fury. 'You're only saying that because I'm a woman,' she snapped, rising to her feet. 'It's okay for a bloke to be aggressive at work, but if a woman shows she's got a pair of balls, chances are there's some arrogant, chauvinist tosspot like you waiting to put her in her place.'

Rob gave a rancid smile. 'You've hit the nail on the head there, darlin'. You've got bigger balls than King Kong; no wonder you're single.'

Tears scuttled up like a ball in Yasmin's throat. She always cried easily when she was tired. 'You bastard,' she said. 'You fucking bastard.'

'Careful,' Rob said, hearing the break in her voice. 'You don't want all that beautifully applied eye make-up to run.'

Almost before she knew what she was doing, Yasmin's hand was making contact with Rob's cheek. The sound of the slap echoed round the empty office, taking her by surprise almost as much as Rob.

'You vicious little cow,' he said, grabbing her arm and jerking her towards him. 'That's assault. I could get you sacked for that.'

'Just you try,' Yasmin hissed. 'Then you'll find out just how big my balls are.'

Suddenly Rob's face was bearing down on hers. For one sickening moment Yasmin thought he was going to spit in her face, but then his mouth unexpectedly brushed against hers. His lips were soft . . . very soft.

'What are you –?' she managed to say. The next moment, Rob's tongue was in her mouth. To her surprise, Yasmin found herself responding.

For several minutes, they kissed hungrily, frantically, hands clawing at each other's bodies. Yasmin's senses were flooded. She could smell the faint musk of his sweat, taste the beer on his breath, feel the warmth of his skin. She knew she was making a big mistake, and yet some devilish little voice in her head was telling her not to stop.

Reluctantly, she pulled her mouth away from his. He was staring at her with a crazed look in his eyes as if he couldn't quite believe what they were doing either.

'Why don't we go to the third-floor boardroom?' she said. 'We'll be more comfortable in there.' A moment of doubt flickered across his face and then he took her hand and led her towards the lifts.

16

Dante was drenched in sweat by the time he arrived home. Keen to maintain the fitness levels he'd developed through years of daily skiing, he'd taken to starting each day with a five-mile run. That morning, he'd followed a particularly challenging uphill route, which led to a local beauty spot – a dramatic chalk cliff with spectacular views. The effort had been well worth it and, as Dante stood there looking out across the countryside and breathing in deep lungfuls of gorse-scented air, he realized that, for the first time since arriving in England, he felt completely carefree.

Back at Ashwicke, Dante kicked off his muddy trainers in the vestibule and headed upstairs for a shower. Juliet had been asleep when he left, but now their king-size bed was empty and on her pillow a silk nightdress lay neatly folded.

After stripping off his sodden T-shirt and shorts, Dante went through to the en suite. It was just as well he'd kept his boxers on because there was a strange woman bending over the bath. Her bottom was thrust provocatively in the air and her coltish legs seemed to extend for miles beneath her black cotton uniform. She was humming loudly as she pulled strands of Juliet's long blonde hair from the plughole with a rubber-gloved hand.

Dante was embarrassed. Even after two months at Ashwicke, he still hadn't got used to the presence of the chambermaids, who serviced his own quarters as well as those of the guests.

'Hi there, are you going to be much longer in here?' he asked, pulling a towel from the rail and wrapping it round his waist.

When the girl didn't even look up, Dante took a step towards her. 'Hello?' he said in a louder voice.

Suddenly, her head jerked round. 'Shit!' she said, pulling a pair of earphones from her ears. 'You nearly gave me a heart attack.' She had a strong regional accent that was quite different to the local burr Dante had grown used to. 'Sorry, I didn't realize I had company,' she added. 'I was listening to my iPod.'

Dante realized he had never seen her before. He wasn't that surprised; Juliet's chambermaids were somewhat unreliable and she regularly used agency staff as stopgaps. 'You're a soul fan, huh?' he said, pointing to the dangling earphones, which were emitting the tinny strains of *Try A Little Tenderness*.

She nodded. 'Yep. I only listen to the old stuff, though – you know, Otis, Marvin, Stevie, all the greats.' She pulled a sheepish face. 'I don't suppose I should be listening to music on the job, should I?'

Dante shrugged. 'Don't ask me. Anyway, don't worry, I won't tell.'

The girl peeled off her rubber gloves and tossed them in the sink. As the light from the halogen spot caught her face, Dante saw how young she was – no more than twenty-one or twenty-two at most. She had huge dark eyes and a mane of mahogany hair that was tied in a loose ponytail.

'You must be Mr Fisher,' she said. 'I'm the new chambermaid. It's only my first day, so you'll have to make allowances for me. This place is huge; I keep getting lost.'

Dante frowned. Juliet hadn't told him she was recruiting new permanents. 'I know just how you feel,' he replied. 'It took me weeks to get my bearings. I've lost count of the number of times I went looking for the downstairs bathroom and wound up in the broom cupboard. So let's make a deal, okay? I promise to make allowances, if you promise to call me Dante. I hate all that *Mister* shit; it makes me feel about ninety.'

The girl flashed a smile. It was wide and wicked, like he'd just told her an unbelievably dirty joke. 'That's cool with me.'

'And what shall I call *you*?' he asked.

She cocked her head to the side kittenishly. 'Orla.'

'That's a pretty name.'

'It's Irish; my mum's from Galway.'

Dante frowned. 'But that's not an Irish accent you have, is it?'

'Uh-uh, I grew up in Liverpool.'

'Ah, a Scouser.'

The girl looked impressed. 'You know a lot for someone who's only just arrived in England.'

'Yeah, well, I watch a lot of TV. To be honest, there's not much else to do around here.'

'Isn't there?' She sounded surprised. 'I've heard there are some cool bars in Loxwood.' She sighed. 'Not that I've got anyone to go with; I've just moved down from Newcastle and I don't know a soul around here.' Another sigh. 'I'm renting a studio flat just outside the town. There's not enough room to swing a cat, but it's all I can afford at the moment.'

'Newcastle? Is that where you were working before?'

'Oh, I wasn't working,' she said airily. 'I was at uni. I've just graduated; I got a first in English and Drama.'

'Wow, congratulations,' Dante said. 'So I guess this job is just a temporary thing, huh?'

The girl shrugged. 'Who knows? If I like it, I might just stick around.'

'Well, Orla,' Dante said, 'I hope you'll be very happy here.'

Her eyes flickered briefly over his naked torso. 'Oh, I'm sure I shall.' She gestured to the bath. 'Listen, I can come back and finish this cleaning later, if you like.'

'Is that okay? Only I've just come back from a run and I really need to take a shower.'

'No problem.' She gathered up her cleaning materials. 'I guess I'll see you around, then.'

Dante stepped aside to let her pass. 'I guess you will. It was nice meeting you.'

'Yeah, you too.'

Half an hour later, showered and dressed, Dante made his way back downstairs. He found Juliet in the entrance hall standing beside a Regency table as she arranged a display of summer blooms in a cut-glass vase. The air was full of their scent, sweet and heady.

She looked up as he approached. 'Hello, darling,' she said. 'Did you have a nice run?'

'Not bad, thanks.' Dante picked up a frothy peony from the table and held it to his nose. 'I went up to the cliff. It was so quiet and peaceful there, and the views were unbelievable.'

Juliet smiled. 'I can see we're going to make a country boy of you yet.'

'I ran into Orla earlier,' Dante said. 'You didn't tell me you'd hired a new chambermaid.'

'I didn't think you'd be interested.'

'I'm not especially. I just thought you might have mentioned it, that's all.'

Juliet stepped back from the vase to inspect her handiwork. 'Hmm . . . a few more carnations I think,' she murmured.

'Do we really need another maid?' Dante asked. 'The ones we've got seem to do a pretty good job.'

'Yes, actually, we do,' Juliet said briskly. 'I had to let Alice go.'

'You fired Alice? But you always said what a good worker she was.'

'She got sloppy. Nathan drew my attention to several occasions where she'd fallen short of the standards expected.'

Dante watched as Juliet began stripping the leaves from a carnation. 'Orla seems like a smart girl,' he said. 'She was telling me that she's just graduated from uni.'

'Really?' Juliet sounded surprised.

'What, you mean you didn't know? Surely it came up at her interview.'

Juliet pushed the carnation into the vase. 'She didn't have an interview. I met her for the first time this morning.'

'But you checked out her references, right?'

She shook her head.

'Jeez, you're taking a bit of a gamble, aren't you?' Dante said. 'How do you know she's trustworthy?'

Juliet looked up from her flower arranging. 'She's

Nathan's sister; that's all the recommendation I need.' She put a hand on her hip. 'Actually, she's his half-sister. I believe they have different mothers, hence the rather large age gap.'

Dante could hardly believe what he was hearing. 'So let me get this straight,' he said. 'You've hired someone without running any background checks, just because she happens to be related to the general manager.'

'Oh, darling, I'm sure Orla's perfectly capable – and she's a nice girl; you said so yourself.'

'It doesn't matter how nice she is,' Dante glowered. 'She's got no relevant experience.'

Juliet picked up a small bunch of chrysanthemums and began trimming the stems with a pair of scissors. 'Domestic vacancies aren't that easy to fill, you know – especially on the wages I'm offering. Nathan has done me a huge favour.'

'Done himself a favour, more like,' Dante muttered.

'What's that supposed to mean?'

'Oh, come on, Juliet. Isn't it obvious? The guy already acts like he owns the place. Now he's trying to get his feet even further under the table by bringing in his goddamn sister. Next thing you know he'll be trying to convince you to get rid of Chef and hire his Auntie Elsie from Edinburgh instead.'

Juliet gave a brittle laugh.

'Do you know what I reckon?' Dante continued. 'Nathan feels threatened by me.'

Juliet tutted. 'You're my husband; Nathan's just an employee. Why would he see you as a threat?'

Dante shrugged. 'You tell me.'

Juliet laid down her scissors on the table. 'You've really got it in for Nathan, haven't you?'

'*He's* got it in for me, more like.'

'Well, I'm sorry you feel that way, but you two are just going to have to rub along. Nathan's brilliant at his job; I simply couldn't manage without him.'

Dante scowled. He didn't understand why Juliet was always so ready to spring to Nathan's defence. Surely there were other general managers who would do the job just as well. 'Well, okay, then,' he said, not wanting the conversation to escalate into a full-blown argument. 'But I'm telling you, Juliet, the guy's gotta sort out his attitude problem. Every time he speaks to me he's got this funny sneery expression on his face. Next time, I might just be tempted to punch his lights out.'

Juliet gave him a withering look. 'Oh, please.'

Suddenly, there was a sound from above them. Dante looked towards the stairs. Orla was standing on the half-landing with a pile of towels in her arms. He had no idea how long she'd been there.

She looked at them both hesitantly. 'Sorry,' she said. 'I didn't mean to disturb you. I was just taking these towels to the laundry room.'

'Don't mind us – you go right ahead,' Juliet replied.

Orla proceeded down the stairs, her chin resting on top of the towels to prevent any escaping.

'Oh, and, Orla,' Juliet called out when she was nearly at the bottom. 'I spilled some body lotion on my dressing table earlier. Will you clean it up for me when you have a moment?'

Orla smiled. 'That's already taken care of, Mrs Fisher. It did leave a bit of a greasy mark behind, but I wiped the wood down with some nail-polish remover and it seems to have done the trick.'

Juliet beamed back at her. 'Clever girl, thank you.' As the maid disappeared through one of the stone archways, she picked up the vase and carried it over to the windowsill. 'You know, darling, I really don't think we're going to have any problems with Orla,' she told Dante. 'It certainly sounds as if she's got plenty of initiative.'

Dante cut his eyes to the side. 'I'm reserving judgement.'

'Have you got any plans for this afternoon?' Juliet asked as she made some final adjustments to her arrangement. 'Only I've got to go into town to buy some new placemats for the guests' dining room. Why don't you come with me?'

'I can't. I'm going to the golf club.'

'Oh? Are you meeting Connor?'

Dante shook his head. 'The bar manager called my mobile earlier; he reckons he might have some work for me. There's a big charity ball coming up in a couple of weeks.'

Juliet nodded. 'The Granville Lodge fundraiser . . . It's a pretty big deal around here. The girls and I have got tickets. We bought them months ago, or I would've asked you if you wanted to go.'

'Cool,' Dante said. 'The bar manager's looking for experienced cocktail waiters, so I said I'd drop by for a chat this afternoon.'

'I'll keep my fingers crossed for you.' Hearing the crunch of gravel, Juliet turned towards the window. A smart silver BMW was parking up. 'That'll be Mr and Mrs Devine. They're booked in for three nights.' She looked at her watch. 'They're a bit early. I'd better nip upstairs and make sure their room's ready. Would you be a love and check them in for me?'

'There's no need for that, Mrs Fisher,' came a voice from behind them. 'I've got it all under control.'

Juliet looked round. Nathan was standing behind the reception desk. 'Hello, Nathan,' she said, smiling at him. 'I thought you were going through the shopping list with Chef.'

'It's all done,' Nathan said. 'I'm putting the Devines in the Byron, by the way. Orla's already made up the room and I've checked it over, so there's no need for you to trouble yourself.'

Juliet clapped her hands together. 'Excellent!' She picked up a white carnation and trimmed the stem. 'This is for you,' she said, walking over to Nathan and working the flower into the buttonhole of his jacket.

'Why thank you, Mrs Fisher,' Nathan said, firing a smug smile in Dante's direction.

Dante looked down and saw that the fragile peony he'd been holding was now crushed to a pulp in his fist.

17

It was the middle of the night and, for the first time in recent history, every bedroom in Ashwicke Park's east wing was occupied. The previous day, one of Loxwood's smartest hotels had hosted a society wedding and, like several other smaller hostelries in the area, Juliet was gratefully absorbing the overspill of guests. Keen to create the right impression in the hope of securing some good, word-of-mouth reviews, she had asked for a volunteer among the staff to stay on duty throughout the night. Not only would he or she be able to check in any latecomers, but they would also be on hand should one of the guests need something at an unsocial hour – an extra blanket, for example, or a mug of hot milk.

Charlie had jumped at the chance to take on more responsibility and claim the modest overtime on offer. At first, Juliet had baulked at the idea of leaving one so inexperienced in charge, but when none of the other staff put themselves forward she relented.

'Just don't fall asleep on the job,' Juliet warned her young employee as she and Dante headed upstairs to bed soon after eleven. 'Remember, from now until morning, you're the public face of Ashwicke Park.'

'Don't worry, Mrs Fisher, I'm used to staying up all night,' Charlie replied, omitting to mention that, in such instances, his wakefulness had invariably been fuelled by artificial stimulants of one kind or another.

It was now nearly an hour since the last arrival had been checked in and escorted to their room. Charlie had specifically been told not to abandon the reception desk for more than a few minutes at a time in case one of the wedding guests called down. However, most of them had been three sheets to the wind and would, Charlie reasoned, have fallen asleep as soon as their heads hit the pillow. With this in mind, he had relocated to the residents' lounge, where there were comfy chairs and a widescreen TV – not that he intended to stay there all night.

The minute the carriage clock on the mantelpiece struck two, Charlie leapt to his feet. He made his way to the entrance hall and heaved open the front door. Outside, the gardens lay in darkness. Nothing stirred. Lifting his fingers to his mouth, Charlie gave a brief whistle. A moment later, three figures stepped out from behind a low clipped box hedge. Grinning, Charlie beckoned them into the house.

Ten minutes later, the four teenagers were sitting in Juliet's dining room, grouped round one end of the highly polished walnut table.

'This is some place you've got here, Charlie,' remarked the eldest – a lumpen lad with bad neck acne – as he pulled a can of beer from his rucksack. 'Do you think you could get *me* a job here? I'd do anything.' He frowned. 'Except clean the bogs. That's women's work.'

Charlie smiled as he cracked open a beer. He'd known all three lads since school. Andy and Tim both had apprenticeships, but Jason had been unemployed for nearly a year. 'I can put a word in for you if you like, but the boss is pretty strapped for cash at the moment. I don't think she's looking to take on anyone new at the moment.'

'But look at all this stuff,' Jason said, gesturing to a display cabinet crammed with Crown Derby. 'She must be minted, especially since her old man died.'

Charlie shrugged. 'All I know is she can't even afford to get the leaking roof fixed.'

Andy reached out and tweaked one of the gold epaulettes on Charlie's uniform jacket. 'I hate to say it, mate, but you look like a right gayer in that get-up.'

Charlie brushed his hand away. 'I thought you'd come here to play poker, not take the piss out of me.'

'Yeah,' said Tim, producing a pack of playing cards from his coat pocket. 'Let's get down to business. How long have we got?'

'Chef gets in at six, so you'll need to be gone by five thirty at the latest.'

Jason rubbed his hands together. 'Plenty of time for me to bleed you lot dry.'

Charlie grunted. 'In your dreams, mate.'

By four a.m., Jason's prophecy was indeed proving optimistic. Charlie, by contrast, was on a winning streak and keen to up the ante. 'How about we raise the stake?' he said, as he dealt a new hand.

'What to?' asked Andy.

'A fiver each?'

Tim raised his eyebrows sceptically. 'It's all right for you to flash the cash. You get a tip just for carrying a bloody bag up a flight of stairs. I'm only a bleedin' brickie, remember.'

'Oh, go on,' said Andy. 'Live dangerously for once.'

Tim thought for a moment. 'Fine, but if I don't win the next hand, I'm calling it a night.' He reached for Jason's rucksack that earlier in the evening had been bulging with cans, frowning when he realized it was empty. 'We're out of beer,' he said glumly.

'No way!' Andy shrieked. 'I've only had three cans. Which one of you greedy bastards has necked my share?'

'You drank the other two in the bus on the way over here, remember?' Jason said.

'No, I didn't. I only had one.'

'You had two. I remember being surprised at how quickly you were putting them away.'

Andy stood up and lurched drunkenly towards his friend. 'Are you calling me a liar?'

Charlie clicked his tongue. 'Keep your voices down, guys. We don't want to wake Mrs Fisher up.'

Andy apologized and sat back down again. 'Can you get us some more booze? A place like this is bound to have a wine cellar. I'm sure your Mrs F won't miss a few bottles.'

Tim gave a loud sniff. 'Wine's for pussies. D'you know what I fancy? A nice drop of whisky.' He looked at Charlie expectantly. 'How about it, fella?'

The porter sighed. 'You lot wait here. I'll see what I can do.'

He left the room, taking care to close the door behind him, and headed back towards reception. At the foot of the stairs he paused and listened for any sound of movement above, but all he could hear was the gentle creak of Ashwicke's old bones. He continued through one of the stone archways and down the dark corridor. About two-thirds of the way down he stopped outside a door. Beyond it lay the snug. The room wasn't used much and

Charlie had only been inside it once before – when he'd been helping Reg hang the curtains after their annual dry clean. He hesitated for a moment, then turned the doorknob.

In daylight the snug had been spooky enough, with its funny, musty smell and all Gus's bits and pieces laid out on the desk as if he might be coming back for them at any moment. By night, the room was even eerier and wreathed with shadows. The curtains were open and soft bluish moonlight flooded in through the window. Its rays highlighted random objects on Gus's desk – a monogrammed fountain pen, the burnished wood of a pipe stem, a squat inkwell with a domed silver lid.

Charlie could feel his skin prickling as he crossed the room to the bookshelf, where he remembered seeing a pair of square decanters on a silver tray. He located them swiftly – one was half full and contained cognac, according to the engraved silver label round its neck; the other held whisky, but it was nearly empty. Picking up the cognac, he walked back towards the door. As he passed the fireplace, he felt a cold breath of air on the back of his neck. It made the hairs in each nostril stand on end. Gulping loudly, he bolted towards the door.

Soon, Charlie was back in the brightly lit entrance hall. As he made his way back to the dining room, he mentally castigated himself for being such a scaredy cat. Everybody knew there were no such things as ghosts. The sensation on the back of his neck was nothing more than a draught, he told himself firmly. Old houses were full of them.

The others were impressed when they saw the decanter.

'Nice one, Chaz,' Tim said. 'That should see us through till morning.'

'What about glasses?' Andy asked.

Charlie pointed to the gargantuan sideboard. 'There should be some in there.' He set down the decanter in the middle of the table. 'It's cognac, not whisky, I'm afraid.'

Tim rubbed his hands together. 'Even better.' He looked over at Andy, who was on his hands and knees beside the sideboard. 'How are you doing with those glasses, mate?'

'No joy yet,' Andy replied. 'But I have found these.' He turned round. In his hands was a long flat box. The lid was open and inside the velvet-lined interior lay a set of art deco steak knives. He picked one up and brandished it like a dagger. 'Pretty cool, huh?'

Jason paused, mid-shuffle. 'Bring them over here, then.'

Andy carried the box to the table. Jason picked one up and tested the tip with a forefinger. 'Jesus, these are sharp.'

'They're steak knives,' Charlie said. 'They're supposed to be sharp.' He pulled the box towards him. 'Anyway, look, we shouldn't be messing around with these.'

Jason yanked the box towards him. 'Don't be so boring.'

'Yeah,' said Tim. 'We're not doing any harm. Why don't you go and find those glasses? I'm spitting feathers here.'

Sighing, Charlie went to the sideboard, pulled open one of its many doors and stuck his head inside. 'I'm sure I saw some in here at Mrs Fisher's last dinner party,' he muttered.

While his back was turned, Andy removed a knife from

the box. 'Why don't we see just how sharp these babies are?' he said, winking at the others. Taking the knife by the handle, he threw his hand over his shoulder and hurled the knife at the door, Apache style. It landed in the back of the door, embedding itself in the soft oak, to a chorus of cheers from the other two.

Charlie looked up from the bureau. 'Hey, what are you doing?'

'Chill,' Andy said as he picked up another knife. 'We're just having a laugh.'

'Don't you dare,' Charlie said as Andy raised his hand again. His threat fell on deaf ears.

At precisely the same time the knife left Andy's hand, the door opened and a middle-aged man in a pair of paisley pyjamas appeared on the threshold. Charlie called out a warning as the steak knife went whistling towards his head, whereupon the man let out a loud scream and dived for cover. A moment later, his forehead smashed against one of the table's carved wooden feet.

Beneath the table the man was groaning.

'You stupid fuck, Andy,' Charlie said as he went to the man's aid. 'I'll probably lose my job over this.'

'How was I supposed to know Wee Willie Winkie was going to come walking through the door?' his friend responded sullenly.

Charlie helped the dazed man to his feet. 'I'm ever so sorry, sir. Why don't you sit down?'

The man sank into the nearest chair, clutching his head, which was now sporting a bump the size of a sparrow's egg.

'Would you like me to get something for you – a glass of water perhaps?'

The man's eyes blazed with fury. 'What the hell do you think you're playing at?' he said. 'I'd like to speak to the owner. Now.'

'Oh, there's no need for that,' Charlie said smoothly. 'I'm sure we can sort this out between ourselves.'

'Sort what out?'

Charlie looked up. Juliet was standing at the door in her dressing gown. 'I heard screaming,' she said, frowning as she clocked the youths. 'What's going on?'

'I'll tell you what's going on,' the man said, jumping to his feet. 'I came downstairs to see if I could get some indigestion tablets and I found these young savages having some sort of party. They were throwing knives at the door, would you believe? If I hadn't reacted so quickly, they might have had my eye out.' He jabbed a finger at the youths. 'I take it they're employees of yours.'

'One of them is,' Juliet said. 'I've never seen the other three in my life.'

Charlie bit his thumbnail. He wore the bewildered look of a captain who knew his ship was sinking but was powerless to stop it. 'They're friends of mine, Mrs Fisher.'

'And what are they doing here, Charlie?'

'I, um, invited them over for a game of cards. I didn't think you'd mind.'

Juliet glared at him. 'You mean you didn't think I'd find out.' She looked at the decanter and the crumpled beer cans littering the table. 'Are you drunk?'

'Just a little bit tipsy, that's all.'

'Never mind them, what about my head?' the man exclaimed. 'I could sue you for damages.'

'I can only apologize wholeheartedly for Charlie's

immature and negligent behaviour,' Juliet grovelled. 'Would you like me to call an ambulance?'

The man glowered at her. 'No, it's all right. I'll live. I wouldn't mind a drop of that cognac, though.' He coughed. 'Purely for medicinal purposes.'

'Of course,' Juliet said soothingly. 'Let me get you a glass.' As she strode towards the sideboard she glared at the others. 'Get out of my sight,' she said through gritted teeth. 'All of you.'

'I'm ever so sorry, Mrs Fisher,' Charlie said quietly as he passed her. 'It won't happen again.'

'It better not,' Juliet replied. 'Or you'll be out of a job.'

Charlie nodded. 'Message received and understood.'

For the next half an hour or so, Juliet tended to her injured guest. After pouring him a generous measure of cognac, she brought ice for his forehead, Alka-Seltzer for his indigestion and promised him a free breakfast, as well as a hefty discount on the room tariff. Eventually the man took himself back to bed, still muttering threats of legal action. When he was gone, Juliet didn't go straight back to her own bedroom where she'd left Dante sleeping soundly. Instead, she crept down the hall to the snug, decanter in hand. As she replaced the cognac on the bookshelf, a great weariness came over her. She slumped onto the sofa and stared into the fireplace. 'What am I going to do?' she said out loud. 'It's all such a terrible mess.' Tears sprang from her eyes and slid sideways down her face onto a cushion. 'Oh, Gus,' she whimpered. 'Oh, Gus, Gus, Gus.'

18

As soon as the cab pulled up outside the house, Dante was on his feet. Even though he didn't know Juliet's friends that well, he was excited at the prospect of a night out. For one evening at least, he would be able to escape Ashwicke and the ghosts of the Ingram family, who seemed to haunt every room and corridor.

When he opened the front door, Yasmin was standing on the step dressed in a thigh-skimming bronze shift that showed off her long legs to dazzling effect.

'Wow,' Dante said, taking a step back. 'You look amazing.'

'You're looking pretty hot yourself,' she replied, eyeing him approvingly.

As she spoke, Juliet appeared at Dante's shoulder and blew Yasmin a kiss. 'So, young lady, which dens of iniquity are you taking my husband to tonight?'

'I thought we'd start off at The Barn,' said Yasmin, naming one of Loxwood's most fashionable watering holes. 'And then, if Dante's up for it, we can head over to Attica.'

Juliet frowned. 'Isn't that a private member's club?'

'Yep – and guess who's on the guest list?'

'How did you manage to swing that?'

'One of my press contacts does the PR for the club; he was only too happy to pull a few strings for his favourite showbiz editor.'

'Sounds like a good plan to me,' Dante said. He glanced

towards the cab and saw that it was empty. 'Are we picking Nicole up on the way?'

Yasmin shook her head. 'She's blown us out. I got a call from her a couple of hours ago; Tilly's running a temperature.'

'Poor little thing,' Juliet said. 'I hope it's nothing serious.'

'Connor reckons it's just a summer cold, but Nic wants to stay home with her, just in case.' Yasmin smiled at Juliet. 'Why don't you come along? I've got a plus-two at Attica.'

Juliet sighed. 'I'd love to, but I've got guests arriving in half an hour.' She patted Dante on the bottom. 'You two have a lovely time, though.'

'We will,' Yasmin said as she started walking to the cab. 'And don't wait up.'

Dante was in high spirits as they set off for town. 'You don't know how much I've been looking forward to this evening,' he said, beaming from ear to ear.

Yasmin found that she was smiling too; Dante's enthusiasm was infectious. 'Me too. Nic and I have been dying to get to know you better; she's gutted she couldn't come.'

'This is my first big night out since I came to England.'

'In that case, we'd better make it a good one,' Yasmin replied. 'Did you use to go out a lot in Aspen?'

Dante nodded. 'It's got the best nightlife of any US ski resort. I was working in the bar most evenings, but I still found time to party.'

'You must find life in Loxwood ever so quiet by comparison.'

'I guess, but it's a small sacrifice to make. I'm with Juliet – that's the most important thing.'

Yasmin felt a pinprick of envy, knowing that when she returned home the house would be empty. 'Juliet said you've managed to find some bar work at the golf club.'

'Yeah, it's only for one night, but if I do a good job they might hire me again.'

Yasmin gave an approving smile. 'You know, Dante, I really admire you for getting off your arse. Plenty of men would have taken one look at Ashwicke and decided they were perfectly entitled to take it easy.'

Dante chuckled. 'That's not my style. I've been taking care of myself since I was seventeen, and I don't see why that should change just because I'm married.'

'But you didn't fancy working with Juliet at the hotel?'

'It's not that I don't want to help out around the place; I just don't want Juliet to pay me for doing it. That way it would still feel like I'm living off her.' Dante rubbed his forehead with the back of his hand. 'Only I'm not sure she understands that.'

'I'm sure she does,' Yasmin said reassuringly.

'I know she'd prefer me to be more of a high-flier, but it's not as if I'm always going to be working for someone else. One day I'd like to have my own bar. I always thought it would be in Aspen, but I guess Loxwood will do just fine.' Dante rubbed his hands together. 'And tonight will give me a good chance to check out the competition.'

'How did you end up being a bartender?' Yasmin asked him. 'Was it a deliberate career choice?'

Dante shook his head. 'Ever since I was a kid I wanted to be a football coach. I studied Phys Ed at college in Montana, but I struggled with the academic side of things and ended up dropping out at the end of my first year.

After that, I bummed around for six months, then a friend of mine got a job as a snowboard instructor in Aspen and invited me along for the ride. I'd been skiing since I was eight, so I didn't have to think too hard about it. When we got there, I took the first job I could find – which just happened to be in a bar.' He smiled ruefully. 'I must admit I didn't think I'd still be doing it ten years later. When I started out, my only aim was to make enough money to pay for my room, my beer and my ski pass. But then I discovered I really enjoyed bartending. I was pretty good at it too. I moved around a lot to get as much experience as I could. With each new job I got a bigger pay cheque and more responsibility, until eventually I was Senior Cocktail Waiter at one of the coolest bars in town.' He gave a contented sigh. 'Then I met Juliet.'

Yasmin raised an eyebrow. 'And the rest, as they say, is history.'

The cab drew to a halt outside a long, low building. 'Are we here?' Dante asked eagerly.

'Yep, this is The Barn. It only opened a few months ago; the owner spent quarter of a million on the refurb.'

'It looks pretty popular,' Dante said, noting the queue outside.

'Don't worry about that; they know me here.' Yasmin leaned forward. 'How much, driver?'

Dante reached for his wallet. 'I'll take care of this.'

'Okay,' Yasmin agreed reluctantly. 'But all the drinks tonight are on me.'

'No, I can't let you do that.'

Yasmin held up a warning finger. 'I was the one who invited *you* out, remember? Which means it's my treat.'

Dante gave her a shy smile. 'Well, okay, if you insist. Thanks.'

With the cab driver paid, Yasmin led the way to the front of the line of drinkers waiting patiently for admittance. The girl on the door smiled and waved her straight in. Inside the bar, the vibe was louche and intimate, with candlelit tables and squishy velvet sofas.

'You must be pretty important around here,' Dante said as a waitress greeted Yasmin by name before leading them to a prominent table on a raised platform.

Yasmin wrinkled her nose. 'I wouldn't say that. It's just one of the perks of being a journalist. The bar manager likes me because I sometimes bring celebrity interview subjects here.' She grinned. 'I like to loosen them up with a few drinks before I go in for the kill.'

Dante assumed a look of mock horror. 'Does that mean I oughta watch what I say?'

'Uh-uh. Tonight is strictly off the record, I promise.'

Yasmin had been a little anxious about entertaining Dante on her own – but, to her relief, conversation flowed easily, especially once they'd both been lubricated with one of The Barn's trademark mojitos. She was keen to hear about Dante's upbringing in Montana and it was a subject he talked about with a good deal of fondness: his close relationship with his brother and two sisters, their carefree existence on his parents' farm, the weekends spent horse riding or skiing in the Rocky Mountains. By the time they were ordering their third cocktail, it felt as if they were old friends.

'How about you?' Dante asked as a waitress delivered tapas to their table. 'Were you born in Loxwood?'

Yasmin shook her head. 'I'm from the West Country originally, but I went to uni around here, and after I graduated I got some unpaid work on a local free sheet. Just like you, I discovered something I was good at and a place I liked, so I stuck around.'

Dante helped himself to a thick slice of tortilla. 'You're single, aren't you?'

'Yeah, much to Juliet and Nicole's disgust. They're desperate to see me settled down. I keep telling them I'm perfectly happy as I am, but they won't listen.'

'But you've been in love before, right?'

Yasmin was a little taken aback. She hadn't been expecting such a direct question. 'Yeah,' she conceded after a brief hesitation. 'But it was a long time ago.'

'How did you meet him?'

'At uni. We both worked on the student newspaper. He was an ex-public schoolboy, not my usual type at all. I thought he was a bit of an idiot when I first met him, but then we got to know each other and I realized that underneath his arrogant exterior he was actually quite shy.'

'He must've been pretty special for you to fall in love with him.'

'What makes you say that?' Yasmin asked through a mouthful of vodka-flamed chorizo.

Dante looked her in the eye. 'Because you're a stunning-looking woman . . . and obviously very clever. And because somehow I can't imagine you ever settling for second best.'

Yasmin shrugged. 'Yeah, Nick was special – or at least I thought he was at the time.' Her eyes narrowed. 'And then he showed his true colours.'

'What happened?'

Yasmin pressed her lips together. Her relationship with her first – and *only* – love was something she rarely talked about. Even Nicole and Juliet didn't know the full details, but the cocktails had gone to her head and Dante was so incredibly easy to talk to that she found herself opening up.

'We'd been going out for nearly a year,' she began. 'Things were great. Nick told me he loved me every day. I really thought he was, you know, The One. I used to fantasize about our wedding, our house in the country, what we'd call our kids . . . real schoolgirl stuff. One night I'd been out with some girlfriends – nothing riotous, just a pizza and a few glasses of wine. On the way home, I was feeling kinda amorous, the way you do when you've been drinking, so I decided to stop off at Nick's house unannounced. The front door was unlocked, the way it always was, so I went up to his room and opened the door. That's when I saw them together.'

'He was in bed with another woman?'

'He was in bed with my *best friend*,' Yasmin said. 'She was supposed to come out with us that night, but she'd cried off at the last minute saying she had a migraine.' Yasmin blinked hard. Even now, after all these years, she could still see them there, entwined on the bed, a light sheen of sweat clearly visible on her so-called boyfriend's buttocks.

'Jeez,' Dante said. 'That must've been horrible for you.'

'Yeah. I ran out into the street and I vomited all that pizza straight back up.' She stroked the stem of her cocktail glass thoughtfully. 'Afterwards, Nick begged me to take him back. He claimed it was a one-off, but I knew he was lying.'

'So you refused?'

Yasmin nodded.

'What about your best friend?'

'I stopped talking to her. Most of our mutual friends did too.'

'And you haven't fallen in love since?'

'Nope.'

'Do you think it's because you're afraid of getting hurt again?'

Yasmin looked up at Dante. She found herself thinking that, for a man, he was pretty perceptive. 'No, it's not that,' she said. Even to her own ears, the declaration sounded false. 'I just don't have time for a full-on relationship, that's all. My work comes first.'

Dante raised an eyebrow. 'So you have casual relationships instead?'

Yasmin shrugged. 'I guess that's as good a description as any.'

'And is there anyone in the frame right now?'

Yasmin laughed. 'So many questions!'

'Sorry, I didn't mean to be nosey.'

'No, it's okay . . . It's just that in my line of work *I'm* usually the one asking the questions. It feels strange to be on the receiving end, that's all.' She took a sip of her drink. 'Actually there is someone . . . a bloke at work. We fight like cat and dog most of the time, but . . .' She gave an embarrassed smile. 'Somehow we ended up sleeping together last week.' She put her hand over her face. 'In the office of all places. Thank God nobody caught us.'

Dante smiled. 'And do you actually like the guy – or was it just sex?'

'Um, yeah, as a matter of fact, I do like him. I'm just not sure how he feels about me.'

'Well, maybe you should find out.'

Yasmin shook her head. 'It was a one-off.'

'How can you be so sure?'

'He's got a girlfriend.'

Dante winced. 'Ah.'

'I'm not proud of myself,' Yasmin said. 'And I really hope his girlfriend never finds out – because, believe me, I know exactly how she'd feel.'

'How do you know his relationship isn't on the rocks – and that's why he slept with you?'

'Because he's barely spoken to me since. In fact, he's gone out of his way to avoid me at work. I think he wishes the whole thing never happened.' She looked around the room. It was nearly midnight and the place was heaving, the decibel level so high they could barely hear each other. 'Do you fancy going to that club I mentioned?' she asked Dante. 'It'll be a lot quieter there.'

Dante glanced at his watch. Juliet would be in bed by now. 'Sure, why not?'

At Attica, they were treated with a similar degree of deference. After entering through a discreet side entrance, a waitress escorted them to a quiet corner of the bar. Moments later, a bottle of champagne was delivered to their table, compliments of the manager. As the night wore on, Yasmin found herself warming to Dante more and more. She could see why Juliet had fallen for him. Not only was he handsome and well mannered, he also had a gentleness that was very attractive.

As they clinked champagne glasses, she touched his arm lightly. 'I'm so glad Juliet found you,' she said.

Dante smiled. 'Not as glad as I am.'

'Nic and I were quite worried about her before she went to Aspen.'

'Why was that?'

Yasmin sipped at her champagne. She'd lost count of how much she'd had to drink – enough to make her feel quite lightheaded. 'Let's just say she took Gus's death very hard. Losing a husband is bad enough, but to lose him in such horrendous circumstances . . .'

'She was the one who found him, wasn't she?'

Yasmin nodded. 'She more or less fell apart. I think for ages afterwards she couldn't quite believe what he'd done. Mind you, it was a shock for all of us. Gus was always so exuberant; I don't think I'd even seen him down or depressed. Juliet said he'd been under a lot of stress at work, but that didn't stop her blaming herself. She was asleep when it happened, you see. The paramedics said he'd probably been dead for several hours when she found him. She couldn't understand why some sixth sense hadn't woken her up sooner.'

Dante chewed the inside of his cheek. 'Poor Juliet,' he murmured.

'For weeks afterwards, she hardly left the house,' Yasmin went on. 'Nic and I did everything we could to bring her out of herself, but nothing seemed to be working. Then, when Gus's will was read, it emerged he hadn't left her as well provided for as everyone thought. During her marriage Juliet had never had a proper job you see. Now all of a sudden she had to find a way of generating an income.'

'And that's when she decided to start the hotel?'

'That's right – and, with hindsight, it was the best thing that could have happened, because it helped take her mind off things. Over the next few months, Nic and I noticed a distinct improvement in her, but she still wasn't back to her old self – apart from anything else, she was exhausted. Even though she'd hired Nathan by that point, she was still running herself ragged. We were thrilled when she decided to go to Aspen. We knew the break would do her the power of good – and we were right.'

'You must've been pretty shocked when you heard she'd gotten married.'

Yasmin nodded. 'And to be honest with you we were a bit worried she was rushing into things.'

'Do you still think that now?'

'Now,' Yasmin said, 'I think we were worrying unnecessarily.'

Dante laid a hand on his heart. 'And just in case you have any lingering doubts I'd like to assure you that my intentions towards Juliet are utterly, totally, one hundred per cent honourable.'

Yasmin smiled. 'I don't doubt that for a second.'

Dante looked at her. 'If I ask you something, do you promise to give me an honest answer?'

'Fire away.'

'Do you think Juliet's gotten over Gus . . . I mean *really* gotten over him?'

Yasmin didn't answer straight away. 'I don't think the death of a loved one is something you ever get over,' she said, trying to be diplomatic.

Dante nodded. It seemed to Yasmin that a strange melancholy had crept over him. 'It's just that Gus seemed like such a great guy,' he said. 'I sometimes worry that I can't live up to him.'

Yasmin put her hand on his. 'Then don't even try. Just be yourself . . . That's who Juliet fell in love with, after all.'

'D'you reckon?'

'Yes,' Yasmin said firmly. She picked up the bottle of champagne and refilled their glasses. 'Now, why don't we change the subject? We're supposed to be having fun, remember.'

'Sure,' Dante said. Even though there was still so much he wanted to ask her.

19

The golf club's banqueting suite had undergone a breath-taking transformation. Dominating the room was a wide central boulevard, flanked on either side by papier mâché trees and gas lamps hanging from curlicued pillars. Around it a series of landmarks – the Eiffel Tower, the Arc de Triomphe, the white-domed Basilique du Sacré-Cœur – had been meticulously hand-painted on vast floor-to-ceiling backdrops. At the end of the boulevard, a lavish stage festooned with heavy velvet drapes had been erected. Above it, the neon-lit sails of a windmill façade revolved slowly.

Tonight, the golf club was playing host to the annual fundraiser for the Granville Lodge Home for Retired Entertainers. A longstanding highlight of Loxwood's social calendar, the event was always hugely popular and tickets had been sold out for months. The Lodge's thespian inmates, who currently included an Oscar nominee, two BAFTA winners and a knight, were held in great affection by the people of Loxwood, not least because they brought a touch of Hollywood glamour to the town. Each year, the home's residents held a ballot to decide the theme of their fundraiser, and this year they had settled on the Moulin Rouge.

In the ladies' powder room, Juliet and Yasmin were busy making last-minute adjustments to their make-up. Like all the guests, they'd come dressed appropriately for the occasion. Juliet was an old-fashioned can-can dancer in a black ruffled skirt and a red satin bustier, which showed off her impressive décolletage to maximum effect. Fishnet stockings, high-heeled lace-up boots and a scarlet feather pinned to her blonde chignon completed the ensemble. Yasmin had plumped for an altogether more daring look, with a showgirl's peacock-blue sequinned bra top and matching high-cut knickers, accessorized with a beaded skullcap and a pair of vintage stilettos she'd picked up on eBay.

'I expect Dante's looking forward to tonight, isn't he?' Yasmin said, as she applied a fresh slick of scarlet lipstick.

'It's all he's been talking about for days.' Juliet smiled at her friend's reflection in the mirror. 'Thanks again for taking him out; he had a great time.'

'It was my pleasure. You've got a good bloke there. I hope you realize that.'

'Oh, I do.' Juliet leaned towards the mirror and turned her face to the side, checking her nose for shine. 'It's such a pity Connor couldn't make it tonight. Why did he bother buying a ticket if he knew he was going to be at a medical conference in Cardiff?'

'According to Nic, he applied to go to the conference ages ago, but it was oversubscribed,' Yasmin explained. 'And when one of the delegates dropped out at the last minute the organizers got back in touch and offered him the place.'

'Oh well, at least Nicole will be able to let her hair down tonight,' Juliet said. 'She's always more restrained when Connor's around . . . Have you noticed?'

'Yeah, I think she's so busy trying to play the role of the

perfect wife and mother she forgets to have fun sometimes.' Yasmin blotted her lips with a tissue and turned to Juliet. 'How do I look?'

'Stunning.'

'Good,' said Yasmin. 'Then what are we waiting for?'

Inside the banqueting suite, there was a palpable air of excitement as the guests – looking like exotic birds of paradise in their fancy-dress finery – promenaded along the boulevard. Juliet and Yasmin made straight for an ornate marble fountain, where champagne gushed from the mouths of fat cherubs.

'The organizers have really surpassed themselves this year,' Yasmin remarked as she picked up a glass and filled it from the fountain. 'This place looks amazing.' Looking around, she spotted a group of traditional French street entertainers plying their trade on the boulevard. One in particular caught her eye. 'Now *he* is hot,' she murmured.

Juliet squinted into the distance. 'Which one?'

'Marcel Marceau over there,' Yasmin replied, pointing to a mime artist in white face paint and a black Lycra catsuit that left little to the imagination. 'Come on, let's take a closer look.'

A few moments later, the two women had worked their way to the front of the small group of onlookers who had gathered around the mime artist.

'Isn't he good?' Yasmin purred as the performer picked up an umbrella and pretended to be battling against a strong wind. 'And so lithe too.' She drummed her fingers on her chin, imagining the possibilities.

'But how do you know what he looks like under all that make-up?' Juliet whispered back.

'Who cares when the man's got the body of a Greek god?' Yasmin rejoindered. 'And check out the horn of plenty between his legs.'

Juliet started giggling. 'You are awful, Yasmin.'

When the mime artist finished his routine, both women joined in the enthusiastic applause. Then, as the crowd started to disperse, Yasmin went over to him. 'Bravo!' she gushed. 'That was wonderful.'

The man clasped his hands under his chin and batted his eyelashes in exaggerated gratitude.

'You're not a big talker either,' Yasmin observed approvingly. 'Even better.' She ran her tongue across her top lip. 'Are you available for private performances at all?'

The man knitted his eyebrows together, as if he were pretending to think, then nodded furiously.

'Excellent. Do you have a business card?'

The mime artist grabbed an invisible rope and used it to haul himself over to the battered leather suitcase of props, which lay under one of the papier mâché trees. Bending down in the manner of an old man whose lumbago was playing him up, he removed a business card from the suitcase and presented it to Yasmin with a flourish.

'Thank you,' she said, tucking it into her sequinned bra. 'I'll be in touch. *Au revoir.*' Yasmin blew him a kiss before walking back over to Juliet.

'Sorry about that,' she told her friend. 'I was just congratulating that nice young man on his performance.'

Juliet snorted. 'Is that what you call it?'

Yasmin laughed. 'Come on, let's go and find our table.'

When they got there, Nicole was already waiting for them.

'Sorry, we're late,' Juliet said as she swiped three Bellinis off a passing waiter's tray and set them down on the table. 'Yasmin insisted on going on the pull.'

Yasmin batted her eyelashes. 'Honestly, Nic, you should see him . . . six-foot tall and abs you could bounce rocks off.'

'Not to mention more make-up than Estée Lauder,' Juliet added.

Nicole's eyebrows shot up. '*Make-up?*'

'It's a long story.' Yasmin gestured to Nicole's beaded flapper dress and pink feather boa. 'You look great, by the way.'

'So do you,' Nicole replied. 'I wish I had the figure to pull off an outfit like that.'

Juliet sat down and pulled one of the Bellinis towards her. 'So how are you? It feels as if I haven't seen you in ages.'

'Not bad, thanks – but I'd be a lot better if my husband was here.'

'We were just saying what a shame it was Connor couldn't make it,' Yasmin said.

Nicole's face took on a fierce expression. 'I could cheerfully have throttled him when he told me he was going to the conference instead. He didn't even have the good grace to apologize. And then this morning, as he packed his suitcase, he was in such a good mood. No doubt he was relishing the prospect of a break from his screaming daughter and his nagging wife.'

'I'm sure that's not true,' Juliet said soothingly.

'No? Then why hasn't he been answering his mobile all afternoon? I keep calling him, but it just goes to voicemail.

I even tried phoning the hotel, but the receptionist must've put me through to the wrong room because a woman answered. Then, when the receptionist tried again, the phone just rang and rang.' Nicole's nostrils flared like a stallion's. 'I mean, what if it was an emergency? What if something had happened to Tilly?'

'How is Tilly, by the way?' asked Juliet. 'Yasmin said she was poorly.'

'Much better, thanks. She's staying at my mum's tonight so I'll be able to stay out late for a change.'

'That's good.' Juliet raised a querying eyebrow. 'And how's Bear?'

Nicole frowned. 'I don't know. You've seen more of him than me, I should think.'

'Hmm,' Juliet said. 'It's just that I saw you visiting his caravan the other week.'

'Ooh, what's this? Do tell . . .' said Yasmin, leaning forward.

'It was nothing,' Nicole said quickly. 'I just dropped by to give Bear some cake.'

Yasmin grinned. 'Is that a euphemism?'

'No!' Nicole cried. 'I was just being neighbourly. Bear's new to the area; he doesn't know anyone. I thought he might appreciate some home baking.'

'All right, all right, no need to get your boa in a twist.' Yasmin slid a Bellini towards Nicole. 'Now get this down you. It'll help you relax.'

Behind the banqueting suite's thirty-foot bar, Dante was hard at work. As he poured gin and dry vermouth into a cocktail shaker for a classic martini, he could feel the familiar adrenalin buzz returning. Around him, the other bartenders worked deftly, mixing, blending and shaking, and all the while keeping up a steady stream of good-natured banter. Dante couldn't help grinning as he gave the cocktail shaker a workout . . . It felt good to be back where he belonged. The pay wasn't bad either – nearly double what he was earning back in Aspen.

As the evening wore on, Dante found he was enjoying himself more and more. His cocktail-making skills were more than a match for the other bartenders'. In fact, his output exceeded that of his nearest rival by two to one – a fact that didn't go unnoticed by his supervisor.

'Good work, Dante,' he said, patting his colleague on the shoulder. 'You look as if you're having fun too.'

'I sure am,' Dante replied as he spun a bottle of tequila on his palm before upending it into a jigger. 'Just keep those orders coming.'

'Could you do me a favour?' the supervisor said, pointing to the end of the bar where a tray of cocktails was waiting to be distributed. 'Take those drinks out onto the floor before the ice melts, will you? I don't think those waiters can keep up with your lightning fingers.'

Dante returned the tequila to one of the glass shelves behind him and wiped his hands on a towel. 'No problem.'

He picked up the tray and set off along the boulevard, pausing every now and then so that greedy hands could snatch drinks from his tray. As he walked towards the stage, he spotted Juliet chatting with her girlfriends. He was tempted to go and talk to her but, not wanting to appear unprofessional, he doubled back towards the bar instead.

Just then, a woman appeared to his right, pouting

outrageously as she helped herself to the last cocktail. She had long dark hair which waved in the right places and manicured fingernails, painted lilac to match her dress. Everything about her screamed *high maintenance.*

'You're a pretty young thing, aren't you?' she said, stroking the side of his face with her hand. 'What time do you knock off?'

Before Dante could reply, a man appeared at her side. 'Come on, Daisy, leave the nice waiter alone,' he said, tugging at her arm. 'You're making a fool of yourself, as usual.'

'Oh, don't be such a spoilsport, Frank,' the woman replied. She reached out and flicked the tip of his nose with her index finger. 'How about if I let you watch. You'd like *that*, wouldn't you?'

'Now you're talking,' the man said. Grinning lasciviously, he turned to Dante. 'How about it, fella? You give the missus a good rogering and I'll watch from the sidelines. Sounds like fun, eh?'

Dante held up his left hand and waggled his ring finger with its wide platinum band. 'Thanks for the offer, but I'm a happily married man.'

Scowling, the man pulled a fat leather wallet from his jacket pocket and waved it under Dante's nose. 'I'll make it worth your while.'

Dante clutched his tray to his genitals, as if to protect them from attack. 'Sorry, the answer's still no.'

Keen to escape, he turned on his heel and headed back towards the bar. As he passed the Eiffel Tower, someone caught his arm. Wheeling round, he found himself face to face with a stunning young woman. She was wearing a spangled leotard, cut high on the thigh and low on the bosom. A plume of pink ostrich feathers erupted from her rhinestone-embellished headdress and the spike-heeled silver sandals she wore made her almost as tall as him.

'Sorry, madam,' he said, holding up his empty tray. 'I'm all out of cocktails, but if you tell me what you'd like I'll have one of the guys mix it up for you right away.'

She fluttered her eyelashes demurely at him. 'It's okay, I don't need a drink. I just wanted to say hi.'

Dante frowned. Something about the girl's dark eyes seemed familiar. '*Orla?*' he said uncertainly.

She nodded. 'I look pretty different, huh?'

Dante hadn't seen the maid since their first meeting, a few days earlier. He couldn't believe how different she looked. 'You look amazing,' he said, unable to stop his eyes roaming her curves.

'That's good because I feel like a right muppet,' she said with a sigh. 'I wouldn't normally wear something so revealing, but this was the last Moulin Rouge get-up the costume shop had.' She gestured to Dante's black suit and shoestring tie. 'You're looking pretty sharp yourself. I heard you were a cocktail waiter in a previous life, but I didn't realize you still worked.'

'It's my first night on the job,' Dante told her. 'I guess you could call it a try-out.'

'Cool,' Orla said, sounding impressed. She nodded towards the dance floor, where Daisy and Frank were now dancing cheek to cheek. 'I saw that woman all over you earlier. Was she propositioning you?'

'Something like that,' Dante said. 'I think she was drunk.'

'I'm not surprised – you're a good-looking guy.' She tilted her head to one side. 'Is Juliet here tonight?'

He nodded towards the tables by the stage. 'She's over there with her friends. How about you? Who have you come with?'

She pointed to a noisy group occupying one of the plush scarlet booths. Dante saw that Leah and Charlie were among them.

'I'm with that bunch of alcoholics,' Orla explained. 'Leah's sister's an auxiliary nurse at Granville Lodge and she gave her a load of free tickets. One of Leah's friends couldn't make it, so she invited me along instead. It was really sweet of her; I could never have afforded to come otherwise.'

'I'm glad to see you're making friends.' Dante gave her a loaded look. 'Although Juliet tells me you have family close by.'

She smiled. 'You mean Nathan.'

'It must be nice to be so well connected,' Dante said wryly. 'I bet he's cutting you plenty of slack.'

'You're joking aren't you? Nathan's a real slavedriver; he doesn't go easy on anyone at Ashwicke – not even his own sister.'

'Are you guys close?'

Orla shook her head. 'Not really. We'd never even met until my dad died two years ago.'

'How come?'

'Dad and his first wife – that's Nathan's mum – split up when Nathan was three. When she remarried a year later, Dad agreed to let her new husband adopt him and promised to disappear from their lives completely. I don't know why . . . I guess he thought Nathan would be better off without him. But when Dad passed away, Mum reckoned his son had a right to know about it, so she hired a private detective to track Nathan down.'

'So brother and sister were finally reunited.'

'That's right,' she said. 'I'm an only child, so it was nice to suddenly acquire a brand-new brother. Having said that, we *were* living at opposite ends of the country at the time, so we didn't get to see each other very often. We'd probably only met half a dozen times when Nathan told me there was a job going at Ashwicke. I was at a bit of a loose end when I graduated so I didn't have to think too hard about it. Mind you, I didn't realize it was going to be such hard work.' She clapped her hand over her mouth. 'Shit, that sounds really bad, doesn't it?'

Dante's eyes crinkled in amusement. 'Don't worry about it.' He glanced towards the bar where several waiters were waiting for their trays to be replenished. 'Look, Orla, it's been nice talking to you, but I'd better get back to work.'

'Sure, the others will be wondering where I've got to anyway.' She raised a hand in farewell. 'Enjoy the rest of your evening.'

Dante smiled. 'You too.'

Orla watched him as he walked away from her. She'd never seen her employer's rear view before. It was cute. Very cute. Sighing, she walked over to the booth to find the group downing shots of viscous green liquid.

'What's that you're drinking?' she said, sliding into the booth beside Leah.

'Absinthe,' replied one of Leah's friends – a moon-faced

lad with a rugby player's physique and black hair gelled into spikes. 'They're bloody lethal.'

'Don't s'pose you got one for me, did you?' she ventured.

Leah flashed an insincere smile. 'Sorry.'

'No worries, I'll get my own.'

'Maybe you can get that waiter you were chatting up to bring you one,' Charlie suggested.

Orla crossed one long leg over the other. 'I don't think I'd feel very comfortable ordering him around.'

'Why not?' Charlie said. 'That's his job, isn't it?'

She gave him an arch look. 'Because that waiter happens to be our employer.'

Charlie and Leah looked at her in surprise. 'Mr Fisher?' they said in unison.

Orla nodded smugly.

'You two were chatting for ages,' Charlie said in a faintly envious tone. 'What were you talking about?'

'Nothing much . . . Dante was just asking who I'd come with. Oh, and he said he liked my outfit.'

'I bet he did,' Moon Face said, looking Orla up and down.

'*Dante*, is it?' Leah said mockingly. 'Only a week and you're on first-name terms with the boss already.'

'I'm only following instructions,' Orla said calmly. 'Anyway, I'm off to get that drink. See you in a minute.'

As soon as she was out of earshot, Leah turned to Charlie. 'There's something funny about that girl.'

Charlie frowned. 'How do you mean?'

'I don't know; I can't put my finger on it. I do know one thing, though – I wouldn't trust her as far as I could throw her. I think we should be careful around her in future. For all we know, everything we say is going straight back to Nathan.'

'Who's Nathan?' Moon Face asked.

'The general manager at work. You know, that bloke we're always moaning about.'

'So why would she go telling tales to him?'

'Because she's his sister,' Leah replied.

'Yeah, well, just because Orla's brother's a shit doesn't mean she is too,' Moon Face said. 'She seems nice to me. I reckon you should give her a chance.'

'You're only saying that because you fancy her.'

'He fancies anything with a pulse,' said one of the others, cuffing his friend's head.

Moon Face ducked away. 'Hey, mind the hair.' He turned back to Leah. 'So if you don't like her why did you invite her out tonight?'

'I didn't invite her. Yesterday at work, she came up to me and said she'd heard I had some tickets for the fundraiser. I told her they were all spoken for and that's when she offered to buy one for two hundred quid.'

'Christ,' Moon Face said. 'I bet you bit her hand off.'

Leah grinned. 'Not quite. I told her I wanted three hundred for it.'

'No way!'

'She didn't bat an eye; I should've asked for more.'

'Three hundred quid,' Charlie muttered. 'How can she afford that on her wages?'

'Fuck knows,' Leah said, her face hardening. 'Like I said before, she's a sly one.'

As the evening progressed and the drinks continued to flow, the atmosphere became increasingly high-spirited. At the champagne fountain, several people had dispensed with glasses and were now drinking directly from the gushing spouts, lapping up champagne as if it were water, while others engaged in heavy-duty frottage behind the trees along the boulevard. In keeping with the general mood of decadence, the stage show too was growing more risqué with each act. The band had been followed by can-can dancers and a bikini-clad contortionist – and now the audience was eagerly anticipating the finale.

Nicole had been subdued all evening and now, as the time approached midnight, she decided she'd had enough. 'I think I'll call it a night,' she said to the others. 'I can hardly keep my eyes open.'

'Oh, can't you stay a bit longer?' Yasmin said. 'Go on . . . one more drink.'

Nicole shook her head. 'I'm picking Tilly up from my mum's first thing; I don't want to be hungover. In any case, if I go now, I'll miss the rush for cabs.' She picked up her handbag. 'Sorry I've been such rubbish company. For some reason, I'm just not in the mood tonight.'

'Don't be silly,' Juliet said, embracing her friend. 'It's been lovely to see you. Shall we walk you to the cab rank?'

'No, I'll be fine. You two stay and enjoy the rest of the show. I'll text you when I get home.'

As Nicole slipped away, a drum roll sounded from the wings, heralding the final performance of the evening. All eyes turned to the stage as the red velvet curtain went up. There was a brief moment of confusion when the stage appeared to be empty, but then an over-sized gilded birdcage began a slow descent from the rafters. A gasp went up from the audience as they caught sight of the exotic bird within: a curvaceous, porcelain-skinned beauty who was completely naked, save for a pair of purple fringed knickers, trimmed with a lavish marabou tail and two heart-shaped nipple pasties. As the audience began to applaud wildly, Yasmin leaned towards Juliet. 'Nude ladies don't really do it for me,' she whispered. 'Do you fancy going for a little wander?'

Juliet smiled. 'Sounds good to me.'

Together, they set off on a tour of the room, drinks in hand. While the majority of guests were enjoying the stage show, others were wandering along the boulevard, ensconced in booths or just chatting at the bar. After a few minutes, Yasmin noticed two men, dressed identically in gangster-style double-breasted suits. One was mid-thirties, with dark hair, greying attractively at the temples. The other was a few years younger, but shared the same broad shoulders and patrician nose. They were standing by the French windows, drinks in hand, their eyes fixed firmly on the stage.

'Check out those two,' Yasmin said. 'Pretty hot, huh?'

Juliet followed the other woman's gaze. 'I suppose so,' she said unconvincingly.

'Why don't we go over and introduce ourselves?'

Juliet sighed. 'Must we?'

'Oh, come on, let's be sociable.'

Juliet jerked her thumb towards the stage, where the artiste had now dispensed with her underwear and was writhing inside a giant martini glass. 'Given the competition, I think we might have a job getting their attention.'

'Rubbish,' Yasmin replied, regarding the stripper disdainfully. 'A two-bit tart like that is no match for us. Come on, I've got an idea.'

Without elaborating, she set off towards the men. As Juliet followed reluctantly in her wake, she was surprised to see Yasmin suddenly trip and stagger. As she did so, she flung her arm in the air and tipped up the glass she was carrying, sending a shower of frozen margarita over her chest.

'Shit!' Yasmin cried, surveying her sodden bra top. 'I'm absolutely soaked.' She glanced towards the two men and was pleased to see that the older one was looking towards her, his brow furrowed with concern. 'Have you got a tissue, Juliet?'

Juliet sucked in her cheeks, desperately trying not to laugh at her friend's theatrics. 'Yeah, I think so.' But then, as she flicked the clasp on her handbag, she caught Yasmin's warning look.

'Erm . . . sorry,' she said, snapping the bag shut. 'I seem to have run out.'

The next moment, the older man was stepping forward and offering the cream silk handkerchief from his breast pocket. 'Is this of any use?' he said in a rich baritone.

Yasmin smiled gratefully. 'Oh, that's terribly kind of you – thank you.'

She dabbed at her cleavage with the handkerchief, observing with some satisfaction how the cold liquid had caused her nipples to stiffen. Conscious that both men were now staring at her raptly, she reached into her cleavage and plucked out a shard of ice that was nestling between her breasts. After wiping her damp hand on her thigh, she offered it to the older man. 'Allow me to introduce myself . . . Yasmin O'Brien.'

The man took her hand in a firm grip. 'I'm Adam Glover.' He looked at his companion. 'And this is my brother, Stuart.'

Yasmin turned to the younger man. She was experienced

enough to know when a man was mentally undressing her – and right about now Stuart was removing her sequinned bra with his teeth. 'I can see the family resemblance,' she said, batting her eyelashes flirtatiously. She turned to her friend. 'This is Juliet,' she said.

Juliet smiled hesitantly, but didn't offer her hand. 'Nice to meet you.'

'I was just going to the bar. Can I get you ladies a drink?' Adam said smoothly.

'I'll have a vodka cranberry, thanks,' Yasmin said.

Juliet shook her head. 'Nothing for me. Actually' – she nodded towards the bar – 'I might go and say hi to Dante.'

'Suit yourself,' Yasmin said. 'I'll see you later.'

'Don't do anything I wouldn't,' Juliet murmured as she melted into the crowd.

While Adam was at the bar, Yasmin and Stuart made small talk. Adam, it turned out, lived locally, but Stuart was visiting from London, where he worked as a management consultant for a big City firm. Both were single and had come to the fundraiser with a large group from Adam's football club. When Stuart questioned Yasmin about her own background, she was deliberately vague. Anonymity, she knew from previous experience, was preferable in these sorts of situations. Before Adam had even returned, Yasmin decided to cut to the chase.

'You know what, it's a bit stuffy in here,' she said, batting her hand in front of her face. 'Do you fancy getting a breath of air?'

'Okay,' Stuart said, looking towards the bar. 'But I should let my brother know where we're going.'

Yasmin grabbed his hand, impatient to leave. 'Don't worry about him. We won't be long.'

As they exited the banqueting suite and made their way down the long corridor that led to the exit, Stuart embarked on a tedious monologue about one of the high-profile clients he worked with. Yasmin couldn't help thinking how dull he was. Still, she comforted herself, in a few minutes' time, conversation would be the last thing on his mind. The revolving entrance door was in sight when she made a sudden right turn.

Stuart frowned as Yasmin set off down a second narrower corridor. 'I thought you said you wanted some fresh air.'

'I've changed my mind,' she replied. 'It'll be chilly outside.'

'So where *are* we going?'

'Somewhere nice and private,' she said over her shoulder. 'Where we won't be disturbed.' At the end of the corridor, she turned left, and then left again. 'Nearly there,' she called out as they rounded the final corner.

'You seem to know your way around this place very well,' Stuart remarked.

'Oh yes,' Yasmin replied. 'I've used the club's facilities lots of times.'

A few moments later, she stopped outside a door. 'Here we are,' she said, twisting the brass handle and throwing it open. 'After you.'

Stuart stepped across the threshold. The room lay in semi-darkness, illuminated only by the fingers of watery moonlight that filtered through the Venetian blinds. Yasmin flicked a row of switches on the wall. As the lights came on, Stuart looked around in surprise. The room was a generous size and each of the four walls was painted a different colour. In one corner sat a paddling pool, filled with brightly coloured plastic balls. Next to it was a row of easels and a large, low table, surrounded by miniature chairs. A fairytale castle with two sugar-pink turrets had pride of place atop a vast toy chest, and on the floor beside it, a stuffed Tigger sat astride a wooden trike.

'What *is* this place?' Stuart asked.

Yasmin laughed softly. 'What does it look like?'

'Um, a crèche?'

'Got it in one.'

Stuart scratched his head. 'So what are we doing here?'

'I thought we could get to know each other a little better.' Yasmin walked up to Stuart and pressed the full length of her body against him.

He rubbed his hands together. 'Sounds like an excellent idea.'

Yasmin reached over his shoulder and pushed the light switches. As the room was plunged into shadow once more, she started kissing him. He responded enthusiastically, grinding his crotch against her, while his hands explored her exposed midriff. They kissed for several minutes and then Stuart's hand began working its way past the waistband of Yasmin's sequinned knickers. Suddenly she pulled away from him.

'What's the matter?' he said.

She bit her lip. 'Nothing. I'm just a bit hot, that's all.'

Stuart smirked. 'I'm a bit hot too,' he said, rubbing a hand against the bulge in his trousers. 'Now come back here.' He pulled her towards him and thrust his tongue into her mouth. A moment later, Yasmin pushed her hands against his chest.

'I'm sorry,' she said, backing away from him. 'I can't do this.'

He shook his head, clearly annoyed. 'Then why did you bring me here?' he snapped.

'I'm sorry,' she said again, before she opened the door and escaped into the corridor.

Yasmin's cheeks were burning with embarrassment as she made her way back towards the banqueting suite. She'd had dozens of casual encounters in the past, but for some reason this time it felt all wrong. This wasn't what she wanted any more. Not tonight – or any night.

It was two thirty in the morning by the time the last guest had vacated the banqueting suite. When the lights went up, most of the mixologists downed tools and began making their way to the staff locker room to collect their belongings before heading home. Keen to make a good impression, Dante hung back to clean up the bar area, which looked as if it had been rocked by a small explosion. With a cloth in one hand and a bottle of glass polish in the other, he began wiping down the shelves. A few minutes later, he felt the supervisor's hand on his shoulder.

'Don't worry about that, Dante. The cleaners will take care of it.'

'Are you sure?' he replied. 'I don't mind helping out.'

'No, honestly, you get off – and thanks for all your hard work. I don't know what we'd have done without you.'

Dante pushed his damp hair out of his eyes with the back of his hand. 'Shall I leave my uniform in the locker room?'

The supervisor shook his head. 'Keep it. We've got lots

more functions coming up at the club in the next couple of months . . . that's if you're interested in working with us again.'

Dante grinned. 'You bet I am.'

'Great, I'll be in touch.'

Dante was in a good mood as he collected his bag from the locker room and headed out through the staff entrance at the rear of the building. Outside, the grounds of the golf club lay quiet and still. The towering oaks cast eerie shadows on the lawn, and high above them hundreds of stars shimmered in the inky sky. Dante was whistling softly to himself as he set off along the gravel path that led to the car park. He walked slowly, enjoying the calm after the madness of the fundraiser and the feel of the cool night air on his perspiration-soaked shirt. As the clubhouse's grand terrace came into view, he saw a shadowy figure leaning over the ornate stone balustrade, a cigarette glowing orange between their fingers. At first he thought it must be one of the waiters, but then the figure stepped beneath one of the art deco lampposts and he realized it was Orla.

'Hey,' he called out when he was within hailing distance. 'What are you doing here at this time of night?'

She turned her head, smiling when she saw it was him. 'Just chilling,' she said in a sleepy voice. 'Care to join me?' She took hold of the lamppost with one hand and leaned back like a poledancer, arching her body so her feather headdress almost touched the ground.

Feeling a prick of concern that she was out here alone, Dante went over to the flight of stone steps that led to the terrace. As he drew nearer, he caught the unmistakeable whiff of marijuana.

‘What happened to Leah and the others?’ he asked her.

‘Oh, they left ages ago.’ She walked along the terrace and sat down on the top step. ‘I told them I’d make my own way home.’

‘Where do you live?’ Dante asked as he jogged up the steps towards her.

‘Newman Street. It’s less than a mile away. I’ll walk – it won’t take long.’

‘No you won’t,’ he said firmly. ‘I’ve got the car; I’ll give you a ride.’

She fixed him with her dark eyes. ‘What about Juliet?’

‘She left ages ago. She was going to get a cab with her friends.’

Orla held up the spliff. ‘Do you mind if I finish this first?’

‘Sure, go ahead,’ Dante said, unhooking his bag from his shoulder and sitting down beside her.

She took a deep draw on the spliff, then offered it to him. ‘Want some?’

He took it from her fingers and raised it to his lips. ‘Ahh,’ he said, sighing in pleasure as the smoke hit his lungs. ‘That’s just what I needed.’

She smiled. ‘Tough night was it?’

‘Tough, yeah – but a helluva lotta fun too,’ he replied. ‘And I think they liked me – the supervisor wants me to work for them again.’

‘Wow, Dante, that’s great,’ Orla said, lifting her hand in a high five. ‘Good for you.’

‘Thanks,’ he said, feeling a glow of pride as their palms slapped together. ‘How about you? How was your evening?’

She shrugged. ‘Not bad. I think the others are a bit wary of me, though.’

'You mean Leah and Charlie?'

'Yeah. I suppose I shouldn't really be surprised. I am Nathan's sister, after all, and something tells me my big brother isn't going to win any popularity contests at Ashwicke.'

Dante took another drag on the spliff, then handed it back to Orla. 'Yeah, well, he's a very strange guy, your brother.'

She shrugged her eyebrows. 'So you don't like him either?'

'I didn't say that.'

'You didn't need to.' She drew her fur wrap round her shoulders. 'In any case, you're right – he is a bit of a weirdo. Even I can see that.'

Dante leaned back against one of the stone pillars and closed his eyes. He could feel his body relaxing as the drug took effect. 'Juliet thinks the world of him.'

'They've got a special relationship those two, haven't they?'

'I guess,' Dante said. 'I know Nathan's experience in the hotel trade has been invaluable to Juliet; she's obviously grateful to him.'

Orla gave a little snort. '*Gratitude* – is that what you think it is?'

Dante's eyes snapped open. 'What else would it be?'

She shook her head quickly. 'It's nothing, honestly . . . just me thinking out loud.'

'No, come on, tell me what you're thinking,' Dante demanded.

'Well,' she said slowly. 'I was just wondering if maybe Juliet and my brother might have had a little thing together . . . before *you* came on the scene, obviously.'

Dante stared at her in shock. 'You're kidding?'

'No, I really think there's a good possibility,' she said, passing the spliff back to him. 'I've seen the way they act around each other.'

'What way's that?'

'Like they've got a special bond, something that goes way beyond any professional relationship. Come on, you must've noticed it.'

Dante frowned. 'They're pretty friendly, I guess,' he said. 'But as for getting it on together . . . I can't see it; he's not her type.'

'Maybe not, but perhaps she was feeling vulnerable. She must've had some very low moments after her husband died. Perhaps Nathan was there when she needed a shoulder to cry on.'

'No way,' Dante said. 'If they'd had a fling, Juliet would've told me about it.'

Orla batted her eyelashes. '*Would* she?'

He handed the spliff back to her. 'Yeah . . . at least I think she would.'

'But if she told you she'd have to sack Nathan.' She lifted the spliff to her mouth. 'And maybe she likes having him around.'

Dante felt the bile rise in his mouth. The idea of Juliet having an affair with Nathan made him sick to his stomach. 'Has Nathan said something to you about this – anything, even a hint?'

'God no,' she said. 'Nathan and I don't have that sort of a relationship. He's a closed book when it comes to his emotions. In any case, he's very professional. If they did have an affair, I'm quite sure he wouldn't want it to get in the way of his career. He loves working at Ashwicke; he'd be devastated if he ever had to leave.' She held what was left of the spliff out to him. 'Do you want to finish this off?'

He took a final drag and flicked the butt into the bushes. 'Come on, let's get going.'

Dante's head was spinning as he set off down the golf club's shrub-lined drive – not just because of the spliff, but because of the idea Orla had planted in his head. The thought of Nathan touching Juliet's naked flesh was almost too much to bear.

They didn't speak much in the car. When they stopped at the traffic lights on the high street, Dante turned to Orla. Her eyes were half closed and she was slouched low in the seat, her feather headdress now lying at a strange lopsided angle.

'What number Newman Street?' he asked her.

'Forty-two,' she mumbled.

A couple of minutes later, he felt her head lolling against his shoulder. He could smell her apple-scented shampoo and feel her soft hair brushing against his jaw. He didn't try to wake her.

Soon, he was pulling up outside a handsome Victorian building with decorative shingles and a stained-glass panel above the door. 'Hey,' he said, giving Orla a gentle nudge. 'We're here.'

She stirred and twisted her face so that she was looking up at him. 'Sorry,' she said. 'I didn't mean to fall asleep on you.'

'That's okay,' he said. Her chin was still on his shoulder. Their faces were inches apart. He could see a faint scattering of freckles across the bridge of her nose and the tiny scar above her left eyebrow.

She pulled back from him, as if she were embarrassed.

'Your place looks pretty nice,' he said as she fumbled with her seatbelt.

'Yeah, it's not bad.'

'I've heard rentals in Loxwood are expensive.'

'They're bloody extortionate. Nathan found this place for me. He's subsidising my rent too, just till I get my first pay packet.'

'That's kind of him,' Dante said flatly.

She smiled. 'See, he's not all bad.'

She opened the car door and climbed out. 'Well, thanks for the lift. I guess I'll see you at work on Monday.'

'Yep, I guess you will.'

She went to slam the door, but at the last minute she caught it and stuck her head back inside the car. 'I've got a bottle of Glenmorangie indoors. I might have a quick nightcap before I turn in. You're welcome to join me.'

Dante shook his head. 'Thanks for the offer, but I'd better get home. It's been a long night.'

'Of course. Sorry, I forgot you've been working like a dog all evening. It was silly of me to even suggest it. Oh, and listen – that stuff I said earlier, about Juliet and Nathan . . .' She licked her lips. 'Just forget it, okay? I always talk shit when I'm stoned.'

A moment later, she was slamming the car door and walking unsteadily up the path that led to her house. Dante watched her, waiting until she was safely inside. It was only when he got home that he realized she'd left her fur wrap behind.

*

On the other side of Loxwood, Nicole was staring at the shadows on her bedroom ceiling. Usually she sank into an exhausted sleep the minute her head hit the pillow, but she'd lain in bed for two hours now, tossing and turning. Sighing, she shucked off the duvet and swung her legs over the side of the bed, pushing her feet into the shabby sheepskin-lined slippers that Connor was forever threatening to chuck into the bin. A hot, milky drink. That should do the trick, she told herself.

Downstairs in the kitchen, she made herself a mug of hot chocolate, adding a forbidden squirt of aerosol cream. Then she wandered from room to room, the mug pressed to her chest, so she could feel its comforting warmth. It felt strange being alone in the house and not altogether pleasant. Drawn by some invisible thread, Nicole found herself pushing open the door of her husband's tiny home office. It was somewhere she rarely ventured, and a place where, just lately, Connor had been spending increasing amounts of time. Now, as she sat in his executive chair, looking at all his things neatly lined up on the desk, Nicole found herself wondering precisely how and when they'd managed to grow so far apart. All at once she heard a beep emanating from the depths of the desk. Frowning, she tried the drawer, but it was locked – an indication, no doubt, that it held confidential paperwork Connor wanted to keep away from their cleaner's prying eyes. She scanned his desk, looking for the key, and eventually found it nestling beside some paper clips in the antique ink well she'd bought him for Christmas.

The drawer unlocked, she discovered that the beep had

come from Connor's mobile phone. Nicole smiled: so he wasn't ignoring her; he'd just forgotten to take his phone to Cardiff. She glanced at the screen: nine missed calls, eight of them from her. She'd better check who the other caller was, just in case it was something urgent. Then she could phone her husband at the hotel first thing and let him know.

Connor had recently upgraded his phone and Nicole wasn't familiar with all its functions. As she pressed keys at random, a photo of Tilly popped up. Nicole smiled. It had been taken hours after their daughter was born: she looked tiny and so cute in her white cotton sleepsuit. Eager to see what other photos Connor had saved, she began scrolling through them. There was one of her in her dressing gown, wrapping up presents on Christmas Eve, and a picture her mother had taken of all three of them in the park. Suddenly an image Nicole had never seen before appeared on the screen: two people dressed in animal costumes, a fox and a rabbit. The fox was holding the phone at arm's length in order to take the picture. Nicole was nonplussed. She and Connor hadn't attended any fancy-dress parties recently. She pressed the key again. The next photo made her cry out in shock. It had clearly been taken in some sort of woodland. A mouse – or rather a person dressed as a mouse – was on its knees. In the creature's mouth was an erect penis. Its owner's face was out of shot but the matted reddish fur at the base of the erect appendage suggested it was the fox.

Nicole swallowed hard. She felt as if she had a stone inside her stomach. It was hard and unyielding and it made her feel quite nauseous. Despite this, she forced herself to scroll through another half dozen similar images. When the picture show was over, she knew exactly what she had to do.

20

Connor was whistling softly as he prepared for his morning surgery. It was a week since the doctor had returned from Cardiff and he was in a good mood. At lunchtime, he was meeting Zoe. She'd told him to bring his stethoscope and a pair of latex gloves, so he could well imagine what the filthy minx had in mind. He glanced at the wall clock: eight fifteen. His first patient would be arriving soon. He had just started to clear his desk of paperwork when he heard a loud shriek. Frowning, he turned his head towards the open door. 'Carol, is everything all right?' he called out.

The receptionist didn't answer straight away. A moment later she appeared at the door. She looked rather flushed and she was holding a copy of the *Loxwood Weekly Chronicle*. A copy was delivered to the surgery for the waiting room every week, together with a selection of women's magazines. 'There's something in here I think you ought to see,' she said.

Connor took the newspaper from her outstretched hand. 'What is it?'

Carol stared at the floor. 'Page ten,' she said. Then, without elaborating further, she turned and hurried away.

Connor spread the newspaper out on his desk. The *Chronicle* rarely contained anything to interest him. Its news stories generally focused on mundane local concerns, like road closures or the length of the queue at the post office.

He turned to page ten. The main story was about a wheelie bin being set on fire. He scratched his nose. Surely this couldn't be what had made Carol cry out in shock. Then his eye alighted on the gossip column on the right-hand side of the page. Penned by an anonymous source, it usually contained items about fly-tipping and local councillors receiving back-handers, the perpetrators' identities only thinly veiled. This week's lead item was rather more titillating.

FUR BETTER OR WORSE

Forget dogging and swinging – a new sex craze called 'furring' is sweeping Loxwood. The bizarre practice sees participants – known as 'furverts' – don animal costumes and meet in woodlands for . . . well, you can probably guess the rest. Mrs Jayne Crisp, owner of the Make Believe fancy-dress hire shop in Henley Street admitted: 'I do wonder where my costumes go sometimes. Some of the fur suits come back in a terrible state, covered in mud and leaves. The seams are often ripped too.'

The *Chronicle* has it on very good authority that a certain local GP is an ardent fan of furring. What's more, the married father-of-one, who opened a swanky new surgery in the town centre five months ago, doesn't go on his nocturnal adventures alone. His partner in crime just happens to be one of his patients. The pair also spent last weekend together at a hotel in Cardiff. Something tells us they weren't just checking each other's blood pressure.

By the time he'd finished reading, Connor was hot with horror. He hadn't been named, but the clues were there. Anyone with half a brain would be able to work out he was the GP in question. He reached for the phone; his lunch date with Zoe would have to wait. He had much more pressing matters to attend to.

The doctor's heart was in his mouth as he drove the short distance home. He'd asked Carol to reschedule his patients. She hadn't asked him why; the answer was obvious.

He found Nicole sitting at the kitchen table, spooning something brown and mushy into Tilly's eager mouth.

'Hello,' she said as he came in through the back door. 'Did you forget something?'

Connor began to breathe a little more easily. It looked as if the paper boy hadn't arrived with their copy of the *Chronicle*. Nicole would find out about the story eventually, but at least he would be able to forewarn her and quite possibly talk his way out of it.

'Erm, yeah . . . I mean, no,' he said.

Nicole stared at him. Her expression was blank. 'Which one is it?'

'It's *no*. I came back because there was something I wanted to talk to you about.'

'Oh? It must be urgent if you've abandoned your patients.'

'It is.' Connor took a seat at the table. 'The thing is, Nicole . . .' He ran a hand through his hair as he struggled to find the words. 'I've done something rather stupid.'

'I know,' Nicole said, wiping Tilly's mouth with the corner of her bib.

Connor's Adam's apple bobbed up and down. 'You do?'

She reached under the highchair and pulled out a copy of the *Chronicle*.

His heart sank. 'Nic, listen, I can explain.' He reached out to her, but she ducked her head away from his hand.

'I'm listening.' Her tone was icy.

Connor took a deep breath and launched into the defence he'd hastily concocted in the car. 'It's lies, all of it,' he told her. 'A lot of people in Loxwood are jealous of my success. Somebody's obviously gone to the paper with a frankly ludicrous story about me, and the *Chronicle* has lapped it up without bothering to check the facts. I'm going to sue them for libel; they haven't got a shred of evidence.'

'Oh yes, they have.'

Connor blinked hard. 'What?'

'Photographs, receipts, mobile-phone bills . . . I think you'll find the editor of the *Chronicle* has quite a damning dossier in his possession. You can sue them if you like, but in the face of such overwhelming evidence I doubt you'd even find a lawyer willing to represent you.'

Connor felt the blood drain out of his face. 'What photographs?'

'Why, the ones on your phone, darling,' said Nicole, shuddering as she recalled a particularly explicit image which showed Connor in his fox costume mounting an unusually submissive squirrel.

The doctor cleared his throat, all the while frantically trying to recall the pictures he'd been stupid enough to store on his mobile. He was quite certain he'd been wearing his fox head in all of them. 'Christ, Nicole, you don't think that was me, do you?' he said, trying to sound shocked. 'A friend of mine's into this furring lark and he emailed those pictures to me for a laugh.'

Nicole sighed. 'Save your breath, Connor. I know it was you. You'd taken off one of your gloves in that last picture – you know . . . the one of you masturbating as you watched those two rabbits getting it on.'

'So?' Connor said defensively. 'What makes you think that was me?'

Another sigh. 'Your scar, Connor. I'd recognize it anywhere.'

With a sickening sense of dread, Connor looked down at his right hand, which bore a livid scar at the base of the thumb – the legacy of a drunken med-school accident. He licked his lips nervously, knowing the game was well and truly up. 'How did the *Chronicle* get the pictures?'

'From me,' Nicole said. 'I thought they'd be interested to see what Loxwood's hardest-working GP gets up to in his spare time. I also sent them a copy of your credit-card statement and a load of receipts I found stuffed in your jacket pocket.' She raised an eyebrow. 'You really pushed the boat out for that little slut in Cardiff, didn't you? Business class flights, romantic dinners for two, bottles of Château Lafite. You were even stupid enough to book the hotel in your real names.' She sighed. 'Zoe Tripp, eh? Let's hope her husband doesn't find out. I've heard he does boxing in his spare time.'

Connor stared at her in disbelief. 'So this is all your doing?' he said, jabbing a finger at the paper, as he struggled to keep his mounting anger under control.

Nicole nodded. 'In a few hours' time, the whole town is going to know exactly what you are.'

Connor buried his face in his hands. 'How could you do it, Nicole? How could you humiliate me like this?'

Nicole regarded him contemptuously. 'Because I've had enough of playing second fiddle,' she said. 'All those times you said you were working late, you were with her, weren't you?'

Connor didn't answer. 'I could get struck off for this, you know,' he snapped. 'And then we'd lose everything – the house, the car, the holidays in the south of France.'

'I don't give a shit about any of those things!' Nicole cried. 'I just want to be with someone who loves me.' She reached out to Tilly, who was gurgling contentedly, seeming unaware of her parents' disharmony. 'We both do.'

'But I do love you,' Connor said in a wheedling tone. 'Desperately. I know I've been a bad boy and I'm sorry. Zoe was just a fling; she doesn't mean anything to me. You're the only woman for me – you know that.'

'It's too late,' Nicole said, praying her voice wouldn't break. 'I want a divorce.'

'No!' Connor shouted, his face crumpling. 'Listen, I know I've messed up, but you've got to give me another chance. I won't let you down again, I promise.'

'Sorry, Connor, I've made my mind up.'

'But this is crazy. I know you want to punish me – and God knows I deserve it – but we can work through this, I know we can.'

Nicole thrust her jaw out defiantly. 'I'm not going to change my mind. I've already instructed a lawyer. You'll be hearing from him shortly.'

At this, Connor dropped to his knees in front of her, hands clasped together as if he were praying. 'Please,

Nicole, you can't be serious. I'll only believe you if you say you don't love me.'

Nicole looked him in the eye. 'I don't love you,' she said calmly. She stood up and walked out of the room. When she returned, she was carrying a small suitcase. 'I've packed some things for you,' she said. 'Just the basics: a few changes of clothes, toiletries and so on. You can collect the rest of your stuff later.'

'But where am I supposed to go?' Connor wailed.

'I don't know – a friend's house, a hotel, *her* place.' Nicole carried the suitcase to the back door. 'I'd like you to leave now.'

'You cow. You bloody conniving cow!' Connor exploded as he marched over to the door. 'If you think I'm just going to roll over while you screw me for every penny I've got, you've got another thing coming.'

'Goodbye, Connor,' Nicole said as she opened the door.

Connor's face twisted into an ugly grimace. 'You're going to regret this,' he said as he stormed out of the house, almost knocking her over in the process.

When he was gone, Nicole went back into the kitchen and lifted Tilly from her high chair. 'It's just you and me now,' she whispered as she hugged her daughter tightly. 'Just you and me.'

By the time Yasmin arrived at Nicole's cottage, dusk was falling. There was still light in the sky but it was the grey, dispirited kind that was worse than darkness.

'Sorry I'm late, Nic,' Yasmin said, following her friend into the living room. 'The picture editor pounced just as I was putting my coat on. He insisted on showing me some pap shots of a guy that used to be in a two-bob boy band, like, a hundred years ago. Then when I finally managed to get away the traffic on the bypass was terrible.'

'There's no need to apologize,' Nicole replied as she sank onto the sofa and reached for the bottle of chilled Chablis that she'd been looking forward to all day. 'I'm just glad you could come at all. I didn't fancy being on my own this evening.'

'I don't blame you,' Yasmin said as she accepted a glass of wine. 'I can't believe you've thrown Connor out. What happened, exactly? Your text didn't give much away.'

Nicole picked up the latest edition of the *Loxwood Weekly Chronicle* that was lying on the floor, open to page ten. 'Check this out,' she said, handing it to Yasmin. '*Fur better or worse*.'

Yasmin's eyes grew big as dinner plates as she read the story. 'Shit, this is Connor, isn't it?'

'Yep,' said Nicole. 'My first foray into the world of journalism – and I must say, I'm feeling rather pleased with myself.'

Yasmin did a double take. 'You mean, *you* tipped the *Chron* off?'

Nicole nodded. 'I wondered about coming to you with it, but I didn't think a big paper like the *Sunday Post* would be interested in the antics of a small-town GP.'

Yasmin's stunned gaze returned to the paper. 'So all this is true?'

'Yes,' Nicole said sadly. 'Unfortunately it is.'

'Oh my God,' Yasmin said, clapping a horrified hand to her mouth. 'How on earth did you find out?'

'It wasn't very difficult,' Nicole said. Taking a deep breath, she described the incriminating photos she'd found on Connor's mobile phone. 'They more or less proved he was being unfaithful,' she went on. 'So I decided to dig a bit deeper. When Connor came back from Cardiff, I went through his jacket pockets and found a whole bunch of receipts – stuff that proved he wasn't staying in that hotel alone. Then I dug out his old mobile-phone bills. When I looked through them, one number kept coming up time and time again. He was calling it every day, several times a day sometimes. When I dialled the number, I got an answer-phone. I recognized the voice – it was the same woman who'd picked up the phone that time I tried to call Connor's hotel room.'

'Christ,' Yasmin muttered. 'Connor, a furvert . . . who would've guessed?' Suddenly, she sat bolt upright. 'Hang on a minute . . . That night you went badger watching with Bear and you saw those people shagging in the woods. You don't think . . .'

'Yes,' said Nicole. 'It was Connor; I'm sure of it.'

Yasmin took a gulp of wine. 'Did he only realize he'd been rumbled when he read the story in the paper?'

'Yep.' Nicole gave a triumphant smile. 'And once word gets around he'll be a laughing stock.'

Yasmin frowned. 'Listen, Nic, I don't blame you for giving Connor his marching orders, but why did you go public? Wouldn't it have been easier just to confront him with the evidence?'

Nicole's jaw tensed. 'I wanted to hurt him the way he's hurt me. If those phone bills are anything to go by, this affair's being going on for months. Meanwhile, I've been stuck at home, raising our daughter and trying to be the perfect supportive wife.' She gave a bitter laugh. 'No wonder he'd gone off sex with me when he had that little slut on speed dial.'

'Do you know who she is?'

'Her name's Zoe Tripp.' Nicole gave a hard sniff. 'She's married too.'

Yasmin touched her friend's arm. 'I'm so sorry, Nic, I really am. You must be devastated.'

'Well, you know, that's the funny thing . . . I'm not really.' Nicole gave a great sigh. 'I've been deluding myself for quite a long time. The truth is Connor and I were having problems even before Tilly was born.'

'You always seemed happy enough to me.'

'I suppose I just became adept at ignoring the signs, but now that I look back they were there all along.'

'All those late nights at the surgery and weekend working, eh?'

Nicole nodded. 'He was always going out on random errands too: nipping to the shops for chocolate and then not bothering to eat it, driving to the garage to check his tyre pressure, always with his mobile of course. And then, when he came back, he'd have a spring in his step and his eyes would be shining. I know now he was calling *her*.'

'So what's next?'

'I've already consulted a lawyer. She's started divorce proceedings.'

Yasmin sighed. 'Oh, Nic, are you sure this is what you want?'

'Quite sure. Connor was making me unhappy and I'm convinced the feeling was mutual. He may be pissed off with me now, but he'll thank me in the long run.'

'Well, I think you've made a very brave decision,' said Yasmin. 'And you do know that, whatever happens, I'm always here for you.'

Nicole blinked hard as tears sprang to her eyes. 'I know, but it's good to hear you say it anyway.'

'Have you told Juliet?'

'Not yet. I feel a bit awkward about telling her; you know how big she is on the sanctity of marriage.'

'She can afford to be,' Yasmin said. 'She found a wonderful husband in Gus, and now she's been lucky enough to fall in love again. I really hope she and Dante make a go of things – he seems like such a lovely man.'

'I'm sure they will.' Nicole picked up the Chablis and refilled Yasmin's glass. 'Now all we need to do is find a nice boyfriend for you. I know you keep saying you don't need a man, but one day you're going to fall in love when you least expect it, I just know it.'

'Hmm,' Yasmin mumbled. 'I think it might be a bit late for that.'

'Oh, don't be ridiculous. You're barely thirty; you've got all the time in the world.'

'Yeah, but I don't think anybody's going to be interested in me now . . . not in my condition.'

Nicole helped herself to more wine. 'You just need to cut back your working hours and get out a bit more. Have you thought about joining one of those internet dating sites?'

Yasmin raised an eyebrow. 'Did you hear what I just said?'

'Yes, you said no one's going to be interested in you in your cond–' Suddenly, Nicole's expression froze. 'You're not . . .'

Yasmin nodded. 'I did a test last night. It was positive.'

'You're pregnant?' Nicole said in a shocked tone.

'Yep.'

'But . . . but I thought you were on the Pill,' Nicole stuttered.

'I stopped taking it last month. It was making me put on weight.'

'And you didn't think to use a condom?'

'It was one of those stupid spur-of-the-moment things; neither of us had a condom. I'd only come off the Pill a couple of days earlier; I thought I'd be okay.'

'Oh, Yasmin, you of all people should know better than that.'

Yasmin sighed. 'You'd think so, wouldn't you?'

'So whose is it? I didn't even know you were seeing anyone.'

'I'm not. It's Rob . . . that guy at work. We had a one-night stand a few weeks back.'

Nicole frowned. 'But I thought you couldn't stand the sight of each other.'

Yasmin smiled sadly. 'You know what they say about there being a thin line between love and hate.'

'And it's definitely his?'

Yasmin nodded. 'I've done the maths.'

'Does he know?'

'Uh-uh, and I'm not planning on telling him. I don't want him trying to talk me out of it.'

'Out of having an abortion?'

Yasmin didn't answer. Instead, her hand went to her belly. At this early stage in the pregnancy, her stomach was still flat, but now, as she stroked it, she could visualize the clump of cells that was growing and dividing inside of her.

Nicole gasped. 'You're keeping it?'

'Yes,' Yasmin replied. 'I think I am.'

For a moment Nicole was so taken aback that all she could do was stare. Then she reached out and snatched Yasmin's wine glass out of her hand. 'In that case, you shouldn't be drinking.' She shook her head, still struggling to digest the news. 'I didn't think you wanted kids.'

'I didn't think I did either, but now that I'm actually pregnant . . .' Yasmin frowned. 'I just can't imagine getting rid of it.'

'But how will you manage? What about your career?'

Yasmin shrugged. 'The two things aren't mutually exclusive; plenty of women manage to juggle work and motherhood.' She lay back against the sofa cushions and sighed contentedly. It was as if something tight and clenched had unfurled within her, like the petals of a flower stretching out into the light. 'You know what, Nic. I think this might turn out to be the best thing that's ever happened to me.'

21

'Honestly, darling,' Juliet said, as she drizzled garlic-infused olive oil on her rocket salad. 'Thanks for the offer, but I'll be fine on my own.'

'I know you will,' Dante replied. 'I just thought you could use some moral support.'

Juliet regarded him from under her eyelashes. 'The meeting's going to be very dull,' she said. 'And actually I think I'd prefer to face the bank alone. If you were there, I'd probably get all flustered and tongue-tied.'

Dante's nostrils flared, not so much in anger as in exasperation. 'Suit yourself.'

It was Friday afternoon and the Fishers were having lunch at Gaston's. In just over half an hour, Juliet was meeting with her bank manager to discuss the possibility of getting a new loan to cover the cost of repairs to the roof, as well as an overhaul of Ashwicke's ancient plumbing. Dante had assumed he would be accompanying his wife. Evidently he was wrong.

'What are *you* going to do this afternoon?' she asked him.

Dante chased a sundried tomato half-heartedly round his plate. 'I think I'll take a nap. I'm feeling pretty tired.'

'I'm not surprised,' Juliet remarked. 'What time did you get back last night?'

'Three thirty.' Dante smiled as he recalled the ruby wedding anniversary celebrations the golf club had hosted in one of its more modest function suites. 'It was a great night,' he said. 'The supervisor even let me design a special cocktail for the occasion. Oh, and he's asked me to work next Saturday. That's okay, isn't it?'

Juliet looked put out. 'I feel as if I've hardly seen you this past week,' she said. 'Can't you find a job with more social hours?'

'But I like working at the club,' Dante replied. 'The money's good too.'

Juliet said nothing, just shook her head sadly.

'You knew I was a bartender when you married me,' Dante snapped, annoyed at her reaction. 'What did you expect?'

Juliet's eyes flitted around the packed restaurant. 'Let's not have an argument in here, all right?'

Dante drove his fork through the sundried tomato. 'Who's arguing?'

They ate the rest of their lunch in silence. Dante felt as if there were a gaping chasm between them. Ever since his conversation with Orla at the fundraiser, nearly two weeks earlier, he'd been torturing himself with thoughts of Juliet and Nathan together. The more he thought about it, the more it made sense. If the pair had once been lovers, it would certainly explain why Juliet was always so quick to spring to Nathan's defence – not to mention the general air of smugness the general manager exuded in his presence. Dante was also starting to see Nathan's attempt to publicly humiliate him at the Best Dressed Pet competition in a whole new light. Originally, he'd assumed the manager – resentful that another man had usurped his position as top dog at Ashwicke – had been displaying some sort of warped territorial instinct. But now he realized it could just as easily have been the act of a jealous lover. Perhaps, Dante hypothesized, Nathan had been hoping his affair with Juliet would develop into something more – that he would be elevated from his position as chief flunky to lord of the manor. And then Juliet had returned from Aspen with Dante in tow, and his little fantasy had been shattered. No wonder the manager didn't like him.

The one thing Dante couldn't understand was what Nathan was still doing at Ashwicke. Why on earth would Juliet deliberately keep her husband and her former lover in such close proximity? Surely the sensible thing to do would have been to let Nathan go the minute she returned from Aspen – albeit, Dante reflected savagely, with a generous severance deal for services rendered. And then, as he worked things through in his mind, he realized there *was* one explanation: that Juliet's affair with Nathan had never ended and was continuing even now, right under his nose. With some difficulty, he pushed the thought to the back of his mind. It was too repulsive to even contemplate.

When the bill came, Dante insisted on paying, using his wages from the night before. It gave him a certain sense of satisfaction, knowing he was looking after Juliet, even in such a small and insignificant way. He was also acutely aware that Gus was the sort of man who would always have picked up the tab – no matter what the cost. As the couple left Gaston's and prepared to part company, Juliet offered him the keys to the Land Rover. 'Why don't you take the car?' she said. 'I can get a cab.'

'No, you have it,' he insisted. 'I've got a bit of a headache; the fresh air will do me good.'

As Juliet turned to go, Dante touched her shoulder. 'Aren't you forgetting something?' he said, tapping his lips with a forefinger.

Smiling, Juliet stood on tiptoes and gave him a kiss. As their lips brushed, Dante felt a jolt of electricity. Even after three months of marriage, she still had that effect on him.

Dante took his time walking home. It had been raining earlier and a soft, damp breeze, smelling of honeysuckle and freshly mown grass, was blowing through the trees. When he turned into the driveway, still deep in thought, he noticed Nathan standing at the open door of the lodge. He was leaning against the lintel smoking a cigarette as he stared out across the lawn. Dante continued walking, head bowed, acting as if he hadn't seen the other man but, as he drew level with the lodge, Nathan called out to him.

'Good afternoon, Mr Fisher,' he said with a faux deference that made Dante want to punch him in the kidneys.

'Afternoon,' Dante replied gruffly.

'Isn't Mrs Fisher with you?'

Dante stopped and turned his head towards Nathan. 'I thought it was your day off,' he said accusingly.

'It is.'

'In that case, why do you give a shit *where* she is?'

Nathan stubbed out his cigarette on the wall, but his fish-like eyes never left Dante's. 'I wanted to let her know that the garden centre dropped off some compost for the vegetable patch,' he said tonelessly. 'I noticed the pair of you going out in the car earlier, so when I saw the delivery van I intercepted it.'

Dante flashed him an insincere smile. 'How very thoughtful of you.'

Nathan reached into the pocket of his jeans and produced a crumpled piece of paper. 'Here's the delivery docket. Perhaps you could give it to Mrs Fisher and let her know that her compost is behind the greenhouse.'

'Fine,' Dante replied, snatching the paperwork out of his hand.

'When do you think she might be back?' Nathan persisted.

'I've no idea; she's got a meeting at the bank. Why do you want to know?'

Nathan's mouth twitched. 'No particular reason.'

'I had a headache, so I came back early,' Dante added, not wanting him to know the real reason he wasn't at the bank with Juliet. 'I'm going upstairs to take a nap.'

'Oh dear,' the manager said unconvincingly. 'I hope you're feeling better soon.'

Dante looked at Nathan, trying to see him objectively, as a woman might. He was handsome in a saturnine sort of way, with a good physique. Plenty of females would doubtless find him attractive. Sighing, he set off towards the house.

The minute Dante was out of earshot, Nathan went into the lodge and picked up the phone. He punched in a number, tapping his foot impatiently as he listened to the ring tone. Finally, Orla picked up.

'Hi, Nathan,' she said. 'What's up?'

'We're good to go,' the manager replied tersely. 'He'll be back at the house in three minutes and he's heading straight upstairs. You know what to do, don't you?'

'Yeah, yeah, don't worry.'

'And don't forget to call me as soon as it's over. I want to know every gory detail.'

Orla laughed softly. 'You're one twisted fucker, do you know that?'

'Just get on with it,' Nathan hissed. He put down the receiver without waiting for her reply.

Dante pushed open the front door. Beyond it, the house lay quiet as a tomb. Only one of the guest bedrooms was occupied – by a pair of middle-aged ramblers, whose packed itinerary meant they were rarely at the hotel during daylight hours. As he pulled off his sweater, Jess came bounding along the corridor to greet him.

'Hello, girl,' he said, smiling as she pushed her muzzle against his thigh. It was nice to have some company, even if it were only of the canine variety. He made a fuss of her for several minutes, then gently extricated himself and walked towards the staircase. The pointer stared after him dolefully. She knew she wasn't allowed upstairs.

'Sorry, dog,' Dante called out as he reached the half-landing. 'I gotta lie down.'

At this, Jess collapsed onto her belly and rested her head on the bottom step. However long it took, she would wait.

As Dante entered the master bedroom, a familiar perfume greeted his nostrils: orange blossom . . . from Juliet's favourite Jo Malone bubble bath. Thinking little of it, he stooped down and began unlacing his trainers. A split second later, a long, contented sigh came from the direction of the en suite. Frowning, Dante looked towards the source of the sound. The bathroom door was fractionally ajar. He stood up and walked slowly across the room.

Whatever he'd been expecting to see, it certainly wasn't this. Orla was lying in the bath. She had her eyes closed and her head was resting on Juliet's inflatable cushion. Her long hair was floating loose around her shoulders and her bare breasts with their dark nipples were clearly visible above the foaming water. On the bathmat lay her chambermaid's black dress, together with a chocolate lace bra and matching G-string. It made an arresting – not to mention intensely erotic – tableau. For a few seconds, Dante stared at her appreciatively. Then he collected himself. 'Jesus, Orla, what do you think you're doing?'

Her eyes flew open. 'Shit!' she said, gripping the sides of the bath. 'I thought I had the place to myself.'

Dante folded his arms across his chest. 'And do you always make yourself at home like this when we're out?'

'No, of course not,' she said guiltily, sinking deeper into the water so the bubbles came right up to her chin. 'The boiler in my flat's packed up and the engineer can't come till tomorrow. I've been having freezing showers for the past two days. So . . .' She licked her lips nervously. 'When I saw you and Juliet go out, I thought I'd have a quick bath after I'd finished my cleaning.'

Dante looked at his watch pointedly. 'A *quick* bath? Your shift ended over an hour ago.'

'Yeah, well, I guess I was enjoying myself too much. This bubble bath's gorgeous. I only used a tiny bit, mind.' Suddenly her face clouded over. 'Is Juliet with you?'

'No, she's got a meeting in town. She won't be back for a while.'

Orla sighed. 'Thank God for that. She'd probably sack me for this.' She winced. 'You're not going to tell her, are you?'

Dante shook his head. 'No, don't worry.' He half turned, suddenly embarrassed at being in the same room as a naked woman who wasn't his wife. 'I'll leave you to it, but don't be too long, okay?'

'Sure. Thanks, Dante, I really appreciate it. Oh, and before you go . . .' She pointed to the tall shelf unit in the corner of the room. 'Do me a favour and pass me one of those towels, will you?'

As he reached for a towel, Dante gave a giant yawn. ''Scuse me,' he said, covering his mouth with the back of his hand. 'I was working late at the golf club last night.'

'So they hired you again,' Orla said. 'That's great news.'

'Yeah, but it's playing havoc with my body clock.' Dante frowned, aware that the dull throbbing in his temple was increasing in intensity. 'I've got a killer headache too. I need to lie down.' He dropped the towel on the bathmat beside Orla's clothes. 'I'll go to one of the guest rooms, so you can have some privacy.'

'There's no need for that,' Orla said, her voice soft with concern. 'Just give me two ticks and I'll be out of your way.'

Back in the bedroom, Dante kicked off his trainers and went over to the window. He could see the lodge in the distance, but there was no sign of Nathan. Remembering their earlier encounter, Dante's jaw tensed. The guy was such an idiot. Not like his sister – it was hard to believe they were related. Orla was a nice girl; he didn't mind helping her out. He pulled the curtains together and went over to the bed. The pillow felt blissfully cool beneath his cheek. He closed his eyes and tried to relax, but the jackhammer in his head wouldn't let up.

A few minutes later he heard footsteps padding across the bedroom floor and then the mattress dipped. Dante rolled onto his back and opened one eye. Orla was sitting next to him. She was wrapped in a towel that barely covered her thighs. Her dress and underwear were draped across her arm.

'How's that headache?' she asked him.

He blinked a few times. 'Um, it feels like it's getting worse.'

'Poor Dante,' she murmured, as she let her clothes slide to the floor. 'Would you like me to give you an Indian head massage? I learned how to do them when I was in Goa last year.'

He lifted a leaden arm and batted his hand at her. 'Don't worry, I'll be fine.'

'Why don't you just let me try?' she said, shifting her weight and giving him a glimpse of the inviting valley between her breasts.

Ignoring his weak protestations, she leaned over him and placed the fingertips of both hands on his head, rotating them in a gentle circular motion.

'Close your eyes,' she whispered, as her hands moved deftly across his scalp. 'Try to relax.'

Sighing, Dante did as he was told. Orla clearly knew what she was doing because after only a few minutes he felt the pain start to recede.

'That feels good,' he said.

She didn't say anything but he heard her breath quicken.

A minute or so later, her soothing hands moved to his forehead as she gently drew her fingers along his brow line.

'Man,' Dante moaned. 'You should do this for a living.'

A moment later, he felt an altogether different sensation on his skin. Startled, he opened his eyes to find Orla planting soft kisses on his forehead.

'What are you doing?' he said, twisting his head away.

She looked at him with a wounded expression. 'What's the matter? Don't you like it?'

'It's not that.'

'So what is it?'

'I'm married, Orla,' he said, pushing himself up onto his elbows. 'We shouldn't be here, alone like this. Why don't you go back into the bathroom and put your clothes on and we'll forget this ever happened.'

'Is that what you want?' she said huskily. 'Is that what you really want?'

As she spoke, she reached up and tugged at her towel. It fell away from her body and then there she was, kneeling on the bed beside him, naked as the day she was born.

Even though the room was dark, Dante could see what a good body she had, her slender torso only accentuated by the full, high breasts and rounded hips. He opened his mouth to give a reply, but no words came out. His brain was saying *no*, but his rapidly stiffening cock was saying *yes*.

Sensing his hesitation, she picked up his hand and placed it on her breast.

'No,' he said weakly. But his hand didn't move.

The next moment, her lips were on his and her tongue was insinuating its way into his mouth. For a fraction of a second, Dante felt himself responding. It was the only encouragement Orla needed. The next moment, her hand was reaching between his legs. As she fumbled with his zipper, a plaintive howl rang out in the distance. It was unmistakeably Jess, who was still standing guard at the foot of the stairs. The sound brought Dante back to his senses. His hand fell from her breast.

'Stop,' he said, pulling away from her.

She drew in her breath, as if she were cross with him, but when she spoke her tone was mellifluous. 'Don't worry, we've got the house to ourselves.' She ran her hand over his crotch. 'No one's going to know.'

He grabbed her wrist. 'I said *stop*.'

She looked at him. There was something in her expression he didn't know how to read. Then she gave an insolent little shrug.

'I thought you liked me,' she said, rolling off the bed and reaching for her dress.

'I do like you, Orla, but not in that way.'

'Whatever,' she said, pulling the dress over her head. She picked up her underwear and began walking towards the door. 'I'll see myself out,' she said. She didn't look back.

For a few moments, Dante sat on the edge of the bed in a daze, scarcely able to believe what had just occurred. It would've been easy to sleep with Orla . . . very easy. But he couldn't do that to Juliet. He loved his wife; he'd given up everything to be with her. He hoped she felt the same way about him – but even if she *was* still sleeping with Nathan, he told himself, two wrongs didn't make a right. Below him, the front door slammed shut, causing the windowpanes to rattle in their frames. Dante winced. From the sound of it,

Orla was really pissed at him. He shouldn't have let her leave. Not without smoothing things over – *or* without making sure she wasn't going to go shooting her mouth off to Juliet. He put his head in his hands. There were so many thoughts whirling round his brain it was no wonder his headache had returned with a vengeance. Ignoring the pain, he stood up and looked around for his trainers. Sometimes it was better not to think. Sometimes it was better to act instinctively, like an animal.

He took the stairs two at a time. Orla was probably making her way to the bus stop at the end of the lane. If he was quick, he could still catch her. As he hurtled across the entrance hall, past a startled Jess, Dante caught sight of his prey through the window. She was nearly at the entrance gates already. Yanking open the front door, he set off across the lawn. Up ahead, Orla was walking briskly, marching almost. In another few seconds she would be out of sight. He was just about to call out to her when she did something unexpected. Instead of carrying on through the gates to the lane beyond, she turned right, towards the lodge. Dante stopped in his tracks. He suddenly felt sick, saliva flowing into his mouth as if he were about to vomit. This was nothing short of a disaster. He took cover behind the nearest tree and watched with his heart in his mouth as the door of the lodge opened and the chambermaid stepped inside. Dante cursed under his breath. If Orla was about to tell Nathan about their sexual encounter, he needed to know. Thankfully, the afternoon was warm and all the windows of the lodge were flung wide open.

Dodging from tree to tree to minimize the risk of being spotted, Dante skirted the edge of the lawn. Only when he was facing the lodge's windowless gable end did he start running towards it. Then, bending low like a fugitive, he inched his way round the building until he heard the low rumble of Nathan's voice. He dropped down beneath the nearest window and turned his head upwards, ears straining to hear what was being said. The general manager was angry, that much was obvious.

'I don't believe it,' he was saying. 'I don't fucking believe it.'

When Orla responded, her voice sounded tight and defensive. 'I tried my best,' she said. 'I almost had him, Nathan, I swear.'

'You obviously didn't try hard enough,' Nathan snapped back. 'We've waited ages for an opportunity like this and then you go and blow it.'

A cold sweat bloomed over Dante's body as he struggled to make sense of what they were saying. He craned his head, not wanting to miss a word.

'It wasn't me, it was that bloody dog,' Orla was protesting. 'The minute she started howling like a wolf, it ruined the mood.'

'Stop making excuses,' Nathan said icily. 'There's only one person to blame and that's you. You're supposed to be an actress, for Christ's sake.'

Orla sniffed. 'I'm not an actress; I'm a drama graduate. They're not the same thing. And, actually, I think I did pretty well, considering the short notice. *You* try getting your kit off and running a bubble bath in three minutes flat.'

'You fucked up, sister dearest, that's the bottom line.'

A sharp intake of breath from Orla. 'What are you talking about? I did everything you asked me to – I took this shitty cleaning job; I flirted with Dante at every opportunity; I offered him sex on a plate. It's not my fault he's a flaming eunuch.' She paused. 'Either that, or he really *is* in love with Juliet.'

There was a long silence. Outside, Dante felt overwhelmed by panic, cornered like he was in a big black box and gradually all the oxygen was being sucked out of it. Suddenly, he heard the sound of footsteps walking towards the window. The next moment, a hand holding a cigarette appeared at the window, directly above his head. He flattened himself against the wall of the lodge as a shower of ash descended on his right shoulder.

'This should all have been so straightforward,' he heard Nathan say. 'You get Dante into bed; I call Juliet with some excuse and tell her to get back to Ashwicke pronto; she catches the two of you at it and sends that prick back to Aspen with his tail between his legs. And I have Juliet all to myself. Job done.'

'So *did* you call her?' Orla interposed.

'No, I was just about to when you turned up.' Nathan sucked on his cigarette. 'You've ruined everything, you silly bitch.'

'Who are you calling a bitch?' Orla said angrily. 'I'm your sister, remember?'

'*Half*-sister,' Nathan corrected her. 'And you needn't think I'm paying you after this. I'll give you fifty per cent of what we agreed, take it or leave it.'

'You fucking shit,' Orla hissed. 'Mum warned me not to trust you.'

Nathan laughed softly. 'Maybe you should've listened to her.'

'You know what you can do, bro? You can take your fifty per cent and shove it right up your arse,' Orla said. 'I've had enough of being your skivvy. From now on, you can do your own dirty work.'

Dante heard the sound of a door slamming. Then Nathan's voice called out: 'Where are you going?'

'Back to Liverpool,' Orla screamed.

Dante scuttled to the rear of the building, out of sight. A few moments later he heard the sound of the front door opening. He waited a few minutes to make sure the coast was clear before emerging into the open.

Walking back to the house, Dante felt as if his legs were encased in armour. There seemed to be something round his chest too, a ligature that stopped him from breathing freely. As soon as he stepped into Ashwicke's deserted entrance hall, he sank gratefully into a seventeenth-century church pew. His mind, up until then a shocked, blank canvas, was suddenly ambushed by questions, which jostled feverishly for position. As he attempted to prioritize them, the phone started ringing, forcing him to his feet. He thought it might be Juliet, but it was only an excited-sounding Yasmin.

'Hi, Dante,' she said. 'Is Juliet there? Only I've got some big news.'

'No, sorry, she's at the bank,' he replied in a monotone, his mind a million miles away.

'That's a shame. In that case, I'll tell *you* instead.' A brief pause. 'I'm pregnant!'

The announcement was met by silence.

'Dante, are you still there?'

'Yeah, sorry,' he said. 'That's great news . . . congratulations.'

Yasmin heard the catch in his voice. He sounded close to tears. 'Is everything all right?' she asked. When he didn't reply, she added: 'You and Juliet haven't had a row, have you?'

'No,' Dante said. 'Not exactly. But . . .' He swallowed hard. 'I think she's cheating on me.'

At the other end of the phone, Yasmin took a sharp intake of breath. 'That's the stupidest thing I've ever heard,' she said firmly. 'Juliet would never cheat on you – never.'

'Hmm, well, maybe you don't know her as well as you think you do,' Dante countered bitterly.

Yasmin made a huffing noise. 'When's she due back?'

'Um, I'm not sure. She said she might do some shopping after her meeting.'

'So you're on your own?'

'Yeah.'

'Right, then. You know that pub in Newman Street – the King's Head?'

Dante hesitated. 'No, but I'm sure I can find it.'

'Meet me there in ten minutes.'

'But –' Dante began.

'No buts, just be there.' Then the phone went dead.

When Dante arrived at the King's Head, Yasmin was already waiting for him in the pub's well-kept beer garden. There was a glass of orange juice on the table in front of her, and beside it a second, shorter glass filled with amber liquid. As Dante sat down, she pushed the drink towards him. 'I got you a double whisky,' she said. 'I thought you probably could use a stiff one.'

'Thanks,' Dante muttered. He never drank whisky but, not wanting to appear rude, he took a sip, grimacing as it burned the back of his throat. 'Shouldn't you be at work?' he added.

Yasmin rubbed her stomach. 'I was feeling a bit queasy earlier . . . one of the joys of being pregnant, so I decided to work from home today.'

Dante forced a smile. 'Sorry if I didn't sound very enthusiastic about your good news earlier, only I have a lot on my mind.'

'I could tell. It sounded as if you could use someone to talk to.' Yasmin tilted her head back so the sun caught her face. 'And I must admit I was desperate to get out of the house. It's such a gorgeous day.'

Dante took another sip of whisky. This one tasted better than the last. 'Look, Yasmin, I really appreciate your concern, but I'm not sure I want to talk about it.'

'I don't blame you,' she said, reaching into her handbag and pulling out a pair of sunglasses. 'After all, we hardly know each other. So . . .' She put the sunglasses on. 'Either we can sit here and talk about the weather for half an hour – or you can tell me what makes you think Juliet's having an affair and I'll do my level best to prove you wrong. Oh, and whatever happens I won't repeat a word of this conversation to her. I promise.'

Dante frowned. 'But she's your friend.'

'I know she is,' Yasmin replied. 'But so are you.'

Dante picked up his glass and drained the rest of his whisky in a single gulp.

As Dante related the afternoon's events, Yasmin listened in silence – except for a shocked gasp when he described

Orla's attempt to seduce him. Recounting the conversation he'd overheard between Nathan and Orla, Dante felt his chest tighten again. 'Nathan couldn't have made things any clearer,' he said. 'He's sleeping with Juliet and now he wants me off the scene so he can have her all to himself.'

Yasmin shook her head. 'No way. Juliet's one of my best friends. If she was having an affair, I'd know about it.'

'Then why is Nathan so desperate to get rid of me?'

Yasmin shrugged. 'If you ask me, the man's deranged. Only a sicko would pay his own sister to sleep with another man.'

'What if Juliet's having an affair and she just hasn't told you?'

Yasmin laid her hand over Dante's. 'I honestly think you're barking up the wrong tree. Think about it . . . Nathan didn't actually say he was sleeping with Juliet, did he?'

'No,' Dante conceded. 'But he did say that if I went back to Aspen he'd have her all to himself.'

'Perhaps he's a fantasist,' Yasmin offered. 'Perhaps he's deluding himself that, with you out of the picture, he'd be in with a shot at Juliet.'

'Maybe,' Dante said, sounding unconvinced. He turned towards the far corner of the garden where two little girls were running between the trees, picking up handfuls of fallen rose petals and scattering them like confetti. 'So what do you think I should do?'

'There's only one thing *to* do,' Yasmin said. 'Talk to Juliet. Tell her exactly what's happened and see what she says.'

Dante frowned. 'Even the bit about me and Orla?'

'*Especially* the bit about you and Orla,' Yasmin replied. 'It's far better that she hears it from you than Nathan.'

'I guess . . .' Dante watched as the little girls went running towards their father, who was carrying a tray of lemonade and crisps. 'When's the baby due, by the way?'

'Not until the end of February. I'm only four weeks gone.'

'You must be pretty excited.'

Yasmin smiled. 'I am. It's going to mean a big change of lifestyle, though – and I'm under no illusions about how tough life as a single mum's going to be.' Seeing Dante's curious look, she added: 'I'm not in a relationship with the father; it was just a one-off.'

'He'll have to pay you child support, though – right?'

Yasmin shook her head. 'I don't need supporting. In any case, he doesn't even know I'm pregnant.'

'But you *are* going to tell him, aren't you?'

Yasmin stared at the dregs of her orange juice. 'I don't know. It's complicated . . .' She sighed. 'Rob – that's the father – he's got a girlfriend, you see.'

'I can see how that might make things complicated, but don't you think he has a right to know you're having his baby?' Dante said.

Yasmin sighed. 'I just think it might be easier for everyone concerned if I don't tell him. Being a dad's a big responsibility. It seems a bit unfair to dump that on Rob when he didn't ask to have a child with me.'

'What's the matter – doesn't he like kids?'

'Oh no, it's not that. He's already got two with his ex-wife.'

'So what is it, then?'

Yasmin didn't answer.

'Look, I'm not trying to give you a hard time,' Dante said, 'but if it were me I'd want to know. It wouldn't matter what the circumstances were.'

Yasmin met his gaze. 'Do you mean that?'

'Sure I do.' He pushed his chair away from the table. 'I hate to be rude, but I'd better shoot off. Juliet will be back soon and she and I have got some serious talking to do. Can I walk you home?'

Yasmin shook her head. 'I think I'll stay here and enjoy the sun for a while longer.'

'Okay,' Dante said, rising to his feet. 'Thanks for the drink.'

'Thank you too,' Yasmin said.

Dante frowned. 'What for?'

'For making me think.'

Dante smiled. 'Whatever you decide to do, let me know, okay?'

Yasmin nodded. 'I will, I promise.'

22

Dante had just left the pub when he saw a girl walking in the opposite direction on the other side of the street, her head bowed as if she were lost in thought. There was something familiar about her and then, as she drew nearer, he realized it was Orla. With a jolt, Dante remembered she lived in this street. As he looked around, he saw the distinctive red door of her apartment block just a few feet away. Without hesitation, he crossed the road.

She looked surprised to see him, but not altogether displeased. 'Don't tell me . . .' she said as he approached. 'You've had second thoughts.'

'About what?' he asked.

She laughed throatily. 'About getting to know each other a little better.'

'No,' Dante said, recoiling. 'I told you before – I'm not interested.'

'Oh well, the offer's still there if you change your mind.'

'What – even though Nathan's not going to pay you for it?' Dante said contemptuously.

She blanched. 'What are you talking about?'

'You know exactly what I'm talking about,' Dante said, fixing her with a hard stare. 'You're not a chambermaid; you're a honey trap.' A look of confusion crossed her face. 'When you left the house I followed you to the lodge,' he went on. 'I heard every word of your conversation with Nathan.'

'Ah.' Clearly embarrassed, Orla turned away and, without another word, began walking towards her apartment block.

Dante followed close behind. 'Is that all you've got to say for yourself?'

'What do you want me to say?'

'You could start by telling me why you did it.'

Orla began rummaging in her handbag. 'For money, of course.' She looked up briefly. 'Besides, you are pretty hot.'

Dante shook his head, shocked by her brazenness. 'You're a good actress, I'll give you that,' he said. 'You certainly had me fooled.'

She pulled a bunch of keys from her bag. 'Don't take it personally, okay?'

'You try and wreck my marriage and then you tell me not to take it personally,' Dante retorted angrily. 'What kind of freak are you?'

That seemed to annoy her. 'Nathan's the freak, not me,' she snapped. 'He was the one who dreamed this whole thing up.' She put her key in the lock. 'Anyway, it's over now. I'm going back to Liverpool tomorrow, so you can tell Juliet she'll have to find someone else to scrub her shitty toilets.'

As Orla turned the key, Dante lunged towards her, grabbing her arms and pinning them to her sides.

'Get your hands off me!' she cried.

'Not until you tell me one thing.'

'What?' she said.

'Is Nathan sleeping with Juliet?'

She gave him a withering look. 'As if.'

Relief swept through Dante's body like a tidal wave. 'Has he *ever* slept with her?'

Orla shook her head.

'So why did you make me think they had?'

'Because Nathan told me to,' she replied. 'It was all part of his plan to split you two up.'

'Well, you can tell that brother of yours he'll never get his hands on Juliet,' Dante hissed. 'I want him out of the lodge by morning, or I'm calling the police.'

'Tell him yourself. Nathan's a twat; I don't care if I never speak to him again.' Orla's lips formed a strange half-smile. 'In any case, it isn't Juliet he wants – it's Ashwicke.'

Dante gawped at her. 'What?'

'You heard. Nathan's always wanted his own hotel. He reckons Ashwicke could be a gold mine in the right hands. He's been using Juliet from the beginning.'

Dante squeezed her arms. 'How has he been using her?'

'You're hurting me,' Orla said, squirming.

'*How* has he been using her?' Dante repeated.

Orla sighed. 'When Nathan went for his interview for the general manager's job, it was obvious Juliet didn't know her arse from her elbow when it came to running a hotel. He knew she was in a vulnerable state – not just practically speaking, but emotionally too – and he saw how easily she could be exploited. As soon as he started work, he set about making himself indispensable – and Juliet was only too happy to hand over the day-to-day running of the hotel to him. She thought he'd be able to make the business a success, when all along he was trying to do just the opposite.' Her eyes flickered from side to side.

Dante squeezed her arms again. 'Go on.'

'For starters, he made sure he hired the laziest, most inexperienced staff he could find.'

Dante groaned in horror. 'What else?'

'Letters Juliet asked Nathan to write to prestigious hotel guides, inviting them to inspect Ashwicke, never got sent. But one time she posted the letter herself and an inspector did rock up.'

'Weinberger?'

Orla shrugged. 'I don't know his name. But Nathan recognized him the minute he checked in because the guy had visited another hotel where he used to work. Nathan was terrified he'd give Ashwicke a glowing review, so he drilled holes in the pipework above his room. Apparently, the inspector was furious when water started leaking through the ceiling.'

'That son of a bitch,' Dante muttered.

Orla laughed. 'That's nothing. Nathan used to buy mice from the local pet shop and let them loose in the bedrooms. One time he even tried to give the guests food poisoning by turning the temperature down in the fridge, but Chef realized what had happened and threw all the food away.'

Dante shook his head, hardly able to believe what he was hearing. 'So what was Nathan's game plan once the hotel was on its knees?'

'He had access to the accounts, so he knew Juliet was up to her eyeballs in debt. He figured that once the business had collapsed the bank would want its money back. Juliet would be forced to sell Ashwicke and –'

'Nathan would snap it up at a knockdown price,' Dante supplied.

'Exactly – but there was one small problem,' Orla explained. 'You.'

Dante looked at her questioningly.

'He knew he could pull the wool over Juliet's eyes, but he wasn't convinced you'd be such a soft touch,' Orla volunteered. 'He could see you were suspicious of him right away. He was worried that some of it seemed to be rubbing off on Juliet too. Before she went to Aspen she'd pretty much left my brother to his own devices, but when she came back she was always sticking her nose in, wanting to know what he was up to.'

Dante grimaced. 'So he decided to try and get rid of me.'

'Yeah. He didn't think it would be too difficult. He reckoned it was only a matter of time before you two split up – with or without his help.'

'And why's that?' Dante asked.

'Where do you want me to start?' Orla said airily. 'The age gap, the culture difference, the fact Juliet was still getting over the death of her first husband. But you see Nathan's the impatient type; he didn't want to sit around and wait for nature to take its course, so he decided to speed things up.'

'By trying to make me feel like a fish out of water at Ashwicke?'

Orla nodded.

'No wonder he always acted so goddamn superior,' Dante muttered.

'He stitched you up at the summer fête as well. I can't remember the details . . . something to do with a fancy-dress competition, I think.'

Dante's mouth set in a grim line. 'I knew it.'

'And when that didn't work, he called in reinforcements,' Orla said. 'Like I told you before, we aren't that close. We hadn't spoken for the best part of a year, so I was surprised when he got in touch. When he told me what he wanted me to do, I said no at first. Then he told me how much money he was prepared to pay me and I had a change of heart.'

'Is there anything you *won't* do for money?' Dante asked scathingly.

Orla sighed. 'I've got a stonking great credit card bill to pay off, as well as my student loan.' Her gaze fell to the ground. 'For what it's worth, I really wish I hadn't got involved now. You and Juliet seem like such a nice couple.'

Dante's hands fell away from her arms. 'Listen, thanks for telling me all this. Everything makes a lot more sense now.'

'I reckon it's the least I can do.' Orla frowned suddenly. 'You know, my mum always said there was something odd about Nathan. I thought she was just being funny because he was my dad's kid from another relationship, but now that I've spent some time with him I'm inclined to agree.' She tapped the side of her head. 'He's not quite right upstairs, if you know what I mean.'

'Just wait till I get my hands on him,' Dante said through clenched teeth. 'He's gonna wish he'd never been born.'

'Yeah, well be careful how you handle him. You don't know what he's capable of.' She shuffled from foot to foot. 'Can I go now? I've got a lot of packing to do.'

Dante nodded. 'Have a good trip back to Liverpool, okay?'

Orla smiled. Then she took a step forward and kissed him lightly on the cheek. 'I'm really sorry – about everything,' she said. 'I hope you and Juliet make it work.'

'So do I,' he replied.

As they drew apart, Dante heard a screech of tyres. He looked round and saw a distinctive grey Land Rover. As it sped past, he caught a glimpse of Juliet through the windscreen. Her pale face looked like thunder.

Dante practically ran the rest of the way home. He found Juliet in the kitchen, gripping the sides of the butler sink, as if in a trance. As he walked into the room, she grabbed a Le Creuset saucepan from the draining board and hurled it at him. It missed his head by inches, bouncing off the door frame and landing with a deafening clatter on the tiled floor.

'You fucking bastard!' she shrieked. 'We've been married for three months – *three months* – and already you're having an affair.'

'You've got it all wrong,' Dante said, stepping over the saucepan and walking towards her.

'What a fool I've been,' Juliet continued. 'I should've listened to Eleanor. She said you'd be looking for a younger model just as soon as you'd got your feet under the table.' Suddenly she began sobbing.

Instinctively, Dante put his arms round her. 'Don't touch me!' she cried, pushing him away. 'I don't want you anywhere near me.'

'Please, Juliet,' he begged. 'You've got to believe me. I am *not* cheating on you.'

She walked over to the battered refectory table and lowered herself, in a way which suggested extreme fragility, into a chair. 'How long?' she demanded, wiping the tears from her cheeks with the back of her hand. 'How long has it been going on?'

Dante sat down beside her. 'I take it you're referring to Orla.'

'Why?' she said. 'Are there others?'

'There's no one else,' he said. 'No one but you.'

'B-b-but I saw you,' she hiccupped. 'You were outside her house; she was kissing you.'

Dante leaned forward. 'I'm going to tell you everything that's happened to me today,' he said calmly. 'And then, if you still think I'm cheating on you, I'll walk out of this house right now and I'll never come back. Is that a deal?'

She stared at him with big, frightened eyes. Then she nodded.

Taking a deep breath, Dante began to tell her about Orla's attempt to seduce him. As he described their brief kiss in the bedroom, Juliet snatched a tea towel from the table and pressed it to her mouth as if she were about to be sick.

'What I did was wrong, and I regret it with all my heart. But I didn't sleep with Orla and I never have,' Dante said. 'The whole thing was a set-up. Orla came to Ashwicke with the sole purpose of getting me into bed. The plan was that you would catch us red-handed and throw me out.'

Juliet looked at him, not comprehending. 'But what possible motive would Orla have for wanting to split us up?'

'Not Orla,' Dante said. 'Nathan.' As he related the conversation he'd heard between brother and sister, Juliet stared at him open-mouthed. Afterwards, unsurprisingly, she was full of questions, but Dante begged her to hear him out.

'Running into Orla later on was a complete coincidence,' he told her. 'I was on my way back from the King's Head.'

Juliet frowned. 'What were you doing at the pub in the middle of the afternoon?'

'It's a long story. I'll explain later.' Ignoring Juliet's look of consternation, he pressed on with his account, describing, in as much detail as he could remember, his conversation with Orla. Then, when it was all out, he sat back in his chair and waited for his wife's reaction.

For several moments, she just stared at him, utterly stupefied. Then she spoke. 'That's the most insane thing I've ever heard.'

'I know . . . crazy, isn't it,' Dante said. 'But, looking back, it all figures.'

'I can't believe Nathan would do such a thing,' Juliet said, shaking her head. 'He always seemed so dedicated to Ashwicke.'

Dante snorted. 'Yeah, dedicated to getting his hands on it.'

'And you really think Orla was telling the truth?'

'One hundred per cent. What would she have to gain by lying?'

Juliet pursed her lips. 'You still haven't explained why she was kissing you.'

'It was just a friendly goodbye. She's had enough of Nathan and his twisted games; she's going back to Liverpool tomorrow.'

Juliet rubbed her temples with her fingertips, trying to work through everything she'd heard. It all sounded so terribly far-fetched.

'You do believe me, don't you?' Dante said at length.

Juliet looked into his face and saw nothing there to make her doubt him.

'Yes,' she said. 'As a matter of fact, I do.'

She stood up and went to the window. In the distance, she could see the summerhouse and beyond it the lodge.

'You've been honest with me and now I think it's time I was honest with you,' she said. 'There are some things I haven't told you . . . about my relationship with Gus.'

Dante felt a tremor of anxiety. 'What things?'

She turned to face him, her eyes meeting his with a sad, quiet candour. 'I married Gus Ingram ten years ago,' she began in a faltering voice. 'Our parents were friends and we'd known each other since childhood. Everyone told me what a good catch he was, and I must admit I thought the same. Gus was tall and good-looking and he had a high-flying job in a shipping firm. He was extremely charismatic too . . . the sort of person who could light up a room just by walking into it. At parties I always felt rather dull and mousey in comparison. Gus would be holding court as usual and I'd be looking on from the sidelines, the devoted little wife. I sometimes used to wonder why he married me when he could easily have found someone prettier and funnier and more outgoing.' Juliet gave a wan half-smile. 'The first few years of our marriage were very happy. Or, at least, *I* was happy. I can't speak for Gus. We had a beautiful home, a great social life and we treated one another with respect. The only thing missing was children. Rather naively, I hadn't broached the subject with Gus before we got married; I just assumed he wanted them. His parents were certainly very keen to have grandchildren; Eleanor was always dropping hints on the subject. Gus was an only child, you see, so they were relying on him to produce an heir.

'It was just after my thirtieth birthday when I told Gus I wanted to come off the Pill. To my surprise, he violently opposed the idea. He said he wasn't ready for children and that he and I needed more time alone together as a couple. I was disappointed. I'd always wanted a big family and I thought the sooner we got cracking, the better, but when he asked me to wait a bit longer, I found myself agreeing . . . Gus could be very persuasive, you see.

'Another eighteen months or so went past and it was around that time that our relationship started to change. We'd always had a healthy sex life, but that side of things began to tail off. Gus always had some excuse to hand – either he was tired, or under the weather, or he had an early start in the morning. He'd started going out in the evenings too, straight from work. It was only once a fortnight at first, but soon he was out a couple of times a week. If I asked him where he'd been, he'd say he was schmoozing business contacts or drinking with colleagues at his firm, but when he started coming home at two or three in the morning, I started to get suspicious. And then one day, when I was doing the laundry, I smelled perfume on one of his shirts. I thought it could only mean one thing.'

'He was cheating on you?' Dante said.

Juliet sighed. 'Over the next few days, I set about searching for more evidence, and it wasn't long before I found it – a half-empty pack of condoms pushed to the back of his desk drawer. As I said before, I was on the Pill, so I knew Gus must be having sex with someone else.' She blinked hard several times. 'He'd gone out that evening, supposedly with a lawyer friend, so I decided to wait up for him. I was in quite a state by the time he rolled home just after midnight, looking rather dishevelled and stinking of drink. I was sitting on the stairs and as soon as he walked through the front door I threw the condoms at him and demanded to know if he was having an affair. He didn't answer me at first. Instead he went to the snug and poured himself a brandy. I followed him and when I asked again if he'd spent the evening with another woman, he turned to me and said, almost matter-of-factly: "Actually, it was another man." And then it struck me that the smell on his shirt hadn't been perfume after all; it was aftershave.'

Dante stared at her, incredulous. 'No way!' he cried.

'I realized then my marriage had been built on a lie,' Juliet continued. 'My husband was gay and he'd managed to fool not only me, but all our friends and family too.'

'Jesus,' Dante muttered under his breath.

'As Gus sat there, drinking his brandy, it all came spilling out. The strain of keeping the secret had become too much for him; he just couldn't hold it in any longer. Apparently, he'd known he was gay since he was fourteen years old. He knew his parents would be horrified, so he made up his mind never to tell them. As he got older, he started having casual sex with men he met in gay bars and clubs. But all the while no one close to him, not even his best friends, knew he was gay.'

'But why didn't he tell someone?' Dante asked. 'It's not like being gay's a big deal or anything.'

'I think some of Piers and Eleanor's ultra-conservative views had rubbed off on him. On the one hand, he loved the thrill of anonymous sex; on the other, he yearned for middle-class respectability. He really thought he could have his cake and eat it. So, when his parents started hinting that it was about time he started to think about settling down, he looked around for a suitable candidate. I suppose I fitted the bill perfectly: young, innocent, eager to please. I was hugely flattered when Gus asked me out. He was considered a bit of a heart-throb and I was amazed he'd even look twice at me. When, eight months later, he asked me to marry him, I didn't hesitate to say yes.'

The line of Dante's mouth hardened. 'But how could he do that to you . . . lie about his sexuality, I mean?'

'He probably thought he was doing me a favour,' Juliet replied. 'And it's true there were lots of advantages to marrying an Ingram – they're one of the oldest families in Loxwood; people look up to them. Then there was Ashwicke, of course.' She smiled thinly. 'It just goes to show how little Gus knew me. Stuff like that isn't important to me; it never has been.'

'You must have freaked out when he told you the truth.'

'I was utterly shell-shocked. Never, not for one minute, had I considered the possibility my husband might be gay,' Juliet said. 'When I found out, one of the first things I asked him was whether or not he loved me.'

'What did Gus say?'

'He admitted that, although he cared about me very deeply, he simply wasn't capable of feeling romantic love for a woman.'

Dante felt a wave of sympathy for her. 'And how did that make you feel?'

'I was devastated; I told him there and then I wanted a divorce. That was when he made me an offer.' Juliet looked down at her feet. 'If I agreed to maintain the pretence of a happy marriage and keep quiet about his homosexuality, he would give me the one thing I longed for.'

'What was that?'

'A baby.'

Dante frowned. 'And you accepted?'

'Yes,' Juliet replied. 'Sex once a week. That was our agreement.'

Dante's lip curled in distaste. 'Why didn't you just leave him and find someone else to have a baby with . . . someone who really cared about you?'

Juliet's hands formed a knot. 'Because, despite everything, I still had feelings for Gus. Some irrational part of me believed that if we had a baby it would make everything all right. I know that sounds pathetic, but my emotions were all over the place. It was as if a bomb had just exploded, destroying everything and everyone I held dear. I was desperate to salvage something from the wreckage. And so, together, we played a shabby, sordid farce before our friends and family. I hated myself for deceiving them, but I thought it would all be worthwhile once I held that baby in my arms. I was sure it was only a matter of time before I conceived, but months and months went by and I didn't get pregnant.'

'What about Gus?' Dante asked. 'Was he still sleeping with random guys?'

'Yes, but he was very discreet and he swore to me on his mother's life he always used protection.' Juliet bit her lip. 'Then one day something terrible happened. It was Nicole's birthday and Yasmin and I were taking her out for afternoon tea at a smart hotel in town. On my way to meet them, I ran into Gus. He was sitting on the patio, drinking coffee and reading a newspaper. I remember him asking how long I was going to be. I told him several hours at least – possibly longer if we went for drinks afterwards.

'It was a lovely day and I decided that, rather than drive,

I'd walk into town. I was almost there when I realized I'd left Nicole's birthday present on the kitchen table. Cursing my stupidity, I turned round and headed back to the house. I'd been gone for less than half an hour.' She paused and took a deep breath. 'As I took a shortcut across the lawn, I noticed the door to the summerhouse was ajar. Assuming the wind had blown it open, I went over. I had some cane furniture stored in there and I didn't want the rain getting in and ruining it. As I got nearer to the summerhouse, I glanced through the window and realized someone was inside.' A flush rose to Juliet's cheeks. 'It was Gus and he was with another man. They were so engrossed in each other they didn't see me standing there.'

'What were they doing?' Dante asked, though he wasn't sure he really wanted to know the answer.

Juliet quivered. 'They were lying on the floor on a pile of cushions, kissing. Both of them were naked.'

Dante gasped. 'What did you do?'

'I exploded; I couldn't help myself. Having sex with a stranger in the toilets of some seedy nightclub was one thing. Bringing a man back to our home the minute my back was turned was quite another. I flung open the door of the summerhouse and screamed at the other man to get out. I must've been a pretty scary sight because he ran past me without even bothering to pick his shirt up off the floor. And then I was alone with Gus.' Juliet caught her breath, as if reliving the memory. 'He was mortified. He kept telling me over and over again how sorry he was, but I wouldn't listen. I began hitting his chest with my fists, while I called him every name under the sun – and then, when I ran out of expletives, I threatened to tell Piers and Eleanor he was gay. When he heard that, Gus went white as a sheet and begged me to reconsider. I could see the fear in his eyes and the beads of sweat on his forehead, but at that moment I didn't give a toss about Gus's feelings. All I wanted to do was hurt him the way he'd hurt me. *Just you try and stop me!* I screamed as I stormed out of the summerhouse.'

Dante looked at her. 'Did you carry out your threat?'

'No, and to be honest I never had any intention of telling Gus's parents. It was just something I said in the heat of the moment. Afterwards, I went into town and had afternoon tea with Yasmin and Nicole while I tried to act as if nothing was wrong. I desperately wanted to confide in them, but a little voice in my head warned me not to. I was dreading going home and facing Gus, so after tea I persuaded the others to have cocktails in the hotel bar. By the time I got back, Gus had taken himself off to bed in one of the spare rooms. I didn't see him, but I heard him snoring. And then, at some time between four and five a.m., he killed himself.'

For a long moment, the only sound in the room was Juliet's ragged breathing. 'If I close my eyes, I can still see him hanging from that tree,' she said in a voice that was little more than a whisper.

Dante dragged the back of his hand across his mouth. 'You don't have to go on with this. I know it must be painful for you.'

'Yes I do,' Juliet said quietly. 'I don't want there to be secrets between us, not any more.' She half turned towards the window. 'When I realized there was nothing I could do for Gus, I went back to the house and called the police. And there, beside the phone, I found an envelope with my name on it . . . a suicide note. In it, Gus apologized for being a terrible husband and expressed his regret for not being able to give me a baby. He said the strain of leading a double life had become too much to bear.' She paused and took a few shallow breaths. 'He asked me to do one last thing for him: protect his secret so that his parents would be spared what he called the "appalling truth".'

'And did you carry out his wishes?' Dante asked.

Juliet nodded. 'I burned the note in the sink. Later, when the police asked me what possible motive Gus would have for killing himself, I told them he'd been under a lot of pressure at work.'

'Did they believe you?'

'I think so. There was something else too . . . Unbeknown to me, Gus had recently been to see his GP, complaining of insomnia and feelings of anxiety. The doctor diagnosed mild depression and asked him to come back for further assessment two weeks later – but by then Gus was already dead. Even though there was no note, the coroner said the evidence was overwhelming. He had no hesitation in recording a verdict of death by suicide.'

'So Gus's parents still think he was straight?'

'Yes,' Juliet said. 'After the inquest, I half expected one of his lovers to come crawling out of the woodwork, but none of them did.'

Dante let out a long breath. 'I can't believe you've been carrying that secret on your own all this time.'

'It's not as big a burden as the guilt I feel,' Juliet said, digging the heels of her hands into her eyes. 'I've never forgiven myself for what I said to Gus in the summerhouse.

If I'd only been a bit more understanding, he'd still be alive today.'

'You mustn't blame yourself,' Dante said. 'Gus was a grown man; he made his own decisions.'

'I know that, but it doesn't make the pain any easier to bear.'

Dante swallowed hard. 'Are you saying that you're still in love with him?'

'God, no,' Juliet said quickly. 'By the time he died, Gus and I were nothing more than friends. Yes, we had our weekly sexual arrangement, but, believe me, there was nothing remotely romantic about it.'

Dante leaned back in his chair and groaned aloud in relief. 'All this time I've been thinking you were still hung up on him,' he said. 'The way you kept the snug and Gus's dressing room like some kind of shrine . . . It was as if you didn't want to let him go.'

'I think I was punishing myself,' Juliet said. 'Whenever I saw his things, it would remind me of what I'd done. It was part of the reason I couldn't bear to sell Ashwicke – that and the knowledge that Eleanor would never forgive me.'

Dante rose to his feet and walked over to her. 'I think you've punished yourself enough,' he said. 'It's time to start over.' He reached out and drew her to him. For several minutes they stood there, their bodies pressed tightly together. Dante's heart was light and free. He wasn't jealous of Gus any more. He didn't hate him. He no longer felt inadequate and unworthy. 'I love you, Juliet,' he whispered into her hair. 'I love you and I always will.'

She gazed up at him. 'You won't tell anyone, will you . . . about Gus?'

He shook his head. 'No. I give you my word.'

She smiled and rested her head against his chest. 'So what are we going to do about Nathan?'

'You leave Nathan to me,' Dante said. 'One way or another, he's going to be gone by morning.'

23

Dante strode down Ashwicke's sweeping drive, breathing heavily as he tried to control his rage. He could feel it growing inside him, dividing and multiplying, threatening to suck the marrow from his bones. It was evening now and the last faint gauze of light was fading rapidly. The grounds stood petrified in their stillness and in the trees beyond the rose garden the birds were making their last little rustling noises before nightfall. Ahead of him lay the lodge, crouching low beneath the gunpowder sky.

Nathan responded to Dante's knock almost immediately, appearing at the front door with a cigarette in one hand and a glass of red wine in the other. He seemed in an unusually convivial mood.

'Aah, Mr Fisher,' he said, throwing open his arms. 'This is an unexpected pleasure.'

Dante offered no response as he pushed past him into the dimly lit hall.

'Hey, you can't just barge in here like that,' grumbled Nathan. 'This is my home.'

'Not for much longer,' Dante said under his breath. He stepped through the nearest doorway and found himself in a sitting room. It was poky and cheaply furnished and the air was thick with cigarette smoke. As he surveyed the room, his attention was drawn to a pair of Royal Doulton shepherdesses, lying prone on a coffee table. The last time he'd seen them, they were bookending the mantelpiece in Ashwicke's dining room. Next to the ornaments was a roll of bubblewrap, some sticky tape and a pair of scissors, indicating they wouldn't be on the premises for long. No doubt Nathan planned to sell them on eBay or in one of Loxwood's overpriced antique shops.

'Do you mind telling me what this is about?'

Dante looked up to see Nathan standing in the doorway. 'I've been speaking to Orla,' he replied. 'She told me everything.'

The general manager ground out his cigarette in a solid onyx ashtray that used to live on Gus's desk. 'I don't know what you're talking about,' he said levelly.

In three quick strides Dante had crossed the room. 'You motherfucker,' he growled at Nathan. 'You think you're so goddamn smart, don't you? Getting that cute sister of yours to come on to me.'

Nathan took a long, deliberate swallow of wine. 'I'm amazed you could resist her,' he said. 'You look like the type who wouldn't need much persuasion.'

His mocking tone was too much for Dante. Grabbing the manager by the throat, he shoved him up against the nearest wall.

'*Waarghh*,' Nathan sputtered, dropping his glass as the air was forced out of his larynx. Around his feet, the wine spread across the sisal carpet like blood.

'Shut the fuck up and listen to me,' Dante hissed. 'I know all about you and your sad little life. I know you've been trying to get rid of me, so you can carry on sabotaging Juliet's business.' He applied more pressure to the manager's throat. 'I'm telling you, asshole, this is where it ends – right here and right now.' He let go of Nathan, who instantly began coughing and rubbing his neck.

'You've just assaulted me,' the manager croaked. 'I've a good mind to call the police.'

Dante laughed. 'Yeah, you do that. Then I can tell them how you tried to take advantage of a vulnerable woman.'

'You can't prove anything,' Nathan retorted. 'It'll be your word against mine. In any case, I've got an employment contract. Juliet can't get rid of me just like that. If she wants me to go, she'll have to make it worth my while.' He rubbed the fingers of his right hand together. 'Fifteen thousand ought to do it.'

Dante tried to stay calm, though he could feel the sweat pooling under his arms. 'So you're a blackmailer as well as a thief.' He thrust his clenched fist into the manager's face. 'How about I just kick your ass out of here?'

'You lay one finger on me and I'll do you for GBH,' Nathan fired back. 'What would your precious Juliet do if you went to prison, eh?'

There was a long silence. Dante could feel a sea of malevolence silently undulating all around him. 'You'd better start packing,' he said. 'You've got two hours to get out of here.'

Nathan giggled maniacally. 'I've already told you,' he said. 'I'm not going anywhere.'

Dante gritted his teeth. This wasn't going the way he'd hoped. 'Two hours,' he repeated. As he walked through the front door, Nathan's laughter was still ringing in his ears.

Back at the house, Juliet was pacing up and down the hall, her palms wet with apprehension. She fell on her husband the minute he walked through the door. 'Well?' she said anxiously. 'How did it go?'

Dante shrugged half-heartedly. 'Not great, I'm afraid. He says he won't go – not unless you pay him fifteen thousand pounds.'

Juliet groaned. 'Oh God, what are we going to do now?'

He put his arms round her shoulders. 'We'll give him till ten thirty and then we're calling the police.'

In the event, they didn't have to wait that long. The first sign that something was wrong came in the form of a frantic ringing on Ashwicke's antiquated doorbell. As its chimes rang out, the Fishers were in the kitchen, picking at a cold supper of pâté and crusty bread, though neither had much appetite. Dante was on his feet in an instant. 'I'll go,' he told Juliet as he flung down his napkin. 'You stay here.'

With a strong sense of foreboding, he hurried to the front door. When he opened it, he was shocked to see Orla standing there, huddled in a thin cotton shawl. She was pale as a ghost and tears were running incontinently down her cheeks. She was so hysterical that at first he couldn't make out what she was saying.

'Slow down, Orla,' he said soothingly. 'Take a deep breath and tell me what's happened.'

She took a few gulps of air. 'Quickly,' she panted. 'Nathan's trapped; we've got to help him.' She jabbed a finger into the gathering darkness. 'Look!'

Dante stepped over the lintel and scanned the gardens. Horror rose in him like a tide as he saw that one corner of the landscape was shot with crimson.

'Come on!' Orla screamed, grabbing his hand. 'We're wasting time.'

Hesitating, Dante glanced back at the house, just as Juliet appeared. 'Who is it?' she said. 'What's happening?'

'Call the fire service,' he shouted. 'And tell them to hurry.' Then he was gone.

Dante's heart was pounding as he raced across the lawn with Orla. Ahead of them the lodge was lit up like a Christmas tree. Flames were leaping from the shattered windows and thick grey clouds billowed from the roof. As they drew nearer, a dense pall of smoke, spotted with ashes, came to greet them like a devouring monster.

'What the fuck has he done?' Dante said, flinging his arm across his mouth.

'I don't know,' Orla sobbed. 'The place was already on fire when I got here. I only came back because I couldn't find my purse. I realized it must've fallen out of my bag when I was here earlier.'

'Are you sure Nathan's in there?' Dante asked her as he skittered round the building, looking for any sign of movement within.

'Yes!' she screeched. 'I saw him through the sitting-room window. He was lying on the floor, and he wasn't moving.'

Dante knew what he had to do. If he stopped to think about it, it would be too late. Tearing Orla's shawl off her shoulders, he ran to a nearby water butt and dunked the shawl, before draping it over his head and shoulders.

'I'm going in,' he yelled to Orla. 'If I'm not out by the time the fire service arrives, be sure to tell them there are two of us inside. And whatever happens, do *not* follow me in there.'

Dante ran towards the lodge and began aiming hefty kicks at the front door. As it gave way, a blast of hot, acrid air engulfed him, making his throat burn and his eyes itch. Instinctively, he dropped to the floor where the air was cooler and cleaner. Visibility was at a minimum but he could see the rooms to the left of the hall were well ablaze. The fire hadn't yet spread to the right side, where the sitting room was located. If Nathan was in there, he might still be alive, Dante reasoned – that's if he hadn't been suffocated by the choking mantle of smoke that was rapidly filling his own lungs. With the end of the wet shawl pressed to his mouth, he groped his way along the hall on his hands and knees until he found the entrance to the sitting room. The door was open and, as he crossed the threshold, he called Nathan's name as loudly as his aching lungs would allow. When there was no answer, he began a slow circuit of the room, using one hand to balance, while the other swept the floor in front of him. His oxygen-starved brain felt numb. He was aware of nothing but the roar of the flames and the sound of his own laboured breathing.

After several minutes of searching, Dante didn't think he could take any more – the heat and the smoke were too intense. He glanced behind him and was alarmed to see flames licking the door frame greedily. *One more minute*, he told himself. *One more minute – and then you can go with a clear conscience, knowing you did everything you possibly could.* He continued on, still calling Nathan's name. Above him, there was a series of loud pops as, one by one, the two-hundred-year-old slates on the roof began to explode. Just as he was about to turn back, Dante's hand made contact with something hard and smooth: a leather brogue. He continued feeling. The shoe was connected to a leg. 'Nathan?' Dante said. He got no response.

Not knowing if the general manager were alive or dead, Dante grabbed him under the armpits and began dragging him towards the door. Nathan was heavy and progress was painfully slow. By the time they reached the hall, flames were shooting across the ceiling, filling the narrow space with an eerie orange glow. For one awful moment, Dante didn't think they were going to make it. But then his survival instinct kicked in. With a primitive cry that seemed to come from the very core of his being, he hefted Nathan onto his shoulder and ran through the flames. A moment later, they were outside.

After depositing his human cargo onto the grass, Dante fell to his knees, head bowed and chest heaving as he breathed in great lungfuls of cool, clean air. A moment later, Juliet was beside him. 'Oh my God, I thought I'd lost you,' she cried, flinging herself at him. 'Are you hurt?'

Dante shook his head. 'Just a bit of smoke inhalation, that's all.' Looking up, he saw Orla bent over Nathan's lifeless form. 'Is he breathing?' he called out to her.

'I don't know,' she said in a tremulous voice. 'I don't think so.'

Dante staggered to his feet and went over to them. Nathan's face was black with smoke and one of his arms was streaked with a long, livid burn. He held two fingers to the side of the other man's neck. 'I can feel a faint pulse,' he said.

Orla gave a loud sob and put her lips close to her brother's ear. 'Nathan,' she said. 'It's me, Orla. You're safe now; the ambulance will be here soon.' As she spoke, the general manager's eyelids fluttered momentarily. 'He can hear me!' Orla shrieked.

Suddenly, Nathan's mouth opened. A wide circle, twitching and trembling. Inside, a quivering tongue and strings of dark mucus laced across the fleshy redness of his throat. Mesmerized, the others watched, waiting for some noise to escape from the gaping, juddering orifice. Suddenly Nathan gave a damp, nasal snort and then his head fell to the side.

'Nathan?' Orla said, stroking his hair. 'Nathan, wake up.'

Dante held his fingers to the manager's neck again. 'I'm sorry,' he said, sitting back on his haunches. 'He's gone.'

Somewhere in the distance a siren started screaming.

24

It was the day after the fire and people in Loxwood were going about their business, completely oblivious to the drama at Ashwicke. In the high street, Nicole was attempting to reverse the buggy out of the newsagent's, swearing under her breath when the wheels caught on the rubber doormat. As she jerked the buggy, Tilly woke up and began to cry, causing a woman browsing a carousel of birthday cards to glare irritably in Nicole's direction.

'Here, why don't you let me help you with that?'

Nicole looked over her shoulder and saw Bear standing on the pavement. His massive frame seemed to fill her field of vision. Before she could answer, he stretched his muscular arm over her head and held open the door, so that now she had both hands free.

She smiled gratefully. 'Thank you,' she said, wrestling the buggy clear of the mat and through the narrow doorway. 'A knight in shining armour, just when I needed one.'

Nicole hadn't seen Bear for several weeks, not since she'd delivered the banana cake to his caravan. He'd left a couple of friendly messages on her mobile, suggesting they meet for coffee, but she'd texted back an excuse. Since Connor's departure, she'd been feeling rather fragile and she was reluctant to let Bear see her in that state. She hadn't stopped thinking about him, though. One night she dreamed she was standing in the Airstream's tiny kitchen, doing the washing up. She was wearing a floaty cotton dress and a pair of Birkenstocks, and instead of the platinum bangle she usually wore – a wedding anniversary gift from Connor – her wrist was ringed with a plaited leather thong. As she lathered up a rolling pin, Bear had come up behind her and lifted up her dress, pressing his crotch against her naked buttocks. Now that he was here in the flesh, she couldn't help blushing.

'Long time, no see,' Bear said as she joined him on the pavement.

'Yes,' Nicole said, rocking the buggy in a bid to quieten Tilly. 'Sorry I couldn't meet for coffee. I've had quite a lot on lately.'

'No problem,' Bear replied. He bent down and cupped Tilly's chin gently in one of his hands. Instantly, she stopped crying.

Nicole looked at him in surprise. 'What's your secret?'

Bear shrugged. 'I've always been good with kids. I've got four nephews and nieces who I love spending time with. My sister's forever telling me what a great dad I'd be.'

'Yes,' said Nicole, smiling. 'I imagine you would be.' She removed a copy of the *Loxwood Chronicle* from the basket under the buggy. 'Have you seen this?' she said, reading the front-page headline out loud: '*Badgers force developer to back-track*.'

Bear nodded. 'Yeah, it's great news, isn't it? After my tip-off, the Badger Protection League carried out a new survey of the site and confirmed that it was home to the largest sett in the county. As soon as the developer realized he'd have to scale down his plans, he withdrew the application altogether.'

'I'm sure you've made a lot of local people very happy,' Nicole said. 'I don't know anyone who wanted those houses to be built.'

'I'm just pleased we managed save a precious piece of Greenbelt from being swallowed up,' Bear replied. 'According to one of my sources, the council's planning to buy the land from the developer and turn it into a nature reserve.'

'How wonderful,' Nicole said. 'That's just what Loxwood needs.'

As she spoke, a massive yawn escaped from Bear's mouth.

'Late one last night, was it?' Nicole said.

'Yeah, I went out for a drink with a couple of my contacts at the Conservation Society. I had a bit too much and ended up crashing on one of the guy's sofas. I'm just on my way back to Ashwicke now.'

'Were you celebrating anything in particular?'

'Actually, it was a farewell drink.'

Nicole's eyes grew wide. 'You're *leaving*?'

'Yep, I've got all the material I need for my article, so I'll be hitching up the caravan and heading back home to Hampshire.'

'When?' Nicole said, trying – and failing miserably – to keep the forlorn note out of her voice.

'Tomorrow.'

Nicole's insides folded. 'That's a shame.'

'I'm going to miss you,' Bear said.

Nicole's eyes rose to meet his. 'I'll miss you too; we both will.' She ruffled Tilly's blonde curls. 'I think this one's taken quite a shine to you.'

'The feeling's mutual.' Bear cocked his head to the side.

'So, what do you ladies have planned for the rest of the day?'

'We're on our way to the park,' Nicole said. 'Tilly wants to feed the ducks.'

'That sounds like fun. Is Connor stuck in the surgery, then?'

'I expect so . . . I don't really know.' Nicole sighed. 'Look, I may as well tell you – Connor and I have split up.'

Bear's jaw dropped. 'No . . . really?'

She nodded. 'I found out he was having an affair with one of his patients.'

'Oh, Nicole, that must have been awful for you.'

'To be honest, the rot set in a long time ago; the affair was just the final straw.' She scuffed the pavement with the sole of her shoe. 'That's part of the reason I haven't felt very sociable lately . . . Things are a bit tricky at the moment. Our lawyers are trying to thrash out an interim financial settlement, but Connor's being very difficult about it.' She looked up as a gaggle of schoolchildren approached the newsagent's. 'I don't really want to talk about it, though; it's far too depressing.'

Bear's face clouded over. 'No, of course you don't. I'll let you get on your way, shall I?' He touched Nicole's arm. 'And, listen, I really hope everything works out for you and Tilly.'

'Don't go,' Nicole said plaintively. She cleared her throat. 'What I mean is, why don't you come to the park with us? If you've got nothing better to do, of course.'

Bear smiled – a wide, sexy smile that made Nicole feel quite hot. 'I can't think of anything I'd like better.'

*

For the next couple of hours, they wandered through the park with Tilly, feeding the ducks, eating ice cream, and talking about anything and everything, while at the same time studiously avoiding any reference to Nicole's impending divorce. It was a long time since Nicole had felt so relaxed. Her life as a mother was so frenetic and Bear seemed to have a magical calming influence, not just on her – but Tilly too. Eventually they found themselves sitting on a bench overlooking the pond. Beside them, Tilly lay fast asleep in her buggy, exhausted from the afternoon's excitement. As she watched the sun sink in the sky, Nicole was reminded that in the morning Bear would be gone.

'Have you enjoyed your time in Loxwood?' she asked him.

'Absolutely,' Bear replied. 'It's been memorable for all sorts of reasons. I came here to research an article and maybe, if I was very lucky, to make some new friends.' He took a deep breath. 'But one thing I never expected, not even in my wildest dreams, was to fall in love.'

Nicole's mouth suddenly felt dry and when she spoke her voice was shrill. 'Who's the lucky girl, then?'

Bear took one of her hands in his. 'I'm looking at her.'

'Sorry?' she said, not trusting her own ears.

'I love you, Nicole,' Bear said, in the tenderest voice imaginable. 'Ever since I met you I've been going around day after day, full of emotion, like a bottle full of butterflies – and now I've finally been able to take the lid off.' He smiled. 'I can't tell you how good that feels.'

Nicole felt weak, as if she were about to melt into a pool at Bear's feet. At the same time, everything around her had lost its definition. The grass, the duck pond, even the mighty oak trees that surrounded them, were suddenly less substantial. Nicole felt that if she touched anything it would fall down, like scenery on a film set, revealing the real, and infinitely less exciting, world concealed behind. The next thing she knew, Bear's arms were around her and she was drowning in one lengthy, mesmerizing kiss after another. On and on they rolled until she felt quite lightheaded.

Yasmin was feeling uncharacteristically nervous as she approached Rob's desk. Ever since they'd slept together, he'd been avoiding her, but today there would be no escape.

'Hey there,' she said, picking up an Xbox game that was sitting on his desk. 'I didn't know you were a gamer.'

Rob didn't look up from his computer screen. 'I'm not. It's a birthday present for my son.'

'That's nice,' Yasmin said. 'How old will he be?'

Rob's fingers froze on the keyboard. 'Was there something you wanted?'

'I, um . . . I was just wondering if you wanted to go out for lunch today.'

The sports editor raised an eyebrow. 'What – just you and me?'

Yasmin nodded. 'I thought we could try that new deli round the corner . . . my treat.'

Rob began shuffling paperwork. 'Sorry, I'm really up against it today. I was just going to grab a sandwich and eat it at my desk.'

'Please, Rob,' Yasmin said. 'There's something I want to talk to you about.'

He looked at her. 'Half an hour,' he said. 'That's the best I can do.'

'Fine. I'll meet you in the lobby at one.'

The deli was packed and very noisy, an atmosphere hardly conducive to the sort of intimate conversation Yasmin had in mind. Rob managed to bag a couple of stools at the end of the stainless-steel counter and a harried-looking waitress came to take their order. Yasmin, who'd been feeling queasy all morning, ordered the plainest thing on the menu – a chicken salad – while Rob went for the deli's speciality – a cholesterol-laden grilled cheese and chorizo panini.

'You'll give yourself a heart attack eating that,' Yasmin told him when their order arrived.

Rob frowned. 'What do you care?'

It was on the tip of Yasmin's tongue to say that, actually, she did care. Quite a lot. But she held her tongue.

'So,' Rob said, as he bit into his sandwich. 'What was it you wanted to talk to me about?'

Yasmin opened her mouth, then shut it again. She'd spent hours rehearsing what she was going to say, but now the time had arrived, she was lost for words. 'Well,' she began hesitantly. 'The thing is . . .' She forked a piece of lettuce into her mouth to buy herself a few more seconds.

As Rob took another giant bite of panini, a dollop of cheese squelched out of the side and landed on his chin. The sight and smell of it made Yasmin feel quite nauseous. She put a hand to her stomach. 'What I wanted to tell you was . . .' she said. Looking around, she spotted a sign for the Ladies. 'Will you excuse me for a minute,' she said, jumping down from her stool and making a run for it.

By the time she got back, Rob had finished his panini and ordered a cappuccino. Beside Yasmin's salad was a steaming mug of herbal tea.

'It's ginger,' Rob said, pushing it towards her. 'A great remedy for nausea. My ex-wife swore by it when *she* was pregnant.'

Yasmin's cheeks burned as if she'd been slapped. 'You know?'

Rob nodded.

'But how?' she said, picking up her mug and savouring its warmth. 'I'm not even showing yet.'

'It's obvious,' Rob replied. 'Your boobs have got bigger and you keep rushing to the toilet during meetings. Oh, and yesterday I watched you wolf a whole tub of Ben and Jerry's at your desk.'

Yasmin grimaced guiltily. 'I used to eat ice cream once in a blue moon. Now I crave it day and night.'

'With my wife it was pickled onions.' Rob steepled his fingers under his chin. 'Is it mine?'

Yasmin cleared her throat. 'Yes. And before you say anything else, I'm keeping it.'

'Good.'

'I know this must have come as a huge shock to you,' she continued. 'And . . .' Her voice tailed off. 'What did you say?'

'I said "good".'

Yasmin frowned. 'You *want* me to keep this baby?'

'Absolutely. I've had two children taken away from me already, and I'm not about to lose another one.'

'Oh,' Yasmin said. This wasn't the reaction she'd anticipated. 'Well, I'm very pleased to hear it, but I want you to know that I don't expect you to contribute anything – financially *or* emotionally.'

'Of course I'm going to contribute,' Rob said sharply. 'What sort of father would I be if I didn't?'

Yasmin snorted. 'Isn't that going to be a bit difficult – seeing as you don't even like me?'

'What gives you that idea?'

'Where do you want me to start?' Yasmin said. 'It's been a battle of wills from day one.'

Rob stared sheepishly into his coffee cup. 'Okay, so I haven't made things easy for you at work, I admit that. But that's only because I'm jealous.'

'Jealous of what?'

'Of your talent,' he replied. 'Believe it or not, I used to be the editor's golden boy – the one getting all the big-name interviews and raking in all the exclusives. Then you showed up with your bulging contacts book and your bloody brilliant writing, and suddenly I was relegated to the first division.' Seeing her look of surprise, he raised his hand. 'Yeah, yeah, I know how childish that sounds, but I'm a bloke . . . I'm naturally competitive. Only thing is, I hadn't reckoned on falling for you.'

'Oh, please!' Yasmin cried.

'It's true,' he said. 'I fancied you from the minute I laid eyes on you. I liked you too. You were funny and ballsy and you knew how to stand up for yourself – only I couldn't admit that, could I, because then I'd be fraternizing with the enemy.'

Yasmin coughed. 'You didn't mind fraternizing with me that night in the boardroom.'

'Yeah, well,' Rob said, raising his coffee cup to his lips. 'The hottest girl in the office was coming on to me . . . I was hardly going to turn her down now, was I?'

'So how come you've been ignoring me ever since?'

Rob sighed. 'Because I assumed you'd be regretting our encounter and wouldn't want anything to do with me afterwards. Why would you? After all, you're a stunning-looking girl and I'm just an ordinary bloke who's fighting a losing battle with middle-aged spread.'

Yasmin smiled. 'Yeah, but you've got lovely eyes. Your arse isn't bad either.'

He smiled back. 'Oh well, that's something I suppose.'

Yasmin took a sip of tea. 'When are you going to break the news to your girlfriend, by the way? About the baby, I mean. I can't imagine she's going to be jumping for joy when she finds out.'

Rob frowned. 'What girlfriend?'

'That girl I saw you with in the tea tent at the Loxwood fête.'

'You were at the fête?' Rob said. 'I didn't see you there.'

'That's because you couldn't take your eyes off the redhead.'

Rob laughed. 'That wasn't my girlfriend, you idiot. That was my sister.'

'Your sister?' Yasmin repeated dumbly.

'Yeah, she lives in Loxwood. Her husband took their three kids off to the bouncy castle so she and I could have a catch-up over a cup of tea.'

Yasmin suddenly felt very foolish. 'So do you, um, have a girlfriend?'

'Nope,' Rob replied. 'I've been single for nearly a year

now.' He gave an annoyed frown. 'Do you really think I'd have slept with you if I had a girlfriend? What kind of sleazebag do you think I am?'

Yasmin chewed her lip. 'We don't know each other very well at all, do we?' she said. 'And now we're having a baby.'

Rob reached across the table and took her hand. 'In that case, I suggest we start making up for lost time.'

25

Juliet adjusted a vase of stiff-necked tulips and stepped back from the table. As she looked around, she couldn't help sighing in pleasure. The dining room was tiny – barely big enough to accommodate a table and six chairs – but it looked so cosy with its low beams and leaded light windows. She turned to Dante, who was kneeling beside the fireplace, lighting a row of squat church candles.

'Isn't it exciting?' she said. 'Our first dinner party in our new house.'

Dante smiled. 'I can't wait to catch up with the others.' He put the box of matches in his pocket and came up behind her, linking his hands protectively across her stomach. 'Are you happy, Mrs Fisher?'

Juliet leaned into him, resting her head against his collar-bone. 'I don't think I've ever been happier.'

It was six months since Nathan's death. Six months during which the Fishers' lives had changed dramatically. For Juliet, the metamorphosis had begun on the night of the fire itself. As she revealed to Dante the true nature of her relationship with Gus, it felt as if a film were sliding off her, a murky slick of grime that had clung to her for years, but which she had now shed like dead skin, emerging all smooth and shiny and new.

Over the days that followed, a team of fire investigators

sifted through the charred remains of the lodge, quickly discovering that lighter fuel had been sprayed throughout the sitting room. Traces of it were also found on Nathan's clothing. He'd removed the batteries from the smoke alarms too. The police found them in his trouser pocket when they went through his things at the hospital. The evidence was incontrovertible: Nathan had started the fire deliberately – and when the police interviewed Orla and the Fishers, they quickly established a motive for the arson attack: revenge. Knowing his days at the hotel were numbered, Nathan had hit back at the Fishers the only way he could – by destroying a precious piece of Ashwicke's heritage. Whether he had meant to kill himself in the process – or whether it was simply a tragic accident – nobody would ever know for sure.

When the investigation was over and the ruined lodge had been bulldozed into oblivion, Juliet finally acknowledged to herself what she'd always known – that being at Ashwicke wasn't making her happy. And so, with Dante's wholehearted approval, she shut the doors of the hotel and sold the house – not on the open market, where it would doubtless have been snapped up by a developer for a tidy sum, but back to its previous owners, Piers and Eleanor Ingram, who would love it and cherish it the way Juliet never really had. Keen to start her life anew, she sold at a price considerably below the estate agent's valuation, but the loss of profit didn't concern her. She was free now; that was the important thing.

As soon as the Fishers moved into Laburnum Cottage, they immediately set about making it home: walls were stripped, a new bathroom installed and the roof lovingly rethatched. There were other changes too. Although the sale of Ashwicke had left Juliet with a healthy bank balance for the first time in ages, she had no intention of taking things easy. As soon as she discovered that the estate agent who was handling the sale of Laburnum Cottage was looking for a full-time receptionist, she wasted no time submitting her CV. Two weeks later, the position was hers. Dante, meanwhile, had also been considering his future. Although he loved bar work, the hours were unsociable and, if there was one thing that mattered to him above all else, it was spending time with Juliet. With few qualifications to his name, however, he assumed his options would be limited.

It was Yasmin who spotted the ad in the jobs section of the *Sunday Post*: a local prep school was seeking a teaching assistant for their PE department. Despite his lack of relevant experience, years of skiing had left Dante in excellent physical shape. What's more, his youth and easy nature were just what the interview panel was looking for. So now, not only did he have a job that offered him genuine career prospects, he also felt on an equal footing with Juliet for the first time in their marriage. For a proud man like Dante, it was a vital accomplishment.

As the couple embraced in the flickering candlelight, Jess emerged from under the dining table and nosed Dante's hand. 'Go away, girl,' he said, cuffing her ear affectionately. 'Can't you see I'm busy?'

Outside, darkness had fallen and cold air rose from the earth. A taxi slid smoothly up to the kerb. The back door opened and Yasmin appeared in a flowing empire-line dress, which only served to accentuate her advanced pregnancy.

'Isn't this place gorgeous?' she said, staring up at the cottage. 'It's like something out of a fairy tale.'

Rob finished paying the driver and came over to join her. 'Stunning,' he agreed. 'They've got a good-sized garden too.' He took her hand in his. 'Come on, let's get indoors. We don't want you getting cold.'

They were halfway to the front door when a second car, a vintage Alfa Romeo, drew up. 'Talk about perfect timing,' Nicole said as she emerged from the car.

'Blimey, Nic, how much stuff have you brought?' Yasmin said, eyeing the bulging bag of baby things her friend was carrying.

Nicole grinned. 'Let's see . . . nappies, wet wipes, bottles, formula, gripe water . . . just the essentials.'

'You two have still got all this to look forward to,' said Bear, as he opened the back door of the car and began unstrapping Tilly's car seat.

Yasmin patted her bump. 'I know, and I can't wait. The sooner she comes out the better. My back's killing me and I keep needing to pee every five minutes.'

'You're still sure it's a girl, then?' Nicole asked, walking over to her friend.

'Absolutely. Rob's not convinced, though, are you, love?'

The sports editor shook his head. 'Judging by the strength of his kick, I reckon it's a boy – and he's going to grow up to be a great footballer, just like his dad.' He turned to Yasmin. 'Did I tell you I once had trials for Southend?'

'A million times,' Yasmin said, patting his rear playfully.

Suddenly the front door of the cottage swung open. 'Hey, guys,' Dante said, raising a hand in greeting. 'Why are you standing out there freezing your asses off? Come on in.'

In the sitting room, Juliet was waiting with glasses of mulled wine to take the edge off the winter chill.

'I see you've been doing some decorating since I was last here,' said Yasmin, settling into a squashy sofa.

Juliet nodded. 'There's only the kitchen left now and then we'll be finished.'

'I'm very impressed with your DIY skills, Dante,' Rob said, running a hand over the wall, which was painted a soft eau-de-Nil to match the curtains. 'This looks like a professional job.'

'I can't take all the credit,' Dante replied. 'Juliet's done loads of stuff, haven't you, babe?'

'It's so satisfying knowing we've done everything ourselves,' Juliet said, resting her head on her husband's shoulder. 'And I have to say I think we make a great team.'

Rob took a seat beside Yasmin on the sofa. 'This place is quite different from Ashwicke. Do you miss it at all?'

Juliet shook her head. 'Not a bit – I only wish we'd made the move sooner. How about you, Yasmin? Are you going to carry on living in the apartment once the baby's born?'

'Uh-uh,' Yasmin replied. 'It's completely impractical; I'd never get a pram in that lift.'

Rob put his hand on her thigh. 'She's moving in with me. My place is twice the size – and it's got a garden.'

Juliet clasped her hands together in delight. 'That's brilliant news! I'm so pleased for you two.'

'To be honest, I don't think I'd be able to cope on my own,' Yasmin said.

Nicole looked at her in surprise. 'I never thought I'd hear those words coming from *your* mouth.'

'Yeah, well, I've changed a lot over the past year.' Yasmin smiled at Rob. 'I fell in love, for one thing.'

Nicole turned to Bear, who was sitting in an armchair cradling a sleeping Tilly in his lap. They'd been a couple for six months, and living together for three. Long enough to have a rhythm, but new enough that her palms still tingled whenever he walked into the room. As she looked at him, Bear caught her eye and smiled.

'You'll be going on maternity leave soon, won't you?' said Dante to Yasmin.

'Next week,' Yasmin said. 'But I won't be going back to the *Post*.'

Nicole frowned. 'I thought you loved your job.'

'I do, but I guess my priorities have changed. I'm going to take six months off and then I'm going freelance. That way I'll be able to work from home.'

'I've told her she's being hopelessly optimistic,' said Rob. 'She doesn't realize babies spend the first six months of their lives crying.'

'And sometimes it goes on even longer than that,' said Nicole, looking pointedly at Tilly. 'Poor Bear's been trying to finish his piece on greenhouse gases for three days now. Still, at least he can go and work in the caravan if the noise gets too much.'

Dante raised an eyebrow. 'You've still got the Airstream, have you?'

'She's parked in Nicole's back garden,' Bear replied. 'The old girl and I have been through so much together I don't think I could bear to part with her.'

'I just hope he feels the same way about me,' Nicole said wryly, prompting much laughter from the others.

'And how's *your* job going, Dante?' Rob asked.

Dante grinned. 'I love it. The kids are fantastic. We're taking them on a camping trip next weekend. I can't wait.'

'It'll be good practice for him,' Juliet remarked.

'Good practice for what?' Nicole asked innocently.

Juliet smiled and put her hands on her stomach. 'I'm pregnant.'

'What!' Yasmin cried. The next minute she and Nicole were on their feet and throwing their arms around Juliet.

As Juliet looked over their shoulders at Dante, she saw that his calm blue eyes were filled with tears. She knew then – as if she had ever doubted it – that she was in love with him. Not smugly or sloppily, but just with a thumping great visceral certainty.

read more 

LEONIE FOX

PRIVATE MEMBERS

Welcome to St Benedict's Country Club and Spa. As a home away from home for the A-list, naturally membership comes at a premium – only the over-sexed, the over-rich and the over-beautiful need apply.

Take a tour of the sauna and work up a sweat before indulging in an intimate Swedish massage. Should your mood need enhancing further, this chic retreat comes with its own drugs baron and you simply must sample the foie gras in the Michelin-starred restaurant. Do watch out for the fiery-tempered chef, though, more prone to filleting his light-fingered staff than the freshly caught sea bass …

WAGs and racing drivers rub shoulders on the famous golf course, site of many a hole in one, and you'll be able to join your celebrity companions for a glass of Cristal in the luxuriously appointed terrace bar after a hard day's posturing for the paparazzi.

But beware. The St Benedict's experience involves more sex, bad behaviour, blackmail and deviance than most women can handle. Are you ready to join the Club?

'Blissfully trashy' *Elle*

LEONIE FOX

MEMBERS ONLY

Remember the sexy shenanigans at St Benedict's? The exclusive country club and spa with more millionaires per square foot than the Hamptons in midsummer? Well, the four gorgeous golfers' girls are back ... let Cindy, Laura, Keeley and Marianne suck you into their naughty world where intrigue, blackmail and depravity bubble beneath the steamy waters of the Jacuzzi.

The girls go gossip crazy when fading soap actress Amber Solomon catches her billionnaire hotelier husband in flagrante with the housekeeper and messy divorce proceedings ensue. He won't part with a penny and she's damned if she's going to join the next series of Hell's Kitchen to keep herself in Krug.

Meanwhile, an oversexed American teenager is prowling the spa and Swinging is having a revival among the WAGs and their footballers. But will the Solomons' battle royal disrupt the delicious decadence of Delchester's favourite Spa resort and end in disaster? Of course it will!

'A decadent blast of fun' *Heat*

'A romp of naughtiness to be devoured and delighted in' *The Sun*